PLAYLIST OF THE DAMNED

EDITED BY
JESSICA LANDRY AND WILLOW DAWN BECKER

WEIRD LITTLE WORLDS

Playlist of the Damned

"Tears Like Rain," by Tim Waggoner ©2023 Tim Waggoner
"The Brazen Bull," by Sofia Ajram ©2023 Sofia Ajram
"Oil of Angels," by Gemma Files ©2023 Gemma Files
"This Loaded Gun of a Song Stuck in My Head," by Paul Michael Anderson ©2023 Paul Michael Anderson
"Everybody Loves My Baby," by Mercedes M. Yardley ©2023 Mercedes M. Yardley
"Pack Up Your Sins and Go to the Devil," by Elis Montgomery ©2023 Elis Montgomery
"The Lung of Orpheus," by Jonathan Duckworth ©2023 Jonathan Duckworth
"I am He," by Premee Mohamed ©2023 Premee Mohamed
"Pied Piper," by Carol Edwards ©2023 Carol Edwards
"Mixtape," by V. Castro ©2023 V. Castro
"To the River," by Corey Farrenkopf ©2023 Corey Farrenkopf
"The Prodigy," by Philip Fracassi ©2023 Philip Fracassi
"Red, Black, & Blue," by Linda D. Addison ©2023 Linda D. Addison
"Instruments of Harm,"by Julia LaFond ©2023 Julia LaFond
"Electric Muse," by Virginia Kathryn ©2023 Virginia Kathryn
"Ambient," by LB Waltz ©2023 LB Waltz
"Vinyl Remains," by Chad Stroup ©2023 Chad Stroup
"Goddess," by Lisa Morton ©2023 Lisa Morton
"Her Only Single," by Devan Barlow ©2023 Devan Barlow
"I Will Not Scream," by John Palisano ©2023 John Palisano
"Lovely Piano of Rich Mahogany," by A.J. Bartholomew ©2023 A.J. Bartholomew
"A Concert in Merzgau," by R.L. Clore ©2023 R.L. Clore
"Sing to the God of Slugs," by Maxwell I. Gold ©2023 Maxwell I. Gold
"Song of the Guqin," by Frances Lu-Pai Ippolito ©2023 Frances Lu-Pai Ippolito
"Scordatura," by Jess Landry originally published in "The Night Belongs To Us," by Jess Landry ©2023 Crystal Lake Publishing
"The Men Who Play," by Jangar Tokpa ©2023 Jangar Tokpa
"Whalesong," by Shannon Brady ©2023 Shannon Brady
"The Devil Went Down to the Subway," by A.J. Rocca ©2023 A.J. Rocca
"Possession No. 239 in E Major, Op. 1," by Hailey Piper ©2023 Hailey Piper
"Slow Head Karaoke," by Robert Beveridge ©2023 Robert Beveridge

Paperback Backer Special Edition
ISBN: 9798863735467

Published by Weird Little Worlds, LLC, Cedar Hills, UT 84062, weirdlittleworlds.com

Cover art by Frank Walls ©2023 Frank Walls Art
Interior art by Sinan Kutlu KuytuGlu
Other Art: "Skull Music Art," Dangraf, "Imagination Fairy Tale Creativity," CDD20, "Texture H" by Darianella, Pixabay Royalty-Free License
Additional design by Willow Becker

PLAYLIST OF THE DAMNED

EDITED BY
JESS LANDRY AND WILLOW DAWN BECKER

WEIRD LITTLE WORLDS

"MUSIC COULD ACHE AND HURT,
THAT BEAUTIFUL MUSIC WAS A
PLACE A SUFFERING MAN COULD
HIDE."
                            — PAT CONROY

"MUSIC DOESN'T GET IN. MUSIC
IS ALREADY IN. MUSIC SIMPLY
UNCOVERS WHAT IS THERE,
MAKES YOU FEEL EMOTIONS
THAT YOU DIDN'T NECESSARILY
KNOW YOU HAD INSIDE YOU AND
RUNS AROUND WAKING THEM
ALL UP. A REBIRTH OF SORTS."

                            — MATT HAIG

"YOU ARE THE MUSIC WHILE THE
MUSIC LASTS."
                            — T.S. ELIOT

★★★

MUSIC AND MAGIC

AN INTRODUCTION

Music is magic. At least, that's what Marylin Manson said, and he probably knows more actual spells than either you or I do. It's a bit of a glib statement, though, isn't it? In a world where we can instantly talk to people on the other side of the planet and AI robots are telling us the movies we want to watch before we even know we want to watch them, there seems to be a lot of magic to go around. So much that it calls into question whether music is even really that magical to begin with.

And yet...

Despite our technology, or maybe because of it, music is as important to humans on planet earth as the day Grock decided that banging a stick against the ground made a pretty groovy beat. In fact, as technology has advanced, so has our ability and desire to take music with us to the edges of evolution. No matter how small the device, how invasive the procedure, how much of our mind or soul it requires, we are always willing to invest in the music.

As Tommy Lee Jone's character, Agent J, says in *Men In Black*, "I guess I'm going to have to buy the White Album again."

We will. And we do. As soon as Apple comes out with the BrainPod, you know that we'll be the first in line.

But what is it about music that makes us so willing to give up our money, our time, and even our lives in the pursuit of it? What is the essence of the magic that music offers?

It has the ability to flip a terrible day into something not so bad, to make you want to get up and dance, to bring out a full range of emotions from the simple twinkle of a piano key or the chord from a guitar. It has the ability to heal, to break, to bend, and to become a completely different and personal and unique thing from person to person.

For myself, I make playlists (not necessarily damned ones) for each project that I'm working on. These lists range from purely moody, atmospheric instrumental ones when I need to feel that unease, that terror that goes into writing something horrific; to an entire jam session of 90s rock anthems fronted by female singers for when I need to feel like I can make it through my next workout. I use music to relax, to agitate, to fill silent voids and have dance parties with my daughter. As I sit here typing this on my laptop at my daughter's dance class, I can hear a pop song I've heard a thousand times, repeating over and over again so the kids can nail a dance move. For them, it's inspiring, it's making them dance. For me, I wish I would've brought earplugs.

Music is everything—it's emotion, it's transformation, it's life-altering, it's transcendent. It has the power to shear away the years, to transport you to a time and place in one of the only truly tangible methods of time travel that humans can produce. Besides writing, that is.

And as long as where (or when) you're going is full of rainbows and sunshine, you're safe to make that journey—one song at a time.

But music, dear, sweet music, can also terrify. Add the right combination of strings and eerie, off-kilter noises, and suddenly, you've found yourself submerged into a nightmare. Find yourself walking alone in the middle of the night, no one else around, and suddenly hear the Halloween theme song playing? You're probably going to pee your pants as you run for dear life.

Every beautiful summer day, every first kiss, every dance...you know that you have a soundtrack for them. And every trauma? There's a soundtrack for that, as well.

The stories and poems in *Playlist of the Damned* are the embodiment of these nightmares, tales that blend both horror and musicality, both intertwined and unable to exist one without the other.

And much like music, these stories transcend. They pluck at your heartstrings like the devil tuning his violin; they use music not as a sound, but as a memory, one powerful enough to move you through space and time; they go beyond the music that we know on earth and bring us into worlds different from ours, where sound and music and noise become something else, something more.

In whichever way music moves you, you can't deny that music is magic. So turn down the lights (but not too much—you've got a book to read!), turn up the broody, atmospheric tunes, and let these melodies that we've stacked on our *Playlist of the Damned* soothe you. Move you. Transport you.

But be careful. Tell someone where you're going before you begin. When you listen very carefully to the music, it has the power to take you. There's no guarantee that you'll have the power to return.

Jess Landry
Willow Dawn Becker
September 23, 2023

SIDE A

3 TEARS LIKE RAIN
by Tim Waggoner

13 THE BRAZEN BULL
by Sofia Ajram

22 OIL OF ANGELS
by Gemma Files

40 THIS LOADED GUN OF A SONG STUCK IN MY HEAD
by Paul Michael Anderson

55 EVERYBODY LOVES MY BABY
by Mercedes M. Yardley

66 PACK UP YOUR SINS AND GO TO THE DEVIL
by Elis Montgomery

68 THE LUNG OF ORPHEUS
by Jonathan Duckworth

83 I AM HE
by Premee Mohamed

97 PIED PIPER
by Carol Edwards

98 MIXTAPE
by V. Castro

111 TO THE RIVER
by Corey Farrenkopf

115 THE PRODIGY
by Philip Fracassi

126 RED, BLACK & BLUE
by Linda D. Addison

128 INSTRUMENTS OF HARM
by Julia LaFond

135 ELECTRIC MUSE
by Victoria Kathryn

SIDE B

147 AMBIENT
by L.B. Waltz

161 VINYL REMAINS
by Chad Stroup

174 GODDESS
by Lisa Morton

186 HER ONLY SINGLE
by Devan Barlow

188 I WILL NOT SCREAM
by John Palisano

205 LOVELY PIANO OF RICH MAHOGANY
by A.J. Bartholomew

207 A CONCERT IN MERZGAU
by R.L. Clore

217 SING TO THE GOD OF SLUGS
by Maxwell I. Gold

219 SONG OF THE GUQIN
by Frances Lu-Pai Ippolito

243 SCORDATURA
by Jess Landry

257 THE MEN WHO PLAY
by Jangar Tokpa

259 WHALESONG
by Shannon Brady

263 THE DEVIL WENT DOWN TO THE SUBWAY
by A.J. Rocca

269 POSSESSION NO. 239 IN E MAJOR, OP. 1
by Hailey Piper

281 SLOW HEAD KARAOKE
by Robert Beveridge

283 CONTENT NOTES/ABOUT
secret track?

TEARS LIKE RAIN

BY TIM WAGGONER

A bell—an honest-to-god bell—tinkled when Michael Wilkins opened the door to Audio Junkie and stepped inside. It was pouring rain, and he was glad to get out of the deluge. He hadn't checked the weather app on his phone before setting out on his trip, and he'd gotten caught in the storm without an umbrella. He should keep one in his car, so he'd always have it when he needed it.

Thunder boomed, rattling the store windows, and the sounds—combined with the driving rain outside—became a plaintive melody echoing in his ears.

Dying...dying...

He closed his eyes, gritted his teeth, balled his fists, and stood there, wet clothes cold against his body, rainwater dripping on the wooden floor.

I don't hear you, I don't hear you!

The Song receded, but it didn't go away entirely. It never did.

"Can I help you?"

Michael opened his eyes and saw a man standing in front of him—fifty-ish, thick white hair, bushy beard, tinted aviator glasses, gray T-shirt, jeans, and sneakers. He was on the heavy side, and he made Michael think of a druggie Santa. There was a warm smile on the man's face, but his eyes were sharp and calculating.

"Sorry about your floor, but it's really coming down outside."

The man shrugged. "It's just water. It'll dry soon enough."

Michael took a quick look around. The walls were painted with murals featuring musicians from various eras and styles: classical, big band, jazz, rock, country, pop, folk, rap...

The art was so realistic that it almost looked like the images might come to life any moment and start performing. Narrow tables filled the small room, atop which rested wooden crates filled with vinyl albums, 45s, eight tracks, cassettes, and CDs. There were no labels anywhere to identify the specific artists whose work the crates held. Were the genres combined and arranged alphabetically? Or was there no organization at all? The place had a funky, mildewy smell, one Michael associated with age, and while he didn't exactly like it, he didn't find unpleasant either. An old-fashioned cash register sat on a counter by the door, and in the rear of the room was a doorway covered by a curtain of multicolored beads.

Michael realized the man was waiting for him to respond to his original question—*Can I help you?*

"I found your place mentioned on an Internet discussion board where people talk about...well, the *unusual.*"

The man laughed, a booming sound not unlike the thunder outside.

"This is Ambergris Falls, son. *Everything* here is unusual."

That was certainly the village's reputation. Ambergris Falls was located about an hour from Dayton in southwest Ohio, home to an eclectic community of artists and craftspeople who sold their creations in downtown shops next to microbreweries, specialty coffee bars, vegan cafes, and gluten-free bakeries. Michael had once dated a woman who said that Ambergris Falls was the place where the Sixties went to die, but he thought of it more as a place where the milieu had been preserved. The village's branding statement on its web page said it all: *Ambergris Falls—We Do Things Our Own Way.*

The man went on. "Besides, you shouldn't believe everything you read on the Internet—unless, of course, it's true." He chuckled at his joke, but Michael only smiled politely. "Let me get you a towel. It's a cold rain coming down today. A man could catch his death out there."

The man turned, walked toward the doorway, pushed aside the bead curtain, and stepped into the back room. A moment later he returned carrying a towel with a faded rainbow design on it. Michael accepted it gratefully, wiped his face dry, then his hair. He patted down his shirt and jeans as best he could, but it didn't do much to dry the sodden cloth. When he was finished, the man took the wet towel from Michael and draped it over his forearm, as if he were a fancy waiter in a high-class restaurant.

"You said you read about Audio Junkie on the Internet," Graybeard prompted.

"Yeah. A lot of the posts were about what a great selection of old music you carry, but some were about the special items you keep in the backroom—items connected to sound—and how you're willing to make trades for them."

"For *some* of them," Graybeard said. "Others I won't part with under any circumstances. What are you interested in and what do you propose to give me in trade?"

"I'm interested in Silence."

"First time I've ever had anyone come in here looking for that. Why do you want it so badly that you've come to me?"

"Because I can't stop hearing it."

"Hearing what?"

Michael didn't want to say, but he sensed the man wouldn't help him unless he answered his question.

"The Death Song of Existence."

As if speaking these words was a trigger, Michael heard the Song in his mind again, wailing this time, mournful and pain-stricken.

Dying, dying, DYING...

* * *

Michael first heard the Song in his mother's womb.

Surrounded by comforting darkness, floating in wet warmth, wrapped in a soft sack of flesh—he would never feel so loved again. He could hear sounds, although he did not know that's what they were—the omnipresent *whoosh-whoosh, whoosh-whoosh* of his mother's heart, the gentle hum of his parents' voices, the melodic rhythms and cadences which he would one day know as music. But behind them all was a single sound, one that came from inside instead of outside, one he felt as much as heard.

Dying, dying, dying...

He did not understand ending. How could he when he hadn't begun yet?

But the deep, ancient sorrow in that sound affected him on a primal level, and he thrashed within his warm home, instinctively trying to force this invader to leave so he could return to the tranquility which was all he had ever known in his brief pre-life. But the sound—the Song—refused to leave, and it continued singing its pain inside his head. And when he was born, he shrieked until his tiny throat bled.

* * *

Graybeard introduced himself as Oren Stull, then led Michael through the bead curtain and into the back room. It was crammed with cardboard boxes of unsorted audio media sitting side by side or stacked atop one another; stuff that, once catalogued and categorized, would make its way onto the sales floor. But one wall held wooden shelves from floor to ceiling, upon which rested empty mason jars, metal lids screwed on tight. The shelves were covered with so many jars there was scarcely room for more.

Stull gestured to the jars. "This is my private stock. I'm a collector as well as a merchant."

"You collect...jars?"

He hadn't been sure what he would find in this place, but a bunch of empty jars definitely wasn't it.

Stull looked at him oddly for a moment, and then gave another booming laugh.

"I collect *sounds*. Pick a jar, unscrew the lid, and give it a listen. Go on, whichever one you want."

This had to be some kind of joke, but Michael decided to go along with it. The faster they got this out of the way, the faster they could get down to business. He selected a jar from the middle shelf and unscrewed it. The lid came off easily, and as soon as he removed it, a sound emerged—water thrashing, someone screaming, meat being ripped apart...

With trembling hands, Michael put the lid back on and replaced the jar on the shelf.

"That's the sound of a bull shark tearing a chunk of thigh from a swimmer's leg. One of my personal favorites. Would you like to try another?"

Michael was so disturbed by what he'd just heard that he couldn't speak. All he could do was give his head a quick shake.

Stull bent over and reached into a cardboard box on the floor next to the shelves. He withdrew another glass jar and held it out to Michael. Michael shook his head more vigorously this time.

"Relax. This one's empty."

Stull removed the lid, and Michael winced, but nothing happened. Stull screwed the lid back on and handed the jar to Michael, who took it this time. The glass felt normal enough in his hands. Maybe a bit colder than he'd expected, but that was all.

"I can give you the silence you crave," Stull said. "But you must collect a sound for me, one that I don't currently have in my collection. That's the price for my help. Are you willing to do this for me if it means getting the relief you've been seeking throughout your life?"

The Song seemed to grow louder then, almost as if it was a thing alive and warning him not to do this. He ignored it.

"Yes. What sound is it?"

Stull smiled. "The last breath of a dying person."

* * *

"His hearing tests all came back normal."

Four-year-old Michael sat on the examination table, his legs dangling over the side. He was bored and antsy, and he wanted to swing them back and forth, but he knew Mommy would scold him and tell him to behave. She didn't like it when he *made a fuss*, which—as near as he could tell—meant doing or saying anything. She stood next to the examination table, one hand on his shoulder, as if afraid he might try to escape any moment. Doctor Tricia stood close by, holding an open manila folder in both hands. There were papers inside, and Michael figured they were the *tests* Doctor Tricia had spoken of. Initially, he'd been afraid when Doctor Tricia had sent him to a different doctor to have his hearing tested. But it hadn't hurt. All he'd had to do was wear these big earphones and tell the doctor whenever he heard soft beeps. It had been kind of fun.

"I don't understand," Mommy said. "He's always talking about this horrible sound he hears. It makes him so *upset*. Sometimes he cries, sometimes he even screams. And he has a *terrible* time sleeping at night. Sometimes he doesn't sleep at all. He keeps both my husband and me up with his foolishness. I haven't had a decent night's sleep since he was born."

Michael felt ashamed. He loved Mommy and Daddy, and he didn't want to make their lives hard. But no matter how much he tried not to hear the Song, he still did, every second of every day—and when he did manage to fall asleep, he heard it in his dreams.

Dying, dying, dying...

Michael really liked Doctor Tricia, but he sometimes wondered if she had trouble sleeping, too. The skin beneath her eyes was dark and puffy, and she yawned a lot, like she was having trouble staying awake.

"There might be a...*non-medical* reason why he hears the Song," Doctor Tricia said. "Have you ever taken him to see a therapist?"

Mommy drew back as if Doctor Tricia had slapped her.

"Why would I do that? There's nothing wrong with him that way. Besides, those people always blame the mother for everything."

Michael wasn't sure what a *therapist* was, but given the way Mommy had reacted to the word, he knew it wasn't something good.

Doctor Tricia looked at him then, and he could sense that she was trying to decide something. She turned toward Mommy.

"Would you mind if I spoke to Michael alone for a few moments? Sometimes children speak more freely when their parent isn't around."

Mommy looked at the doctor, then at Michael, then back to the doctor again.

Doctor Tricia gave Mommy a reassuring smile. "It won't take long."

"Well...if you think it will *help*."

"I'll come get you when we're finished," Doctor Tricia said.

Mommy gave his shoulder a squeeze then left the examining room.

When she was gone, Doctor Tricia's smile vanished.

"I know what you hear, Michael. I hear it, too. Lots of people do, they just don't talk about it."

Michael was stunned. All his life he'd thought he was alone, feared that he was imagining the Song. But now a grown-up—a *doctor*—was telling him it was real.

"You were born different," Doctor Tricia said. "Me too. No matter what we do, we'll always hear the Song, and we have to learn to live with it." She gave Michael a weary smile, and although he was only four, he understood why she was tired, had dark spots under her eyes, sounded so sad. She'd been hearing the Song longer than he had–much longer.

"What is it?" he asked, his voice barely more than a whisper.

"From the moment anything is born, it starts to die, and it begins to sing a song–a song of fear, sadness, anger, and despair. But most of all, a song of *pain*. All of these different voices join together to make a single voice. That's what you hear."

He didn't understand, not fully, but he nodded anyway.

"Damaging our ears won't stop the Song because we hear it in our minds. And do *not* kill yourself to escape the Song. If you die while listening to it, you'll join with it, and then you'll never be free. But if you're at peace when you finally die, you might–just *might*–escape it."

Doctor Tricia reached into the pocket of her examination jacket, removed something, then held it out to him.

"Lollipop?"

* * *

Michael looked at the jar in his hands.

"How does it work?"

"Simple," Stull said, "when you're ready, remove the lid and point the open end toward the sound you wish to collect. The jar will do the rest. When you're finished, put the lid back on."

Michael tapped a fingernail against the jar's surface. It felt and sounded like glass.

"What if I accidently drop it?"

"It'll break," Stull said. "The sound will escape and our deal will be null and void. Only one jar to a customer."

Michael didn't want to believe Stull. The jar with the shark attack sounds in it could've easily been a fake created by some technical trickery. The place was called *Audio* Junkie, after all. But Michael did believe the man. The same way he knew the Song was real, he knew Stull could do what he said. But how was he going to find someone who was dying and capture their last breath? And even if he did find someone, how would he know when their last breath occurred? He looked up at Stull.

"Can I capture more than one sound in the jar?"

"No. And you only have one attempt to get it right."

Michael considered. Maybe he could go to a hospital or better yet, a hospice. He could bribe one of the employees—an overworked nurse, an underpaid orderly— to let him sit with someone who was getting ready to check out, and if he was lucky, he might be able to capture their last breath.

Maybe you could kill someone. That way you could better control the moment they die.

It was a terrible, awful thought, but he considered it for a few seconds. No, he didn't think he had it in him. He'd find another way, he'd have to. Still, if he couldn't find a better opportunity...

Dying, dying, dying...Dying, dying, dying...

Stull stuck out his hand.

"Good luck, Michael."

Stull's hand looked completely normal, but Michael was still reluctant to shake it. He took it, though, and was surprised to find the flesh cold and wet. He jerked his hand back and looked at the palm, expecting to see it coated with moisture. But it was dry.

He gave Stull a parting nod, then turned and left the back room.

* * *

As he stepped out of the store and into the rain, he began making plans. When he got back to his car, he'd start researching local hospices on his phone. How much money would he need to bribe one of the employees? Did he have enough in savings? He wasn't sure. He'd have to check his bank balance.

The rain was colder and coming down harder than before, the thunder more intense, the wind a wild roar. All the sounds—rain, wind, thunder—merged to become an impenetrable wall of noise so loud that it took Michael a moment to realize something.

For the first time in his life, he could no longer hear the Song.

He stopped on the sidewalk and stood there, shivering, head hunched over to keep the driving rain out of his eyes, and listened.

No Song.

It had been with him all his life, pressing down on him like a great millstone, relentlessly grinding, grinding, grinding, reducing his mind and spirit to infinitesimal bits. It was only now, when the Song was silent, that he realized what it meant to be truly free, and he laughed with joy.

Was this just a bizarre coincidence, or had Stull done something to make it happen? Michael thought of the man's parting handshake and his wet, cold grip. Like the rain.

But why would the man give him what he wanted *before* Michael paid him? Stull hadn't struck him as the type to act out of the kindness of his heart. He was a businessman, a trader of goods and services. He wouldn't just give this blessed Silence away.

Michael's left hand felt strange, and he moved it closer to his face so he could examine it. The fingers were tingling, especially his pinkie and his ring finger. The rain wasn't *that* cold, was it? He still had normal sensation it the rest of his body, so why...

The tingling in his two fingers intensified to the point where it became painful, and then—just when he thought he couldn't stand it anymore—the sensation stopped, and he felt a gentle, almost pleasant release. He watched his fingers lose cohesion, liquefy, and be washed away by the rain, leaving only patches of smooth flesh where they had been attached to his hand.

He had never experienced anything so wonderful.

Something Doctor Tricia said came back to him then.

If you're at peace when you finally die, you might—just might—escape the Song.

He then remembered Stull's words.

It's a cold rain coming down today. A man could catch his death out there.

And he recalled the village's motto on its website.

Ambergris Falls—We Do Things Our Own Way.

In a normal shop, you paid first then received your goods. But in Audio Junkie, maybe it was the other way around.

Michael knew he couldn't stand here forever. Sooner or later, the rain would end, and the Song would return full force. He didn't think he could take that. But then he didn't have to, did he?

He held the jar with the remaining three fingers on his left hand and unscrewed the lid with his right. Still leaning over, using his body to block the rain, he moved the jar close to his mouth. He took a deep breath, held it for a second, and then exhaled. As he released his breath, he let go of everything—pain, sorrow, fear, hopelessness—and his entire body began to tingle. He quickly screwed the lid back on the jar, bent down, and placed it on the sidewalk.

Then, weeping tears of joy, he collapsed into liquid and became one with the rain.

* * *

A few moments later, Oren Stull stepped out of his shop. He gripped the metal frame of an umbrella in his hand, but even without fabric, it still somehow protected him from the rain. He walked down the sidewalk a bit until he came to the jar. He picked it up, held it to his ear, and listened. Smiling, he lowered the jar and gazed down at the rainwater rushing along the gutter toward a nearby sewer grate.

"Pleasure doing business with you, son."

Stull turned and headed back to his shop, the new addition to his collection held tight in his hand, whistling a tune that Michael—if he'd still been alive to hear it—would've recognized.

THE BRAZEN BULL

BY SOFIA AJRAM

I can tell you what will happen. I can play your mentor.

On a night you won't remember, the fading chambers of its heart will bellow, and the sound will cleave across the sky like a sonic boom, and when it finds you, it will bifurcate your life into two.

You will hear it forever. Yes, it will be loud, and it will be constant, but you will grow used to it, the way we grow used to all of the daily meditations of our bodies—in time, with unbridled patience.

It will be different each time you hear it, and yes, you can medicate to keep it quiet, and no, it will not help abate the sound completely, but I promise you that it is not some Guantanamo-style torture, because you will learn to enjoy it. Sometimes it will be discordant, barbaric, redolent of a guttural war cry. Other times, it will be manufactured in violent intervals. Often, a sort of funeral dirge. These things will stain your imagination and stir something in you.

When you will be seventeen, you will try to reproduce it. You will collect materials to make an instrument. You will scrape, sand, and glue. Make tuning pegs of steel ball bearings and frets of nickel cable springs. Your hands will tremble as you work to string oiled wire over a metal rig, and although your device will come together, that sound will be irreproducible.

When you will be twenty-nine, or thirty-two, or fifty, or whatever age, you will no longer want songs that bite. You will want a madrigal that bleeds. You'll think: life has ridden me so hard for so long that I have had to come up with my own coping mechanism, and from that coping, you'll know that it exists—this machine that bellows this sound—in the way dreams are unrelenting premonitions of real places unvisited. Ask others. Some will hear it, the same as you. You'll find word of them following it. To stand in Los Angeles, or Sinai, or some gloomy castle. You'll know it'll have been to find the source of the song.

You will endure until you no longer can, packing up your things—the important ones; the essentials, so to speak—and you will head for the sound. You will bring your Walkman and your tarot deck, some victuals and a sleeping bag. You won't need a compass. On second thought, you won't need the Walkman, either. The sound will keep you company.

And you will follow its trail like a milk-hungry kitten.

It will shepherd your aching soles across open fields as vast as lunar horizons, through deserts and dreams that are almost bucolic.

Sometimes, on nights where the songs seem so intimate, so familiar—a whisper across the wind reaching directly between your ribs to grasp the seat of your heart—you will think you may lose your mind if you don't find its birthplace. Every day, it will acetone the chambers of your heart and wear away at your soul.

Eventually, the sharp command of sound will filter in from all directions. You will find yourself in a forest, somewhere on the other side of the world where the climate, the language, the soil, will all be foreign to you.

Cresting upon the hillside like a sliver of moon, you will see them winding serpentine across the mountain.

"Hello!" you will shout.

A domestic face will turn toward you and stop. You will stumble down the face of a hill and comically stagger up another until you reach her. She will be stout, buttermilk-skinned and fair-weather pretty. When she'll greet you, her voice will be stripped.

You will ask her if she's here for the sound—and when she will say yes, she is going *there*, too, you will feel an immense joy well up in your chest.

These will be them. Your people. You're not insane, they will hear it too, are moved in animal persuasion to follow it to its source, just as you have been.

You will throttle a barrage of questions at her all at once. How long has she heard it? Was it loud or did it ramp up? Did she first hear it in a song? How had she assumed the direction?

"Helluva mystery, isn't it?" she'll say, and smile thinly.

Together, you will creep through the brush and find the machine that oils your purpose; colors your life with sound.

So disoriented, you will stumble along, and for the first time since breaching this space, you will sense something larger than yourself—no longer just the sound of that *thing*, or your breath or your footfalls, but a hushed elegiac utterance.

There will be proselytizing spectators, audience to this orchestral number, supplicants of this holy space, gorging themselves on song.

The forest will shed its density, branches shouldering back, halted and crippled as though by heat, before bending open into a glade-like sanctuary.

And this will be what it is: at the center of the clearing, like the votive offering of a Trojan horse, will be an immense metallic creature—

A brass bull.

It will sit like a sentry, guarding a pyre beneath it, fanned and fed by spectators, biting at the air like an auto-da-fé spectacle.

A queue of people—like small and insignificant farm animals, their faces intent—will dot into an assembly line like an ellipsis, scaling up rungs on the strong, tall pillar of its leg and into its open mouth in funereal procession. Dark rags will ribbon and dribble out the ass of the great bull into a red sludge on the soil, and from its nostrils will rise thin plumes of smoke.

You will approach and inspect it with a farrier's gentle touch; its hollow bronze metal, muscled with the most exquisite Florentine detailing. The unearthly proportions of woven planks of brass making up its ribs, high as a sequoia, titanous as a ship. Its proud, upturned head, and slightly parted lips. The way the sun will gleam off of the polished metal, lightly tarnished, warming the soil. Poised on its hoof, you will notice a most unusual etched detail: a marking, small, like the intaglioed peaks of a polygraph test. The brass will be autographed. Branded and signed, *your name.*

You will hear it come alive: enormous, the sound that pours out of it slow and deliberate, exquisitely lush as though greased by the oils of gods, and the deadly lullaby will cradle you like a snake charmer.

My god, you will wonder. What could make that sound? What instrument within?

You will have done nothing but covet it since you were a child, and the yearning, wine-dark and wild, will urge you forward. There will be a way in. If the eyes are the windows to the soul, then a tender mouth is the gateway.

You, too, will climb diligently into it, past those thinly parted lips, skimming your shins on gilded teeth.

You will come to it, a pilgrim resolute, composed and on your feet, but like the throne of any fiefdom, it will force you to your knees.

What wild dementia will possess you to venture inside? Courage—? Hubris—? An aroused curiosity? Or will it be stupidity which gathers you in its fist like a dictator?

Inside: mouth, lolling tongue, uvula, all made of brass, will bottleneck at the throat and tilt back into darkness dense as crude oil. And here, the dislocated sound again, an echo in desperation to hear itself will call you forth.

Past a few yards, you will see the silhouette of the pretty woman disappear beyond the gilded glint of a downward turn, into the beast's throat like a drainpipe.

A spindly mustachioed man on hand and knee will nip at your heels with his fingertips in impatience.

"Shit or get off the pot!" he will balk, and you will not be able to help yourself, ducking into and crawling down the fathomless dark that siphons you in like anaphylaxis.

Its golden throat will extend before you to map the interior of this beast in a trombone-like series of curving passages. The metal will loop up and down and around in neat right-angle bends like a taught ribbon. On and on, those smooth and cylindrical pipes will spill back-and-forth in rises and falls, squeezing you through its curvature of tunnels and valves while the songs crossfade in contrapuntal symphony. You will wonder just exactly which way is up. A playground affection will swell in you: of slides and play structures, and with it, a sense of profound awe. Behind the man who is so rude to you will be another crawling body, and another, pumping into this beast's gullet like gasoline. Because of this, there will be no moving backwards out of this space, only forward. Your breathing will grow thin. You will try not to think about it.

Slowly, as though unwrapping a savored gift, the sound will lap forth in gorgeous waves from deep within the beast. It will produce a resonance in you that will make you think vaguely of delicate fruit, heavy on the branch, sweetest at the source. And then, somehow, from one tunnel to the next, the sound will ripen quite rapidly, fermenting the plucked fruit to cloying rot. It will seem nearly synesthetic, that an overripe sound could make you so nauseous. You'll be uncertain if that's what it is until you'll take a second breath and clap a sweaty palm over your nose and mouth. Not a blend of senses, exactly. The music will have sagged into discordance, yes, but you will not be imagining it. There will also be an odor of filthy machinery and burnt oil and the festering of decay corked in with you all.

And here, it will be hot—sweat-slick—and disorienting. The tube will pitch up in slight inclines, and when your hand will slip, you will rest a moment to gather yourself. The man behind you will bump into your ass. He will immediately start barking at you like a mad dog. "Move! What's the *matter* with you?"

Turning to him over your shoulder, you will see, just so, the blazing silver coins of his eyes, wild as though transformed by the light of the full moon, damp with hysteria and hemmed by furrowed brow with contempt.

"Go on. Hurry it up!" he will say tartly.

And you will not want to argue. You will stretch your palm toward the woman ahead of you, but you will find that she's gone. You'll creep forward and find yourself at the end of a juncture. Your fingers will curl around the ledge of a chasm, the width of a storm drain. You'll reach across it and feel the metal overhead curve straight down in front of you in a sudden ninety-degree drop.

The lasting notes of the song will hang in the air, and then flicker out. Slowly, you will begin to reassess where you are and what you've done.

As you will lean your body forward to anticipate the depth of the drop, it will choke your senses with the overwhelming metallic reek—something tinged gastric. Grotesque terror will dance in your belly.

And then, an eager hand will harshly shove you from behind. And before you will have time to even think, you will fall, tumbling from your perch, plummeting inexorably down the chute.

And you will be inside it, then. Really inside it.

Black will bruise your senses. It will be blindingly dark.

Here, where the song should be at its finest and purest, it is not. To your horror, you will find its absence. It will be strangely, eerily quiet. Instead, that nauseating pestilence will pepper the air, heavy and persistent, turning your stomach. Viscous plasma will suckle up to your shins, the membranes of something thick and macerated clotting between your fingers.

Others will continue dropping in from the chute above you. Some will heave their inert bodies into the beast with reckless abandon, while others will be shoved in by force, colliding into one another. The panicked fists of the mustachioed man will grope around the slush and find purchase against the side of your head, pushing you into the muck to hoist himself up. You will crawl out from beneath the mound, reaching, stumbling desperately in the pitch. Your hand will meet along the smooth, bare framework of the interior wall, body-warm, and you will reel.

And then there will be shoving, pushing hands and elbows and chests, all pressed up against your skin. Movement will gradually diminish. The human density will become so thick, your arms and legs will soon no longer have space to move.

Then there will be a sound. Not a song—not yet. More like mechanical workings: a squeal of metal under protest; an orchestral tuning underfoot. Suddenly, an infernal glow will dye the ground menstrual. Not sunlight, you will think. Nothing so hospitable.

By the dim light of this, you will be able to perceive, just so, a sight that you will not want to see. A wall of people pressed up against the brass lining of the bull's belly, staring at you, glassy-eyed, coming to the slow, lucid realization of exactly what this is: a statue, yes; an animal, maybe, but also a machine; a system that will slowly compress, digest, and roast you inside of it like a roaring incinerator.

Crushed between the masses, you will fix your gaze to the hatch and realize it is too high to reach. The flap gate will have already been triggered shut. There will be nowhere to go.

And beneath you will bloom the glow of the most primal womb of colors: red. *Red.* Obscured by the metastasizing crowd of legs, the rhythmic claustrophobia and percussive drumming of too many people in too dark a space, and then you will see what this is.

A digestion. An erosion. A death, in order for there to be some sort of song. A sacrifice. Invisible to the layman. I'm sorry, but it's not something we see from the outside. Nobody wants to know how the meat is made.

The pyre beneath the beast will burn. Fire—the one power which rivals god. Lit by who? you'll wonder. The supplicants outside, desperate for another song? If you were still outside, would you, too, light that fire? Slake that thirst?

A frenzy will erupt, converging, rippling outwards, past you and to those fastened to its walls like pilot fish. They will be the ones to feel it first. The heat. It will kiss at their skin, as the air starts to corrode, rusting with the scent of blood. Sweat will cover your faces.

Your veins will feel like a fiery stream just beneath the paper-thin rind of your skin.

Like any good machine, it will break you down. Convert you, all of you, to a pulpy paste; make songs of the screams. It is the suffering that makes the art. Somewhere you will have heard this. It's what made Orpheus turn. This knowledge will not assuage your torture. You will still be burned alive, crushed in a belly—hot, and friendless, and in the dark.

Some bodies will not be built like yours—they'll ache and groan and the heat and external pressure will become too much to bear, and they will burst. Pus and lymphatic fluid will cover their skin. Clumps of hair will burn away in glimmering cinders. Fingernails will wrench from their nail beds as they will try helplessly to scrape against the metal in animal fear. What will stick, instead, will be their skin. The soft pads of their fingers will cling to the molten metal in dextrinization, like tongues to iron lampposts.

The stink will be so nauseating, you will almost pass out. You will smell yourself roasting and a cry will froth up out of you, crawling skyward.

Soft flesh will be rent; your joints will throb and you will feel as though you are expanding somehow.

Your own body will tremble, and a wild sound will burble up through your belly and rip out of your mouth, joining the choked screams of everyone around you, piping through the meridians of metal and splintering out the brazen bull like squeezed bellows,

And the beast will come alive with the cries of its makers.

You will almost be able to hear it—the song—and this time it will be yours, it will be the song of an entire generation, pain silted to its most economical element—wild, demented screams, salted with tears. You will scream until it's all you have left, until the flesh and the meat and the bone have sloughed off, until you are reduced to the purity of resonance that bleaches up into the sun.

And here it will be. The cruel indignity, carried by delirium, of knowing what it's like to sing with the clear voice of the mad. What will you have given up for it? Your life? What life? A life moved through shadow, the afterimage of a hideous dream. Who will it have been that stuck this dream in you like pins in a voodoo doll? You'll think, it's because it's all you have. It's all you'll ever have had, and if you're going to come apart, you might as well make something beautiful of it.

The miserable thought will cross your mind to warn others, but would it have stopped you? You, who will have climbed into the brazen bull and sung a song that will have killed you. But maybe, of that song, someone will come looking to trace its origin. And maybe they'll find the bull that was your end—your art, your song—and maybe they'll think to themselves:

And I, if I climb in?

OIL OF ANGELS

BY GEMMA FILES

Text of a note left behind for her parents to find by Ester Oricielo (still missing):

DEAR MOM AND DAD—

BY NOW YOU KNOW I WENT ANYWAYS, EVEN THOUGH YOU
SAID I COULDN'T. TO YOU IT'S A CONCERT, AND I GET THAT.
TO ME IT'S SOMETHING ELSE. I NEED TO SEE THEM LIVE,
AND I'M GOING TO. IT'S MY MONEY. I'LL TEXT YOU AFTER.
DON'T KNOW IF I'LL BE BACK, DEPENDING ON HOW THAT
GOES. I LOVE YOU.

                                              E.

Text exchange between freelance journalist May Burnside and Cultural Slide *webzine editor Dwina Wandrell, 01/11/2023:*

- 3:35 a.m. -

hey, M‹y, you up?

get up

get up RN not kidding

- 3:38 a.m. -

kay

up NOW

you hear about the concert?

what concert

cicada, doom in a room

you hear?

that was today?

*night?

boot up, go to cp24.com

- 3:41 a.m. -

oh *shit*, dee

EXACTLY

* * *

Second text exchange between DW and MB, 1/11/23

- 4.55 pm -

> don't want to rush you
> May but?????

yeah yeah, sending what
I've got so far. mostly quotes
and notes, not hooked up yet

> we need CONTENT on this

well, it's complicated
can't just keep updating
w/same crap

> why not?

everyone else is

> b***, f**k YOU

---

* * *

Notes towards an article about the mass disappearance of audience members from the Cicada Music "Doom In A Room" showcase, 31/10/2023

According to police sources and family members [specifically Jerry and Margo Oricielo], many came because of social media rumors about an appearance by Oil of Angels, Skull Covenant frontperson Sarai Lispector's occult gloomcore side-project (possibly named after the song by 1980s experimental band Cocteau Twins, given its reliance on drone and low-volume, looping vocals [check])

—Skull Covenant is/was a fairly well-known Toronto doom metal band, the first band signed by Cicada Music, a company formed in 2015 to develop, promote, and distribute what they called Toronto Dark. Every Doom in a Room thus far has been arranged to introduce a new Cicada band (Skull Covenant being the first, also in 2015).

—This was Cicada's first official Doom in a Room since the end of the Covid-19 pandemic

.

—Other acts performing sets that night were fellow Cicada bands Vestment of Worms, Gore Crow, Widdershins Nazarene, and Eeyore, all introduced at previous Doom in a Rooms (2017, 2018, 2019, and 2020, respectively). The lineup was supposed to end with a full set from Skull Covenant, possibly followed by Oil of Angels.

—Since the venue where Doom in a Room usually takes place (Killya Darling's) folded during the pandemic, [third "during the pandemic," fix it later] the show was moved to Wychwood Barns Art Collective's largest performance venue, the Slam, which has a formal 150-person capacity. Eyewitnesses claim the crowd inside exceeded this by at least a hundred, probably more. [check, is this actually possible?]

—Masks were required inside, and audience members had to show vaccine passports in order to get through the front door. People turned away were allowed to stand outside and watch the show on flatscreen TVs mounted on the Slam's outer walls, with two generator-powered speakers providing sound. These speakers apparently blew when Oil of Angels took the stage; outside attendees claim they couldn't hear anything from that point on, except screaming.

* * *

This is what happened, and maybe how. What we still don't know, as of now, is why.

"I came with three friends," says Genevieve Joscelin, University of Toronto Kinesiology student and self-described Skull Covenant "superfan." "I left alone. Woke up in Emerg, and nobody can tell me what happened. Mab [Coorie] and Ai [Fang]"—both also U of T, both still missing—"were into the band, like me...but Derek [Kuletski, Joscelin's boyfriend of two years], he only came because I asked him to. He didn't like anything harder than Dad rock." She starts to cry. "I just want to know what happened."

Philip Takashima admits he's still angry, despite having good reason not to be. "I was this close to making it inside," he claims, rubbing one fist like he wants to punch something. "After months of planning, seeing that club door slam in my face, I was ready to f***ing commit murder. So I stood there stewing for close to an hour, moving back to look at the screen and then up to the door again, just praying they'd open back up...and then I saw the screens go out, just as the screaming changed. Because everyone's screaming, right? But I heard the difference, I heard it right away." Now he looks haunted. "And it got worse. Me and a couple of other guys, while we were trying to break down the doors, we realized the noise was fading. Getting quieter. There had to be at least a couple hundred people in there, and when we finally got the doors open? Maybe a dozen came out. At most. I could see bodies on the floor and the stage, but nowhere near enough. And the air inside was full of smoke, and it stank like..." He shakes his head. "Shit. And blood."

One witness speaks from his hospital bed only on condition of anonymity, as he admits to being a notorious illegal livestreamer. "I use—used to use, crutches and a fake leg cast," he confesses. "GoPros and a mike built into a crutch handle, batteries taped in my armpit, my phone in a compartment in the cast, and who hasn't got an earbud in twenty-four seven these days? Nobody complains about a dude holding up a crutch—well, not usually. But I think that was why I saw the shit kick off before anybody else did.

"Sarai had just started her big stunt piece where they were trying to play music off an actual rock, like a physical stone, something she said she'd brought back from...Israel, I think? Turkey? I don't know how it was supposed to work, but I heard about fifteen seconds and then my earbud blew, like, just this deafening static screech in my ear. So I drop one of the crutches and I rip out the earbud, cursing a blue streak, and I think that was when the security guy by the stage realized something was hinky, 'cause he climbs down and starts pushing through the crowd towards me. Well, I've already seen my GoPros are dead too, so I do a one-eighty and start fighting my way out of there, and then—" He pauses.

"Everything goes dead silent," he says at last. "And then it was like somebody turned on the biggest spotlight in the world, behind me. Like, I could feel this light, physically shoving me in the back. I went down on my face in the middle of the crowd, and I remember I thought, 'F**k, am I deaf?!' before it all goes black. And then I woke up in the ambulance, and they tell me I might be stuck with crutches for real, this time. For a long time, anyway."

He tries to smile.

* * *

- 5:15 p.m. -

R U kidding me?
THIS is what you got
out of your interviews?

i know, it's weird

it's thin. doesn't actually
tell us much

more than anybody else
has, so far

get me some cops/relatives
on the record, at least

working on it

---

* * *

27

Notes fr. Conversation w/ TO Police Dept Public Relations

—Inside of Slam's covered in blood but no bodies. (Everyone they actually found was alive, went to hospital. Any other event like this?)

—They're trying to type the blood, possibly break it down for DNA. Relatives giving samples. Says it'll take "incredible" amount of time. (Not willing to say how long that might be, or even take a guess.)

—Not willing to speculate further on nature of incident until more evidence is found or existing investigation is resolved. WAIT, EXISTING INVESTIGATION?????

Notes fr. Conversation w/ TO Det. Davis Whitfield, Sex Crimes

—Holy crap. Whitfield says Sarai Lispector's been subject of investigation as "person of suspicion" for close to a year

—Been reaching out to small select group of fans: email, Instagram DMs, texts. Lot of them just "kids," like Ester Oricielo (we're talking seventeen to nineteen, which isn't really kids per se, IMHO). All invited. Most of them came, lot of them defying parents.

—Ester's relatives sent copies of Sarai's emails to police. "She was grooming our daughter. That's what they call it, right? Teaching her all this...stuff. Against God." Weird stuff about how she's the perfect person to come see Oil of Angels. "We're kin," Sarai apparently told her. How so?

—Who are the Lispectors?

* * *

Excerpt of online creative writing from Sarai Lispector, age 19, c. 2015:

After the fall of Constantinople, we opened up all the reliquaries and made a brand new saint from what we found inside, a saint made from saints. Then we made armor from the bones of our martyrs, those killed in battle under the new saint's banner. And then, last of all, we made a chapel from the rest of the bones to contain our saint, because after the fall, bones were all that we had left.

We rode out wearing eyeless bone masks and wings on our backs, covered all over with our new saint's relics; we didn't need to see; we had faith. Perpetual adoration. And beneath those eyeless masks our pupils turned inwards, spinning like pinwheels, opening like irises. Letting out a black so dark, no exterior light could ever hope to penetrate it.

We hooked an archangel and pulled him down, fighting all the way. We made the hook from half-angel bones and tempted him with Oil of Angels, extract of compounded Nephilim—he smelled it from far off and went into a frenzy, determined to destroy what God had told him should be extirpated. What clever heretics we were, to weaponize God's law and turn it against Him!

Angels cannot destroy each other, after all; the Apocrypha tell us as much. Satan was thrown down, not killed. They are all made from the same substance, the Word Made Flesh, the thoughts of God. So it only follows, sensibly, that nothing from Heaven can be overcome, except with its own substance.

Pinned to that hook and surrounded by wards, fenced in with all the myriad names of his (and our) progenitor, we pruned him, cut him back, pin-feathers and all. We knew his wings would grow eventually, those quills of his carving their way back into the world, drawing blood from the air with their motion; we did not dream we could hold him forever. But we got what we wanted, even so: to bind our blood to his, to the One Name's, the Maker's.

For Who Is Like God but you, Micha'el, old ancestor? Whoever could be?

That was our ambition, you see. Our generative sin. To make Nephilim of ourselves. To set ourselves apart from all others, a living affront, stronger than any by sheer virtue of our arrogance, our heresy.

My grandmother told me this, as her grandmother told her. And on, and on, and on. So far back, the words we wanted to use to tell this story had not yet been written.

So far back, we had to make up our own words for we wanted to say.

* * *

- 7:31 p.m. -

i'm confused. R u saying
lispector was a child predator?

i'm saying i don't think
this was an accident

she chose everybody in
that audience; every other
person, anyhow

and she had some kind
of a reason for choosing
who she chose

which is?

don't know

but i got hold of the band's
agent – he says he'll ask
joey kau to call me back
from hospital

the keyboardist? thought
he was in a coma

seems not. agent promised
he'd call tonight

setting my watch [/sarc]

* * *

Transcript, phone interview, 1/11/2023 10:42pm

M. BURNSIDE (MB), J. KAU (JK)

JK: Am I the only one left?

MB: From the band? Uh, yeah. I mean, the other guys from Skull Covenant are okay, basically—they were backstage already, in the green room.

JK: Sounds about right. No, I meant...from the concert.

MB: We don't really know what happened to anybody else. Yet.

JK: ...that sounds about right too. From what I saw.

MB: Which was—?

JK: Well.

(PAUSE)

What did you hear?

MB: A lot of different things, really. I was hoping you could clear them up for me.

JK: I can try.

MB: Okay. Um...a lot of people are saying Sarai was handing out invites right and left on social media, that's why the place was so overcrowded. True or false?

JK: True.

MB: And these people she picked out, they were—really young, a lot of them? Like...

JK: Oh yeah, they were. The special fans.

MB: Special like how? I mean...some of the parents, they're throwing words around like, um—grooming? Like they, like kind of implying—

JK: Oh wait, what? No, no, no: That wasn't Sarai's thing at all. She had me, she had Eya...two full-grown adults just hung the f***k up on her, both of us. Which was pretty funny, considering how much we couldn't stand each other.

MB: Eya, this is Eya Gall, right? Secondary vocalist for Oil of Angels?

JK: The very same. Classically-trained, don'tcha know.

(PAUSE)

She's gone too, now—they, shit. They're gone. The both of them.

MB: Yeah, still missing. You're saying you guys were all—

JK: Well, obviously. But I really don't want to talk about Eya, okay? I mean, I barely want to talk about Sarai. (PAUSE) I will, though, don't worry. You'll get your story.
MB: ...all right. Thank you.

JK: Oh, don't thank me yet.

(PAUSE)

Do you know why she called the band Oil of Angels?

MB: Because of the Cocteau Twins—

JK: No. She knew people would assume that, but no.

MB: Okay, then why?

JK: You ever read that stuff she wrote, Sarai, back when she wanted to write books instead of songs? The "family stories?"

MB: I looked it up, yeah, sure. It's on your website.

JK: Uh huh. Well, they told her something else when she was growing up, the Lispectors, something even weirder. She said they told her if you found a way to kill a bunch of Nephilim and boil them down somehow, you could make your very own guardian angel.

MB: ...what?

JK: Nephilim. People like her, supposedly. And her grandma, and her grandma's grandma...

MB: —because her family f* * *ed an angel right after the fall of Constantinople, or something. Right?

JK: Or something, yep.

MB: And you believed that?

JK: Sarai did. And Eya did, because Sarai did. And me...(PAUSE) We started Oil of Angels during Covid, you know that, right? Hooked up with Eya on the Web, formed ourselves a little magical musical polycule. Wrote and recorded the album. And then, when international air-flights finally opened up again, we all went to Chorazin together...Khirbat Karazza, whatever it's called now. You know where that is?

MB: Um...it's in Turkey, somewhere? Supposedly where the Antichrist is going to be born. Oh, and M.R. James said Count Magnus went there to...right, I get it. That's why the album's called Black Pilgrimage.

JK: Yeah, that was Sarai's idea, like everything else. So—that's where the rock was from.

MB: The rock from the concert.

JK: Black basalt. We played it on an acoustic turntable, an analog amplification system with resonant membranes—a stylus picks up surface variations, transmits the vibrations to a copper horn and bang. This Colombian artist, Leonel Vasquez, invented the original version. The idea was to make a noise nobody'd ever heard before and weave the song around it...something cool for our first live performance, y'know. For the fans.

MB: Was it a new song, too?

JK: No, it's on the album. The last track. You've probably heard it.

MB: ...maybe.

JK: Doesn't matter. Anyhow—that rock made a sound, like a shofar, or a kangling. Like one of those...you know that noise from Inception, that "BWWWAAAOOOAAAAWWW" sound? They do it with a machine, something they invented for the first Star Trek movie. Not that, but like that. It made me want to throw up. I mean, I felt like I was browning out, like I was gonna swoon. And then I saw Eya start to scream, and float, and melt. Like all of her was coming apart, and just—boiling upwards.

MB: Um...Mr Kau?

JK: Sssh, just listen, okay? Just listen.

(PAUSE)

Sarai met Eya on some Nephilim-gene board on the Dark Web, supposedly, so I guess it makes sense about her. But what I still don't get, what I'll never know, is how she found all those other ones. All those kids. Didn't think angels f***ed around that much, to be frank. Then again, demons are angels too, right? And

34

there's the Watchers, like in that weird-ass Aronofsky movie...think those were the ones who first thought monkeys looked hot, according to Sarai...but anyhow. Anyhow.

(PAUSE)

I see what's happening to Eya and makes me feel sick, even sicker, so I look away instead and then I see what's happening to everybody else. All those special, special fans coming apart the same way, spewing into the air in a huge f* * *in' gore milkshake or something—blood sprayed all over the walls, but the rest, it went up towards the stage, towards Sarai. Splashing onto her like a reverse waterfall made from nothing but guts, skin, bone-marrow, cells. And first it was pinky-red, and then it was gold, and then it was white, bright white. And Sarai—she was in it, but she wasn't part of it, you get me? It was holding her, wrapped up in itself, clutched tight in two long things like tentacles, or maybe like, um...claws? Those two things a praying mantis has, the ones they tear bugs apart with. Tight. Kind of like it loved her. Kind of like it wanted to eat her.

(LONG PAUSE)

MB: What happened then?

JK: Um...it came apart too? Flicked out two bits of itself, wide, like a pair of wings. And it went up.

MB: Up?

JK: Through the roof. That big window up there, the one they cover at night—I heard it break. Glass came down everywhere. Got a big piece of it in my back, all down one side; I lost a lot of blood too, the docs told me. They took it out while I was sleeping. So...up through there, and into the sky, so high I couldn't see it anymore.

MB: And Sarai?

JK: Oh, she went with it. She was yelling. Telling it to stop. Telling it let go, then don't let go. Don't, don't, don't...

(LONG PAUSE)

MB: Listen, I have to ask—

(JK SIGHS)

—no, but seriously, you know I do. Did you...expect what happened to...happen?

JK: Like, did I think it would work? Of course not! I mean, who could possibly... well, Sarai, sure. Obviously. But no, I never thought...f**k. (PAUSE) F**k.

MB: I'm sorry.

JK: Oh, are you? Me too.

(PAUSE)

I know what happened after that, you know. Saw it...dreamed it, I guess, in my coma. Because why not, after all this other crap? Sarai...I think she thought she'd be absorbed by it, kind of, like everybody else, but better. Become its brain, or its heart...its conscience? The monkey on the angel's shoulder. And instead it just grabbed her and went straight up, so far she died, and when it figured out she'd stopped yelling, figured out how it couldn't make her work again, it just dropped her. Probably find her drifting in from the Islands next week, all freezer-burnt and suffocated, with every bone broken from slamming into the water—surface tension gets pretty hard once you're up over a mile, I bet. Yeah, I think that's right...

(PAUSE)

'Cause that's the thing about angels—they don't have free will. Not even the ones that want it. And this one, created beyond the boundaries of either side...no will, no wisdom, no experience beyond that moment it came together, just—power. An angel only beholden to her who made it, except...

MD: ...she's dead.

JK: That's right. She sure as f**k is.

(LONG PAUSE)

And now it's just out there, somewhere—unwelcome in hell, unwelcome in heaven. Yeah, that's got to suck.

(PAUSE)

Here's the thing I worry about, though: What comes next, now she's gone. Now it's rattling around the cosmos with no one to look after, no one to take orders from. No one to love it. No one to love. How mad that's gotta make it. And what that might make it want to do to us, if—I mean, when...

(LONG PAUSE)

MD: When what?

JK: When it comes back, you dumb-ass. Because...it will. I mean—

(VERY LONG PAUSE)

—I would.

* * *

- 11:59 PM -

there's no f**king way
we can print this, May,
you get that right?

don't think that's true,
actually
like
not necessarily

WTF dude
I mean, * TF *

look, he said it
I didn't
so all the crazy's in quotes
so
its cool

this is anything BUT
cool you weirdo

...

okay, it's pretty cool

...

...

let me think

will do

* * *

Lyrics for "Egregore," the final release from Oil of Angels' first (and last) album, Black Pilgrimage:

> *And in the air*
> *A smear of wings*
> *A narrowing*
> *A harrowing*
>
> *We turn the key*
> *An opening*
> *Unlock the gate*
> *To bitter things*
>
> *Now we begin*
> *This is how it starts*
> *We break the sky*
> *The whole world's heart*
>
> *Above*
> *Below*
> *Above*
> *Below*
> *As above*
> *So below*
> *Oh low*
> *Low*
> *Low*
>
> *We bring above so low*
> *From high to hell*
> *From high to hell*
> *Ah el*
> *Ah el*
> *Ah el*
>
> *I call your name, A'el*
>
> *(saraia'el)*

THIS LOADED GUN OF A SONG STUCK IN MY HEAD

BY PAUL MICHAEL ANDERSON

The big takeaway, if you need one, is this: it can be any song. Any song that takes you to a different time, fires up memory in a way where you can almost smell, taste, touch, feel those moments again—whatever's playing through the speakers the first time you met the woman who would become your wife, or what was still playing on the dashboard radio when you crawled bloodily through the gaping hole of the windshield. Any song can cut through the muscle of space and time.

* * *

Patrick said to you in a recent session, "You're letting this song have control over you. You suffered a trauma and linked it to it. Do you think of Carrie and Evelyn when you hear it? No—your brain's decided to focus on *that* song."

You shook your head, your face heating up. In your mind, the vicious little troll cued the song, and your mental blocks took over, screaming nothing into the void. "I *do* think of them—I think of them in the street and everyone standing around and the speakers above Soul Mountain playing good ol' 95.3, The River—" Your lips squirmed around the name. "—and that song playing and—"

Patrick held up a hand. "Replay what you just said. You explained the setting *itself.*"

You saw the Kleenex on the side table, but wiped your eyes with your shirt sleeve.

"A well-timed song can be wonderful for memories," Patrick said. "They're right there with other sensory memories. If I smell Aquafina hairspray—that bitter, crunchy smell? I'm back in middle school, and all the girls I liked used gallons of it to look older. Do you have a similar one?"

The question distracted you, so your answer was immediate, "Vanilla perfume. That was middle school, freshman year. I think of my girlfriend, Steph."

Patrick nodded. "Same with songs. Blondie's 'Heart of Glass'—you know that song?—and I'm a college sophomore, on a date with a woman who would eventually become my first wife. We were parked on the shoulder—don't get any ideas, we'd gotten food poisoning, and we were throwing up. Sounds awful, right? But we were holding hands—" He demonstrated, his elbows parallel to his shoulders. "—so we didn't fall into the mess. It's a *good* memory."

He laughed to himself. "Forget this song—do you have another one?"

"The one by that band Nada Surf, 'Popular,'" you said, and suddenly you couldn't see Patrick at all—in your mind's eye, you saw the street your father and his second family lived on, and you're walking down to the house on the corner, where the girl there, Annette, was waiting. The song was in your head, and Annette would take you to third base for the first time in your life. The memory was so clear that you felt the sun on your shoulders, heard the scrape of your sneakers over the hot top.

You said, "It played all summer when I turned 13."

Patrick said, "Songs can be *good* memories, can't they? But this one song is a weapon you're using against yourself; you're beating yourself up with it. As long as you react to it—and everything you mentioned—it won't let you actually *have* a memory."

He stared at you levelly. "You need to disarm that weapon, John."

* * *

Finney sits at the kitchen table, eyeballing his smartphone, and pulls a cigarette from the open top of his Winstons. His hands shake as he lights it.

He exhales above his head, where it hangs with the dust. He can feel his heart,

41

solid knocks against his ribs. Birds call in the field that Evelyn should've been playing in.

He leaves his cigarette in the ashtray and pulls the phone closer. He wakes up his lockscreen—family photo, like a wooly mammoth preserved in ice—and keys in his passcode. His browser's still up, still showing YouTube, still frozen on an overhead black-and-white shot of an ashtray, a lit cigarette smoldering like the minute-hand of a clock. The video is three minutes and forty-six seconds. A lifetime. An epoch.

He takes a deep breath, remembers what Patrick told him—focus on Evelyn and Carrie, not how the song makes him feel—and it'll become just a song again, just a three-minute pop confection released in 1983, a few months before he was even born.

He taps the PLAY symbol. The song starts with a rifleshot snap of a snare—how come he's never noticed it before? How come he's only ever been able to think of the tight knot of the guitar and bass riffs? It's the most-played song in the history of radio. He'd read that somewhere.

The camera zooms down, and the ashtray transforms into the head of the snare drum, the shot dissolving into the drummer working the rhythm, the camera panning up to take in the guitarist in the background before cutting to a lower angle of a standing bass. Finney's gut churns. His face heats up. He struggles to control both.

He hears his chair squeak, but it's far away, something heard in the other room. "*Every breath...*" the singer begins, and his voice—very low, very British—is even further away. All Finney can hear, really, is that bass and guitar riff, the lyrics beneath not so much sung as *delivered*, like a spell.

And Finney...

...sees the intersection of Main Street and Church Street; Main running to the horizon and Church curling to make a fancy T-shape; the restaurant Soul Mountain on the left with its speakers above the jungle-green painted trim of the wide windows; brick planters, separating the café tables from the curb; the old First National Bank with its ionic columns on the right, draped in shadow...

...feels the heat of the morning sun on his shoulders, the breeze on his arms, the unforgiving solidity of the road as he sprints...

...hears the song playing, the echo of screaming brakes and the *clump*-ing sounds of impact subsumed by pop music, his own tortured breathing...

...smells hot rubber, exhaust...

...tastes the lemon-acidic flavor of fear that has surged up his throat because he's too late, too late by *far*...

Finney screams, tipping the chair over. He rolls onto his stomach and splays his hands, feeling the grit on the old linoleum, this goddamned house falling down around his ears. His mind latches onto this because, somehow, he can still *feel* the heat of morning sun on his head and shoulders.

The song's no longer playing.

He pushes onto his knees slowly, sees his phone and his ashtray, the butt of his cigarette but no smoke. "It played through?" He doesn't remember the song *playing*, only remembers that riff like a garrote, remembers running down Main...

"But not Carrie and Evelyn," he says, and heat fills his face as he stands. Patrick wanted him to see the song for what it was, just something he heard, and what happened? He remembers everything except what mattered.

He bares his teeth. "I'll do it again, goddammit." He wakes up his lockscreen *again*, puts in his passcode *again*, sees the YouTube screen *again*. He hits the replay button, and he hovers over his phone. Don't focus on the bullshit—focus on *them*.

Rifleshot snare, the snapping-fingers emergence of the bass and drums. Camera zooms on the ashtray, dissolves to the drumhead, tilts to take in the drummer and guitarist.

And Finney...

...feels Carrie seizing against him, the narrowness of her neck against his forearm, hot blood soaking through his shirt, her slight weight on his thighs, the twinge in his back from the awkward angle...

...sees everything fractured crystal because the tears are flowing—the misshapen globe of his wife's head, the lumpy red of Evelyn a few feet away, the growing shadow of approaching people, the old pickup accordioned against one of First National's columns...

...smells the hot iron of blood, the sharp tang of sweat, the marshy stench of burst organs...

...hears his own keening; Carrie trying to speak, and he knows she's trying to ask if Evelyn's all right, but her final seizures turn four syllables into thirty-two, and she won't live to get them out...

...tastes the bile lapping at the back of his throat...

Finney jerks back, the speaker on his phone playing out the vaguely Gregorian chanting at the end of the song. He lets out a shuddering breath and goes to wipe his eyes but freezes.

Carrie's blood is *grimed* into his palm and forearm. His gaze slides down, and his shirt is soaked in Carrie's blood.

* * *

"Do you want to talk about the accident?" Patrick asked, longer ago.

"It wasn't an accident."

"You went off the road on 522."

"Nothing happened."

Patrick stared at you, waiting.

You looked down at your hands, your fingers spinning your wedding band. "I had the radio on scan because nothing sounded good." You hissed breath between your teeth. "And that...song came on." The troll in your mind cued it, and every ounce of you screamed in the darkness.

You looked up, and Patrick asked, "And what happened?"

"I started sobbing," you said. "I couldn't see the road, couldn't breathe. The car swerved, went into the ditch between lanes."

He snapped his fingers. "Just like that?"

You sighed. "Pretty much."

"Well," Patrick said, "I definitely think you shouldn't be listening to the radio at all, currently—"

You snorted a humorless laugh.

"—but that's only a symptom of the problem, John."

"My problem's that my family's dead."

"But you're not," he said. "Your problem's not that they're dead, but that you haven't grieved. Emotions don't come like that unless they're building and building."

"I've mourned them since they *died*."

"Mourned them—or mourned *you*?"

Every part of you stopped. "What?"

He leaned forward. "A tragedy happens, completely upends your life, but grief is *dealing with the change*, and I don't think you have. You grieve for Carrie and Evelyn, of course, but you haven't grieved for the *you* you lost."

You swallowed hard. "I'm not following."

"The John Finney that's been coming here is not the John Finney the day before his family died," he said. "And *this* John Finney has not grieved *that* loss, is still thinking he's the same person. But the body needs to heal, so your mind is making this song a trigger to try and force the issue."

"My mind's pretty conniving."

Patrick shrugged. "The mind can get up to some pretty weird shit. The point is, the longer you withhold the grief for the loss of *you*, the worse it's going to get."

"I'm not projectile vomiting, anymore."

Patrick nodded. "No, you're not, but that's not necessarily better, John. You're refusing to deal with what your life is *now*. That song is a force in you—good or bad—but you have to *let it work*."

* * *

Finney stumbles up the old logging road that marks the edge of their property, studying his hands. They tingle against the fragile warmth of the morning sun and the more persistent chill of the breeze. He spent fifteen minutes washing them in the kitchen sink, dimly feeling like Lady Macbeth. His mind's a volatile mixture of absolute disbelief and absolute certainty.

He rolls his hands into fists. He closes his eyes, breathes deeply. Therapy trick—focus on the moment, catalog what the senses perceive. He hears birdsong and the wind, smells the tall grass and the dirt, feels the cold air on his hands and neck, tastes the last cigarette and the acrid mulch of swallowed vomit, sees nothing but the reddish imprint of the sun on his eyelids.

He opens his eyes. A crooked tree in his back field, looking like a black lightning bolt. Sour apples? Cherries? Carrie would've known. He remembers seeing it when the realtor brought them out, thinking of how Evelyn could play with her toys out there, commanding her teddy bears and plushies in elaborate scenes like she did in the apartment.

He looks back at the rambling farmhouse. From this angle, from this state of un-remodeling, it resembles a horror movie house, someplace Leatherface could call home.

"Oh stop it, Jack," Carrie whispers in that amused-but-done-with-it tone, riding a breeze past his ear, and he whirls around. He's alone, of course.

The tears come, and he blinks against the sun. "Oh shit, babe," he breathes. "Oh shit."

The question that's been waiting to be noticed takes its chance, not believing or disbelieving, just asking the obvious: *What if it was real? Patrick said songs can be sensory memories. What if they could be more, though? Hell, when you hear "Popular," Jacky-boy, you know how Annette felt, don't you? That was twenty-five years ago, and you still...*

He looks at his chafed hands. "I had my wife's blood on me."

Not allowing himself to think, he pulls his clear blue lighter from his pocket. He sits on the grassy crown of the old road, and, holding the lighter on his knee, closes his eyes. He thinks to the troll, ever-ready to unleash the worst earworm in the world, *Go ahead.* A vault door shudders open, and he hears that Gordian knot of guitars and bass, now punctuated by the snare drum, keeping it all together.

Finney grinds his teeth, but he...

...sees the planters in front of Soul Mountain, obstructing his path; the tire marks, as black as an evil man's heart, leading right to the reddish mound just beyond the crosswalk; the first shocked, converging crowds; the twisted, less-bloody form of Carrie...

...feels the stitch in his side, the crinkly spit burning his mouth, the heat of the sun on his neck, the lighter falling from his hand...

...hears the lighter clatter to the sidewalk; the panting of his breath; the speakers broadcasting a crescendo of sound, a lilting voice singing, "*95.3, The Riverrrrr...*" before a digital burp cuts through, and the snare of that song starts up again...

...smells hot rubber, overheated engines...

...tastes the first laps of bile climbing his throat...

...and thinks, *Too late, still too late...*

Finney jerks, empty hands flying back to keep from falling. He swallows back the old bile. The song's gone from his mind, and there's blissful silence.

He realizes he feels nothing in his hands. He brings them around, seeing the pinkish indentations left from the embedded stones. *You tossed it, you idiot,* a part of him thinks, but where? He looks around—no glint of clear blue plastic. And, also, could he have been so wrapped in the memory that he really wouldn't have felt himself heaving the lighter into the field?

The question lingers in his head—*But*—and Finney bares his teeth.

A seemingly sensible part of his mind says, *None of this is what Patrick said, Jacky-boy. You're playing with—what?* Time travel? *This is worse than a song making you sob and vomit. You know that, right?*

"I have to bring something *back*," he whispers. "That'll prove it."

Oh my god, a part of him thinks, but Finney's remembering the planters, and how the bushes were just beginning to bloom. He closes his eyes. "Let's do it again."

Snare-drum, then bass and guitars, holding for four measures before that British voice begins to intone—

—and the memory, those few minutes (over seven of them, now that he remembers how the radio station hiccupped) unfolds through him, all his senses awake and humming. But this time, two extras...

...seeing his right hand dart out, grasping a thin, knobby branch of the planter bush...

...the abrading feel of the rough bark as he *pulls*...

....and the effort sends him onto his back on the logging road. His face's wet again from fresh sweat and tears, but he doesn't even clock this because he raises his right hand and sees the oval-shaped leaves of a two-years-past shrub.

There's no such plant in this field.

"Real," he breathes. His whole body shakes. "It's real."

He barely has time to roll before he vomits violently.

* * *

"How do you feel about Travis Cooke?" Patrick said.

You were suddenly very aware of your muscles. "What does that have to do with anything?"

"You're not the first grieving survivor I've counseled, John. It's not uncommon to feel vengeful towards those that *made them* survivors."

"Are you asking me if I've thought about killing Cooke?" It felt like ants were crawling across your skin.

Patrick stared as you shifted on the couch. You forced yourself still. "No, I don't spend my ample free time daydreaming of how Cooke should die. Feel better?"

"Do you? Your family was taken away from you because his brakes were shot on a truck he had a bogus inspection sticker for, and Cooke, now a quadriplegic, is going to spend the rest of his life in assisted living—under security, but the operative word is living. Do you think he's suffering—let's say, *enough*—for what he did?"

"I hope so."

Patrick studied you another moment. "Have you thought about forgiveness?"

"Are you about to go on a Jesus trip?"

Patrick rolled his eyes. "No, John—but why are you coming here? To cope with the loss. That's from *your* intake form. If I'm quoting scripture, it's yours. But I don't see how you can do either of those things if a part of your life wastes the energy of hating Cooke."

"Wouldn't *you* hate him?"

"Sure. For a while. That's natural. Forever, though?"

"I try not to think about him at all. What matters is Evelyn and Carrie. Cooke doesn't factor in."

Patrick cocked his head. "Is that true?"

"Yeah," you said, but your mouth was dry. "It's true."

* * *

Finney collects leaves and branch tips and mulch, a yard sale flyer off a lightpost, and a pile accumulates beside him. He leaves cigarettes, stones, loose change in the past. The song plays almost continuously in his head, and his face is soaked with tears not because of grieving but frustration.

He jumps into any instance during those seven-minutes-and-thirty-two seconds—the length of time The River plays "Every Breath You Take" twice—but none of it matters, because he's always too late: Travis Cooke's ancient truck plows into Finney's wife and daughter when Finney's still halfway down Main Street, after that first snare drum rifleshot. The outcome is always the same. He's a trauma tourist in his own life.

Finney hugs his knees and lowers his feverish forehead. He cries—not cinematic sobs of lost and grief, but the tired, frustrated cries of someone trying to accept there are no options left, no avenues untaken. It cracks open a canyon in his chest, and he shivers, his cries insignificant.

Eventually he raises his head and blinks his leaking eyes. He sees the lightning bolt tree Evelyn will never play under, the field he won't mow, the house he and Carrie will never remodel. A whole list of nevers pile up in his mind.

At the very edge of his view, he can see the top of his old Jeep Cherokee, disappearing and reappearing with the movement of the tall grass. If they'd just driven that Saturday morning, they would've never known Travis Cooke. Finney wouldn't be crying in an untended back field, and Travis Cooke wouldn't be spending the remainder of his days unable to move anything below his collarbone.

Finney's gaze drops to the pile of useless shit he's pulled. A spark, a tiny flame of an idea, blooms. He freezes, as if movement would kill the unarticulated thought, or give the rest of his mind time to put it out.

He slowly uncoils his body, gets to his feet. He shuffles a step, breaking apart the leaves and branches and mulch—the flyer gets caught on the breeze. He sees all of this and none of this, thinking of Cooke, thinking of where Cooke is now and where he was then. Angry dismissal to Patrick aside, he's always known where Cooke was. Not because he fantasized about harming the crippled murderer, that much was true, but because...he liked knowing where Cooke was, how Cooke spent his time.

When Cooke was alone.

Don't try it—the seemingly sensible part of his mind starts, but it's too late. The spark is still small, but it's a Roman candle in his mind, and Finney breaks into a shuffling run.

* * *

"It's the helplessness, right?" Patrick said. This was your third or fourth session. Evelyn and Carrie had been dead for eight months. Travis Cooke had pled guilty, but hadn't yet been transferred to Lavender Hills, the assisted-living facility on Route 340. "The reality that something happened that you couldn't control even a little bit."

You thumbed moisture away from the corner of your eye. "What are you talking about?" Your voice was thick.

"The hardest part of the grieving process," Patrick replied. "For some, anyway. The idea that there's no 'if I'd only done this' that could change the outcome."

"No," you said. "The hardest part of the grieving process is my wife and daughter are gone, and it was random and instantaneous and pointless."

Patrick propped his chin against his hand. "You accept the capriciousness of life."

You thumbed more moisture from the corners of your eyes. "Is there any other choice?"

Patrick straightened. "That's what we're here to learn, isn't it? You tell me."

* * *

Lavender Hills, a long one-story sprawl of sandy-brick and white trim, sits far back from State Route 340, with a man-made pond complete with a brief dock in front.

Finney turns off onto the narrow blacktop lane, and pulls his Cherokee in a VISITOR'S spot behind the home. He's the only VISITOR, he notes—the only other cars have to be employees, parked near the mouth of the lot.

There's no direct path from the parking lot to the semi-shaded patio, where residents are wheeled out in rotation. Finney strikes out across the lawn without even a glance towards the front doors. He's never been inside the home, and he has no intention of changing that at this late date.

The sensible I-have-to-rebuild-my-life part of him says, *You can't be seriously thinking this might work, can you?*

He has no idea. The point is to try.

Is this what Patrick would suggest? that stubborn, surface-pragmatic part asks. He wants to tell that part of himself that Patrick just wanted his patient to heal, to rebuild his life, but that's a lie, hiding a bigger truth: he has no life to rebuild. He *was* a husband and father, and if one takes those pieces away, who is he? No one. A ghost. He haunts his own life more than Evelyn and Carrie ever could.

Finney slows when he reaches the corner, peering around. A handful of residents recline in their wheelchairs, a male nurse slumped at an iron patio table and scrolling his phone.

Finney spots Cooke right away. Cooke's contraption, which looks like a strange hybrid of a chair and a go-kart, stands out. Cooke's facing mostly away, slumped bonelessly and staring at the pond with the morning sun catching on his reddish beard.

Finney freezes. His plan, such as it is, had been direct—grab Cooke's chair, let the song play in Finney's head, and Finney would see if he could drag Cooke into the past with him. He realizes he has no idea what he thinks might happen after that—only that something has to. Could he shove Cooke's chair in front of Cooke's own truck? Could he, by having Cooke with him, somehow remove the truck entirely, and Evelyn and Carrie cross the street safely? He doesn't know, doesn't know how he can know, but knows *something* has to be different.

The thought's like a starting pistol, and he sprints out onto the patio, dodging around the nearest old folks, arrowing for Cooke's chair.

Behind him, he hears the orderly squawk, more startled than angry, "The hell—?" but Finney's hands catch hold of Cooke's chair's bicycle grips, and his momentum carries them forward—off the patio barreling down the short hill to the dock and the pond beyond.

"*What's happening?*" Cooke screams, fear making his slurry voice crack like a child's, and Finney realizes he's never heard the voice of his family's murderer.

Behind him, the orderly shouts, *"Stop! Get BACK here!"*

The pond, its stubby little finger of a dock, rushes up to greet them. Cooke coughs and cries out, gargling; Finney smells the water and the grass; his palms sweat against Cooke's chair handles. In his head, the song starts with its rifleshot, the tight braid of its bass and guitar riff tightening around the thought, *The song is a weapon, but it's not a bludgeon. It's a bullet to be fired—*

Everything around them fades to a blinding white, and exhausted tension climbs up his arms, as if he's flexing against Cooke's chair. His muscles cramp, and he feels an excruciating *pull* at his shoulders, like someone's trying to rip his arms out of their sockets. Vertigo and lightheadedness slam through his mind, clearing out everything else except the song, which swells to deafening levels, vibrating his skull.

It wasn't like this before, Finney thinks with something like excitement, and the song *shifts*, no longer in his head, but something his ears *hear*. At the same time, his hands snap closed around nothing—the chair is gone.

What— he thinks, and the world resolves at the crosswalk between Church and Main Street, Evelyn and Carrie right in front of him, Carrie's thin face stretching into dawning horror as she looks to the left, her hand already attempting to yank Evelyn behind her.

Time slows, and "Every Breath You Take" becomes a dirge. Finney follows Carrie's gaze, sees Cooke's truck bearing down on them, sees *Cooke*, slumped in the driver's seat the way he'd slumped in his modified chair, unable to grip the wheel, his dead weight pressing the accelerator down and making the engine roar.

Too late! Finney thinks, his mind not slowing like everything else, but his hands encounter the space between Carrie's shoulder blades, and he acts instinctively— he *shoves* his wife, sending her and Evelyn flying across the crosswalk.

And Finney...

...sees Cooke slump against the driver's side door as the truck drifts to the right, the morning sun spearing off the windshield, the hungry faded chrome teeth of the grill slamming into his face and plunging his sight into darkness.

...feels the rushing steel crush the bones of his raised forearms, his chest, in an explosion of white-hot pain that fries every nerve-ending, momentum and gravity dragging him under the truck, the street just as unyielding as the back of his skull fractures against the hot top...

...smells the poorly cared for engine, the hot oil and spent gasoline, his own internal fluids on the morning air, the cold finality of metal...

...tastes blood and bile surging up his throat, filling his broken mouth...

...hears the truck pass over him, hears it crash into one of the columns of First National, hears The Police shift to the Gregorian-like chant at the end of the song, hears Carrie's scream, a howl of horror that pockets itself right in a slight lull in sound...

...and then everything fades again, but Finney doesn't get yanked back into the present. His vision remains dark, but the street no longer feels so unyielding, his broken body no longer burning, the stench of hot engines no longer so overwhelming, his mouth numb, Carrie's screams softening until they're a recording of a recording of a recording.

Finney hears Evelyn's own shocked crying, and he manages to think, *She's safe. It's different now.*

The flutter of butterfly wings batting against his shoulders, the top of his head, and it takes all his remaining mental energy to realize, no, those aren't butterfly wings—they're Carrie's hands, she's grabbing him, holding him, and he starts to wonder if this is what Carrie felt...

Finney dies before he can finish the thought.

* * *

"I still can't make sense of it," you say, shifting on the couch.

Patrick cocks his head. "What do you mean?"

"Jack was getting coffee from the Daily Grind—that's halfway down Main Street. How'd he get to us so quickly?"

"Traumatic events often leave gaps in the memory of survivors," Patrick says. "Isn't it possible that he caught up with you beforehand, and your mind just blotted that out?"

You shrug. "Sure...but it doesn't *feel* right. I can remember everything about that morning, but now how Jack got to us." You look at your hands, turn your wedding band on your finger. "I even asked Evelyn—indirectly. She doesn't know where her dad came from, either."

"But your memory is otherwise complete?"

You nod. "Every detail. Evelyn, too. We were in the car the other day, and the song that was playing when Jack was hit came on, and Evelyn burst into tears. I started crying, too. Had to pull over so I didn't crash. It's like—god, the song takes me back so that I can almost *feel* everything, and I'm holding Jack, and he's as dead as the driver, but I don't know how he got there to save us..." You trail off, your vision crystalizing, heat filling your face.

Patrick is silent a moment, then he asks, "What's the song?"

EVERYBODY LOVES MY BABY

BY MERCEDES M. YARDLEY

A new song started up, and there was only one thing for Betts Ingber to do: dance. She moved her knees and shook her hips while her hands flew over her head. She grinned with her lipsticked mouth, and her dark eye makeup hid the black eye Benny had given her the night before.

The music was loud, full of brass, all trombones and trumpets, and the *woo-woo* and *wah-wah* of it took Betts to another place entirely. The Vegas speakeasy was a portal to another world, a place without jobs and tips and serving meals to men in cheap suits. It was a place where she could simply dance.

The music slowed, become something more intimate, and Benny caught her around the waist. Oh, this song again. He buried his face in her neck, took her hand, and hummed along with it.

"*Everybody loves my baby*," Aileen Stanley's voice crooned over the phonograph. Betts rolled her eyes, then swayed with her lover.

It was a nice song, sure, but overplayed, and Betts didn't want to slow dance. She wanted to feel fire, to move her body, but this was Benny's favorite song and so they twirled.

"He's mad for her," people said about Benny and Betts, but it didn't hurt her none. Benny was powerful and handsome and on the good side of the mob. He gave her diamonds and booze and black eyes only now and then, so what did it matter if he liked this slow song like some old man? It didn't hurt nothing.

"*Everybody loves my baby, but my baby only loves me,*" Benny sang into her skin. He grabbed her closer, uncomfortably so, and Betts gasped in pain. The bruises were still fresh.

"That's right, baby," she said. "I only love you."

They say that time slows—that it stops—and that's what happened here. Benny was breathing her in, and she had her lips next to his ear. He smelled of cigar smoke and Brilliantine, and for a moment Betts thought, *This is perfect, this is a beautiful moment. When he's sweet, he's the sweetest.* She kissed his ear, just once on the tip, and was surprised he reacted so violently. He lurched, pulling away from her, his grip loosening, and Betts had just a second to think, *Why? He always loved it before.* Then time sped back up and she realized he wasn't reacting to her kiss at all.

He was jerking, he was bucking, shuddering to a beat that was far too fast and extreme for the song. Betts jumped back, her hands to her mouth. She watched Benny caught in the crossfire of bullets, the sound of the Tommy gun loud and punctuating the song with percussion.

The speakeasy erupted, tables overturned and feet flying as the crowd stampeded toward the exit. Betts was caught up in the massive wave of moving bodies, pulled away from Benny as she screamed his name.

"*Now everybody wants my baby, but my baby don't want nobody but me...*" warbled over the chaos. The record skipped, and the words sounded morose as she called for her lover

"*Baby— Baby— Baby—*"

Betts shrieked, too. "Benny!"

But his suit ran red, the white shirt crimsoning up his chest, blooming near his throat, and then he was spasming on the floor, covered in a bouquet of blood.

* * *

It was wrong. Everything was wrong. Betts wore black at Benny's funeral, her lips lined in bright red, and she couldn't quite make herself loiter by his casket. He looked like a stiff, not like himself at all, and she turned her eyes away as she threw a flower onto his body. She didn't lean down to kiss his forehead or his lips because he was dead, now, wasn't he? The thought of his cold skin made her cringe. It wasn't natural.

Tony C. took her home and walked her to the front door.

"You okay, Elisabet?" he asked. His hair was slicked back, and he reminded her so much of Benny that she dabbed at her eyes.

"I'm fine, Tony. Thanks for askin'."

"It hasn't been quite a week yet," he said. "You don't have to be fine."

Betts looked at his earnest face. Tony had always been soft. It was going to get him popped, and then the world would be a little dimmer.

"How are you?" she asked him.

He scratched at his face awkwardly.

"Not so good, Elisabet. I've known Benny longer than anybody. I never thought he'd go out like this."

Betts' laugh was sharp.

"That's a lie and you know it. What, you thought he'd keel over of old age? A little old man watering his plants and shouting about taxes?"

Tony's lips twitched.

"You're right. That wouldn't be Benny at all. But I didn't see this coming now. He's settled."

He looked meaningfully at Betts, who drew the dark veil on her fascinator farther over her eyes.

"He was still wild. We both know that. I suppose it was only a matter of time." She met his dark eyes with her light ones. "I don't know what I'm gonna do without him, Tony."

Tony stepped forward, dashing in his suit, and took both of her hands.

"I'll help you any way I can," he promised.

Betts gently pulled her hands away. Tony was still sweet on her—had been pretty much since the day they met—and easily half of Benny's outbursts had been because of it. He didn't even trust his childhood best friend and right-hand man when it came to Betts. Benny didn't trust nobody.

"Aw, thanks. You're a good friend. I'm going to go lie down now. I'm just..."

She waved her hand, uselessly, and her gloved fingers looked so slim and empty that her breath caught. They were usually swallowed up in Benny's strong grip, equal parts comforting and constraining, but now her hand looked displaced. Lonely. She laced her fingers to keep her hands from shaking.

"Call me if you need me," Tony said, and ambled to his car. He made a show of not looking back, feigning confidence in her ability to get inside safely, and she was grateful. If he saw the way her knees trembled, he would never let her be.

"Everybody loves my baby," a man's voice sang tunelessly. Betts snapped to attention.

"What was that?" she called after Tony, but he had already put his car into drive.

The evening felt unreal. Betts drifted around the place, folding and unfolding Benny's clothes relentlessly. She buried her nose in one of his shirts. It smelled like him. She straightened his cigar box and made sure his ties were hung nicely.

Nerves, yes, but Benny also liked an orderly home. If he came back and his shoes weren't shined and lined up just right, or if supper burned or there were dirty dishes in the sink, well...Betts reflexively fingered her ribs.

She turned on the radio and ran water in the claw-foot tub, more than Benny usually allowed her. Enough that it would slosh messily over the sides when she stepped in, and she wanted this more than anything. She piled her hair on her head and added scented gels, bubbles, and dried flowers. She slid into the tub, hearing the tell-tale sound of water pattering onto the floor. Betts ignored it. She'd clean it later.

Now she sighed, closing her eyes, and letting tears wet her lashes. She thought she'd cry quietly, but soon the panic and grief hit her. She curled up, covering her face with her wet hands, and bawled. She smelled Benny's blood over the scented bathwater. She saw his body jerk, watched his eyes go wide and surprised and betrayed. What horror! What trauma! And yet there was that sense of relief, even as she felt her life rip apart. *He's dead. He's dead.* She missed him and loved him and hated him and feared him. *He's dead.*

Betts sobbed until she felt the tub contained oceans of salt. She washed her face and hiccupped herself to silence. Betts gazed out of the tiny bathroom window near the ceiling. Vegas lights obliterated the stars, but she knew they were there. They hid behind neon and desert dust, but they still filled the sky as they had when she was a barefoot girl growing up in the country.

"You're still there, too, right, Benny? Somethin' as bright as you can't just fade away."

She stepped out of the tub and wrapped herself in a soft towel. She peered in the mirror.

"Goodness," she said. Without her makeup masking her sadness, she looked years younger. Far too young to be living alone in Las Vegas. She'd been barely eighteen when she first met Benny. An adult, legally, but her eyes were full of forests and trees and her lips were girlishly pink. He had introduced her to a hard and fast life with friends who dolled her up. They'd taught her to watch her figure and wear silk stockings and use wands, powders, and paint on her face. Tony C. had been there, too, with a girl on his arm but his eyes dizzy for Betts. He tried to hide it, but Benny saw. He always saw.

"You look good," Benny had told Betts when she'd first tottered out in too-high heels and a new cloche hat. Tony quickly looked at the floor.

"Do I?" she had answered. Her fingers fluttered nervously at Benny's lapel. "I feel like I'm playing dress up."

"You're not a kid anymore. You're my girl," he had simply said, glaring at Tony, and that was that. They hadn't parted since. She had given him love and attention and anything he wanted. He gave her furs and nerve pills and security. They were a match made in hell, and wasn't hell just the bee's knees?

The last lines of "It Ain't Gonna Rain No Mo" faded away, and familiar upbeat notes started.

"I'm as happy as a king, feeling good and everything."

Betts watched her face crumple in the mirror.

"Just like a bird in the spring, gotta let it out..."

She couldn't move. She clutched the towel to her body, watching the steam from the hot bath curl around her. It formed into a burly shape and the shadow hulked behind her.

She opened her mouth and sang along with the radio, her voice quiet and breaking.

"Everybody loves my baby, but my baby don't love nobody but me."

A tear slipped down her cheek. The misty shadow reached out and rested its hand on her shoulder. It was a weight she had felt so many times, and then Benny would slide his hand gently to her cheek, or not-so-gently to her throat. Whether her knees went weak because of his kisses or a good sock to the eye, it always started with that hand.

"Nobody but me," Benny murmured in her ear.

The song was over, and Betts stood there alone, blinking rapidly.

The radio went to static.

"I'm losing my mind," Betts whispered. She hung the towel up, changed into a nightgown, and slipped into Benny's side of the bed. She hoped it would always smell like him, no matter how many years passed.

She fell asleep, exhausted, and didn't move as a deep voice hummed the words to his favorite song. A man's hand gently patted her hair.

* * *

Tony hoped today was the day Betts let him inside. It had been nearly two months since they buried Benny, and the doll had practically gone into hiding. She didn't answer the door or the phone. She hadn't gone to a single get-together, not one, and the girl was known for dancing. Wasn't nothing improper about dancing in their circles, even with the dead. Jazz had a way of exorcising most demons. In fact, most of them had come to count on it.

"Elisabet?" called as he rapped on her door. "It's me. Won't you let me in?"

There was no sound. Then the door slowly opened an inch, and he grinned.

"Tony?"

His smile fell immediately. He didn't like the way she said his name, painting it with weariness and dimmed hope. Like he was gonna save her, or die trying. Like maybe she expected the latter.

"Hi, Betts," he said, keeping his voice casual. "It's good to see you."

She squinted as she peered through the crack, her white fingers slipping around the edge of the door. They trembled, and her fingernails were broken.

This wasn't the brash Betts he knew. This was a woman who had a gun to her throat or a knife to her side. This was a woman trapped.

"Everything okay in there?" he asked, gripping the blade he always had on him. He narrowed his eyes and watched her carefully in case she looked to the left of the right, tipping him off to an intruder.

"I'm feeling silk. The cat's pajamas. I'm...Tony, you look real dangerous. You're scaring me."

Her frail fingers tightened, and Tony's heart twisted inside. He had frightened her. Showed up on her doorstep with good intentions and a knife, and she was cowering back as if he was going to shower her with blows.

"Sorry, Elisabet," he said. His voice was raw, the emotion all laid out. "I'd never want to scare you. I just wanted to come by. It's been ages."

She opened the door fully, studying him as if she had never seen him before. Tony stood straight and tried to look both trustworthy and protective. He didn't even blush when her eyes rested on his scarred lip, on his left collarbone, on his large hands. He loosened his grip on the knife in his pocket and showed her that his hands were empty. He held them out to her, low and unthreatening.

Betts looked at his open palms with something like confusion and slid her hand into his. Soft as a cat's paw, and just as gentle.

Tony thrilled. Her hand fit just right, like it had always belonged there. Like a puzzle piece sliding home. He wrapped his fingers around hers.

She started and yanked her hand away.

"Sorry, Elisabet. I...." He looked at her, really took her in, and frowned. "You look terrible. Are you eating?"

She laughed, quick and sharp.

"Why, that's an awful thing to say to a lady, Tony. Not nice at all."

Her skin was so pale that he could see the veins running underneath, but the shadows under her eyes were the color of bruises. Her hair was disheveled, and she had lipstick smeared across her face. She wore one heeled mule, and the other foot was bare. She was shivering.

"Step aside and let me in," he said gently, and when she didn't respond, he swept her up in his arms and strode through the door.

"Put me down," she gasped, and fear came into her eyes. Tony kicked the door shut behind him.

"Put me down right now! He's going to hate it," she begged, and her voice cracked. Tony froze.

"Who? Who's going to hate it?"

Betts struggled until he set her tenderly on the couch. She scooted away, pulling her dressing gown close around her. She made herself small.

Tony realized he was looming over her just as Benny had always done. He knelt on one knee and tried to meet her eyes. Her gaze kept skittering away.

"Elisabet. I'm your friend. Why don't you let me help you?"

He kept his voice gentle, although he felt anything but. Her fear made him want to lose his cool.

"It was a mistake for you to come," she said, her shaking hands knotting together.

"It wasn't a mistake." Tony sighed. "I told Benny I'd look after you any time he was out of town, and that hasn't changed just 'cause he was chilled off. Hold tight."

He went into the kitchen. Betts looked like she needed some food, giggle juice, and one of her pills. Probably two or three of her pills. The kitchen was covered in old newspapers and bits of broken crockery. It smelled like garbage. What had happened in here? He opened the window and then rummaged through her bare cupboards.

"What have you been living on, Elisabet?" he asked over his shoulder. He heard her murmur something in reply but couldn't make it out. He opened her fridge and tossed out the old vegetables and sour milk. She had half a carton of eggs, and Tony broke two of them into a frying pan.

"It's good to see you," he called. "Nobody's heard from you in a while. We were all getting worried."

Silence. The eggs scrambled up nicely and Tony slid them onto a plate. He grabbed a fork and stepped into the living room.

It was empty.

Tony tapped the fork on the plate like he was summoning a cat. "I have something for you to eat. Try a few bites."

She didn't answer. He put the food down and gripped his knife.

"Elisabet."

He peeked in the bathroom. Nothing.

"Hey, Betts."

The spare room was also empty. That only left the bedroom. The door was closed.

Tony knocked on it gently.

"Elisabet. I'm worried about you. I'm coming in, okay?"

He grasped the door handle, and fear jolted through him. Wariness. Warning. He wanted to turn and run. He wanted to scram so fast that the door swung close behind him. Then he pictured Betts with her pallid face and hopeless eyes lying in the floor of her room. Maybe she had a bottle of poison beside her. Maybe she had her own blade, and her vermillion wrists would smile at him.

Panic forced him to open the door. He stepped into the room and gasped. It was cold, colder than anything he had ever felt before, and the air pressed down on him ominously. His lungs struggled to fill amidst the pressure, and he could see his breath as it curled around him like cigar smoke. Betts blinked at him furiously, her mouth turned down at the corners and her neck tilted at angle.

"Elisabet?"

"Tony," Betts said.

Well, that wasn't on the square. Her lips moved, but her voice was deep and familiar. A shadow stood behind her, tall and heavyset, with an arm draped possessively around her neck instead of around her shoulders.

"Benny?" Tony asked. "Is that you?"

"Who else would it be?" the shadow answered. It swung Betts away from Tony and began to slow dance with her. Betts looked like a rag doll in the shadow's arms. The shadow spun her, and her toes dragged across the floor.

"How did you come back?"

The shadow laughed meanly, and the sound made Tony suppress a shudder. Benny's eyes glowed, red flames in the black mass.

"How did I come back? Not 'Good to see you, Benny' or 'What is hell like, Benny-boy?' You just wanna know how I came back."

That song he liked, that "Everybody Loves My Baby" was playing over the radio. It sounded strangely sinister, the voice trilling about how *everyone loves my baby, oh, but my baby don't love nobody but me.*

"You came back for Elisabet."

Benny twirled her again. Bett's eyes had rolled back into her head and she had foam collecting in the corner of her mouth.

"I never left, Tony. Not completely. I had to take a step back for a few days while I figured things out, but then I came home. To *my* house. To *my* woman."

Benny's challenge was clear. Tony raised his hands.

"Yeah, yeah, I get it, Benny. Back to your home and your girl. But Elisabet, she ain't looking so good right now. I think she needs a doctor."

The shadow glared at Tony. He was getting more solid by the minute, feasting on his anger or jealousy or whatever was happening. This was nuts. This dead guy was off his chump.

"Stop looking at my girl," Benny hissed. "Stop acting like she ain't mine. I've

EVERYBODY LOVES MY BABY

seen your eyes on her all this time. You want things that don't belong to you. The Bible calls that coveting, friend."

The music swelled, slowing down like a record on low speed.

"Everybody wants my baby," Benny growled at Tony, "but my baby don't want anybody but *me.*"

Betts' hair had fallen from its curls. They hung around her shoulders haphazardly, sticking to her face and swaying as Benny danced her around.

"She never eyed another gink, Benny. You know that. Even when you were out with other dames, she never so much as looked at anyone else."

"She knew better. I'd pop her in her pretty little eyes for looking."

"It killed her when you died," Tony said.

Benny flared. He solidified completely, looking like a live man. The tense air tightened around Tony's throat, invading his windpipe and stabbing into his lungs. It nearly drove him to his knees. He heard Betts say something weakly. He thought maybe it was his name.

"It should have killed her, but it didn't. Who survived that night? She did, not me." He shook Betts roughly, and her head fell back. "I knew they were coming. You cross the mob and they come gunnin' for ya, don't they? I was pretty sure it would be that night, too. And I was right. I saw the droppers coming, right when my favorite song came on. The one I wanted us to die to."

"Us?"

"So, I wrapped myself around her, held her in my arms, and I thought, yes, this is how it's supposed to be, right? Just you and me, Betts. Me and my girl, heading together into the afterlife, or whatever's waiting for us. I couldn't leave her here alone."

Tony stiffened in horror. "You meant for her to die?"

"But the bullets, they come ripping through, and they hurt just as bad as you'd expect. And what does Betts do? What does my lady-love do?" Benny jostled her again, and Betts' limp body shuddered in his arms. "She dusts out. She's screaming my name, but she still leaves, and the last thing I see in this life is my jane running and leaving me to be pumped full of lead."

Benny was holding her too close. Betts' dressing gown fell and revealed the rainbow of bruises decorating her décolleté. They ran under her nightgown like watercolor.

"You beat her nearly to death," Tony whispered.

6 4

Benny yanked up Betts' nightgown, exposing her white legs. Now they were black, blue, purple, green.

"Just writing my name on my property," Benny said smugly.

"You could let her go," Tony suggested quietly.

Benny laughed, and it wasn't as cruel as Tony expected. It was happy. Content. Almost childlike.

"I couldn't even if I wanted to. She already made her choice, don't you see?" He nodded toward the booze and bottle of pills on the dressing table.

Tony cut his eyes to Betts.

"Elisabet? Elisabet, can you hear me?"

Benny shook his head almost sadly.

"It's too late for that, my friend. Her heart no longer beats, and she'll be with me for the eternities. I know you carry a torch for her, and I forgive you for that. I really do. I should fill you full of daylight for your double-crossing ways, but I understand. She's everything a woman should be. Beautiful. Fearful. Loyal. You couldn't help falling in love with her."

Tony gritted his teeth. "That's not who she is. That's not why I love her."

Benny snarled, and held Betts closer.

"You don't even deny it now," he said. "Big man, admitting it now that it's too late. Where were you when you could have been a hero? Put me in my place, and all that? You could have whisked her off at any time, if she would have had you. And she wouldn't have had you. But we'll never know because you never asked."

Tony fell to his knees, his gaze unfocused. Despair as heavy as death itself.

Benny's footsteps came closer until he stood right in front of Tony. He's dead, and his shoes are still shined up real nice, Tony thought dreamily. I'll never beat him in anything.

Benny held Betts' body to him and buried his nose in her hair.

"Maybe it didn't have to be this way, but I couldn't let you keep hanging around her. Because everybody loves my baby." He kissed Betts hard on her cooling face.

"But my baby don't want anybody but me."

PACK UP YOUR SINS AND GO TO THE DEVIL

BY ELIS MONTGOMERY

The speakeasy appears when you bob
your hair. Feel naked in a short dress,
feel sheathed behind thickly painted eyes
and lips. Hear the thrum and join the mob
and mess. Twist hips in tungsten caress
and think: none of it, this time, is lies.

Momma thinks you're slipping but you need
this free fall. Eyes closed, mind clenched, fists coiled—
she doesn't know the music she calls
"devil" is grease. You've come to be oiled
with the rest of the lost: join their falls
in the dark, and on the dancefloor, bleed.

Think you belong here. Think it's your reign
and yes, if you drink, spin, kiss, revel,
then you're queen of cymbals, trombone riffs,
too loud yourself to hear the old pain
he wrings from monochrome keys as if
it's black and white here with the devil.

He's on stage, that old bandleader, bright-
horned and sharp-tailed, hot as where he's from,
coaxing from faceless bandmates fresh tunes
as the singer with liquid hips croons
pack up your sins as if they are light
and you could possibly carry them.

Sinner among sinners, you're thinner
than mother'd like and stronger headed.
She won't have you as you are so she
won't have you. Unbuttoned, unwedded--
devil girls don't go home for dinner.
Burn and breathe like that's how you'll be free.

Like her: see, there, a girl you once knew,
twirling barefoot through the haze, heels
ground down from her deathless dancing years.
The devil leans in, cooing appeals
as swelling saxophone licks your ears.
Still you hear him say, "she looks like you."

Spot the truth of his gifts through the thrills:
in the ceaseless dancers, jelly-limbed;
in their split grins; in their eyelids pinned
to weeping brows. Hear the violin
screams, the snare-snap of tendons and wills.
Accept his gifts as more strays file in.

Feel seen in each raw claret eyeball
and fully fall: the trip to Hades
is deep enough for good young ladies.
Have no ties or bones left to sever:
call the devil mother and never
ever *have to go to bed at all.*

THE LUNG OF ORPHEUS

BY JONATHAN LOUIS DUCKWORTH

Soon the trees and hills along the E18 erase Stockholm's skyline. She can't hide her angst, so she doesn't try, not with Peter. But she also can't bring herself to address the suicidal elephant in the room. In Peter's last call before Kali booked a red-eye, one-way flight from D.C. to Stockholm, he'd made it sound like Viktor was an imminent danger to himself. That was the only thing that could have brought her here, given how things ended between them. He'd been a shitty partner, yes, but she wasn't going to let him off himself.

Imagine her surprise when Peter drops the bomb.

"The thing is, I may have massaged the truth somewhat."

The car almost swerves off into the swale beside the road when Kali punches his shoulder. She means to hurt him. It's less the fear of causing an accident and more the frailty Peter projects—the way he crumples into himself, tucking his chin in and flinching from her raised fist—that keeps her from hitting him again. Peter's a scarecrow, with a face of sharp angles, shoulder-length hair he ties into a ponytail, and thick square-rimmed glasses.

"I know it's terrible to lie about that, I understand. Believe me."

"Do you? What the hell did I come out here for?"

"Viktor *does* need you," he says, steadying the wheel. "That bit wasn't a lie. I wouldn't bring you out here if it wasn't something serious. I truly wish you could've stayed out of it—God knows, Kali, it's not fair to you."

She counts backward from ten to calm herself. "What is it then?"

"I'm not entirely sure I can explain," Peter says. "There's not really a word for what he's undergoing. Not one conventional science would furnish."

She speaks through her teeth. "Try. Use your words."

"Metamorphosis, you might call it."

She asks what that's supposed to mean. He does not answer or look at her. He clenches his jaw and watches the road, the lines strobing across the lenses of his glasses. After a while, he sighs and says, "Some things can't be explained—they must simply be witnessed."

* * *

There's a picture Kali keeps folded in her wallet from the year 2013. She's nineteen, tall and gangly, wearing her Ormen hoodie—the one from the *Crocus* tour—sandwiched between two equally gangly, awkward dudes who happen to be heavy metal legends. On one side is Peter Milton, former frontman of prog legends Cartilaginous, looking the same as now only with fewer gray hairs. To the other, not facing the camera, mouth hanging open in a goofy grin, is Viktor. His hair was a long mop, while his ridiculous handlebar mustache hadn't yet reached the terminal length it would attain a few years later when they started dating and Ormen released the eternally divisive concept album *Soul Marrow*, the record that decisively signaled their shift away from death metal into something jazzier and experimental. The photo does not show his eyes, hidden as they were under a beetled brow; does not show their ferrous hue like the Baltic under a storm's aspect.

In this photo, there's no indication of what's to come. It's just a fan geeking out in the presence of her musical idols, having been lucky enough to catch a rare live performance of their collaborative side project, Verdigris Sky. In this moment, Kali is an awkward metalhead with a rinky-dink music blog and Peter and Viktor are gods to her. Maybe it still feels like that now—for someone like her who could never write a song (well, a good one), the act of creation still retains its mystique even after spending uncounted days watching "the process" from an intimate proximity.

What the photo does not show is how the amateur blogger would reach out to Mr. Viktor Lindqvist and sheepishly ask for an interview for her blog, not expecting any answer at all, less still an offer to sit down and talk when Ormen came to Baltimore, where she lived at the time.

The first few years of their acquaintance were just that: an acquaintance, a trans-oceanic correspondence punctuated by occasional brief meetings. The third time they met it was in Brooklyn, in the middle of Ormen's 2016 North American tour for the album *Azimuth*. This time was different. There was a familiarity, a rapport between them that had not existed before.

After the show, he invited her to meet the rest of the band at a bar a block from the venue—Bjorn Karlsson, the bassist she'd already met, but she finally got to speak with; and Alex Mattsson, the drummer, formerly of the black metal quintet Necrocide (another of her favorites, broken up too soon). First Alex left, then Bjorn, and then suddenly Kali and Viktor were alone. They talked for a while about things she can no longer recall, but in a deranged moment of sincerity, perhaps lubricated by all the beer and wine, Kali admitted Ormen's music had inspired her to attempt songwriting.

"You say attempt," Viktor said, in his mystical way. "I don't think it's possible to *attempt* something, unless the act is not completed."

"A few were completed. Poorly."

She explained her theory to him, that there were lower case "artists" (like herself) and uppercase artists, like Viktor or Peter.

"You're assuming anyone has any fucking idea what we're doing," he retorted.

A platoon of empty bottles lay between them—in retrospect, the signs of his alcoholism were always there if she'd cared to notice—and it struck her how inscrutable he was. It seemed to her he saw through the surface of things and his eye became muddled in the layers beneath.

"I like your crop-top," he said after what seemed like five minutes of strange silence. "And I like how the vertical cut, well, I always like seeing the shadow of a woman's collarbone."

For as gorgeous as his compositions and his guitarwork were, Viktor Lindqvist was a painfully awkward flirt. It didn't matter. She was smitten. She brought him back to the hotel where she was staying. Sex was what she wanted and what she expected. But they didn't have sex, not that night. He was too drunk to even get his belt off. Instead, he sort of leaned against her, and she propped him up, and they stood there, cheek to cheek, breathing each other's smell, feeling each other's heartbeats through the blood-gorged lobes of their ears. The experience was both less and more than she expected, but that didn't matter to her. It was a terrible and wondrous thing to be desired by the hands of a living god.

* * *

After another hour of driving, they arrive at the cabin on the far shore of Lake Mälaren. Here, the highway has yielded to small, crooked roads. The firs and spruces walling the shoreline are strangely dark even as their needles should be shimmering from the light of the golden hour before sunset. There is a faint but unmistakable rumor of fog swirling above the lake's surface. The cabin itself is tiny, a single room with an A-frame roof and a brick chimney.

Peter parks the Fiat in the shade of a rowan tree burdened by an onerous frutescence of red berries. Kali idly wonders if they'll fall and stain the car. She is grateful when he opens her door and offers her his hand. She's feeling unwell, her legs like bendy straws, her stomach full of drunk wasps. Is it from not knowing what she'll face? Or is it just the natural angst of seeing an ex for the first time in almost two years?

But as she finds her feet and faces the little cabin where her former lover is holed up, she feels the tumult in her gut quiet somewhat when the door opens and a lumbering shape appears.

"Bjorn!" she calls out, waving her arms at him as if she's in a crowd.

Bjorn runs to meet her halfway, picking her up and spinning her into a bearhug. Bjorn is the only person she'd ever let pick her up like that. During the years she lived in Sweden with Viktor, Bjorn was one of her closest and most attentive friends in a strange, unfamiliar city.

"Thank God you're here," he says, setting her down. "I was worried you wouldn't make it in time."

"In time for what?" she asks.

Peter stands off to the side, his attention on the lake.

Bjorn shrugs. The motion reminds Kali of an obscure factoid: that gorillas can't turn their heads because of the size of their shoulders. "I—I'm not sure how to explain."

The door to the cabin creaks on its hinge, slowly swinging to a close. But it doesn't. Something props it open from inside. For a blink in time, Kali holds her breath, wondering what she'll say—if she should say anything.

But it isn't Viktor who steps out onto the cabin's porch. It's an old woman. No, not old. *Ancient.*

She is pale and wrinkled, but her eyes are strangely young, bright and vivacious. Her ears are long in the lobe, sagged by heavy ornaments that look to be made from black cast iron, and her hair is immaculately coiffed into a dramatic steel-gray wave struck with strands of white. She walks with the aid of a carved walking stick with a steel cleat on its tip, but her spine is so straight and her gait so certain Kali wonders if she needs it at all. With each little step and each passing heartbeat, the woman seems to get younger, or rather Kali starts to question why she thought she looked ancient, because the woman who comes to stand in front of Kali is at oldest a soft 50, maybe not even 45.

"Here she is at last," the woman says, her English good but with a much more pronounced local accent than Bjorn's or Viktor's. "This must be the *muse*, all the way from America."

Kali opens her mouth to protest the woman's descriptor, but then gums up. She's tired, and whatever, the lady's European.

Peter steps up between them. "Kali, this woman here is...well, actually she never gave us a name."

"I am the Caretaker," the woman says, her teeth straight and strong.

"Cool, right," Kali says. "So, who are you, then?"

"The Caretaker," the woman says again, her smile unbroken.

"She's been watching over Viktor during his, uh, changes," Bjorn puts in. "Perhaps you should come in and see him."

"Does he know I'm here?" Kali asks.

Peter and Bjorn trade a look.

"What?"

"Well," Peter scratches his head. "It's just, we're not really precisely sure the extent to which he's aware of anything in his current state."

Kali hurtles past the Caretaker, thunders up the staircase to the cabin's porch, then throws the door open. What does she expect to see? Viktor on his deathbed, perhaps, or Viktor strung out on a gurney with an IV tapped into his arm.

But there is no Viktor here. The cabin is sparsely furnished, the wood dark and lustrous as if recently polished. At first all she remarks is an upright piano flush against the western wall.

Then she notices the curtained partition. At the same instant, the smell hits her. It reminds her of an obscure smell from when she was little. Maybe from when her dad took her hunting and she smelled a murdered deer, the bullet having torn through muscle of the belly and then ruptured the large intestine, releasing a potent fetor like sweet cut grass mixed with sulfur. There's something like that, but something else too, more like leather and the stench of armpit.

She does not hear or feel the Caretaker approach. The Caretaker merely appears beside her, one hand taking firm hold of Kali's wrist. "Be warned, you may not recognize him."

Her mind darkens with a catastrophized clip show, ranging in severity from Viktor having shaved his head and mustache to Viktor in a vegetative state with a blackberry belt bruise around his throat to Viktor with half his face scooped out by a shotgun shell. When they were together, even when he was happy, he'd still make unfunny jokes about blowing out his brains. Watching old black and white Hammer horror movies together, shopping for vinyls at their favorite record store in Stockholm's Old Town, playing minigolf (he always lost and ended up chucking his club into the little pond), or just hanging out at home—always the "Kurt Cobain" joke was never far from his lips.

But what she sees makes an understatement of the Caretaker's warning. Kali wants to scream when the curtain parts, but she can't, as if what she's seeing is beyond what can be processed through any violence of breath.

It's a cocoon. It is perhaps seven feet long from its spiny crown to the spurred heel of its base, and it hangs from the ceiling by a corded spindle of translucent wire that seems to have knotted itself around the rafter beam. Kali thinks of a punching bag, of a whoopie cushion, of the gutted carcass of a pig hanging from a hook. But it's none of these things. It is an enormous lung—that is clear when she watches it swell and then sag, expelling warm air that she feels waft off the tears in her eyes. Its leathery membrane is a sad gray color, glistening with a bright sheen and shot through by branching deltas of veins and capillaries. The sheen accumulates and beads from the tufts of coarse coir-like bristles that gird its underside. There is a puddle staining the wood below where the lung dangles and slowly twists on its tether.

"That–that's–" Her words will not descend far enough down to find her.

"This is Viktor Lindqvist," the Caretaker says. "He is, perhaps you would say, negotiating a difficult stage in his ongoing metamorphosis. Becoming something Other."

Peter comes from behind her and gently touches her shoulder. "He wanted you here. He begged us to bring you here before it swallowed him up. Made us promise you'd come."

Why? That is the question she wants to ask, but she's not sure what answer–if any–she seeks. She wishes she'd never come here. That she'd stayed home. She wants to turn away, but her body won't listen to her.

Mercifully, Bjorn takes her hand and guides her away, to the welcome respite of one of the chairs. She wishes he'd guide her outside, maybe all the way back to the airport. She breathes in slow and tries to center herself.

"Now you see why I couldn't explain it," Peter says, sitting down at the piano bench. "Language becomes inadequate past a certain threshold."

He strikes a single key. The G-note. The sound is rusted and tortured but it lingers in the air, and as its shrill voice fades, there comes an answer from inside the lung. It is Viktor's famous tenor that hums a reply, mirroring the note.

* * *

Kali always loved metal. As a kid she headbanged to the three M's (Metallica, Megadeth, and (Iron) Maiden), and as she got older, her tastes became more rarefied. Even now she still loved the simple, steam locomotive-like relentlessness of old school thrash and the earnest bombast of the Tampa scene of classic death metal (and of course nothing beat Pantera when you were three, four beers deep and angry), but there was something irresistible and transformative about the richer sonic textures and lyrical complexity of a group like Ormen.

The first time she listened to all 17:32 of "Where the Puddled Night Weeps" from Ormen's 2002 release *Noctuary* she felt like her soul had been refined in the way raw ore is smelted and made into something new and purer. Ormen was steeped in and yet separate from the strain of the so-called "Gothenburg sound."

The lyrical and compositional grandeur that she spent hours lauding on her grubby little blog felt so different, so elevated compared to the rest. It was like you'd listened all your life to generic chamber music and then suddenly heard the genius of Liszt or Beethoven's "Moonlight Sonata," or savored a filet mignon after a lifetime of insipid fast food.

In every Ormen track there seemed to be an inarticulable tragedy, a haunting that glided wraithlike through every cord progression and hovered in the breathing spaces created by every odd time signature. Even the more brutish, simplistic songs like "Ichor" from the 1998 album *Gallowsreach* contained in them some elusive resonance of a deeper murmuration beneath the blast beats and chugging riffs.

Or maybe she was just a pretentious kid who wanted to gas up her favorite band in front of her digital audience of 20 or so netizens.

What could not be denied or undersold was the enormous influence of Peter Milton upon Ormen's sound in the post-*Crocus* era. In many ways, Peter and Viktor were the same person. They were around the same age, had grown up listening to much of the same music, and had similar attitudes about art (important) and success (unimportant, but nice as a fringe benefit of the art). But where Viktor nursed a morbid fascination with dead and dying things and all what might be termed "the Gothic," Peter's lyrical preoccupations tended toward more diverse climes: adolescent ennui, doomed marriages, the relentless commodification of modern life, and also (for some reason) trains.

Peter once told her that he was drawn to Viktor because he perceived a potential no one else—Viktor included—saw in Ormen's music. That it could be more than metal, something sublime and transcendent it only needed the right guidance and insight: his.

Peter helped produce Ormen's eighth album, *Vastation*, which featured very little of the guttural vocals that had predominated early releases, but instead centered Viktor's beautiful clean tenor. The band never really looked back from there, but although Kali had first fallen in love with Ormen for its classic sound, she found herself mesmerized by the progressive, jazzy verve of the new soundscapes Viktor created under Peter's tutelage. Not for nothing did Kali, in her five-star review of *Vastation*, call Mr. Milton "the mastermind" behind that watershed record.

* * *

Peter says he's staying inside to receive Viktor's "dictation" (his word for the strange sequence of groans and sighs emanating from the fleshy sac), but Kali needs air, and Bjorn follows her out.

She remembers the breathing exercises she learned in therapy and employs them on the porch while Bjorn leans on the railing beside her.

The sun is setting now, irradiating the fog with a cloying gold that would be breathtaking if she weren't already struggling to breathe. By and by, she steadies.

"When did this start?" Kali asks. "And who the hell is that lady?"

"It started a couple weeks ago. It was when we were finishing the new album when Viktor decided he hated every single track. Fell out of love with it, you might say."

He does that, she thinks but does not say.

"As for the Caretaker, well, I can't tell you much. She just showed up when Viktor started coughing up the sticky shit and knitting it around himself. It was transparent, like jelly, at first. It's only later that it started to get like it is now, this sort of chrysalis thing. Viktor liked having her around, said she was an expert."

"And you never thought to get a doctor?"

"Viktor was very clear he didn't want a doctor."

"And you didn't think that was weird?"

"I think I'm a guy who plays bass and this is entirely out of my understanding."

From inside, the cruddy clang of the piano keys ring out, and Peter calls out, "Four-four now."

Bjorn shakes his head. "Viktor was depressed. He never really recovered from you leaving, I don't think. And please don't take that as me blaming you for any of this. I don't. I wouldn't."

"I appreciate that."

"Like I said, he was depressed. It was a damn good album, I thought. Alex thought so too. Alex, you'll notice he's not here—well, he took it pretty hard when Viktor deleted the album."

The fan in Kali feels like she's been slugged in the gut. "He did what?"

Bjorn grimaces. "Yeah. I wasn't happy either. But the problem has always been the same—it's Viktor's satisfaction that matters. He thought the album didn't live up to what it could be, so he burned it down to start again. And that's where it began: he got to thinking that he wasn't capable of putting out the best work. What he told me was something weird—*I'm not what I need to be."*

That sure sounded like Viktor. Always his own harshest critic, always the devil on his own shoulder. When she broke up and moved back stateside, some of her old friends took her out and invited her to dish on him, to get drunk and talk shit about her ex. She did get drunk, but even as much as she was angry at him for letting what they had wither and for closing himself off, she couldn't hate him.

The golden fog has become a brooding shade of red. From inside, the caterwaul of the old piano intensifies. She's not sure what to say. What could she say?

Bjorn nudges her. "By the way, I never got a chance to thank you."

"For what?"

"For being so kind to us. You know, in your review of *Magus.*"

In spite of everything, she finds the wherewithal to roll her eyes. "I broke up with Viktor, I didn't stop being an Ormen fan."

He looks at his shoes. Kali recalls that Magus was the first album where Viktor let Bjorn contribute to the writing of some of the tracks. "Magus didn't do so well with the old fans."

She gives his meaty arm a squeeze. "Old guard fans are useless babies. They want artists to pump out the same shit as always and then reserve the right to complain when the formula gets stale."

"Seven-eight!" Peter calls, almost shouting.

"We should get back inside," Bjorn says.

As they reenter the cabin, Peter is alternating between tapping out notes on the piano and scribbling lines of music on a composition book splayed against the fall board. At the same time, the Caretaker stands beside the pulsating, groaning lung, rhythmically tapping her walking stick on the floorboards, like a human metronome.

"Skapa! Växa! Bli!" the Caretaker intones, her eyes closed, her head tossed back.

Create. Grow. Become.

Viktor's cocoon—his prison, his lung—has become the tortured scarlet of enflamed gums ready to bleed. From inside the sac comes a different kind of sound, not a groan or a sigh, more like a shriek. It both is and isn't Viktor's voice, because for all his range Kali has never heard him hit such a shrill pitch.

"F-5!" Peter declares before matching the note on the piano.

"What the hell is wrong with you?" Kali asks. "He's in pain, can't you see that?"

"He is becoming, child," the Caretaker replies, before continuing with her mantra.

With each passing second, with each tap of the Caretaker's stick, the veins of the lung thicken and darken as if swelling with pitch or black bile.

She feels a noxious wave passing over her, an onerous, all dissolving agony. Ormen songs, she's always thought, are like vaccines of tragedy—they contain a deadened, inert form of the ontological pain their lyrics and compositions shrug at. But this, what she's feeling now emanating from the shrieking lung—this is the real thing, the darkness alive and manifested as flesh.

Another shriek, this time loud enough she feels it deep in her ear canal.

"We need to cut him out of it," she hears herself say, and it's the first thing she's heard since coming here that makes any sense. She looks around for something sharp. Bjorn stands aside, immobile. Peter seems entranced by the dusty keys of the piano.

She'll use her fingernails if she has to. She lunges forward.

The Caretaker moves into her path. Kali tries to get past her, tries to wrestle her away, but the Caretaker pushes her back effortlessly, with one vise of a hand that seizes Kali's wrist and bends it away until Kali cries out.

"You cannot halt the process prematurely," the Caretaker rasps. "It must run its course. He must become what he is to become."

When the Caretaker lets go of her, Kali's wrist is the same color as the darkening horizon outside. As she holds her wrist, she looks to Bjorn for help, but Bjorn's attention is arrested by something he sees out the window. She follows his stare. In the darkening outdoors, illuminated by the light of the porch, swarms of moths scatter and converge, pulsing in time with Peter's piano strokes and the groans from within the lung.

Another scream. Viktor. For all that they might have drifted apart and for as much as he became a stranger to her the last few years, the sound of him in pain still cuts deep. She doesn't care about her mangled wrist, she launches herself again at the Caretaker, and this time grabs the old woman's walking stick, trying to wrest it from her bony grasp.

As they struggle, Peter—seemingly in a fugue now—glides his fingers along the keys, tapping out wild glissandos and tuneless sequences of disordered tones.

"You don't listen!" the Caretaker seethes, and though she is stronger than Kali, Kali won't let go of the woman's stick, even when the old woman spins her around and shoves her hard against the edge of the table.

As they fight, the lung stirs. Objects, organs, move beneath the membrane. Appendages, limbs, and things that aren't quite limbs (wings?) distend the skin, stretching it to the point of breaking. A face like but not quite Viktor's impresses itself briefly against the epithelium of the vesicle.

Finally, Bjorn moves. He grabs the Caretaker from behind, lifts her off her feet and chucks her aside, not roughly, but hard enough that she dashes her head against the wall and lies there, dazed.

Kali has the walking stick now. She turns it around so that the sharp cleat faces out like the tip of a spear.

"No, don't!" the Caretaker protests.

Kali's not sure where to plunge the sharp point, she doesn't know if any of the organ is vital, if all of it is. All she knows is she can't stand to watch and listen to the screams for another second. If it's misery, then it's past time to put him out of it.

The membrane resists her thrust almost successfully. At first she thinks she's failed, that the cleat has glanced off the rubbery integument. But then she pulls back and the skin stretches and bursts, releasing a glut of ichor, at first colorless, then black and viscid. The smell—there's no comparing it to anything else. Not ten day roadkill, not week-old piss. If she'd eaten anything on the plane, she'd be puking it out.

As the liquid spills, first as a glut, then as a weak runnel, then only a trickle, the sac deflates, the screams cease.

The cabin is silent. "Where is he?" Kali says.

She unfurls the deflated skin with the point of the walking stick. Inside, there's nothing at all. It's an empty membrane. No Viktor. No corpse for anyone to mourn. When she takes in her next shuddering breath her lungs swell with the room's silence.

"Jag förstår inte," the Caretaker says, sitting up, blood running down her forehead.

I don't understand.

In the quiet that follows, Peter seems to break from his trance. He stands up from the piano. Kali hears him mutter something under his breath that sounds somehow more disappointed than distraught. Something like, *He promised it would work.*

Bjorn breaks into violent sobs. Kali puts her arms around him, shuddering as he shudders, holding the wounded bear in her arms. She holds him because the one she wants to hold won't ever fill her arms again.

* * *

Back in Stockholm, in Peter Milton's flat, Kali sprawls out on the couch, waiting to feel the grief she thinks she should feel, what she expects. All she feels is detachment. Not the miserable numbness of depression, more like shock, an absence of joy but also an absence of pain.

It's late. Jet lag is catching up.

Peter's footsteps burp down the stairs and he stops halfway down to look at her. "How are you managing?" he asks.

She stares back at him. All she can think about is how obsessed he was with the sounds coming out of the cocoon. But now he's looking at her with concern etched into the lines of his forehead.

"Fine," she says. "I keep waiting to cry. But it—it just feels so unreal. Like he's not really gone."

Peter nods. "Yeah. Yeah, I know what you mean. Sure you don't want me to make up the spare bed?"

"A couch is fine," she says. She's not sure if that's true, but she doesn't want to walk upstairs.

"I'm turning in then," Peter says. "Good night." He walks a few steps and then pauses and looks back down. "You know, if you think about it, that was probably the most Viktor way he could have gone out. Becoming suddenly nothing."

She laughs because it's true. It's exactly how he would have wanted to go—in a way no one could explain or contextualize.

Peter turns out the lights, and Kali's alone in the dark, sprawled out on an uncomfortable, hard couch with no pillow or blanket. She's thinking maybe she's changed her mind, that maybe she should ask Peter to show her to the guest room, when she feels movement in the air around her.

It's a rippling, a displacement of the air. Like something without form or mass but pure will has moved toward her and hovers above. The presence enters her; she has breathed it in, or it has breathed her. The hairs on her arms rise and her body shudders and her next breath feels heavier somehow, strained as if she is now breathing for two.

A melody, strange and almost atonal, flits through her and she gives it breath; she begins to hum. Without realizing it, her heel starts to tap on the floor. Something syncopated in 7/8 time. She realizes something—the humming, it's not her voice at all, but Viktor's. The voice of Ormen.

The unfurling music sears itself into the sound booth of her mind and etches itself into the spinning disc of her consciousness. It's an Ormen song, not one she knows or has ever heard before but one she adores; music she wishes could become the blood in her veins. The melodies unfurl, the progressions, the guitar solo, the bass line, the chorus. As the lyrics assemble themselves, she feels compelled to commit something to paper. An album name is already rising from the froth of her imagination: *Chrysalis.*

Peter watches her from the staircase. Moonlight shines on the panes of his glasses so they glint like the eyes of a night-stalking wolf. She continues to hum, and as she does, Peter descends the stairs and moves to where his guitar rests on its stand.

I AM HE

BY PREMEE MOHAMED

bitha had chosen a paring knife both because it could be concealed whole in her small hand, and because it was the only good steel she owned. The edge she had put on the short, curved blade could have shaved a fly. So the monster would have a quick death; and she was unhappy about this undeserved mercy, but it couldn't be helped.

She stepped from night into night. The whole saloon was blackened with coal dust, as if each opening of the rickety door let in some part of the darkness that clung unfading to the walls. In the irregular dusk, lit by candles in smudged glass globes, men moved like shadows—drinking, cursing, arguing, stalking. In the main room the player piano tinkled dismally, as if it too was choking on the dust. Abitha, dressed all in black, was a shadow too. Her heart was pounding as she scanned the room. Worse to find him? Not find him?

There he was, the bitch's bastard. The sight struck her with a soft, light shock, all her hatred and despair returning fresh, like someone had blown on a dying fire. The paring knife was in her hand, handle greased with sweat. She didn't remember taking it out of her sleeve.

McCord was playing cards with his usual crowd; a bottle of rotgut, the pale clay smutched all over with coal, squatted in the center of the table, hip-deep in coins. Such petty villains. Poor imitations of men. He was drunk, he'd get up to piss, she could ambush him then. She must wait. Tempting to do it now, but she would rather hang for his murder than be beaten to death by these men...

But even as she thought it, the men exploded from the table. Dustdevilling, the brawl and its cursing and flurrying of fists spun out the side door, and Abitha began to follow, half-instinctively, then stopped. She was a fool to believe she could kill McCord in all the commotion and then blame it on someone else, but the thought of accidentally killing the wrong man sickened her, she who had never killed, never considered it till now. *Me, a murderer? Yes, me.* She reached for this sensation and held it in her hands, dazed: it was like a single trickle of water, silvery and thin, inching down a dried riverbed.

She'd known for some time she wasn't in her right mind, and at first she had believed that knowing somehow protected her from its consequences—that as long as she clung to that knowledge she would never actually *do* anything mad. But now she wasn't sure.

Was she mad? That was all right. Virgil had been a little mad too, and she had loved him, and he would understand her desire for revenge even if he would not condone it; and McCord, the murderer, he was mad too, as mad as a rabid dog. Hell, maybe he had given her this madness. Like smallpox. He had left it on Virgil's body and she had breathed it in with the stench of his blood; and now she had the same disease, differing only in degree. Grief as a kind of bloodlust, as a red haze in which everything was dull and indifferent except for McCord, who shone out from the general murk like a blazing torch, marked by her hatred.

The brawl petered out and disentangled, the knot of spidery limbs resolving into a half-dozen spidery men, bloodied, confused at someone approaching—not only approaching but riding actually through the fight, parting them, on a tall oddly-colored horse of mottled grey and red.

Abitha stood in the doorway and stared too: the stranger was tall, well-matched to the horse, and had a similarly long gaunt face—very white, as if it had never been touched by the sun. His teeth were so white that they reflected back the dim lamps like broken mirrors. He did not speak to McCord or his men, only walked the horse around the corner toward the big hitchpost in front of the saloon.

Abitha crept back into the main room. The stranger had interrupted her revenge; whether that was for better or worse she wanted a look at him. At the bar she sat on the last stool and asked the counter-girl for a whiskey and water.

"Abby," said the girl.

"I know," said Abitha. "Just the one. I know what you're gonna say. But one."

The glass appeared on the black-dusted wood, and her coin was refused: not the girl's doing but the barkeep, who also shook his head at her as if to emphasize: *You said just the one, which I will allow.* Then his attention was taken with the stranger, who stood in front of the bar, his white, hard-looking hands cradling a brown leather roll, like something a carpenter might use to store his chisels. The stranger surveyed the room: sooty, crowded, sullen. A town, the room said, where nothing much happened; where there was nothing to do but work and sleep and come here of an evening.

"Greetings," the stranger said in a curiously soft voice, at odds, Abitha thought, with the hardness of his face and those sharp teeth. "I'm spreading the good word across this dry land, and I wonder if, as a man of spirit yourself, you would be so inclined as to let me play a hymn or two on your piano. I have the music here."

The barkeep stared at him, perhaps trying to see if he was being had. Abitha did not think so. Finally the barkeep shrugged. "You're the one who has to deal with the complaints," he said. "Not me."

"I thank you kindly. Bless you and your kin." The tall preacher stalked over to the piano, flipped the compartment open with a practiced hand, and stopped the lackluster tinkle of "My Long-Lost Rose-Marie." In a moment he had swapped rolls—not before Abitha had spotted how odd his music looked, the cylinder not ordinary brass but definitely gray, spotted with green, as if it had gone moldy.

The preacher crossed his arms as the first sluggish notes rose into the air. Like he expected a mass conversion, Abitha thought; like everyone would leap up and run to the river, crying out to be baptized. Wouldn't that be something.

She turned back to her drink—then turned again, eyes wide. The gloom had not lifted, but anyone could see something was happening, something real. A brightness in the air, not like flame, star, lightning bug, nothing natural, but a drifting glitter emerging from the ceiling, white motes like burning dust. And everyone in the room began first to moan, then to rise, clumsily, as if they could not feel their legs, and raise their arms and shuffle—as if they were trying to dance, Abitha thought numbly, with weights on their legs. Eyes rolled up to whites, hands sunk into hair, tugging out braids and unwinding them, hands dipped into the reservoirs of dust in the corners, smearing it across faces, across teeth, tongues. Still the brightness fell, still their voices went on.

Abitha, frozen, waited in genuine terror for their rapture to seize her as well, but the song went on, innocent piano plinks.

They were all singing now, words muzzy and wet, as if a load of drunks had broken into the church and packed it to the rafters.

I am he of seven heads
I am he who brings pain
I am the voice of the dead
I am a flood across the plain
I am a hill of bones
I am he who will bring —

The preacher was smiling. *Smiling*, a real smile, showing all his teeth. Tapping his boot in time to the arrhythmic, pulsing beat of the song—Abitha would not call it a hymn. It could not be a paean to any good God, not even the thunder and blood God of the Old Testament. How did everyone know the words?

The preacher reached over and shut off the piano, cutting off the music with a metallic *crack*. Everyone moaned; a few folks wailed, a small sickly sound like a calf. Abitha held her breath, waiting for them to—what? She had no idea. Demand he play it again? Attack him? Steal the music he was even now fussily removing? She had never seen faces ravaged with such anguish and loss. As if what they had lost was anything like what she had lost.

The preacher waved the grayish roll before replacing it in the leather case. His face was inscrutable now that they were looking at him—a blank wall of stone. "I thank you kindly for your time and your attention," he said. "It is most gratifying to a traveling preacher to see a flock like this. Why, it's rarer than wings on a worm. And how do you all feel? Now that you have been filled for the first time with the spirit?"

They stared at him hungrily, yearning, hoping. Wanting more. *Here it comes*, Abitha thought—the scam, the song-and-dance. This was an old, old story. The mysterious preacher always comes to town and...

"Then we shall continue," he said beatifically. "Gratis and free, excepting if you feel like donating of your own free will. But I will play and preach out of the love of my own heart and the love of him who is greater than me. Are we agreed?"

They moaned in unison, another choral performance. *Yes, yes please. Please. Yes.*

"Soon," he said. "I invite you all to come listen to my sermons. Just before sundown at my humble camp. You will perceive the great benefits it brings into your lives. We will share fellowship and faith...and song."

I want to hear you say it, Abitha thought suddenly and for no reason. *I want to hear you say God, I want to hear you say Jesus. I want to know who* he *is in your song.*

She knew how it was supposed to sound because they had a preacher already—Brother Wenther, who presided over their little clay-brick church that could fit about twenty people, and never got more than half that of a Sunday morning. They had seen dozens of traveling preachers come through Whitstun. They begged alms and sundries (repairing bootsoles, shoeing horses, tallow for candles), they preached for a while, they moved on. Wenther was not possessive of his flock and always gave a few coins to the interlopers. He had said kind words over Virgil's grave which, in Abitha's grieving measurement of time, had been so recently dug as to still contain the warmth of his body. What little warmth had been left after McCord cut his throat.

The saloon was all in confusion, people asking with sleepy voices, *What happened? I feel pretty good. I feel like I took a dip in the river, I feel like I slept all night, I feel like I—*

Abitha wanted to be happy for them—be happy that the hymn had made them happy. She was not. She did not know why it had not affected her. Perhaps because she was mad, or perhaps the flavor, the texture, of her particular madness. She did not care. She slipped out of the saloon by the back door, and returned home to sit next to Virgil's bloodstain in the bedroom and think up a new plan. Already the clouds that covered the stars formed strange new shapes.

I am the wolf who breaks bone
I am he of the night
I am the valley of stone
I am he who makes blight

* * *

Abitha walked into town, her steps heavy. At first she had kept up her usual schedule—two or three times a week as needed for provisions and errands and to keep an eye on McCord. But now, as spring ended, she came only when she could not stand it anymore. There was something wrong with the town, the townsfolk, and they watched it happen like a steer watching the hammer fall for the stunning blow, eyes up, unblinking, not even asking themselves, *What does it mean? Does it mean my doom?* Maybe it was not their doom, Abitha thought, but it was right sinister anyway, and she did not like to be around it.

"A bag of flour," she said to the storekeep. "Some cheese, two cans of sardines..."

"Any eggs?"

"No thank you kindly."

Strange things were coming out of eggs—chicken eggs, duck eggs, the eggs of the songbirds and carrion birds around town. Nothing like ordinary chicks, but half-made things she could not identify. Brother Wenther said they were curses sent by the devil. Lizard heads, legs like tongues, eyeless or with a thousand eyes. People had screamed, panicked, thrown them onto the fire. But burning would not kill them. They skittered off into the twisted wildflowers that had inexplicably bloomed on the outskirts—in this rainless season, they had come out of nowhere, overnight, like mushrooms. And in the mine, she had heard tell of monstrous groans and cries from the earth itself, the crumbling soft black seams transmitting the voices with the mindless obedience of the brass hammers of a player piano.

Everyone in Whitstun, some five or six hundred souls (*everyone*, as far as she could tell) went to see the new preacher. A steady trickle had become a flow, until now everyone was accounted for—even Brother Wenther, as caught up in it as the rest of them—sang and moaned and begged for more like the rest of them. Abitha went too.

At first this was because some of the town ladies had asked her to. "We know you're grieving, Abby, and it ain't healthy to be locked up in here all alone where the accident happened." It was no accident, she told them; the sheriff lied, he lied like the Prince of Lies. "There there," they told her, "you'll feel better if you go worship, and feel the spirit move through you."

Over their arms they held baskets covered with cotton handkerchiefs, thin and much-washed, and inside Abitha could see the stones they carried. Big, round stones from the river, as big as their hands could fit. She looked down, stunned, making sure that was what she saw, then back to the placid, scrubbed, smiling faces. Smiling out here where no one from town would hear the screaming. Even her madness was not so far gone to miss it. "Well of course I'll come," she said. "Just let me get my bonnet on."

The hymn was ugly to the ears but its power was undeniable; she wanted to deny it, she hated it, but there is that about power of any kind that draws folks near. She did not know why. Even the few good men of the town who maybe would not have coveted power itself wanted to be near it, wanted to feel it, knowing they could not control it.

The preacher had no piano, though he had come with a wooden cart that could have fit one, pulled by a team of unnaturally tall silent mules—all black, not a single hair of silver or brown. He had drafted a few men who could play fiddle and mouth harp, and now they accompanied all his sermons. They always started with the hymn, playing it seven or eight times in a row. *I Am He, I Am He.*

Tonight a storm was brewing, far over the distant mountains north of the town, blue-purple teeth glowering under a lid of clouds. Abitha hugged her shawl close and studied the massed townsfolk around her, sitting in the dust or the grass, mamas holding babies, children spellbound, silent, not running or playing or squirming or whining. Back home all the chores undone, like hers: feed for the animals; water from her naturally parsimonious well; dusting, sweeping, washing; chopping wood for the week.

People's lives were falling apart. They didn't care. Power, power. What was it? It could not be the hymn. It must be something aside from it or on top of it that worked together, like a key useless without its lock and vice-versa. Virgil, she thought bitterly, would have known. He had read books, seen things; he had traveled even, gone overseas and up north to Canada and south to Mexico. How he had ended up in this shithole town he had never told her, only that he was glad he had, for he had met her.

My love, my love. Killed by McCord and the sheriff saying it was a scuffle that went wrong and boys will be boys. *Looking me in the eye to say that boys will be boys.* An 'accident,' and his throat cut wide open with not one ragged accidental cut but four straight firm deliberate ones, open like a wet red book so you could see everything inside.

Thunder in the distance. From the back of the crowd Abitha could not hear the preacher drone on. She smelled the faraway lightning and waited for the smell of rain. She touched her madness again, deep inside her own darkness: a cold, faceted, unseen gem.

The sun sank away. Everyone left, trudging back home through the dust of mingled stone and earth and coal. Abitha looked up at the sky and said, "Take him and cut him out in little stars," and still in her black mourning clothes, half-invisible in the long prairie twilight, she walked upstream through the flowing crowd and climbed the three steps to the preacher's enclosed cart and pounded on the door.

He opened it at once, as if he had been waiting for her with his hand on the latch. An unpleasant smell flowed from the enclosed space—not the expected odors of unwashed male body, stale food, but something else. A wet, green stench. She climbed up anyway.

Two low benches faced each other inside, both half stacked with wooden crates, leaving half empty and surprisingly clean. She sat across from the preacher and waited as he lit the lantern and hung it from its hook. His white face was papery dry, unwrinkled except for the sharp black lines from his nose to the edges of his lipless mouth.

"Folks will talk," he said pleasantly.

"Folks will talk anyway," she said. "No matter what I do. It wouldn't matter if I was in here with the Roman Pope."

His eyes glittered in the faint light; they were every color or no color, like washing faded on the line. In the face of anyone else she would have thought perhaps they were the eyes of a blind man. He said, "What can I do for you, Miss Lukey?"

"I want..." She closed her eyes, testing: yes, still the cut throat, Virgil's face half-hid under a blanket, only the throat and the blood. Flooded over the white pine floor, the sea of blood. "What you're doing here. I want to help you. Take me on as your assistant—your apprentice, whatever you'd like to call it."

"And why should I do that?"

"Maybe you need the help," she said quietly. "Maybe not. But I don't have anything else to trade. I want...your help. Your power."

"The power of faith," he said. "Of true belief. Well—"

"You know damn well what I'm talking about," she said, and opened the bundle she'd tied to her skirts. Inside was a chunk of coal she'd found in the streets a few days ago near the train tracks. Local stuff, perfectly ordinary from the distance she'd originally spotted it. It was only when she had picked it up (*well, waste not, want not*) that she had realized she should not have. She held it out to him.

He did not take it, only looked at it on her black-smudged palm, unsurprised. The coal, like all coal, resembled a collection of tiny buildings all pressed together, like the cities you saw in engravings in the newspaper. But this one actually *was*. Minuscule lights shone inside it, voices of the same scale, and it sang: they both heard it singing: *I am He, I am He.*

"*That* power. What are you doing to the town?" she said. "To the mine?"

"It is not me," the preacher said. "It is the greater power I serve, Miss Lukey. We both happen to be quite surprised and...gratified by the response of the good townsfolk here. We've decided to stay a little longer than usual in this very special town. Now tell me what you really want."

She took a deep breath, gagged, and put the city of coal on the bench, wiping her hands on her skirts. "On March thirteen," she began, cold and steady, as if she were telling a totally different story. Virgil, her lover, her only lover, her first love, murdered by McCord weeks before the wedding; the sheriff, that bitch's bastard, doing nothing; Abitha's plan for revenge and self-destruction. She showed him the small knife she took everywhere now. "Just in case I catch him alone."

The preacher took the knife gingerly, as if he was not used to touching such things, or women.

"Why did he kill Virgil Dunn?"

"Because he's a bastard," she said bitterly, and finally tears came, slow, creeping. "Because he said he was in love with me—him! And Virgil was in *his way*. The sheriff knew all that. Oh they go way, way back, those two boys." She snatched the knife back.

"Your cause is righteous," the preacher said. "I believe it is. And there is something about you, Miss Lukey. Yes, perhaps you will be an asset to me here. In this great...work of improving your town."

"I don't care about them," Abitha said. "Only Virgil."

"But you still love," he said, his voice suddenly sinuous, caressing. "You can still love."

She shrugged. Her answer did not matter. She could not convince the preacher that she was under the influence of his hymn, she knew that now, so that part of her plan was no good; but she could allow him to think whatever else he wanted to.

"You know them well then," he said. "These folk."

"I've lived here all my life. Born and raised here, buried my folks here."

The lantern flickered—or was it his eyes? She watched him warily.

"The price of power is seven lives," he said. "Seven is all that is required. My master asks no fewer and no more than that. Choose them. The seven. And you will rule at my side."

She stared at him, shocked yet unsurprised. *My master*. The howling piece of coal. Singing with the throats of maggots and flies. Again that cold sense of apprehension and pressure, a storm separate from the ordinary storm outside and its ordinary lightning and thunder. The preacher was a monster, truly, a begetter of monsters. Father of monsters, spreading his seed in secret and through unspeakable and arcane ways. The thousand-eyed prodigies bursting in blood and pus from the splitting groins of ewes and cows all ready to do his bidding in this, the one town where everyone had proven susceptible to his song. Her knife put up now, unneeded.

It wouldn't bring him back, nothing would bring him back. But revenge was something. And perhaps to rid the world of this Preacher, too, this creeping blight who seized and used the minds of the innocent... if he let her approach near enough to take advantage of his power for her ends, she could stretch those ends for other means. She smiled.

"I will give you the names," she said. "Tell me what to do."

He said, "I will tell you what you may sing."

* * *

Midsummer eve. Longest day, shortest night. Abitha had never paid it any mind; no one in town had ever celebrated it or even known which day it fell upon. The preacher had called them all to a strange place—a dead spot in the land that had not always been dead but eventually the turf and even the weeds had given up under the relentless traffic of hoof and boot and cart and carriage in front of the entrance to the coal mine that was Whitstun's sole reason for existence.

The wind was hot and dry. Abitha stood next to the preacher for the first time and felt everyone's eyes on her. *What's she doing up there?* She near as saw the thought rising above the crowd like smoke. Sweat sprang out on her skin despite the unnatural heat after sunset. Voices rang in her head, all urging violence, all urging escape, some in her own voice, some in others. A chorus of contradictions. She thought, *I am mad, I am mad, but my body is not mad and it thinks something is coming.*

"Now," said the preacher, and the song began—familiar and still hated, she had never learned to hate it less or even fear it less. Each time she dreaded the discordant opening notes, dreading that this time it would do the same to her as to the others.

> *I am he of seven heads*
> *I am he who brings pain*
> *I am the voice of the dead*
> *I am a flood across the plain*

She wanted to turn, run, flee the preacher and the crowd and the town and the mine, pick another direction, just run. She clasped her hands and stood still, heart pounding so loudly she could barely hear the whine of fiddle and voices.

The master said humans had a weak intellect, were weak in their souls and minds, and needed...guidance. Control. The hymn was a beginning only. It opened up a minor chink in humanity's armor. Soon one would come to sing a different song, brought here from another place, the preacher had said. Tonight his colorless eyes glowed hot as horseshoes in the forge, white-hot. *A different song, a better song.*

The ground trembled lightly at first, no more than the sensation of a heavily-laden cart passing nearby. Then harder, longer, and a sound accompanied the next one, rising over the dull ecstatic uncomprehending voices: a roar. A sundering. Abitha turned to look behind the: the mine. Of course the mine. The wooden struts and beams making a throat through which the sounds could more easily reach the surface.

Those standing began to fall, some sitting, some kneeling; Abitha grabbed the preacher's arm to stay upright. The singing went on. No one screamed. But it was coming, whatever it was. It was almost here.

Silence. The ground stilled. The fiddlers set down their instruments and sat, slackjawed and waiting.

The thing burst out of the mine in a single motion, effortless and fluid, as if not only the human-built things like the tracks and the beams and the carts, but also the mountain itself, the whole land, was not there. It shrugged off the crumbling stones upon it, grass, bushes, trees, and cried out something to the night sky. Its breath was as loud as a tornado.

Abitha managed one quick glance, then clapped both hands over her eyes. Her mind reeled for uncounted seconds, time stretching out in the horror of it. *The master will help you with your revenge. Seven names. It will be very easy. You need do nothing but sing back the song I will teach you. So that he knows you—so that you are recognized as my adept.*

Seven names. The preacher was reaching for her now, closing his white hand around her upper arm. "You must speak," he shouted. "So the master can hear that it is you."

"Yes, preacher." She opened her eyes and held out a hand and for a second it was all Shakespeare again; she saw blood visible as well as invisible upon it, like Lady Macbeth, except it was Virgil's blood, an innocent, not a king.

She spoke and pointed. McCord and his men, that was four. Mears, Fulton, and Cresswell. The sheriff Couzens and the deputy Lewden who had laughed at her weeping: six. And Mrs. Alloways, who had been holding the biggest, fullest basket of rocks: seven. Oh, the joy of it, the gladness, the meanness. Abitha felt it all and felt it break around the hard airless stone of her insanity and pass by it.

They came up of their own accord—she was glad for that. They walked through the fallen crowd, buffeted by the night's strange winds, towards the roaring creature. They walked past Abitha and the preacher and the preacher's cart and did not turn to look.

"The master, who is all-powerful, demands a token only of our worship," the preacher said over the noise. "In all the world only seven at once is asked. A nothingness. For such riches and powers as you all cannot even imagine. As you cannot imagine with your weak, human minds!"

A nothingness. For we are nothing. Abitha stared at the creature in disbelief, at its writhings and twistings, dislodging the few boulders that were still balanced on its back, wedged between the scales there. In front of it a hole yawned open, unknowably deep, the pit blacker than the night sky above them. It caressed the edges obscenely with its limbs. Gloating, anticipating. The seven chosen looked pitifully small as they marched towards it.

She had known it was not the devil the preacher served even though he had done his utmost to make her believe that it was. But this, this...

"He will begin," the preacher shouted into her ear. The wind ripped away his foul breath. "Remember! Your responses!"

"Please," she said, putting a hand over his. "Come with me...I am so... overwhelmed in the face of the master. What if I forget them?"

"You will not," he snapped.

"Come with me," she said again. "Please, please. It would be a comfort to have my teacher there with me."

They approached the pit; she continued to cling to his arm as if she might faint without his support. Her mind whirled like the dust devils spinning all around the crowd, like the spirals of the burning flecks erupting from the pit. Not the devil, no, but an opening to hell anyway. What could you call it if not hell? The creature had come from there. *The master.*

His arm felt dead, as cold as if there was nothing under the sleeve but bone. Two black-clad servants marching towards their lord and master. Only one already dressed for mourning.

The creature called out to her, though in all its chaos of eye and scale and tongue and limb she did not think it had a mouth. No...it was using the pit, it sang from there. A stream of darkness and notes poured from it, high, shrill, relentless. When it paused, Abitha took a deep breath *and sang back.*

Your cause is righteous.

No. Righteous was not the word. She was not so mad yet. *His* cause, though...

The seven approached the edge. Again came the verse; again she sang the chorus. Her throat ached and stung from the blowing dust. Next to her, one blurred form vanished into the pit—could that have been McCord?—and she felt as well as heard the creature howl its satisfaction and triumph into the sky. Did the stars seem closer? Did they burn hotter? Perhaps.

Her trembling was real; no acting was needed for that. In they went, one after another. *I am no saint, not I. No one will worship my name. They will curse me, they will always remember...*

The seventh had gone in. The creature sang for the last time. She opened her mouth for the last response—then spun and shoved the preacher towards the pit.

In, she had meant, but he teetered on the edge with inches to spare between his bootheels and the abyss, his face finally realizing, shocked, betrayed, then furious. His hand snapped out and seized her arm. Unthinkingly she jerked it back, a reflex only, and the ragged black sleeve tore out of his grip.

Before he could rebalance, she kicked him sharply in the knee, and he was gone as if the pit had risen up to seize him.

The creature's shriek rose—rage or shock or vengeance, Abitha had no idea. But something had broken that should not have been. The pit began to crumble away like wet sand, the noises within it dying away, screaming, fading as if falling, and she finally snapped from her amazement and began to run.

She did not wait for anyone. Some folks outpaced her, some must have fallen behind and then fallen forever. Their screams vanished too suddenly. She did not waste precious minutes unhitching the black mules, only leapt onto the right-hand animal and drove her heels into its flanks. They clattered away into the darkness, towards the coal-dirtied lights of town.

* * *

She stayed in town only long enough to help herself to supplies from the general store, then rode back to her house and packed her few things. The preacher's possessions she burned without removing them from their crates and everything, unlike his little monsters, went up easily enough. The smoke was strange, she had to admit—flashing and twisting as if it were full of metal shavings, and with a terrible stench, as if she had built the fire out of bones. The gray cylinders of the hymn went last, furiously shading from red to amber to white and finally dribbling out over the coals in viscous strings that did not resemble molten metal, silenced at last.

She supervised the dying fire for a long time, till everything vanished under the ashes. Then she poured a bucket of water on the remains, climbed into the seat of the cart, and picked up the reins. The two night-black mules moved off silently as she clucked to them. She did not know where she was going; she only put her back to the town, and her bloodied house, and she sang as she went, a song of gladness, riding into the rising sun.

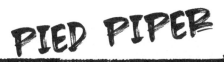

PIED PIPER

BY CAROL EDWARDS

Trip the tempo from the hangman's flute
jangling bodies sway in tune
line strung from head to
neck to bar to stem

dangling feet
seared by hellish heat
beat cacophony
discordant notes thrilling bones
seize and jerk
marionettes on strings

helter-skelter limbs askance
spines snapped, heads collapsed
black lightning drips
from tissue paper skin

microtears' tears
mist invisible beams
dark seams gleam in
sharp origami folds
curling ribboning souls

MIXTAPE

BY V. CASTRO

've always loved music. Since I was a child, music had been part of my life. The radio was always on in the car. Family parties had the boom box on a table at the front of wherever we were so people could dance after a few drinks and a full belly of food. I had to be satisfied biting into the limes since I was too young for the beer or tequila. And when I began practicing brujeria as a woman, it became an essential part of my private rituals at home. But never did I think music would become a ritual I would share, or have the power to call to unseen entities. My heart always focused on healing. The only darkness I faced was my own. Music was incense for my soul. As I would learn, we often underestimate ourselves. I did.

How many soundtracks do we have stored in our heads to remind us of others? In high school I made mixtapes on real cassettes (yes, I'm that old) and when CDs came out, I continued to make my mixtapes. I love them because they are an anthology of sound, emotion, and memory. They take you on an intimate journey and can show you one's soul. Music can reflect the soul, and the soul can be a beacon in this dimension for those we cannot see.

Pam always wanted the wrong men and strangely they were all the same (especially how they looked). She came over on a Tuesday night with a bottle of wine and puffy eyes. Her condo block was in the same complex and just a walk across the pool. "Can you read my cards? I don't know what to do. Your tarot readings are the best."

I gave her a side glance as I took out the wine glasses. "You know exactly what to do."

She sat down on one of the stools on my counter and grabbed a chip from the bag I had opened before she arrived. "I need to just fall out of love with Dave. How did you get over your thing?"

I placed the wine glasses down and paused. I never really thought about it. It just happened. "I don't know. A lot of wine and music. A mixtape I made to keep myself busy one night."

Now she gave me a look. "Girl, nobody makes those things anymore."

"Sorry, but I'm old school in some ways. I like the intention behind it."

"You can make playlists on any streaming service."

"I guess, but it's more than that. It's the physical act of holding it in your hand and handwriting the name of the mixtape with a red sharpie."

"Is that what you do?" she asked with a chuckle.

I lifted my wine glass filled to the top. "Cheers. To getting over losers with music."

She clinked my glass. "To the end of someone who thought a weekend away was too much of a commitment."

I took a large gulp then walked into the living room. I had two six-foot-tall bookshelves filled with CDs and DVDs. My eyes scanned the CD collection until I found the mixtape labeled, "Get over that shit." Every song belonged to a particular tape because these tapes began in a notebook. I would write down a theme then let the songs come to me. Sometimes they played on the radio, came up on my shuffle at the gym, waiting for coffee. I'd make a voice note of it on my phone then write it down later under the appropriate theme. Sure, I could leave it on the phone, however, there is magic in writing. Thought becomes visual and with a song, ineffable emotions find the right words. The written word is just as powerful as the spoken word. A song combines the two. Like a spell.

I smiled and brought it back to the kitchen. Pam was browsing Instagram, creeping on Dave.

"Here. I want you to light candles and listen to this before bed. The next day listen to it again and again."

Pam rolled her eyes and took a deep breath before putting her phone down. "I *would* do exactly that, but I don't have a CD player. Most people don't."

She was right. Most people no longer gave CDs the time of day. Call me a big nerd, but I still had the original Pearl Jam CD I purchased when it was released. I looked at the case again. "The songs are here. Maybe a playlist? But the exact order. Don't add or delete any. And *please* don't share it. These are personal. They may be for others, but still have part of me in them and whatever out there that inspires me to put it together."

I wasn't sure if she would do this, but I hoped she would. She glanced through the list.

"What do we have here...'Violet' by Hole followed by Pat Benatar's 'Heartbreaker.'" She smiled. "I like that. I want to be the heartbreaker for once. Quite the playlist. But I don't get why you are so freaked out about sharing? What about sharing is caring? I doubt the demon of heartbreak would mind." She gave me a cheesy grin.

"Just listen to it." I said placing my hands on my hips trying to be serious. Only time would tell if she saw this more than a joke.

* * *

The following morning my phone pinged. It was a video of Pam listening to the mix while she put on her make-up and mouthing the words of one of the songs. I had to chuckle. Then she sent me a text.

Happy now? :)

I texted back. *YES!!! Was that too difficult?*

She responded straight away. *I have put all the songs on a Spotify playlist and shared it on my social media. Hope he sees the songs and knows it's over for him. I'm already hating him more. Quite a few people have listened to it already. My friend Nina across the street loves it.*

Now I rolled my eyes. Not because she was losing interest, but that she made my playlist public on Spotify.

I put my phone down feeling slightly exposed. People would listen to what was in my head, what dwelled in my heart. I grabbed my phone again and checked Spotify. There it was. She wrote a little caption. *The best mix to get over their shit!* It had hundreds of likes.

It was public now and taking it down might cause a fight with Pam I didn't want. What was the worst that could happen? People dump sleazeballs. I couldn't be afraid.

Keep listening! I texted back. It seemed harmless. My only hope was that she would truly never go back to that toxic situation. My watch alarm when off then letting me know it was time to leave for work.

* * *

At the end of the day, as I packed my bag and laptop, I received another message from Pam.

You won't believe what happened!

What? I typed back, dreading her reply, sure she would say he wanted another try at their relationship. It didn't occur to me the playlist would be as potent for her as it was for me.

I don't feel anything for him anymore. I looked at his Instagram and wanted to vomit! I swear I am not blowing smoke up your ass.

Good! Now let that shit stick.

A week later, she began dating again, not worrying about Dave. He was deleted and blocked. Something she never did before with Dave. It was also at the same time I received a message from someone I didn't know.

Our mutual friend Pam mentioned you made the mixtape. My name is Nina. Hope you don't mind she gave me your number.

I am. And it's no problem. I messaged back with a surge of excitement at my fingertips from the flattery. Maybe I didn't want to share the playlists because I was afraid of criticism from people I didn't know. Not some supernatural reason.

Can we meet for coffee? I'd like to discuss getting a mixtape for myself. I have a big problem and his name is Tad.

This seemed odd to me, but I trusted Pam. *Okay. How about Saturday at Big Joe just outside the complex?*

Great. See you then.

* * *

Nina sat at a table with a large mug of coffee. Whatever this woman was experiencing had to be bad. The heaviness of her presence was not something I had encountered before. It felt like a cosmic thunder cloud hovered above her. Maybe she needed an exorcism and not a list of songs to make her move on. Most people just needed reassurance it was okay to follow their intuition. I could sense that looking at the deep sadness in her eyes that were darkly rimmed from lack of sleep. Her skin appeared sunken in at the cheeks. I sat down as she picked at a muffin.

"Hi, Nina. I'm Pam's friend Scarlett. How can I help?" I asked.

She stared at me on the verge of a deluge of tears and pain. Without hesitation she spoke. "I want to kill my ex."

I didn't know how to respond or if she was serious. "Um...I don't deal in murder. Just getting over pricks or needing a boost to your workout."

She pulled out her phone and scrolled through something I could not see. "This is why."

She placed the phone on the table. It was a photo of her with a busted lip and an eye closed shut. The other eye bright red from crying. The sight made me sick.

"That's for the police. I can't help you with murder."

Her hand shook as did her voice. "You don't understand, I have tried everything to keep him away from me. I don't have social media anymore. Everything paused. I'm afraid to leave my house. I thought of moving out of state, but then I'd leave my family and friends. Why should I be punished for this obsessive psycho? It's either his life or mine. I know it. I have a restraining order, but I find little reminders of our relationship on my car at work or on my doorstep. There are the cards I gave him for special occasions, small gifts, candy I like. It's creepy. I can't afford to put cameras everywhere or keep moving in this city." Tears streamed from her tired eyes. "I'm desperate," she said in a whisper.

And I could hear the desperation. If I knew for certain I could find that bastard and make him pay, I would. But that type of power I didn't possess. At least I didn't think I did. I stood up. "I can't help you. You are asking me to help you commit murder. I don't even know if my mixtapes are capable of that."

She grabbed me by the wrist. Her hand was wet and clammy. Her bloodshot eyes made her look possessed. "You have to try. People are commenting on the playlist and how it worked for them. I've never seen Pam happier. Pam told me you were the most reliable and strongest friend she has ever had. If anyone had the ability to help, it would be you."

I shook my head. "For minor things...you need the authorities to put him behind bars."

She let go of my and slumped into her chair. "I have. I have done everything like I said before."

I looked at her again. "I'm sorry."

I walked out feeling awful, but it wasn't something I could solve. Would it even work? I didn't want to give her a false sense of hope. Wouldn't the authorities deal with it?

When I got back into my apartment, I checked Spotify again. The likes were in the thousands with comments on how the playlist did wonders. I slammed my laptop shut. How could that be? I thought it worked for me because I *willed* it to work. I *wanted* it bad enough. Pam's emotions were strong enough as well. She was ready to untether herself. It made me think about collective energy, wind farms. When the wind was strong enough, it turned a turbine with a constant force to create electricity. All those people sitting in their cars, lying in bed, listening at a bus stop and believing the music could give them what they needed, steer their intention... Now *that* was a powerful thought.

* * *

A week later, at 1 a.m., I looked at my phone and saw a text and some missed calls from Pam when I woke up with my bladder aching. *Answer!!!*

I called her back half awake, knowing she would never do this unless it was an emergency. "You all right?"

She was crying. "I'm fine, but Nina is not."

I blinked my eyes and tried to put a face to the name. A chill gripped my body. The woman from the coffee shop. I sat up in bed.

"What happened?"

"I'm at the hospital. He kidnapped her and kept her for two days before she escaped...what he did..."

My heart dropped and stomach soured. Nina came to me for help. I ignored the terror in her voice and eyes. She paid the price for that.

"I'll be over in a few hours." I hung up the phone and began to collect what I needed to take to the hospital.

In the darkness, I thought of all the music I would want to curse someone one with. What heinous power could I conjure with thought and musical notes? Many people believe dark entities lurk unseen, waiting to be fed. If all those people listening to the playlist on Spotify could change their lives—could feel empowered and good—could rage be enough for vengeance? Was there something wanting to carry that out for us? Nina came to me with the confidence I could help her, but I doubted. Now I had to believe with every fiber of my body. It would be a short list, but effective.

I snatched my work backpack off the back of my dining chair and rushed through the house looking for the items I wanted to take to the hospital. My spare candles were located beneath the sink and crystals on the windowsill. I probably couldn't light it in a hospital room because of the heavy scent, but I grabbed a bundle of palo santo as well.

* * *

I sat next to Nina with Pam on the opposite side of the hospital bed. Nina came in and out of consciousness, her mottled bruises shrouded in shadow with the lights in the room at the lowest setting. Her lips were chapped. The blanket had been pulled to her collar bone so we couldn't see any other damage he had done. But the painkiller drip feeding into her body was all we needed to know.

I lit tea light candles instead of my usual seven-day pillar ones. We didn't need the nurses storming in. We both held her hands. I bowed my head.

"Please forgive me. I am sorry I left you in that coffee shop. You needed help. I didn't think I had the power to do anything. I am sorry I didn't try. I won't fail you again. I am here for you." I could feel her index finger twitch and her hand squeeze mine.

According to the police, he was gone. They only offered a "we'll do our best to find him." This gave me little hope. We needed something more powerful than an underpaid cop who didn't really care about their job. If all those listeners really meant what they wrote in the comments below the list Pam uploaded on Spotify, then maybe we had a chance. Collective rage and pain have worked miracles when it comes to creating change. Perhaps all this belief in the power of the music would give us more of what we needed. Some wrote how it gave them courage and hope to leave unhappy situations. Others said it made them angry enough to call out abuse and seek help for themselves. Everyone got something different out of the music, the words morphed into what they needed in that moment to give themselves personal power. If that isn't special, what is in this life?

I placed the small portable speaker on Nina's lap. She stared at the speaker and raised a trembling hand. She winced trying to sit upright. Her arm was still connected to the IV and couldn't quite reach. I moved to do it myself when she stopped me.

"No. Let me. I want all the pain in my body to be felt by him. Let this be my way of cursing the music."

I nodded and moved the speaker closer so she could press play. Let her see and feel what she needed. Most magic when real, presents itself intuitively and is different for everyone. Just as there is light, there is shadow. Like the soul. He had no light to do what he did. Let the darkness now consume him and take him where he belonged. It was the darkest mixtape I had ever made and my intention possessed more hate than I had ever experienced, or wanted to. I didn't like wishing ill on people, but he had it coming. Tears streamed from the corners of Nina's eyes.

"Hell Awaits," by Slayer began our journey. It moved to "Are You Afraid," by Type O Negative. These songs sealed his fate with her intention. I added "Santa Muerte," by Cartel De Santa for her protection. *May Santa Muerte be with her.*

The final songs were "Black Widow" and "Only Women Bleed," by Lita Ford. Lita Ford, an angel of metal. Her presence in a genre where most women didn't go felt appropriate. Her strength and success were the seal to give those things to Nina.

"I want him to die," she whispered. The candle flared brightly, then flickered.

I had to control my emotions seeing her lying there, knowing what he put her through. The marks on her wrists and ankles were still visible. I found myself also whispering, "I want him to die, too."

I gave her a photo of him I printed from Instagram. Her knuckles were white as she squeezed it. We sat there with her until the music stopped an hour later. I blew out the candles and took the picture out of her hand. Pam and I left her to sleep.

In the parking lot I took out the photo and burned it with my lighter. Pam wiped tears from her cheeks. "You think it will work?"

I watched his face become consumed by the flames as the paper curled to black and fell to the ground. "Pray. I hope to God it does."

* * *

Nina was released from the hospital four days later. She stayed with Pam until she could move again. Tad had not been found yet. Every sound in the house, phone ringing, knock on the door made her jump. I brought over peanut butter cookies and she only emerged from Pam's spare bedroom to say thank you before shuffling back. I felt awful.

That night I went to bed with mixed emotions, not knowing what would transpire. I closed my eyes, replaying in my mind every song on my death mixtape. I tossed back and forth, seeing Nina on the hospital bed with whatever strength she had, squeezing Tad's photo. Did my mixtape have the power to summon a demon to find him if the cops couldn't and his family and friends played dumb? In that moment, I thought if it could, I wanted it to. It was just a thought.

* * *

I jolted awake from a deep sleep to banging on my door. I looked at my phone. Three a.m., with no emails or messages. My imagination hopped on hot coals of fear. Who was it? The darkness of the room made me feel paralyzed despite my mind racing. The pounding continued. I had to do something. I closed my eyes and said a prayer. *Be with me, Santa Muerte.* Then I got out of bed. My pajama bottoms didn't have pockets, so I shoved my phone in my soft sleep bra in the event I needed it close by. Then I grabbed my baseball bat from beneath my bed and gripped the handle hard, ready to swing. That man who hurt Nina was still out there. I turned on all the lights as I walked through the condo towards the front door.

"Who is it?" I shouted with as much authority as I could muster, despite not feeling that way. It made me think about how lonely it is when you think you are all alone to defend yourself, like Nina did. "I...I have a gun."

My hands trembled as I gripped the bat until it hurt. Whoever it was would get as many swings as I had strength for.

"It's Nina. Help me."

I rushed to the door. I felt like I failed her before and wouldn't do it again. I unlocked it before flinging it open.

She stood in my doorway covered in blood. Tears streamed from her vacant eyes. She appeared numb or in shock, looking directly at me, devoid of emotion except for the silent tears. I glanced outside. No one on the street or passing cars, just a barking dog in the distance. I grabbed her arm, dragged her inside, and slammed the door.

"What did he do? Are you okay? Let me call an ambulance."

She shook her head. "It isn't my blood."

"Oh my god. What happened?"

She smiled with tears in her eyes. "A miracle."

"What happened, Nina?"

She looked at her reflection in the darkness of the TV before speaking.

"I sat on the bed feeling nothing. I took my mirror out of my purse and looked at myself. The bruises were reminders of what happened and the regret of allowing that man into my life. All those years wasted and having so little self-respect. I almost hated the person in that mirror as much as I hated him. At least I did find the courage to leave him. Never did I think he would stalk me for years before doing what he did. I threw the mirror to the ground and listened to the mixtape you brought to the hospital. I thought about one of the nights where the sedation made me not sure if I was dreaming or awake.

"The music in the hospital room went from garbled to clear as day. I remember the scent of candle wax with a hint of cinnamon. Shadows played on the walls. I watched them as they morphed into different shapes. One looked like a large claw that seemed to motion for me to come closer, but I could hardly move from the stitches and the pain meds. A large human form rose on the wall. What might have been a foot tapped to the beat of the music. The rest of the form grew until it seemed to fill the room in a darkness that didn't scare me. I wanted to dive into it and forget what had just happened to me. My only intention was vengeance.

"When I got out of the hospital, I wanted to see that darkness again. Pam was out on a date. I left her place without any hesitations and went back to mine. I lit black seven-day pillar candles and played the music. I closed my eyes as I lay down and imagined the dark figure I saw on the hospital room wall. My soul ached to see it again. I could feel the room spinning and gathering in the center of my forehead. It felt like a vortex wanted to pull me into oblivion, and I welcomed it. Something massaged my temples. It felt good. I relaxed into the music and touch. Then a vision flashed before my eyes. It was of blood and sacrifice, wealth and pain followed by joy.

"I knew what to do. I got up and picked up my phone and downloaded Instagram again. I made my feed visible so I could send Tad a message. I knew that asshole...he wouldn't be far."

I'm sorry. Let me make it up to you. This is all my fault. You were doing what you thought was best for me, us. Come over?

"I waited for a response. Before I got too excited, I ran out the door to get supplies. He messaged back within a few minutes."

The cops stopped looking for me? Or you want more? Tell me where you are.

"I typed in the address and time to meet at my apartment. No more living in fear or regret anymore. I jumped out of the bed and began to hum "Let The Music Play," by Shannon. It just popped in my head and so did my plan for Tad.

"That evening I did my makeup perfectly. The house smelled of his favorite meal: roast beef and baked potatoes. I dressed in his favorite outfit: soft, wide leg leggings and a low cut crop top. Then I played the hospital playlist on low and lit the candles. All I had to do was wait.

"It was exactly at nine when he arrived with a cocky look on his face. It took so much control for me not to vomit and sob. Then I let him in. He slammed the door behind him and I asked him if he wanted a drink. He smirked. Of course he did. It was the same ugly face he made when I woke up in his bed with a throbbing head after he kidnapped me. 'In a moment. Hope it will make it easier for you to apologize,' he said.

"I walked backwards as he moved towards me. All I could think to say was, 'I will...in a moment.'

"Then he asked, 'Why did you run from me? I didn't want to hurt you. You see, it was the only way to show you how much I love you. To keep you.' His voice remained so calm as he got closer. I stopped when I bumped into the dining room table. I told him I was scared. 'How would you feel if you were me?' And you know what he said? He said, 'I think you were dumb to break it off in the first place. You thought I was controlling, but I just wanted to take care of you in ways you wouldn't think of taking care of yourself. The world is scary. Other guys are. Not me.' He moved my hair from my shoulders then touched my cheek where one of the bruises still showed through the makeup.

"I touched his hand and asked him if he wanted that wine now and we could get more comfortable on the couch. He smiled and said, 'That is a great idea.'

"I walked back to the counter and grabbed the bottle of wine. I turned to him and gave him a pleasant smile. As fast as I could, I tossed the contents into his face and jumped back.

"The acid sizzled against his skin. He screamed as he clutched his cheeks and bulging eyes. His skin melted like the candles.

"I turned the music louder before grabbing the chef's knife out of the knife block and walked over to him as he fell to his knees. Then I plunged it into the side of his neck to silence him. I never stopped looking at him as he fell to the ground and bled out.

"When he stopped moving, I took out a pair of plastic gloves from a black bag on the floor next to the sofa. I kneeled next to him and said, 'I will chop off your tongue for the lies you told, sever your dick for using it as a weapon, and rip out your heart because it belongs to the darkness.' Then...I did it."

I looked at her not knowing what to say or do. It wasn't my intention to turn her in to the police. "What do you want?"

"To say thank you. Making the playlist to kill him gave me the power I needed."

"Now what?"

"Ever heard 'Ride Like the Wind' by Christopher Cross?"

I nodded.

"Headed to Mexico and never looking back."

"You think you will make it?"

"It's only a few hours by car."

I paused before walking to my purse on the hook behind the door. I rustled inside and handed her my car keys. Without saying anything, I walked into my bedroom and returned with my passport. "Take these. Wear a baseball cap and keep your head down. More makeup. You just might get away with it."

She looked up at me with tears in her eyes. "You don't want to call the cops? You don't think I'm evil?"

"Pam and I prayed over your bed that fate would find him. We prayed hard with the playlist wanting justice, or some punishment."

"Thank you."

"Go shower. I'll get a towel, trash bag, and clothes ready. But hurry. Try to get over the border before dawn."

She stared at me. "Huh."

"What?"

"It's just...I started to make my own mixtape. It begins with Nina Simone's 'Feeling Good'. I liked the idea of getting there and watching the sunrise once I crossed over. "

I smiled.

TO THE RIVER

BY COREY FARRENKOPF

Every year, on the anniversary of Denny's drowning, they returned to the bridge and solemnly tossed stones into Bass River. The water below was brackish, never freezing, slowly weeping into the Atlantic. A sea captain statue standing atop a nearby condominium watched over the scene. Everyone on Cape Cod used the massive wooden seagoer to give directions. The friends were no different, always saying *Meet under the captain* before they played *To The River*.

After Denny drowned, directions went unsaid.

They knew the date.

The time.

The place to perform their song.

To The River was named after their favorite punk anthem. On summer nights, the friends slipped down to the algae-wrapped docks at the public landing, goading one another into the current as the others gathered stones from the shoreline. Once someone had submerged, the others climbed the grassy incline to the road, then jogged to the middle of the bridge directly above the swimmer. They'd sing the lyrics to the song, six from above, one from below, and toss the gathered stones into the water. If the swimmer dodged the projectiles, they'd be granted one wish from the sea goddess who'd appeared in many of their childhood fairytales and familial prayers. All the Water Wench sought as an offering was their favorite song.

It didn't matter which.

They'd been making the pilgrimage since before they were in middle school. Rarely had a wish come true, but that didn't stop them from repeating the rite, over and over again, year in and year out as if their desires waited just beyond their grasp.

The wet *plop* of rocks sinking would rise in chorus, then another barrage would go up until the stones were depleted. No one actually tried to hit the swimmer. It was about the thrill and the song, not the violence...at least until Denny caught a stone to the face and sank.

His limbless torso washed ashore on a beach below a golf course the next day.

Someone called in the corpse after noticing a gyre of seagulls circling above, their caws disrupting a peaceful round of eighteen holes.

The rest of Denny's body was never found. Schoolbound whispers claimed his head now belonged to the Water Wench, adorning Her altar up stream. Divers were unable to recover the missing bits, so there was no way to refute the rumors.

No one tried.

The friends, between the ages of thirteen and fifteen, were not charged.

Accidental drowning was written on the death certificate.

Though no one was found guilty, the friends carried the grief for the rest of their lives. It was impossible to know who had thrown the fateful stone. They had become a firing squad of teenagers, each believing they'd pulled the trigger. They imagined the act a thousand times. The stone leaving their hand, arcing up, rising and rising, before plunging down, arrowlike, into Denny's face, spearing clean through his open right eye.

* * *

Ten years passed, and the friends continued to meet beneath the captain to toss their stones and sing their song. They lit candles on the ledge beneath the bridge at the moldering shrine they'd made years ago. Denny's freshman photo had to be replaced with each visit, the previous installment having turned to mush from the constant salt wash, or carried off by rats for nesting material.

"Is this going to be the year?" one of them asked, tongues of flame dancing around Denny's acne spotted cheeks.

"Not sure why this one would be any different," another replied.

"Why doesn't he come? It's not like we're singing it wrong. He's got to know we can't keep living with this," the next said, because, in truth, they weren't there to keep Denny's memory alive.

They'd all had the same dream every night for all those years, the ghost of Denny pointing the finger, the guilty slipping into the river, the fateful rock cast once again from the bridge. An eye for an eye. Consciences swept clean. For them, the world wanted balance, and there was no other way to achieve equilibrium.

They had to alter the ritual though. No one could bring themselves to get into the water, knowing what happened to Denny's body, knowing there actually had to be something in the river like the prayers said. And if She had to be down there, so did their friend, in some shape or form. In the haze of regret, the logic tracked.

Everyone wished the same wish.

No other desire remained.

Once the candles were lit and the stones flung, they sat on a low wooden fence that stretched around the edge of the public landing, singing the song they'd sung years ago, chanting the chorus into the night as if it were a summoning spell. They'd sing the lyrics again and again, gasoline fumes from the boat launch filling their lungs. Each gazed out over the water running slow beneath the barnacle-stuck bridge, waiting for a translucent shimmer to rise from the depths, the lanky ghost treading water before them, lifted from the riverbed by the hand of that ancient sea goddess they'd prayed to all those years ago.

But the Water Wench never surfaced and Denny never came.

His spirit didn't seem anchored to the place like the others.

The dead don't always linger.

"What would we do if he actually showed?" one asked.

"Apologize? Beg forgiveness?" another replied.

"I'd get in the water if it was me," a third said. "Let Her take me too."

All eyes turned to him. No one spoke.

"Maybe it's better he doesn't show," another said after the moment passed.

"We've got to try one last time. It's tradition," said another. "Bad luck to leave otherwise."

Then they sang the song for the last time that year, as if repetition might prevent them from having to sing again the following year, as if the six would stop meeting at the same place on the same night until the day they died, singing an old punk song by a band they barely remembered, words cast to an oblivious god, trying to call to a ghost who no longer cared about wishes and stones and the sea and the view from beneath a bridge.

Sometimes ghosts were quicker to forget than the living.

Sometimes the living never had a choice to forget.

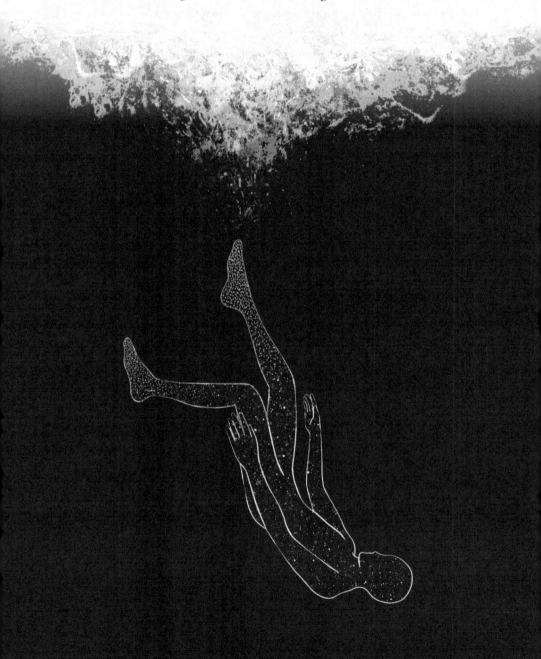

THE PRODIGY

BY PHILIP FRACASSI

The boys stand in the funeral parlor picking at the buttons of their stiff black suit coats and tugging the coarse knots of their ties. Outside, the late summer Georgian sun mercilessly bakes the earth, and inside the air conditioning struggles to keep up. The parlor is hot and their cheeks are reddened, their scratchy dress shirts stuck uncomfortably to their backs, glued by sweat. The entire room feels damp, sticky with the tears of family—many of whom they'd never met or even heard of prior to their mysterious grandfather's death.

Grandpa Johnny lies in a shiny brown coffin at the front of the crowded room, the top half of his body exposed to mourners—an exhibit in the museum of death. He wears a blue pinstripe suit that looks too big on his bony shoulders and a white dress shirt knotted with a tie the color of blood; his long gray hair slicked back over a narrow skull wrapped in wrinkled, liver-spotted skin. Travis stands in line with the others, eager for a peek at the cadaver—having never seen a corpse, he's morbidly curious. When he finally arrives at the front and looks down at his grandfather, he finds himself disappointed by the pale, dusty face, the fishy lips, and the closed, sunken eyes.

"They sew the eyelids shut," Josh explains after he slumps next to Travis a few minutes later, having completed his own examination of the old man's body. "They pull the brains out through the nose, rip out all the organs, and replace the blood

115

with turpentine so the body doesn't stink."

Josh is Travis's distant cousin who'd come into town for the funeral. Despite being raised far apart, and having never met, the boys bonded instantly from the second their two mothers held their own reunion the day before. As their mothers exclaimed fussily over one another, the two boys eyed each other slyly, exchanging a knowing look that easily translated into: *Looks like we're in this together, so please—oh please—don't be a dick.* After a few minutes they'd been instructed to *go play* while their moms chatted about funeral plans and faded memories.

They'd found solace in each other's company, a respite from the awkward loneliness only the death of a grandparent can introduce into a child's life and, regardless of their differences, it quickly turned out to be a match made in heaven—a relief to the boys and their mothers alike.

Being from Detroit, Josh is amused by the accents and cultural differences of the deep South, and Travis is fascinated by all the crazy winters folks had in the North. Both kids are small and skinny for their age, and both hate sports, love music, and gravitate toward a studious rebelliousness that keeps them entertained but free of any serious trouble. They had discovered they're both readers, although Josh leans more science fiction while Travis enjoys thrillers, but even this disparity had allowed their relationship to comfortably intertwine, each of them expanding the other's perspective on books and stories in a way that had opened worlds for one another that would never fully close. Of the man who brought them together, however, they had known little.

Now, stuck at the funeral, they keep their ears open for new information, but for the most part decide to hang out with each other and simply wait for it all to be over.

"I guess he was sort of famous," Travis mumbles, sticking a finger under the side of his collar and tugging absently. "But he sure don't look like much now."

"I heard that too," Josh replies, nodding. "But my mom wouldn't tell me any more about it. Only that he was strange, and she'd been happy to move away when she did."

"Yeah, my mom stayed on longer, I guess," Travis says. "But we hung out a few times, mainly for holidays. A few years ago, we moved to South Carolina, and it was too far to travel back unless you really had to."

After a few moments of silent people-watching, Josh says, "Hey, I dare you to push a finger into his cheek when no one's looking. I bet the dent will just stay there, like putty, or pudding." He pokes Travis in the cheek to emphasize the point.

"Gross," Travis says, swiping at his cousin's hand, but finds himself intrigued by the idea, and decides to give it a try if the situation presents itself. This is his first funeral, but the experience isn't as jarring as he thought it'd be. The old man just looks sort of fake. As if they'd swapped out a person for a wax figure and expected everyone to cry and holler over it. If anything, he's bored.

"Hey, can I ask you something?" Josh says, his tone secretive.

Travis looks him in the eye, nods. "Sure."

Josh looks around to make sure no one's eavesdropping, but since they'd found seats on a couch at the back, most of the guests are well out of earshot.

Regardless, he leans in closer.

"Do you know the story?"

Travis feels a tingle at the back of his neck, where the hairs on an older man might be standing when a similar feeling overcame them. Of course he knows the story, but he finds himself shaking his head, swallowing hard. "What do you mean?"

Josh smirks, as if knowing Travis is avoiding the question, but pushes on. "You know what I mean," he says, then whispers: "About how he beat the Devil."

Travis has indeed heard the story countless times. People loved to talk about the time the old man "whooped the Devil fair and square." How he'd saved his soul and become an instant legend.

Travis doesn't know how much is true and how much is nothing more than a tall tale, but regardless of the details, the stories always begin and end the same way.

With the Devil's challenge. And the golden fiddle.

Travis likes Josh, but he isn't comfortable discussing a topic he's long thought of as taboo; a dark slice of family history that is best left alone rather than poked like a dormant animal thought dead, one that might just spring to life, all claws and fur and teeth.

Plus, Josh is from the North, and doesn't understand that things like ghosts and demons and monsters are just different in the South. In a place like Michigan, folks think of the Devil as an ethereal spirit that lives far beneath the surface of the earth, or a metaphor tucked into the pages of scripture. In the North, the Devil lives as a myth, a representation of evil, a symbol of the sin inside each one of us. For people like Josh, the Devil exists in air-conditioned churches, or on the television.

In Georgia, the Devil is much different. He isn't quite as mysterious. And he isn't just a symbol or a myth, some metaphor for the darkness of mankind.

He's as real as your next-door neighbor. And just as close.

He strolls the streets of your town and lurks outside your home. He sits behind you in the movie theater, stinking of smoke and sulfur. He'll settle beneath an old tree in your backyard, rest in the shade on a hot day, his golden eyes wide and intent on whomever dares look out at him from a nearby window. In the South, the Devil is downright *clingy*.

Josh leans over again. "Come on, you can tell me. We're family, after all. And I know you've seen it."

Travis sighs. He knows, of course, what Josh is referring to. He stares forward for a few moments, watches the black-clothed mourners bow and weep at Grandpa Johnny's coffin as if it were a shrine. The line, he thinks, is never-ending.

Everyone wants a glimpse of the man who beat the Devil.

Suddenly, Josh is gripping Travis by the bicep. "Dude, tell me," he hisses. "I heard it's real but I call bullshit, and if it *is* real you've got to show it to me before I head back. So come on, have you seen it or not?"

"Yeah," Travis says finally, yanking his arm from that too-tight grip, then turning to look his distant half-cousin from the north in the eye. "I've seen it."

* * *

When Travis and Josh arrive at their grandfather's house—a massive old mansion that's beginning to show signs of neglect—their mothers immediately begin bustling about to prepare for the onslaught of well-wishers and hangers-on that will soon crowd the living room, parlor, kitchen, and dining room of the dead man's home. As the sisters pull out platters of cold cuts from the oversized refrigerator, push trays of pre-cooked fried chicken into the oven for warming, and stock the wet bar with clean glasses, buckets of ice, and enough liquor to appease a hundred souls, the boys are left to their own devices, told only to *keep out of the way, now* and *go about their business elsewhere.*

But instead of yanking their ties off to go play in the vast backyard, or hunker down in front of the old tube television in efforts to find a good science fiction or monster movie, they decide to duck beneath the frail rope that's been strung at the bottom of the staircase (hung to restrict visitors from exploring the more private areas of the large house), and make their way past bedrooms, bathrooms, and closets to the end of the long, dark second-story hallway, to a door Travis knows leads to the most important, most revered room in the entire house.

The library.

* * *

The room is large, the ceilings high and arched, the attic floor having been removed to make room for the tall shelves lining the walls. Each one is packed with books—some leatherbound and musty, some fresh and modern, still wearing their colorful dust jackets—and equipped with a rail ladder that rolled smoothly from case-to-case in order to reach the higher volumes.

There is only one window, round as a flower in full bloom and just as colorful, the glass a patchwork of panes stained in red, purple, blue, and yellow, creating an abstract mosaic that turns sunlight into smears of color which rest across the hardwood floor, mud brown walls, and voluminous spines. At the far end of the room sits a massive oak desk, half-shadowed in the dim light. Against the wall beside it is a display case built with dark, glossy walnut, the contents viewable only via the glass top.

"Come on," Travis says, and the boys step lightly across the room, respectful of the energy their grandpa's old haunt of a library demands. They approach the case the way age-old explorers likely approached the X on their treasure map; the way a medieval knight would step gingerly toward the Holy Grail—with reverence bordering on awe, anticipation hinging toward madness.

Set inside the case, illuminated by the soft red light streaming in through the stained-glass window, lies the object of much speculation in the South, the talisman Grandpa Johnny had been given by the Devil himself on one hot, humid Georgian afternoon—the one on which he'd outplayed the demon and kept his soul.

The golden fiddle.

It was said that Johnny never played the demon's gift in public after that lore-drenched day, but it was *also* said that if one happened to be walking past the mansion on a rare moonlit night, one might hear a sweet, slippery melody streaming from the house—from the fiddle itself—riding the humid air as Johnny sat in the library, bow skipping and gliding over the strings with such veracity, such skill, it was as if he were the Devil himself playing for all the hordes of Hell.

Those who'd heard the strange music (or sworn they'd heard it) said the sound would change a person forever; as if that innocent passerby had been given a glimpse of Heaven—like Saul on the road to Damascus. Some claimed hearing the violin made you want to believe in God, or simply be a better person. Others claimed the music could eradicate illness, lift away depression. An old woman from Buckhead had once camped outside Johnny's house for three nights before finally hearing him play. The next day she returned home, her doctor informed her that the cancer in her blood had vanished, that she'd been cured. That it was a miracle.

Decades later, Johnny declared to anyone who would listen that his playing days were over, that his fingers weren't as nimble—his hands no longer fast enough—to do the golden fiddle justice.

"So he locked it up," Travis says. "My mom said he'd left instructions that, upon his death, it should be melted down."

"Melted!" Josh exclaims, hands trembling atop the case, wide eyes filled with the red light reflecting off the instrument.

Travis nods. "He wanted the gold to decorate the carvings of his headstone. It would have his name, the years of his life, and one phrase: *Here Lies the Man Who Beat the Devil.* Personally, I think he just wanted it destroyed."

The boys stare silently into the case, and now the fiddle seems to glow with an inner luminescence that wasn't there before—as if taunting them, begging them to open the case and place the fiddle in their hands, run their fingers along its strings. As if saying, over and over again: *PLAY ME.*

Despite the blood rushing in their ears, their palms moist with desire, the boys hesitate. There's something about where they are, what they're doing, that seems...not necessarily wrong...but *forbidden*. And, just possibly, dangerous. After all, if the fiddle really does have supernatural powers gifted by the Devil himself, there will likely be ramifications to touching it, to playing it. And yet they stay, transfixed by the instrument as if it were a golden apple, fat and ripe, clinging to a low-hanging branch for one of them to pluck free.

And take a bite.

"How do we open it?"

"I saw him do it once," Travis says quietly. "To show my mother. There's a key..." he looks toward the desk, points in its direction. "In there."

They walk to the desk. Josh watches as Travis opens a bottom drawer and removes a sheath of papers, leaving the drawer empty.

"It's gone?"

"Wait," Travis says, then presses the bottom of the drawer, grinning as the fake bottom clicks upward, revealing a hidden compartment and a thick, black iron key. He plucks it from the drawer and holds it up reverently, as if it were a rare jewel.

"Holy shit," Josh whispers.

Moving quickly back to the case, Travis inserts the key into the lock and twists. There's a soft pop and the lid rises slightly, warm air puffing out like a held breath. Travis leaves the key inserted and gently lifts the glass, exposing the famed treasure.

"Do you think it still plays?" Josh asks.

Travis shrugs, but his eyes don't leave the golden fiddle, the long golden bow resting on its side, both objects nestled in plush crimson fabric.

As if sleeping.

"No idea."

Josh licks his lips, his fingers gripping the edges of the open case. "Let's take it out."

"Okay," Travis says, then reaches down and picks up the long, thin bow. When he holds it aloft, they both notice the thick, jet-black ribbon running from tip-to-tip.

"It's made of hair," Josh says. "Horsehair, I think."

"Isn't it usually white?"

Josh nods. "I played violin for a couple years," he says. "Wasn't very good, but I know what a bow looks like. And yeah, normally it's paler than that. Hey, can I..."

Travis looks down at the violin, but suddenly the idea of touching it seems vile, like plucking a dead fish from the muck, or a rotted apple from a barrel. "Go ahead."

Josh grips the violin in two hands and lifts it from the case. He studies the instrument, wide-eyed, then nestles the end of it beneath his chin. He closes his eyes and sighs, as if in relief, or ecstasy.

"Heavy," he mutters.

"Can you still play?" Travis asks.

"A little," Josh replies, opening his eyes. To Travis, they appear a shade darker than they were moments ago, and there's a glimmer there that seems alive, like a vibration of gold beneath a clear, rippling brook.

"Hand me that."

Travis gives him the bow and, not realizing he's even doing it, takes a step backward.

For a moment, Josh studies the bow's oily black ribbon. "Cool," he says absently, eyelids fluttering as he rests the bow atop the body of the golden violin, the fingers on his other hand now arched atop the fingerboard, tips pressed onto the strings. "In school I learned an old country song called 'Orange Blossom Special,' but I was never very good at it, so don't laugh."

"I won't," Travis says earnestly. "Promise."

Josh blows out a breath, presses the violin more firmly against his chin, brings the bow down onto its strings, and plays.

At first, the sound coming from the fiddle is disappointingly ordinary. A long, flat, dull note seeps into the room as Josh pulls the bow across the strings.

But as Travis watches, Josh begins to gain confidence, momentum. The hand holding the bow moves in tight, quick bursts; his arched fingers begin dancing along the fiddle's neck, and what was momentarily nothing but sound...becomes music.

As he plays, the music becomes richer, fuller, as if stretched, the dense chords filling the library as if by magic. The opening of the song is slow. Long chords stretched like taffy. Then Josh's fingers move faster along the neck, the bow twitching along the strings, and suddenly the song is coming like a freight train, furiously punching into the room like jagged bolts of lightning, crackling and spitting from the golden fiddle.

"Josh?"

Without slowing, Josh's eyes spring open and lock on Travis. The blue irises are blown out by wide, dilated pupils. He stares blankly at Travis as his hands move impossibly fast, the fiddle now playing the old song in a pure rage, an impossible fluidity, a devilish glee.

Josh grins.

Outside, a cloud passes in front of the sun and the light from the stained-glass window fades, sinks the room into darkness; the colors turn dim and lifeless, reds and purples and blues and yellows lie stagnant on the floors and walls, rest against the book-filled shelves like dust.

A deep, raspy voice comes from the shadows.

"Hey, he's pretty good."

Travis gasps and turns to see the Devil step from the shadows. As if sensing his gaze, the Devil tilts his head toward Travis. His body is black and sinewy, his reflective skin almost silver as it absorbs whatever light remains in the old library. His legs are bent at odd angles, clawed hands curled into loose fists. His golden eyes are obscenely wide and Travis finds himself wanting to go to the massive demon, to be held tight in those long arms and feel that slick, forked tongue ride along his cheek.

But when the great beast steps forward to stand just behind Josh, Travis steps back, shaking his head in horror. "Josh!" he yells, not caring if anyone hears; almost hoping someone *will* come running, that an adult will burst into the library and disrupt whatever's happening, plunge them back into normality, into reality.

He shuffles toward his cousin, close enough that he's within arm's reach. "Josh, stop!" But Josh only plays faster, and faster, the violin's gold body growing brighter as the music flays the air of the small room. Travis reaches out and touches Josh's darting elbow. There's a spark of electricity that shocks his fingertips and he yelps with pain and falls backward.

The music stops.

The lone window disappears. The room empties into darkness, as if swallowed whole.

Travis is panting and terrified, but he's grateful that Josh has stopped playing. The silence, however, is maddening, and he can't see anything. He looks down at his hand, wiggles his fingers, but there's only darkness.

The voice comes again.

"Shame on you children for playing with something that isn't yours," the Devil says with a grating chuckle. "At least, not yet."

Before Travis can decide what to do next, he hears rushed whispers from nearby but can't make out the words. He only knows there are two voices, both urgent, both eager. A discussion.

A negotiation.

Moments later, a dull red glow opens in the dark like a rose, and as the red light grows, Travis once again makes out the demon's face—the golden predator eyes, the wide grin showing off long, fanged teeth. To Travis's mind, the demon looks greedy, looks...*hungry*.

The crimson glow grows larger, and Travis can now see Josh. He's nestled against the Devil's side, still holding the fiddle, his eyes wide and empty. The Devil slides his arm around Josh's thin shoulders, holds him tight to his bared torso, the boy's nose and mouth crushed against his slick skin. "I think we have ourselves a deal," the Devil says, his eyes never leaving Travis. "What do you say, Joshua?"

Josh turns his head to face Travis, his pale face now filled with a sort of sadness, or regret. "Yes," he says. "I agree."

And then, like the blowing out of a candle, the glow is extinguished, the room plunged once more into darkness, and when Travis feels his arms gripped tightly by long, clawed fingers, he starts to scream.

Something heavy collides with his forehead, lifts away, then smashes into his skull again, and again. He badly wants to raise his hands, to defend himself, but his arms are held tight by those serpentine claws. He begins to speak, to beg, to cry, but then there's another blow at his temple, and another, and then the world beneath his feet disappears and he is falling down—down through the floor, through impossible depths, through an abyss that seems to stretch on for eons.

Down, down, down...

Into Hell itself.

* * *

Josh comes down the stairs and into the living room, where people are milling and conversing, stuffing their mouths with fried chicken and pie, drinking bourbon and gin and beer and wine. Someone laughs too loudly from the far end of the room. By the kitchen door, an old woman weeps and is ignored.

A hand falls onto his shoulder. He turns to see his aunt's worried face staring down at him. "Josh, where's Travis?"

"Upstairs," he replies, knowing it's the truth. "In the library."

His aunt's eyes move from his face to the golden fiddle dangling from one hand, then to the black-ribboned bow held tightly in the other.

Josh follows her gaze, notes the blood dripping from the edge of the instrument to the wooden floor, forming a tiny puddle. He raises it protectively, holds it tight across his chest. Others in the room turn to look, to stare at the strange boy with the bright, bloody fiddle cradled in his arms.

"It's mine," Josh says.

Travis's mother nods slowly. The room falls quiet. She offers a sad smile.

"Of course it is," she says. "Ain't no one here said different."

RED, BLACK & BLUE

BY LINDA D. ADDISON

stop it, burn it, run run run

he jerks against tight restraints,
    arms, legs, feet—running
    running, muscles pulling
    joints popping out of place,
    fractures, like spider webs,
growing under black & blue flesh.

Nurse gently cuts away red sneakers,
    red dripping from swollen feet
    into a pail, she dabs open blisters,
    he keeps running, running against
    the leather straps holding him down,
in spite of sedatives, muscle relaxants.

don't listen to...the music, the music

the music echoes non-stop even without
    the earphones, tape player on table
    in hospital room, while his body
    won't stop running, running, wish
    fulfilled, to be the longest non-stop
runner in the world, steady without end.

Doctors did all they could, nothing
    could stop movement shredding
    heart, kidneys, muscles, bones,
    so they gave him to her, to comfort
    his last moments, she would not turn
away from sounds of cracking bones.

running running winning winning

with his last breath, body finally still,
    she closes his eyes, holds his hand
    breathing in the end of suffering,
    he could not say how it started,
    tongue destroyed by dehydration,
after three days of running on the track.

Waiting for the coroner, putting his
    belongings in a ziplock bag, the
    tape player, the last thing, the
    whisper of music made her put
    the headphones to her ears,
lyrics moaned breathless promises.

ake a wish, you can be anything, any Thing

There was only one thing she wanted to be,
since as a child watching her grandmother
    painfully die over weeks in their home,
    now as an adult caring for the suffering,
    fearlessly, when others could not, until
Death finally took them, the music showed her
    as the Angel, the Mercy needed, changing
    to her blue suede dress, headphones on,
    syringes in a bag, first her bedridden father,
then many, many others' pain to relieve...

INSTRUMENTS OF HARM

BY JULIA LAFOND

The thing the recruiters don't tell you about the Marchers is how miserable it is.

It's all speeches about how you'll "act in harmony" to "protect Simphoni" and "combat discord." Then the cadet squad glide steps in, wearing their sky blue uniforms with the shiny silver buttons. The auxiliaries flit around them, rattling their sabers in time to the drums and bugles. And then, just as excitement reaches its peak, the field commander steps forward to conjure sparks and fireworks with their bare hands!

It got a chump like me to sign up.

Admittedly, the promise of enough money to keep me and my family set for life factored into that—I'm not a complete fool, after all. But some nights I wonder: if those shiny coins get sent back atop my closed casket, will it be worth it?

I've had plenty of time to wonder today. Because, like most days, we're marching. At least it's temperate and partly cloudy, with no chance of rain. No bugs, either. No additional hazards on top of the grueling, mind-numbing task of staying in step with your rank and file.

As I took a swig from my canteen, I almost hoped it would storm after all; a big, thunderous squall. Getting soaked to the bone was miserable, but it would keep us from engaging the Reds today. Keep me from being in their line of fire. But I couldn't bring myself to wish—really wish—for it. Not since poor Allegra got fried by lightning.

The Marchers only paid her family half, since she didn't fall "in the line of duty." Even though they were the ones who sent her squad scouting, using that storm as "cover," knowing full well she was a sousaphone player.

Bastards.

Two reasons I haven't deserted yet: because I wouldn't get paid, and because of that confounded Oath of Loyalty. Arcto, who never lets us forget he got twice the education the rest of us did, says it violates the rules of magic, that it can't possibly be binding. Maybe there's a real version of it for higher-ups, but not for us rank and file. Not that we'll test it—no one can find any records of anyone who successfully deserted. Could have been covered up, obviously, but it's not exactly encouraging.

If the Oath were the only thing keeping me here, I would have fled the moment dust clouded the horizon, unbroken save for glints of reflected sunlight. The Reds weren't surprised, like they were supposed to be—they were coming to face us head-on.

That, *that* is the worst part. Seeing it coming, *knowing* how easily you could die a brutal, ignoble death, and nothing to do except keep your steps in time with the drum cadence. At least the drummers get to decide how fast or slow it comes... not that I envy those poor souls. Their small measure of control means they get targeted first.

"Detail Halt! To the Ready!"

I jolted to a stop, though the order took me off guard. Our field commandant must have decided our current position was favorable, though it looked like the middle of nowhere. The only thing notable about the grassy green field was the stubby gray rocks littering it. Maybe he thought the enemy would trip over them, the way we were struggling not to. Whether the field was favorable or not, it forced the enemy to come to us. And coming they were—the horizon was red with them.

"Squads one through three, Left Face! Squads four through six, Right Face! Squads—"

My squad, as usual, wasn't repositioned. Very few formations called for us to be anything other than dead center, uncomfortably close to the front. That gave me a break from marching, at least, until—

"Cover Down!"

—all the squads aligned themselves precisely around us. I did my best not to turn my head; that way, I could pretend there weren't ninety-nine other squads of desperate souls depending on the ten of us in the Interference Squad.

"Band, Atten-hut!"

"Hut!" we all shouted back. Even me, despite the sweat trickling down my face that I couldn't blame on the weather. I sipped from my canteen anyway.

We remained at attention while the Reds drew closer. Until we could make out all the instruments they wielded: their drums, their xylophones, their tubas and clarinets and cornets.

"Horns Up!"

We would make the first move, before they could set up. I let the barest sigh of relief escape as I raised my trombone. It was my best, and only, defense against the Reds. Other Marchers were depending on me as well, but I never let myself dwell on that. It was bad enough to be responsible for my own skin.

Around me, the band opened with the Simphoni Anthem—woodwinds, brass, and percussion in perfect harmony. In a few bars, they would summon enough magic to use, the melody unleashing chilling winds and creeping frost upon the Reds.

My squad, however, still had to wait.

Because I'd been a trusting greenhorn, I hadn't considered holding back during my auditions. It landed me the single most dangerous task barring drumming: the Interference Squad. It was our "solemn" duty to cancel out the Reds' music. Either by turning their melodies to dissonance that would backfire upon their troops, or by drowning them out to keep their magic from crescendoing. Every single one of us possessed perfect pitch. We studied the fundamentals of musical composition. Memorized every piece the Reds had ever produced. Practiced improvisation until our fingers creaked and we could barely hear music over the ringing in our ears. With us against them, not even an orchestra could summon a single spark.

The problem was, the Reds also had Interference Squads. One missed note, and they would wipe us out with fire and brimstone before we could so much as blink.

Our anthem took out their front ensemble before they mustered defenses. As so often happened with the Reds, their "defense" was "even more offense." We scrambled to counter concording melodies: "The Song of the Phoenix," which would have incinerated our drummers. "The Funeral Pyre," which would have immolated the Field Commander. And strangely, "The March of the Dead Men." It was far too early in the battle for there to be corpses to—

The realization hit me like a slap in the face, making me miss a beat. A fiery meteor hurtled toward us, the air shimmering in its wake. Arcto improvised a counter that dissipated the magic, sparing us from roasting to death (I owed him one), but he couldn't dispel the truth of this place. It was a gravesite, and the stones were markers. What were our superiors thinking, sending us here? Simphoni had yet to crack the secrets of necromancy, unlike the Reds. If they succeeded, we would face a battle on two fronts, with each casualty further swelling their ranks.

A subtle gesture with my pinkie finger was all it took to inform the others. In an instant, our priorities shifted. When there were too many songs to counter, we blocked the necromancy.

Squad four fell to fire. Immolation, at least, was quick.

Half of Squad twelve fell to volcanic gas, which was lingering and painful.

I choked down guilt at our failure to protect them.

But we were winning. Gusts of wind disrupted the Reds' formations, and their songs with it. Crystalline ice rose to encase entire squads. Taking advantage of the chaos, the auxiliaries charged. Their twirling flags and dancing steps channeled a different sort of magic: enhanced speed and strength. Their sabers ripped through instruments and armor alike as if they were waterlogged paper. The bloodshed turned our foes' half of the battlefield a different sort of red.

The extended conflict wore on the Interference Squad's stamina. We took alternating rests to try to catch our breath, but our fingers and minds were slowing. Liselle was the next to make a true mistake: when her G sharp came out as just a G, the Reds took advantage to kill and reanimate a squad of drummers, forcing surrounding squads to divert to defense. We were wearing out fast, and the Reds knew it. If they could endure a little longer, we wouldn't be winning anymore—they would overrun us.

The battle stretched on, worse than the march to reach it. My canteen ran dry. When my parched throat seized up at the worst possible moment, we lost another squad of drummers. Then Arcto missed his entrance cue, and more meteors hurtled toward us. Summoning up our strength, we burst into a rendition of the Anthem, barely turning it dissonant. It fizzled, but the heat left our skin covered in blisters.

My legs twitched and trembled. Any second now my knees would buckle, and once I fell, the Reds would press the advantage. It was over.

I kept playing, desperately clinging to the few seconds of life I had left. Around us, the other squads continued their melodies, oblivious to their imminent destruction. Wind howled, ice exploded into the enemy ranks, and the auxiliaries continued their dance of death, but all too soon the tables would turn. All the Reds had to do was hold on a little longer, and then—

"About Face!" screamed the enemy commandant.

The Reds retreated.

Though I could barely stand, I stayed at attention along with everyone else. We had all heard of ambushes that began with those words. But the other band vanished over the horizon, leaving only the frozen dead in their wake.

I laughed as cheers broke out around me. I didn't know or care what this meant for Simphoni, because it didn't matter.

We'd done it. We'd survived.

Maybe next time we wouldn't. Maybe one of these days, my ashes wouldn't even fill an urn. But this time, we'd won the day. One day closer to home.

Of course, if I deserted, there wouldn't be a next time...

Arcto passed me his spare canteen.

I took a grateful swig. I owed him for this and for his earlier improv, which meant I couldn't desert until we were even.

I'd been telling myself that for a long time now. Better than admitting I'd lost track of how many times my squadmates and I had saved each other. Balancing the ledger was a never-ending task; the only way to survive the battlefield was to watch each other's backs. If I left, I'd disrupt the squad, which would tilt the odds against them, and then they'd never get to go home.

So now I had three reasons to stay.

Once a chump, always a chump.

ELECTRIC MUSE

BY VIRGINIA KATHRYN

Rock is dying, they say.

I say it's just changing.

All shapes of it come through this dive—the riot grrrls, the goths, the flannel girls—all grunge and glory.

And then there's me.

Standing in the August heat at the club doors like I belong there, handing out Greenpeace pamphlets like candy. Mechanical pencil tucked behind my ear. Seven plastic bracelets dangle on my wrists, each a different color, each for a different cause. Those were mine to keep, not to be given away like the words on my pamphlets.

I know how they see me: a little creature flitting from one flame to the next. So I let them call me Moth.

Flashing my paper wristband and black marks at the doorman, I push through the crowd. There are a lot of us with the black marks tonight. I see a guy from economics, and a kid from poli-sci with purple streaks in their hair. All huddled around the bar to sneak a shot. I've played that game before. They're just gonna get themselves kicked out.

Around the corner, through a doorway papered with band logos and old postcards, that's where the bands hang before the show. Must be four or five playing tonight, by the looks of it. One of the opening acts has thrown their bass player behind the merch table, slinging T-shirts with a guitar strapped to his back.

Craning my neck, I try to see the CDs and tapes spread out. No one does vinyl anymore, not really. Hard to see. Everyone is so goddamn tall at this show. I'll be pushing to the front of the stage soon.

When I walk up to the table, the bass player smiles. I won't return the favor. Nobody should smile at a punk show.

What does he see when he looks at me? Turquoise lipstick (Walgreens), Black Flag T-shirt (Hot Topic), pleather jacket (Macy's), stoic expression (three years in customer service). Damned if I didn't try to look the part.

"Got any promo copies?" I ask, craning over the shoulder of a tall white guy. "I'm with WKXR. College radio." Shit. I should have led with that.

The bass player's smile turns into a grin. Feels like he's sizing me up at the butcher shop. He reaches across the table and grabs my right hand. His breath reeks of cheap weed.

"So soft," he whispers. "So small."

Of course that's what I am to him. Just another tiny girl in a sea of college kids. "I have calluses. From playing bass," I tell him. It's not a lie. But he's not wrong, either—my hands are small and soft and usually cold.

"Let's see what you got."

I stretch out my fingers. Try to show him the calluses on my fingertips. But he is stroking my palm, feeling the muscles and skin. He tests my grip. His fingers wrap around mine in something like an arm-wrestling match. I finally allow myself one smile, a short smile, the smile of someone who is about to win. He pulls away before I can.

"Wouldn't wanna get hurt before I play." His voice is thick with sarcasm.

At my left, a girl with magenta hair picks up an enamel pin. The bass player slides over to her side of the merch table, giving me a last glance before he goes. Magenta doesn't seem to mind.

Tucking a CD into the sleeve of my oversized jacket, I make my way to the stage. That's the beautiful thing about being small and nondescript. No one sees you coming.

At the front of the house, they've just finished soundcheck. A pentagram hangs over the stage imprinted with the headliner's name in a skeleton script. I slip one of my Greenpeace pamphlets underneath their set list.

People start to gather around the stage as the opening act picks up their guitars. The bass player sees me in front of him. He looks away. Didn't even notice the missing merch.

Their first song is empty screams over a long bass line. It needs words. They could make something out of the words I wrote last night, crawling out of bed, across the carpet to my stack of papers. How did the first line go? *When I sleep, thunder breaks the sky.* No, it's a terrible line. Totally unfit for a band. Too personal, too weird.

I had written the rest on sticky notes scattered across my room. More in the margins of the pamphlets, the ones at the bottom of the stack. I pull out the last one and look at the upper margins in the spotlight glare.

The pamphlets with my words were scattered all over the place. Saw one tucked into a plaid skirt in front of the stage, another crumpled into someone's back pocket. My words spread across the venue.

Swallowing, I turn over the pamphlet in my hand. No time to take it back now. I could trace my steps, go back to the door, see if the last one fell on the sidewalk. But the doorman won't let me back in if I leave now. They think that keeps kids from drinking between sets.

Next to me, Magenta jostles a boy. Pushes him, pulls him closer. Shoves him away again. Drags the needle of the enamel pin she bought across her collarbone and smears the blood on her lips. I find myself thinking: if I kiss her, would she leave blood on my skin?

The bouncers are there, and then they're gone, and Magenta's with them. They don't mess with that shit. The singer looks on and smiles.

There was a sticky note on the back of his hand, covered in my scrawl.

> *Shining in the mud*
> *Crystal sand and blood-red rust and*
> *painted paper lullabies*
> *Flowing in the flood*

My words screamed electric from his tongue.

* * *

Another show, another night. This time it's a psychobilly act. Cowpunk, if you will. Call it what you like, it's a country crooner with three punks behind her, and a name that's banned from local newspapers. I'm at the door again, arms full of Sierra Club pamphlets, wrists full of causes. Free Tibet, end apartheid, animal liberation—all dangled like rhinestone-covered bangles from my wrists. Some of my pamphlets are for things that have happened. Some are for things that are yet to come.

I'm more careful this time. I sketched my poems on index cards and sticky notes tucked into the folds of my jacket. Nothing can end up onstage for them to steal and scream out.

The psychobilly act is sharing the bill with a garage rock outfit from Tokyo. It's quite the combo. Got people in cowboy hats and leather waiting in line next to grungy guitar players from the local scene. Two very different audiences.

"Whatcha got tonight, kiddo? Save the coral reefs? Re-forest the planet?"

One of the guys in line had taken a pamphlet right from my hand. How rude. He opened it up, took one look, and threw it on the ground.

People get weird when you start to talk about Armageddon. Especially when illustrated with images from dreams. None of the others standing outside seem interested in what I have to say. So I make my way in the door.

The crowd is older tonight. No one from the college, just a couple of high school kids here with their dads. These are the kids all grown up, looking to relive their younger days, when punk was real and the world was still alive.

I want to talk to the psychobilly band's guitarist, but she's hiding in the back. Saving her voice or some shit. Not gonna give up her pre-game drinks and smokes for a kid with a camcorder and a part-time gig at the radio station. I push past the merch tables and walk right to her. The bass player towers over her, a full foot taller, and still she dominates the space.

"You gonna tell me it's the year of the woman again?" she says, nodding at my camcorder. "We just had one of those. *New York Rocker* did a whole thing."

Readjusting the purse strap on my shoulder, I say to her, "It's all right. I get it. Hard enough being a woman in this world."

She takes a long, slow drag of her cigarette. "What more is there to say? Daring. Imaginative. Raw. We've heard it all." Taps the ashes to the floor. "We've given everything we've got."

After her set, she stumbles offstage in a drunken haze, and some idiot yells for an encore. In the background, someone is yelling. A young girl in a slashed-up *Sailor Moon* T-shirt walks up to the sound booth, where the club owner is taking stock of the crowd. The shouts are coming from her.

"You're gonna give us the goddamn money upfront or we walk. All the way back to Tokyo."

Band manager, probably. I get it. She's pretending to be small too—until she needs to look big.

She must have sorted it out, because the band makes their way to the stage, one by one. They start with an empty microphone. I wonder if the singer is coming. Someone pushes past me, shirtless and covered in sweat, carrying a guitar in one hand and a beer in the other. He climbs onstage and plugs into the waiting amp. He howls into the mic.

Only the day the world slipped away
And happiness stood still

There it is. The next line of the same song that metal band had played a couple weeks back. Lyrics drawn in the cramped corners of an index card. Taped to the back of his guitar.

My lyrics. My words.

I've seen the worlds end in sleep. I try to tell them in pamphlets and posters, but no one listens. Now I'm drowning in the sound of it, this day I dreamed, where the sky burned and the oceans boiled and the world came tumbling down.

This wasn't right. This wasn't how I meant to tell them. I wanted to be a prophet, a visionary.

But the crowd loves it.

* * *

So this is how I get them to listen.

This is how they will hear.

Never the small girl, the vulnerable girl, the girl with too many words, who gets heard. I just had to give the words to someone else to speak.

Or to sing.

They wouldn't have listened to me without the music.

* * *

Secret Muse, they call me. It feels like someone else: an alias or a disguise. It doesn't feel like the girl they called Moth, the girl who lies awake at night trying not to dream about the end of the world.

Vice did an exposé on the first few acts. What did a Nashville psychobilly band, a Japanese garage trio, and a Satanic metal band have in common, that they shared these same lyrics over the span of a few weeks? Couldn't have been stealing. None of them had met each other. The psychobilly lead singer didn't remember meeting the Tokyo guys—but that could have been the whiskey talking.

Just like Banksy, they said. An artist leaving words to be found by another, to be spoken or screamed in another's voice.

New Musical Express talked about the lyrics like poetry. They didn't understand it at all. Sure, I shaped the words into something pretty. But they weren't meant to be just words.

Some of the smaller zines are starting to get it. *Black Market Magazine* looked at what was happening: the Mississippi river valley, the dam breach. (Two of those, actually, one in the Philippines and another in Spain.) Floods full of mud and minerals, red as blood. Just like in the songs.

But no one really listens to the zines. People want the glitz, the glamor, the mystique of a muse.

Guess I have to give it to them.

* * *

The club is half-empty. Snow keeps most folks at home. This isn't a blizzard, not even close. But they'll take any excuse not to dab on a little makeup, pull on the tight pants, go out on the town.

On the walls, I can see a timeline of the things that have already come to pass. Club owner let me put up posters wherever I wanted. There's a tapestry of disasters drawn across the wall. No one has noticed yet. No one sees.

I'm just another college kid trying to make a better world.

Tonight it's a Bowie cover band, fronted by a guy who goes by Starman. They probably only play here because the bass player runs sound.

I do my usual dance: hand out pamphlets, skirt the edge of the bar, take my marked hands and my camcorder back to the green room where Starman is doing his makeup. I click the camcorder. He sees me in the mirror and goes back to painting a thunderbolt around his eye.

"So tell me, what made you move from death metal to glam rock?"

"Oh, we'll just skip the niceties, then." He dots foundation on his chin and cheeks.

"If it's all right by you."

He shrugs.

Swallowing, I try again. "Bowie is such a contentious figure. Always shifting and changing from one era to the next. Sometimes occupying multiple personas in the same show." I can't keep asking these same questions over and over. It's the same story for every interview. *What inspired you? How did you get started on this line of work?*

He can feel it, too. The doldrums creeping in.

Fuck it.

"If you knew the end of the world was coming, would you tell people?"

He stops. Holds the brush in his hand. Posed, like an artist's muse. I scan the room. Twelve-string Hagstrom and a Telecaster lean against the wall, cases propped open like coffins behind them. Silver space suit hanging from the mirror's edge. His hair is smoothed into a net, wig on the table beside him. The change is almost done.

"No."

He swoops the brush across his face. Powder explodes in the air.

"I'd just let them live their lives. Pretend that nothing's changing. 'Til it does."

Nodding, I turn off the camcorder. Sit down on the chair beside him. I slip him the last index card in my sleeve. Given freely and openly this time.

He knows what this gift is. He doesn't thank me, because he is the one who should be thanked for bringing these words to a wider audience. At least, that's how he sees it. Giving these words a voice.

* * *

After the Bowie show, the magazines start to draw the connections. Local ones, at first. It just doesn't make sense for a cover band to write their own verse for a well-loved tune. Campus bulletin even said something about it, underneath an article about another protest at a women's clinic. Don't know how they printed any of it.

On the bar, there are copies of a local zine. No name, no author. Looks like a chapbook of found poetry, lines of an article blacked out to show the words.

A chill runs down my spine. I close the chapbook and slide it across the counter, let it slip beneath the bartop to the floor. Seeing it here is too much somehow. I hear the kids talking about it at the bar. I see it in their side-eyes as I walk by, trying to get to the sound booth, to talk to the riot grrrls before they go on stage.

The sound guy tears a poster off the wall. Touring act, didn't catch the name. "Canceled their tour," he says, catching my eyes on the wall. "Damn shame." Was it the economy this time? Did they lose their gear to thieves, to fire, to the great unknown?

In the pit, there are a handful of people. None of them are talking to each other. Standing seven feet apart, staring at the still-empty stage. One of them is mumbling about the heat. Another pockets a guitar pick from beside the monitor.

Magenta is here again. Surprised they let her back in, after her attitude last time. She whispers something in her boyfriend's ear. I halfway expect her to throw him to the ground again. But the music hasn't started yet. She is looking at me with hungry eyes.

What do they see when they look at me? No more the tiny blue-lipsticked, leather-clad girl with her sixteen plastic bracelets. Maybe I am a mystery now. I don't know if I want to be a mystery anymore.

Do they even know?

I should stop now. While I'm ahead, while I've still got one more trick up my sleeve. One more dream I haven't worked into words.

Let me give them one last line to remember me by. And then I'll disappear.

* * *

The club is empty for the last show. We've known for a while this day would come. I thought I would see more of us with black marks on our hands, scrambling to get that last stolen shot of tequila, that last contraband beer.

After this, I tell myself, the muse will be gone.

The muse was the place, and the people, and the sounds of chaos all around. It shaped my dreams, and my dreams shaped their words.

Sure, there have been whispers of bushfires in the global south. Flooding in Thailand and typhoons in Japan. Things are changing, but the lyrics of a secret muse won't make a difference. No one can predict the future except weathermen, and most of the time, they can't even get a thunderstorm right.

I could come forward. But would they believe me now? I could be stealing the words from someone else, for all they cared. I could be stringing together conspiracy theories from anarchist zines, desperate for attention, desperate to be heard and understood.

So I go to the shows, and I hand out my pamphlets, and I wait.

* * *

The last set of the last show at the last club on Earth. Before they went on, I gave the band a Greenpeace pamphlet, margins full of words. I could be open about it now. There was nothing left to lose.

The singer smiled.

Now she stands tall, leather vest over tank top, jeans shredded at the knees, singing my words into the microphone. Something about the end of the world again.

Magenta comes up to me. Her boyfriend is nowhere to be seen. She stretches her arms across my shoulders like I am hers, and we move with the slow moan of distorted guitar. I smile, and it feels real for the first time.

"It's you."

Of course she would be the first one to see the wildness in me, because it's in her, too. Maybe it didn't let her see the end of the world. But it drove her to become the person she is now.

I close my eyes, and I remember everything that I dreamed. I see thunder and floods and raging fires. I see two towers falling.

I see the end of everything.

Scrawled in the corners of magazines and pamphlets and index cards, taken from sleep into waking. I tried to turn them into words to be given away and forgotten. I tried to make them someone else's responsibility, someone else's muse. But my dreams of the future are here, in the songs, in the lyrics that they sing.

The band throws glitter into the pit. Just a handful of us now. We move with the music, and we crash into each other, the last shining stars in a sea of dark. They sing the words that I wrote, and the people in the crowd shout them back.

Everyone is dreaming with me now.

AMBIENT

BY L.B. WALTZ

hen I grow up, I wanna work on the radio.

I haven't decided what job yet. There are a lot to choose from. There's the man who talks about the news, and the lady who reports the weather, and the troupe who performs the nightly dramas. That's already six whole jobs. And that's not even all of them!

Momma says there are bunches more. I didn't believe her at first, because those six are the voices I hear most when we turn on our radio, but she explained there's a place that some grownups live called a 'station,' and the people there work really hard so we have broadcasts to listen to. They investigate the news so there's something for the man to talk about, and they find out about the weather so the lady knows what to report, and they write the nightly dramas so the troupe can perform them.

I asked her if there are also people who press the buttons, because I bet there are a lot of buttons at the station. At home, we have at least a-hundred buttons, and our house doesn't do anything cool. Not really. But sometimes, a button at our house doesn't work, so Mister Grayson and Mister Arnt and Toby and Felicia and Doctor Litter all have to go *outside* for a long time and try to fix it. Last time that happened, Toby got hurt so bad he needed to get a giraffe for his skin.

I think it's called a skin giraffe, anyway. It would make sense, since his skin looked weird and kinda spotty after.

But that's not the important thing. The important thing is, that's just our house. And our house isn't even special, so I bet the station needs tons of people to press the buttons and help if they break. Maybe even as many as ten people.

Ten plus six is sixteen, which means there could be sixteen jobs. And that's a lot of choices. Too many choices, maybe. Sometimes, I tell Momma I've finally decided for sure what job I want–like last week, when I heard that the weather lady gets to see pictures from *outside*–but then I'll change my mind again, because I'll hear something else, like how the troupe gets to travel to different stations every year. Hana said that they even get to go by car, during the *day*.

I think she was lying about that part. I hope she was lying when she said it doesn't matter what I want, because I don't get to choose, nobody gets to choose, and that she was told that next year she is gonna start working as a delivery person. It can be hard to know when Hana is telling the truth.

But I was thinking, and actually, maybe it's okay. If I don't get to choose my job, I mean. If I get told what I have to do. I won't care, so long as my job is for the radio.

* * *

We get new radios, sometimes.

"Just in case," Momma explains, organizing the other goods that were delivered along with the new radio. Since there isn't much in the crate this month, it's only Momma doing the sorting, and me putting away. I show off how strong I'm getting by holding all four bolts of fabric at the same time.

"In case what, Momma?" I ask, my knees not even wobbling a little bit.

"In case something breaks."

"You and Mister Arnt and Felicia fix a lot of stuff that breaks."

"We do," Momma agrees, making a mark on a list that she calls an 'inventory.' "But fixing stuff can take a long time. And once in a while, stuff breaks for good. There are consequences to missing a broadcast, so it's easiest to just have a backup radio."

"Oh. Okay." That makes sense, I guess. Except for one part. "What's a con-see-quince?"

Sometimes, when Momma tilts her head like that, the scar next to her ear catches light in its curve, like a little cup of water. Or a 'c' written in silver crayon. I can write really good 'c's, even in crayon. It's most fun to write 'w's, though. They're like two 'c's that are sleeping.

"Consequences are things that happen when we don't do what we're supposed to," Momma explains, with the same sort of carefulness that she is using to finish the inventory. "For example, what would happen if you went outside during the day?"

"My skin would get all black and yucky, and I would need giraffes," I answer quick, because I know that answer. I get told about the sun basically every day. Plus, I see Toby every day. I haven't been told about the consequence of missing the radio, but I don't need to be. It's obvious. "And if we don't listen to a broadcast, we won't get to know the weather or the news or the dramas or the music! That would be a consequence, yeah? A bad one."

"That...would be a consequence, yes," Momma says. She sounds like she's trying not to be sad. I understand that feeling. After all, missing the broadcast would make me sad, too. But the good news is that she doesn't need to worry about it, now that we have this just-in-case radio.

Being extra careful, I slide the fabric into the closet, next to the cookie tin of needles. The tin goes *ching-ching-ching* when the bolts make the ground shake.

"Where are we gonna put it?" I wonder after I'm done, watching Momma heft jugs of dusty water into the cabinet with the metal padlock on it. I count nine of them. Usually we get twelve, which is a harder number to remember, so I'm happy about the nine. "The new radio? And the old one?"

Secretly, I hope I can keep the old one. I dunno where I would keep it, but I want to have it. I know I can't, though. Felicia already told me that the new-old-radio is gonna be stored—"Just in case," she'd said, like Momma did—and that she's gonna turn the *old*-old radio into spare parts. That's also for just-in-case reasons, but those reasons are more about the buttons and the other stuff that makes the house safe. She promised she'd teach me about it when I'm older.

Anyway, Momma is busy making notes about mason jars and canned beans and Tylenol bottles and doesn't hear my question. I think about asking again, but then I decide I don't want to.

This way, when I find out, it'll be a fun surprise.

* * *

Actually, I lied. Like Hana does. But only a little bit. On accident.

I do wanna work for the radio, and almost any job would be okay. Except I don't wanna play the music.

No one likes the music.

So I don't wanna do that.

* * *

Doctor Litter put the new radio in the shared space, down in the deepest part of the basement, in the room next to the garden. The old radio used to live in the sleeping room, since that's the biggest room in the house, but she said that this will make transportation easier, and the other grownups agreed, in that serious way that grownups agree to things.

It's been an entire week since then. I haven't had to help move anything yet, so I dunno if Doctor Litter is right. But I do think it was a good idea to put the radio in the room next to the garden, because the air in that room is the best. It smells like mud and thick water and sometimes makes my tongue feel spongy. So I'm glad we're keeping it there.

Plus, it's nice that everybody can see it in the shared space. I guess the sleeping room is also a shared space, but it's for sleeping, so it's different. This is a room for being awake in, and having the radio here makes it feel like we're always about to have a party.

It helps that the radio looks like a decoration. It's *beautiful*. Momma showed me pictures of a place called 'church' and the new radio makes me think of that: it's dark and thin and tall, and it has fancy cuts in its front where somebody could put colored glass.

There's not glass in it, though. Of course there's not. How would the sound come out? Instead, there's a skin-colored mesh that feels like foam if you poke it. Except you're not allowed to poke it, because it might tear, and that would hurt the radio, and it would take a really long time to get another one, and even though we still have the new-old one, everybody would be mad.

If I was a baby, this new radio would have towered over me, like the church in Momma's picture. Like a holy thing. But I'm not a baby, not anymore, so the radio and I are the same height.

Well. Almost. My forehead is as tall as the knobs, anyway. I can't see some of the dials yet, but that's okay. The settings on the radio never change, so I'll see them soon. I just need to grow a tiny bit more.

*　*　*

I can't choose a favorite radio program.

It's like choosing a job at the station. There are too many. And they're all good. Even the music. Even though nobody really likes the music. Momma says the music is one of the most important parts about the whole broadcast, so there's gotta be *something* good about it.

My guess is that it's pretty. It *is* pretty. Before, I tried to dance to it, because it can be really spinny and twinkly, but that just made Mister Grayson cry and Mister Arnt glare at Momma, so I stopped. Now I sit and be quiet, usually.

Though sometimes, when no one is looking, I sway to it.

I wish somebody else liked the music. Or that they'd at least say why it's bad. Everybody tells me they don't hate it—even Mister Arnt—but I can see that they do. The grownups always get super quiet when it plays. Not quiet like they're paying attention, or quiet like they're listening hard, but quiet like they're scared.

Momma put her hand over my mouth when I asked one time if she was okay. She said hush and promised she was fine. But her fingers were shaking, so I didn't believe her.

At least the people at the station always play the music first. The grownups relax when it's over.

*　*　*

Sometimes, after the inventory and the sorting and the putting away, Felicia and Hana turn the crates into furniture.

If the crate is big, they might make it into a couch. If it's big-big, it could be a shelf or a table. And if it's big-big-big, we get a closet.

Because of the new radio, last month's crate was big-big, even though a lot of it was empty. But since we don't need another shelf or table right now, we broke it into pieces, just like we do to the old-old radios.

This month, the crate is big-big-big-*big*. Almost gigantic! But before I can get excited about what it'll be turned into, I hear the adults say that it's broken. So I stop being excited about that. Instead, I get excited about the people inside the crate, because actually, new people are exciting too. Almost as exciting as a new radio, even. Especially because one of them is a baby!

I'm not a baby. Not anymore. But until this month's crate, I was the littlest in our house. It's hard to be the littlest of eight people. At least, it's hard when one of those people is Hana and she keeps telling you that you're a baby, even though that's not true. But now there are eight people plus two, which is ten, and one of them is a real baby, and I get to be older than her! I didn't think I'd ever get to be older than somebody. I'm glad the new people are here.

I don't think anyone else is glad, though.

Miss Blum is a skinny, tired-looking lady. She has brown hair and a million dots on her skin and one really bad blister where the crate got broken during her trip and some sunlight was let in through a crack. Doctor Litter got mad about that, because people are only supposed to work at night, like we do, unless there's an emergency. A real emergency. That time with the buttons, she says, when she and Mister Grayson and Mister Arnt and Toby and Felicia all had to go outside—*that* was a real emergency, and look at what happened to Toby.

"Anything hotter than dawn and the poor girl would have fried," Doctor Litter hisses. That's how you know Doctor Litter is mad. She hisses. "What if we hadn't checked the container until the next evening?"

I don't answer, because I don't know what would have happened. But that's okay—Doctor Litter isn't talking to me. I'm just in the kitchen because I'm supposed to be getting plates. She's really talking to Mister Arnt, who is pulling baked potatoes out of the oven.

"Well. At the risk of sounding redundant: she'd have fried," he says, in that way he says most things. Toby calls it 'flat.' "And we'd have made the best of that. But what do you expect us to do about it now? Report the delivery service for... what, endangerment? Report to *who*, precisely? How? Our transmitter only sends messages to the station. What are *they* going to do about it?"

"The people there are in daily contact with world leaders. They could—"

"'Daily contact.'" Mister Arnt laughs. I don't understand what's funny, but Mister Arnt doesn't sound happy, so I probably don't get it because the joke isn't good. "Just say it like it is, Kathleen. They're *run* by the government. Just like the delivery service. And when it comes down to it, what incentive do they truly have to help us? Besides, I suppose, maintaining a bullshit façade of leadership. If anything, 'accidents' like incinerating a woman and her child make life easier for them. Wouldn't be shocked to hear them call it 'natural selection,' at this point."

"'Natural?'" Doctor Litter isn't hissing anymore. Now she's growling. That's how you know she's super mad. "It wouldn't have been *natural*! The delivery service—"

"Yes, yes, it would've been pinned on the delivery service. The only delivery service in this county. The only delivery service, run by the same agency that controls everything," Mister Arnt continues. He hasn't even noticed me yet, because I'm so, so quiet. And I'm moving so, so slow. I'm like the ninja in yesterday's drama, invisible and sneaky, my back sliding along the wall. "Let's say we sent in a transmission complaining about this clear human rights violation. The only thing they'd do is air some garbage report about the number of supplies that needed to be delivered last night, warn the public at large that things might get damaged due to speed of processing, and thank our local delivery service for 'risking all' by working until sunrise. Aspen, don't think for a second that I don't see you there. Grab the cutlery and set the damn table."

Mister Arnt sounds like he's in a bad mood when he says all this. Especially that last part. So I stop being a ninja and hurry up and take what I'm supposed to, but I don't let it bother me otherwise, because actually, Mister Arnt always sounds like he's in a bad mood.

Hana calls him a grumpy teddy bear, sometimes. And even though I know that's not true—Mister Arnt is a grownup, obviously. Not a teddy bear—I do kind of see what she means.

* * *

Two days later, when we're all in the shared space listening to the radio, the man who reports the news says:

"In response to customer feedback regarding recent practices and apparent breaches in protocol, our local chapter of the USPS has issued the following statement:

'We hear your concerns, and appreciate your interest in the well-being of your friendly neighborhood delivery staff. Our number one priority, as it has always been, is the safety of both our people, and of your parcels. As we enter the summer months—with their longer days, shorter nights, and higher temperatures—we ask not just for your patience, but for your understanding. This is the most volatile season, and as such, schedules might require readjusting, crate contents could change, and certain regulations may need to be temporarily suspended for the benefit of the majority.'"

I am sitting on a pillow next to the radio, watching the way that the mesh wiggles with sound. It makes my body feel tingly to see it. It's a teeny-tiny movement, like Momma breathing when she sleeps, but it helps me pretend that the radio is alive. Maybe even with a heart inside it. And its voices are friends who are in our house, talking to us and telling us stories.

It's one of my favorite things to imagine, so it's hard to stop. But I try. I try just long enough to look at Mister Arnt. He's standing in his corner, arms crossed over his chest, staring grouchily at Doctor Litter. I dunno if Doctor Litter sees that, though, because she's busy checking on Toby's skin giraffes.

"On the subject of adjustments and change," the man on the radio goes on, *"surface temperatures have continued to climb at an unprecedented rate, and the domino effect of resultant consequences—"* I gasp, recognizing the word, *"—is yet to be fully understood. However, present projections indicate that next month's crates will contain six fewer gallons of water per household, and thirteen pounds less canned food due to climate-related fires in government storage units. It is also being reported that plans to procure spinach, carrot, and pepper seeds have fallen through. Attempts to obtain fertilizers have similarly failed. In an effort to counteract the presumed effects of these events, next week's programming will begin with two waves. The first, as always, will be randomized, while the second will be dedicated specifically to those living in households of ten or more."*

This announcement makes the grownups shout, and Mister Arnt says more of those words that Momma has asked me not to repeat, please. They're so loud about it that the baby starts crying, and that makes the grownups louder, and then I can't hear the radio, so I start yelling, and it's a mess. I don't get to hear the weather lady at all. My entire day is almost *ruined.*

But when the nightly drama starts, everybody except the baby finally stops screaming. Miss Blum takes her out of the room, though, so it's okay. Mister Arnt leaves too, his mouth shut tight, but that's normal for him.

Tonight, the drama is about an astronaut who flies all the way to the moon. The lady in the troupe makes the moon sound like a weird, cold place that's a long way off. Since Felicia is sitting closest to me, rubbing at her eyes, I whisper-ask her how far away the moon is, and what it looks like, because we don't have any pictures of it in our books.

It's one of those questions I sometimes ask that makes Felicia do a laugh-cry noise. Then she says something about missing the Internet and TV, but that isn't a helpful answer. It never is, no matter when she says it. That's frustrating to me, and I wanna be angry at her, but not when the drama is on.

I tell myself I'll ask Mister Grayson about the moon later and just keep listening right now.

So that's what I do.

* * *

Kinda like Mister Arnt, Miss Blum is usually in a bad mood.

Her bad mood is the unhappy kind, though. Not the cranky kind. I call her "Miss Glum" once when talking to Momma, but Momma doesn't think it's clever. She stares at me with down-pointing eyebrows and says that I'm being rude, and then I feel bad about it, so I'm gonna be careful with her name from now on.

It's good practice, actually. People on the radio are always careful when they list names.

Miss Blum and her baby were assigned next to me and Momma in the sleeping room, probably because Momma is the only other mom in our house, so Momma and Miss Blum spend a lot of time making friends. Most nights I ignore them, curling up like a "c" or half a "w" and trying to fall asleep right after the nightly drama, so that hopefully I can dream about it.

But other nights, I only pretend. That I'm sleeping, I mean. What I'm secretly doing is closing my eyes and listening, because grownups can be shy too, and only talk about some stuff when they don't think I can hear them.

"It was awful. We knew it was coming, but it was still awful," Miss Blum is saying to Momma. She is speaking so soft, I almost can't hear her over the nursing baby. I'm still surprised about how noisy that baby is. Who knew babies were so loud? "From the moment I realized that I was...but by then, what could we do? Our doctor refused to act. He just talked about the 'circle of life' and 'making sacrifices for our future' and all that horseshit. Meanwhile, my husband was convinced that we'd get sent a spare from that house on Red Brick Avenue. You know, the one that turned off their radio."

"God rest their souls."

"I hoped Aren was right. I really did. But I never believed he was. Then...well. Ivy was born. And it was only when I held her for the first time that I realized why I could never bring myself to share his convictions."

"The numbers."

"The numbers," Miss Blum agrees. "I mean, in the long run, an entire household getting 'turned off' barely buys society any leeway, as far as supplies are concerned. It doesn't take a mathematician to figure that out. So. If the powers that be see an opportunity to kill two birds with one stone, they're going to take it, 'lottery system' be damned. A switch was absolutely going to get flipped in our house, and long before Ivy's skull fused. We just didn't know who would be... facing the music, so to speak."

My eyes are still shut, so I can't see Momma's face, but my guess is that she's frowning. Momma frowns a lot when she's talking to other grownups.

"Christ, Olive. I'm sorry," Momma says, just as quiet as Miss Blum. I can feel her heartbeat in the fingers that are tracing around my ear. "It doesn't help, I get that, I fully acknowledge that, but...but my husband was also—"

"Oh, it wasn't Ivy's father," Miss Blum snorts. She sounds a little scary for a minute, because I can hear that she's grinning, but there's a meanness in her voice. "That's the only good thing to come out of this nightmare. The thinnest silver lining. No, it was our asshole doctor. Watching him keel over as the last note played...it was the first time in years that I've enjoyed music, you know? Or meat. Or composting, for that matter. But," Miss Blum sighs, and that meanness dries up faster than water in our garden's containers. "That does mean Ivy's implant came from him...and I can't say I love that reminder."

"No. I imagine not." Momma stays silent for a second. In that second, the baby gives a wet burp. Babies are loud and sorta gross. "When the government men came to do Ivy's operation...I don't suppose they told you why they didn't just ship you all a different doctor, rather than break up the household?"

"Nah," Miss Blum says, flat like Mister Arnt. "But they didn't need to, did they? It's common sense. Easier to corral cattle when they're kept in fewer pens."

* * *

The next day, before I have to start working on my numbers and my writing, I show Miss Blum my forehead.

I probably shouldn't. I don't want her to know that I was listening to her and Momma. But she seems sad, and I don't want her to be sad either. So. When she is finishing her breakfast, I put my knees on my chair and lean over the table, pulling my hair back to point at the smooth skin right above my ear. The place that's just about where the radio knobs reach.

"See?" I tell her. "It's okay. My scar got better, and it's all gone now. Ivy's scar will go away, too. Then you won't have to remember it!"

Miss Blum blinks at me. She looks surprised, but she *doesn't* look at where I'm pointing. Which makes sense, I guess. You really can't see my scar anymore, so what would she even be looking at?

"It's okay," I tell her again. Sometimes you gotta say things more than once for people to hear them, or to remember them. "Your scar might go away, too. Momma's didn't. Mister Grayson's and Mister Arnt's and Toby's and Felicia's and Doctor Litter's didn't, either. But Hana's did. And mine. And I bet Ivy's will, probably. Is your blister better? No giraffes?"

Miss Blum opens her mouth. Maybe she's gonna answer my question. Or maybe she's gonna ask me a question. Or maybe she's gonna say 'thank you' because I gave her my help. But then Mister Grayson comes into the dining room, ready to start our lesson, and Miss Blum closes her lips real thin instead. Which is probably the best way to stop me from getting in trouble.

Also, she smiles at me. A little bit. Which is as nice as a 'thank you,' I think.

* * *

There's no way of knowing what the nightly dramas are gonna be. Not at the beginning of the week.

It could be the start of a two-day series, or a three-day series. Once, there was even a *seven*-day series, and I couldn't wait to hear the end, so on the last day I sat in front of the radio for a whole hour before the broadcast even started.

That's just one thing that might happen, though. The troupe could also use the beginning of the week to say that they're not doing a series, but that they are gonna perform stories that use the same characters. Those are good also. Especially when the character they use is Ember Oklahoma. He's a cowboy, and I love him.

But usually, the beginning of the week is when the troupe tells us a list of titles and themes. That's all. They call it a 'preview.' Then we have to wait and be surprised about which story we hear each day. I like that, too, because I like being surprised.

Anyway. Today is the beginning of the week. I dunno if we'll get a preview, or if we'll have more stories about Ember Oklahoma, or if we'll find out about a series, and I won't know until after the music and the news and the weather, but that's okay, I can be patient, since I like that other stuff, too.

Well. I like *most* of that other stuff. The grownups are mad about having to listen to two songs, and I don't like that.

Momma is sitting with me on the pillow next to the radio today, her arms in a floppy hug around my shoulders. It isn't cold in this room, but she's shivering. I can feel it against my back, along with her bones. So I snuggle in to help keep her warm, even as my eyes stay stuck to the radio, because Mister Grayson is finally turning it on.

My whole body feels like that static sound. That's how excited I am. Nobody else looks excited yet, but they never do until the music is done.

"Good evening," says the man on the radio. It's not the man who reads the news—that's another man. This is the man who plays the music. He doesn't always talk, but sometimes he does. Like now. *"This is night one of a two-wave week. As a reminder, our first wave—which tonight shall be the second movement from* Der Tod und das Mädchen *by Franz Schubert—will be randomized, as is customary. The second wave—for which we have selected the finale from the* Pathétique Symphony *by Tchaikovsky—is an emergency response, and will not affect households containing fewer than nine people. From all of us here at the station, our thanks and sincerest condolences."*

"Fucker," Mister Arnt whispers in his corner. That makes Hana gasp like she's the lady in the troupe. Toby and Felicia ignore them both, probably because they're busy holding hands, but Doctor Litter starts hissing, and that makes Mister Grayson start grumbling, and that makes the baby start crying. Or maybe it's that Ivy doesn't like violins, I dunno.

Momma turns her head to say something to Miss Blum, who is leaning against the wall. I should be able to hear it, because Momma and Miss Blum are both so close to me. But I just...

I...

I just hear the music.

I've heard music before. I've heard music every night. But I haven't heard music like this. This music sort of...flows. Over me. It sort of *rolls* over me. It rolls over my neck and my shoulders and my knees, over and over, moving like water does when we pour it from the jugs.

I don't think I could dance to it. Or sway to it. Even if I wanted to. Even if I needed to.

Suddenly, I remember that I didn't ask about the moon. I dunno why I remember now, except that maybe it's because I feel very floaty, and the story said the moon floats in the sky. I wanna ask Mister Grayson about it right this very second, except my mouth won't work. It opens, but that's all it does. I can't even say *Momma*. My throat is too tight for words to squeeze out of it.

It hurts. It hurts too much. My head hurts too much. Right by my ear, it hurts *too* much, like somebody is pushing on it. Like they're pressing a button. Or maybe like something is breaking, something that can't be fixed. Whatever it is, it makes my chest feel sharp, and my tongue taste like metal, and my eyes go blurry, and the only thing I can hear is the music, but it's gotten real quiet. Like it's far away. Except I'm right next to the radio.

It's still pretty, though.

I think...maybe it's a lullaby. Maybe that's what the music is. Yeah. I think that's it. I think I'm gonna go to sleep.

I'll ask about the moon when I wake up.

VINYL REMAINS

BY CHAD STROUP

Brett vetted the vinyl, eyed it as closely as physically possible. He'd never dreamed he'd find a copy so clean. Never even seen one in person that hadn't turned out to be a convincing bootleg. But this was no facsimile. The matrix number in the runout etching matched his meticulous notes, the center label art featured just the right shade of crimson, and the record itself—when held up to the light—was not quite black but more of a muddy, see-through brown, confirming the vinyl had been cut in the mid-1990s at a pressing plant that had since gone under.

"You look like a man who knows what he's holding."

Brett winced at the vendor's comment, forced a smile before lifting his head to face the man, ready to pretend he was fine with inevitably being talked down to.

"It's an original, isn't it?" Brett asked, playing along. Another determined digger rubbed elbows with him, flipping through an adjacent crate. Brett grunted and side-eyed the man, bullying him into shifting a few steps to the left.

"Damn skippy it is," the vendor said. "Don't see those every day, right? Total bonzer."

"What are you asking?" As much as he looked forward to the hunt, Brett often dreaded attending record fairs, because he knew without fail at least half the vendors would not be pricing the goods they were peddling. Which meant the items would likely be assigned arbitrary worth in the vendors' heads at far above market value. Even if they had clearly been mishandled, not kept protected in Japanese re-sealable plastic sleeves, wasting away in damp quarters to encourage mold growth within the jackets, or left out for days only to allow dust to settle in and take root.

Not this specimen though. Quite the opposite. Pristineness personified. Perhaps—he could hope—an unearthed stock copy that had yet to be deflowered. If so, it would be well worth the top dollar it would surely command.

"Hmm, well I dunno. Something as piss rare as that..." The vendor ran his fingers through his thinning, frayed hair, a sun-damaged cobweb. He sniffled, wiped his nose. "You know...only a hundred of those were pressed, supposedly, and rumor has it at least half of the copies were—"

"—were destroyed. As was the master lacquer. Lost in that terrible warehouse fire before they had the chance to be distributed. Yes, I'm well aware of the folklore." Brett smirked, held back his ire as best he could. As if some lowlife mouth breather would dare to know more about the history of this treasured LP than he. The fool didn't even seem to be aware of the fanciful campfire stories about what became of the musicians involved. And Brett wasn't about to be price gouged. With tender care, he placed the record back into its black dust sleeve, then the outer jacket, and prepared to file it back in the bin, wedged between the Butthole Surfers and Captain Beefheart.

The vendor's confident grin loosened. "Hey, wait...you sure you don't want that? It ain't gonna last the day."

Pure poker, Brett shook his head, shrugged. The record hovered halfway back in its place, but his fingers refused to release it. "I don't doubt that, but I'm afraid it's going to be a choice between this rarity or the rent."

Calculations going on inside the vendor's head. Betrayed by his eyes. The burly man chuckled. "Well, hey, I'm sure we can work out some sort of deal that keeps us both happy, can't we?"

Brett smiled, nodded. He supposed he could subsist on Top Ramen and tap water for the month if need be. Wouldn't be the first time he opted for such a lifestyle choice. Sonics over sustenance.

The terms were determined, then Brett paid the man and left without exploring the remaining vendors. He'd found his Holy Grail. No need to sniff around for lesser discoveries.

He couldn't wait to get home and savor the sounds of this special treat.

* * *

Body quivering with excitement. Fingertips damp with sweat. Tongue coated with a dry, stale paste. Brett had reason to celebrate. He finally possessed a copy. The infamous album he'd been pinching pennies, skipping multiple meals for.

Canciones de la Semilla. Songs of the Seed.

Only an album title emblazoned on the cover in elaborate cursive, the enigmatic artists behind it too modest to take credit with even so much as a simple band name. No liner notes, no recording info, nothing that would indicate any pride had been taken in its creation. And Brett couldn't bring himself to play it. Not yet. His fingers trembled as he dangled the tone arm over the spinning record, and so he returned it to its rest. For the first time in his pathetic life, the needle made him nervous.

The front cover art harbored intense detail. A scene that would have made Hieronymus Bosch gasp with envy. Once formidable towers crumbling to insignificant dust. Woolly beasts running rampant in the streets, their vicious, enormous teeth bared and ready to sink into virgin flesh. Shrieking children being roasted over an open fire, the crudely made spits extending from esophagus to anus. All the while—bald, androgynous partners copulating in the gutters, their deadened eyes gazing into nothingness. A bleak yet colorful rendition of Hell on Earth. Nothing he hadn't seen before on pedestrian heavy metal album covers, but Brett couldn't help but be impressed with the level of detail in this instance, especially when it came to the true focal point of the art. Shadowed in the background, looming over the chaos—a behemoth god from below or beyond. Its wingspan stretched from one top corner of the album to the other, and its head was a misshapen mass that claimed to be neither man nor serpent nor cephalopod but some amalgamation of the three. Its mouth formed a Stygian hole, its teeth hidden deep within the black chasm. The tips of its massive horns had been clipped away to fit the restrictions of the twelve-inch format. A pity.

On the back cover—a silver pentagram against a black background. Neither inverted nor right side up. Instead placed slightly askew. A curious choice. Running his fingers across the pentagram, he discovered the artwork had texture. Some sort of embossing effect, yet upon closer inspection he could spot no sign of relief in the cardboard. Such peculiar detail. An impressive illusion.

Now, finally summoning the bravery to listen to the actual music, he had to admit he was a tad disappointed. He'd expected dark, epic crescendos, heartbreaking melodies, crushing beats, life-affirming lyrical content. Something he could feel deep within his soul. An experience that would gut him and then promptly revitalize him. What he got in lieu of his wish was utterly pathetic. Sporadic, nasal chanting, so quiet and high-pitched it might as well have come from the squeaking mouths of mice rather than men. Though these voices didn't sound quite like men either. Altered by studio magic. Maybe he had to be of canine descent to discern its genius. The sounds spewing from his speakers did not in the slightest resemble the rave review he'd once read on the now defunct *KISS THE G.O.A.T.* blog. Before today, he'd trusted that particular writer's opinions without question, but now he'd been failed and lost his faith.

He wondered why he'd even bothered believing in the first place. It wasn't as if playing the record would actually conjure the long-faded spirits of those who had purportedly created the music—whoever they were. But it was fun to buy into the fictional tale while it lasted. And now, with barely enough funds in his bank account to purchase a Happy Meal, Brett realized it was probably time to reconsider his priorities.

But he believed there was still more he could learn. From someone who'd once owned a copy—found on the cheap and flipped almost immediately. Someone who could help him make sense of this utter travesty. What Brett truly wished was that he knew someone he could rely on, someone who could guide him in his moment of need.

Instead, he called Jerry.

* * *

As long as Brett had known Jerry, the main room of his friend's cozy apartment was as follows: covered wall-to-wall with custom cedar shelving, packed to near-bursting efficiency with LPs, save for the shelves on the outskirts that contained handcrafted boxes stuffed with singles. Not an inch of space wasted. Plastic dividers indicated genre, from Blue Note jazz and comedy to thrash metal and show tunes. Jerry considered himself an equal opportunity collector, something Brett silently resented. Though Brett undeniably understood the pleasures that came with excess, he also believed in the power of a focused collection, a discerning ear. As such, he only ever sought out the eclectic, the truly eccentric.

Jerry had always fancied himself the lucky type, which Brett loathed with bitterness. Scouring the local used record shops, thrift stores, flea markets, and yard sales had become Jerry's side business, and he'd often found items wasting away in hidden, forgotten dollar bins that would make some sorry grown men weep. He'd also once discovered a discarded crate full of singles behind a dumpster that contained mostly rubbish but also a near mint copy of the Sex Pistols' "God Save the Queen," of which only nine copies were said to exist. Brett had never actually seen the record, though. Jerry claimed to have sold it to a private buyer. With the number of these transactions that had allegedly transpired during the time Brett and Jerry had been acquainted, he wondered why his friend still wallowed in this polished pigsty.

"So wow, bud," Jerry said. "You finally found a copy, huh? Sure it's not a bootleg?"

Brett huffed. "Very."

"Well, are you going to let me see it or not? I'll be able to tell." He extended his hand toward Brett, snapping his fingers.

"Not with those greasy paws of yours, I'm not."

"I see. I'm just a prisoner in my own house. That's what this is." Jerry hobbled to the sink, turned on the faucet. Brett never let anyone handle any piece in his collection without immaculate hands or rubber gloves—preferably both. And like hell was he going to allow this expensive artifact to be ruined to avoid hurting Jerry's feelings. "Want a beer?"

Brett nodded.

When Jerry returned from the kitchen, he passed Brett an opened bottle and set his own drink down on a scratched-to-hell Hall & Oates 45. An odd choice for a coaster, considering the big round hole dead in the center. Brett tasted his beverage and placed the chilled bottle next to Jerry's.

Jerry shoved his freshly washed and dried hands in Brett's face, confirming he'd scrubbed all the nooks and crannies of his fingers. The nail on his forefinger had grown far past a respectable length, and Brett wondered if his friend had recently taken up snorting cocaine as a hobby.

"Okay, Keeper of the Holy Grail, can I see the record now or do I have to sell my soul first?"

Brett waved him away. "Stop that." He slid his hand into a leather knapsack, its inside lined with hard plastic, perfect for fitting up to five albums with no risk of causing ring wear or corner dings. He always brought the knapsack with him when he went shopping for vinyl, rarely purchasing more than he could carry home safely. It had always proven to be the perfect protection. Today, however, the knapsack only held one record.

He hesitated, then—holding the album flat in his palms—passed it to Jerry, who whistled as he examined it, checking in all angles of the light for the telltale signs Brett had already scrutinized before purchasing.

"Yup," Jerry said. "It's the real deal all right." He swigged his drink. Brett's asshole clenched, worried Jerry would spill even the slightest drop on the record. "Want me to find a buyer for it?"

"What I want is to know is why it sounds like absolute rubbish. The music is just—it's not even...I can't..." Brett sighed. "Clearly this album is only desired for its rarity."

"Well, that's pretty typical, though, ain't it?" Jerry burped, excused himself. "You don't often get the two great tastes that taste great together. Rarity and quality? That's asking for too much."

"Is it, though? I'm just a little...I don't know...dissatisfied, I suppose." That was putting it lightly. Brett had experienced buyer's remorse more often than he preferred to admit. But the sensation had always passed by the time he focused his attention on the next fixation. This was different. He felt betrayed. And he hadn't been able to sleep at all last night either. Lost in a wakened fever dream, obsessed with the terrible sounds that had screeched from his speakers when needle met wax.

Jerry leaned in close. "Same thing happened to me when I had my copy. Went straight to the front of my TBL pile, and not even worth the damned effort."

"Well, thank you so much for warning me."

Jerry shrugged. "Hey, what do you want from me? I'm only human. Tell you what, though. I'm gonna let you in on a little secret about this record. Something I found out after I sold mine."

Brett rolled his eyes, but his ears perked despite his best judgment. "And what might that be? Play it backward and there'll be hidden Satanic messages? Sell your soul for the music, and the devil will bring you unfathomable wealth? How banal." The whispered folklore Brett had heard always implied that *Canciones de la Semilla* harbored unspeakable evil. So offering up one's soul would make sense, were one to believe in such farces as devils and gods and the fictional wars they waged against one another.

"Cut the sarcasm and just listen. There's a hidden groove, dig?"

"Get out of here." Though Brett supposed it wasn't out of the question. Plenty of more commonly pressed records had contained a hidden groove with an additional song or other recording just waiting to be discovered. Tool. De La Soul. The Sugarcubes. Fine Young Cannibals. Monty Python. The list went on. A fun gimmick that had yet to overstay its welcome, unlike the "hidden track" contrivance often employed on the dreaded compact disc format.

"Thing is, there's a catch."

"Always is, isn't there? Who, may I ask, did you acquire this privileged information from?"

"Uh, I know a guy who knows a guy."

"Of course you do. Please, don't keep me in suspense any longer." Brett's voice was drenched in ennui, sprinkled with irony.

Jerry hesitated. And for once, it seemed honest. He really didn't want to reveal the big secret, which intrigued Brett further. Brett persisted, dragged it out of him.

"Okay, okay," Jerry said. His face re-sculpted itself. All business. No play. "Here's the deal. Apparently you can't play it with an average stylus."

"If you're about to tell me I have to listen it on a Crosley, so help me God I'm leaving and never coming back."

"No, no...nothing as awful as that."

"So how did it turn out with this source of yours?"

"No idea. Never got the chance to ask him. He wouldn't return my calls. So I just gave up, moved on."

"Naturally. Okay, so how about this? I've got to go out of town for a few days for a conference. Why don't you—"

A smile slapped across Jerry's face. "Yeah, man! Sure! I'll take care of everything, try my guy again, look into the details, and get it all figured out for you. You can trust me."

Jerry's dictionary had always contained a skewed version of "trust," but at this point Brett merely wanted some form of return on his investment. Not necessarily monetary. He hoped to satisfy some urge he couldn't yet name.

"You'll be extra careful with it?"

"Of course, bro. What do you take me for?"

Brett raised an eyebrow. "Fine. Keep me posted."

"Roger that. Don't call me, pal. I'll call you."

* * *

Somewhere in Wisconsin, only a few days deep into entrepreneur conference hell, trapped in the vacant confines of a hotel room, sipping watered down vodka brought by faceless room service, Brett noticed he had a voicemail. From Jerry.

Brett pressed play, listened. Nothing but background noise for a few seconds. Not quite static. Brett couldn't quite confirm the source, as it sounded like it was coming from another room if not another universe, but it most closely resembled wind. Hot wind, if sound could be assigned a temperature. He moved his thumb to delete the call.

Then—a voice cut in. Jerry's, presumably. But distant. And slightly off. Like a facsimile of his friend. A recording of a recording.

"Hey, hey big B-r-e-double-t. You're never gonna belieeeeeeve this shit, but my guy, he finally got back to me. Seriously. What are the chances? And he hooked me up with the deets. Told me what to do 'bout the hidden groove."

A pause, followed by violent hacking and a sickeningly wet noise. A placenta colliding with a concrete floor.

Jerry continued. "Yeah, so it took some time, but I got it all figured out now. My notes were a bitch to read, man. Not even sure I wrote them to be honest. Doesn't look like my handwriting. But trust me, it's not going to be what you think. You gotta get back here so you can see for yourself." Jerry paused. The wind's volume surged before his voice returned. Altered. Deepened. Layered. Like a second distorted vocal track recorded a half-second off from the timing of the first track, causing latency. Two simple words that filled Brett with unexplainable trepidation: "Come now."

Now Brett was certain Jerry had found God in recreational drugs. Again. He deleted the voicemail and set his phone face down on the nightstand. He kicked off his shoes, switched off the lamp, and settled into bed, but sleep once again refused to take him, no matter how much he begged for it.

* * *

Two days later—the final day of the conference, as Brett was packing up his belongings and preparing to hail a rideshare to the airport—he decided to reach out to Jerry, hopefully catch him at a sober moment. He hadn't heard from his friend since that ridiculous message, and he was really hoping there had been some new developments in this hidden groove business. And that they could be conveyed in a simple, rational manner.

He made the call. The ringing stopped short, but there was no clear answer on the other end. Only a barely audible hum that prevented complete silence from prevailing.

Brett huffed. "Hel—"

Before he could complete his greeting, an inhuman shrieking exploded from his phone, shredding his eardrums. He howled and hurled the phone across the room. Brett counted his blessings as it landed on carpet rather than tile. Even from where he stood he could hear the wretched noise clawing from its speakers. Static building into cacophony, wild laughter, and an all-too-familiar chanting, only the voices sounded like they were being played on the wrong RPM, sped up to near Chipmunk insanity.

And even though it was his first time truly hearing these sounds, he knew exactly what they implied.

Jerry had played the hidden grooves.

* * *

Brett rang Jerry's doorbell. No answer. He tried again, waited, then knocked with the base of his fist, in case the doorbell had taken an unannounced sabbatical.

"Jerry? Are you home? It's Brett!"

He jiggled the knob, applied slight pressure, and the door opened without protest. Something wasn't right. Jerry never left his apartment unlocked for fear of tweakers ravaging his precious collection. The space between door and jamb widened from crack to chasm, and a powerful stench washed over Brett. A blend of aged cheese, copper wire, and Nag Champa.

Brett hesitated. His instincts urged him to shut the door, turn away, never return. Forget he'd ever spent time in this part of town, cut his losses on the album, and figure out the bottom line later. But loyalty trumped instinct, and so he moved forward through the hallway. Jerry was the closest thing he had to a comrade. It was his duty to make sure he wasn't suffocating in snow he'd just tried to snort, his heart stopped with no hope of kick-starting.

If only Jerry had been so fortunate.

When Brett first saw the man huddled in the corner of the living room, he believed a derelict had in fact broken into the apartment and was in the process of pilfering through Jerry's precious goods. The man barely clung to his humanity. Limbs that a mantis would pray to possess, hair disheveled to the point of fine art, a bird's nest of a beard exploding in all directions as if being pulled by static electricity, eyes that had milked over—Brett was nearly tempted to grab a spoon from the kitchen and scoop into their slick pudding, see what delicacies hid within the creamy center.

A full minute passed of Brett standing still, silent, heart-stopped. Then the derelict grinned in his direction. Teeth resembling charcoal briquettes. Lips that had kissed sandpaper. Brett held his hands up in defense, darted his head back and forth in search of a weapon.

"Oh, hey man. Was wondering when the hell you'd finally get here." A familiar voice spat from the intruder's mouth. And Brett then saw the shape of his friend's face cached behind the mutation. How could this be Jerry? And after only days had passed? He looked as if he'd been living on the streets for years, subsisting on rat droppings, expired meats, and extremely cheap junk.

"Wha—wh…"

"C'mere, bud. You gotta see what I found. Gotta hear this." Jerry remained in a crouching position as he hobbled to the next room, a toad doing a poor impression of a man. Brett followed. They reached Jerry's turntable. *Canciones de la Semilla* sat atop the platter, its hole tightly fit around the spindle, its grooves begging to be played so it could finally share its primordial secrets. But one important component had gone missing—the tone arm. And this might have been the most grievous affront of all. It had been torn from its home, tossed somewhere among the massive debris that had claimed Jerry's apartment in the few days Brett had been in the Midwest.

"I don't understand. How will you be able to play the record?"

Jerry's grin stretched. He held up his right hand, wrapped tight in blood-soiled bandages. The next few moments played out like a sickening striptease. Jerry unwrapped the bandages, and they floated to the floor. He extended his pointer finger as far as he could in Brett's direction. A gasp escaped Brett's mouth before he could quell it. The skin on Jerry's finger had been peeled away. At the knuckle closest to the palm—all raw dermis. From the second knuckle on, bone fully exposed in all its blinding white glory, shaved meticulously narrower the closer it got to where a fingernail should have been.

Filed to a point so fine it could have been mistaken for a...

A needle.

Brett couldn't fathom how Jerry had performed this sickening self-surgery. How much determined effort must it have taken to attack it with such precision? And how had he remained conscious as the mutilation progressed? Surely he had to have been out of his wits to even contemplate the task. But this went beyond the mere influence of hard drugs. No, this was a man possessed.

"Don't you see?" Jerry said. "The music's within me, man. Always has been. That's the trick. It's in me, in you—all of us. It surrounds us and moves through us. I know that sounds like some wannabe hippy dippy poetic cliché bullcrap, but you know what? Fuck it. Truth is truth until it ain't. Amiright?" And with that, Jerry pressed the power switch to the turntable. The record spun at 33 RPMs in silence for a few seconds, then Jerry placed the bone lightly into the album's spinning grooves. And the sounds that spilled from the speakers couldn't have been further from the whiny chants Brett had heard when he'd first attempted to play the record at home. No, these were the voices of otherworldly angels hidden within the secret groove. Those that had fallen, to be certain, but angels nonetheless.

And they were calling to him, imploring him to abandon his existence of conferences and staff meetings and endless lonely nights in front of a series of meaningless screens. Beckoning him to leave that all behind and come join them in their passionate dance. To trade one form of excess for another. Brett had never before fancied himself a hedonist, but the sultry sounds pulsing within him begged to prove otherwise. Lyrics sung in languages that had never been uttered above ground. Tempos that shifted seamlessly from a maddening speed to an unbearable crawl. Chords that could have only been played from the gut and *of* the gut. These were the sounds of the primeval dead and those that had never been worthy of living in the first place, channeling their damned souls into miscreant melodies.

These were the *Canciones de la Semilla*.

Pressure against Brett's thigh. He'd grown an erection in record time. It quickly pushed itself to painful hardness. He winced, tried to hide his penile faux pas, then realized he didn't care. The music that had possessed him was the only thing that mattered in this moment. Sexual nirvana birthed from sonic transcendence.

Jerry bobbed his head, kept his hand very still above the turntable, continuing to share the aural revelation. "Ain't it beautiful, man?"

"Yes," Brett whispered. "Very. But—"

"Just wait 'til you see what happens next."

The music wasn't just coming from the speakers anymore. It filled the entire space. Brett hummed along with it. It would surely be his earworm for eons to come. He steeled himself, but nothing could have prepared him for the next few moments of his insignificant life.

He hadn't noticed it before—the pile of vinyl on the opposite side of the room. It had been hidden by Jerry's considerable girth. Precariously stacked LPs and singles unsheathed from their jackets, at risk of unquantifiable damage. It would have been an awful enough sight to witness as it was, without all of the other madness occurring, but then a spontaneous flame burst from somewhere within the pile, and the records started to melt. They coagulated, forming a mass with no definable shape, at least not one native to this plane of existence. Decidedly not humanoid nor animal, but most certainly flowing with life.

Jerry cackled—a painful sound, despite the wicked pleasure plastered across his face. Brett inched forward, planning to remove Jerry's finger from the still spinning record, the wax that spat sounds from elsewhere. Maybe he could still save his friend. Maybe it wasn't too late to salvage his own soul.

"You don't want to do that." Jerry's voice lowered to a growl. He wagged the unmarred pointer finger on his other hand. "That would be very, very bad."

"But...but what's happening? What is that?" He motioned frantically at the being that grew more massive with every breath, pulsating like magma in motion.

Jerry's lips formed an idiot smile. "Bow down, old friend, and give a warm welcome to your one true lord. The maestro of the forbidden. The gateway to your destiny."

Now complete in its unorthodox form, the deity shuffled forward. It did not resemble the majestic, terrifying beast depicted on the album cover in the slightest. But its essence was surely intact. Dripping appendages reached toward Brett, and Brett stumbled backward before his back slammed against a wall of records. Whether the creature's extensions were intended to be arms, tentacles, or something else, Brett could not say. He could only admire with innocent wonder. The mysterious god's appendages slithered around Brett's torso, and his body went limp. His new master beckoned him into its warm embrace. A shape resembling a head leaned toward him, the gaping emptiness in its center whispering infernal harmonies as it widened. Endless, tiny holes formed eyes, and Brett knew he was being observed, judged. Its grooves pressed against his lips, a vintage vinyl kiss.

And Brett did not resist. For now he was one with the music. Finally. And he couldn't wait to share his song.

GODDESS

BY LISA MORTON

Last night I saw my dead mother outside the windows of my tour bus, in a pecan grove near the center of California.

This morning I saw her again, as I lolled in the hotel bed scrolling on my phone.

Two hours ago I saw her in the audience when my band took the stage for our L.A. performance.

I don't mean that I saw her in my mind's eye, as a memory, although that's partly true; I also didn't see her as a ghost. No, I saw her image, emblazoned on a billboard, a blog article, a T-shirt, her gorgeous hazel eyes staring into your soul as she cradled a glowing orb in her hands. She's had quite the resurrection since that hit TV show used her 1989 song "Sliding on Glass" in a climactic scene.

I wasn't born yet when that song came out. Now I'm twenty-three, and my mother's been dead for five years.

Why am I thinking about this? Because it's been a strange month, with that song and *that* face, eternally young and beautiful, everywhere, with me fielding hundreds of interview requests not for my work but for *hers*. "Goddess," as her worldwide legions of fans still call her. "What's it like being her daughter?" they ask, or, "Was she really magickal?" Or, worst of all, "Your mother was an icon—is it hard living with that?"

Of course it is, you tool, I want to say, but instead I try to put on my most enigmatic smile and shrug, a small gesture.

Here I am, Keeva Oakes, daughter of the great Liz Oakes, who burst onto the world in 1980 with a #1 hit single as if she'd crawled already singing from the agonized forehead of Zeus. Liz Oakes, both insanely charismatic and totally reclusive, with an ironically much-publicized loathing of fame. Even though she'd moved to Northern California in the mid-80s after finding a picturesque town where no one cared who she was, she'd been born and bred in Great Britain, and had a particularly British reserve. In her entire career she'd done no more than a handful of live performances, and it had made her even more successful. She'd defied every rule of the music biz and yet had never failed.

Meanwhile, I'd managed a Grammy nomination and two club tours, but I knew people who came to see an Oakes weren't there to see me. I dutifully covered several of Mom's biggest hits (or at least the ones I could sing—she'd had a four-octave range I couldn't touch); I enjoyed the screams and the applause, but couldn't help noticing how many of them left for a break when it came to my songs.

Which, mind you, is not to say I didn't love my mother—I did. She'd been a caring if somewhat preoccupied single parent (my dad having been a handsome session guitarist who wanted nothing to do with me); we'd eat together and play a bit before she'd vanish into her studio and I'd be turned over to Auntie Consuela, the woman hired to look after me when Mom felt creative (which was most of the time).

Then that day had come when I'd been pulled out of class during the end of my last semester at my expensive charter school, and found Auntie Consuela waiting for me in the principal's office, crying. "Your mama," she'd said, before choking on a sob.

Principal Edwards, a kind woman who'd personally shielded me from the paparazzi the day Mom was accused of having an affair with British royalty (she hadn't), came out from behind her desk, led me to a couch, and sat beside me. "I'm so sorry, Keeva," she said, "but there's been an accident—a plane crash."

"Is she dead?" The words blurted out in a way that probably made me sound callous.

"There's no easy way to say this..." she said, trailing off as she placed a comforting hand on my shoulder. Auntie Consuela sobbed louder.

I felt...cold. What came into my head just then was a line from one of Mom's songs: *"You could have cared, but your heart was shale."* It was one of my favorite songs of hers, "The Stone Inside," from '95.

"Are you okay?" Principal Edwards asked.

"What happened?"

Mom had been flying to a friend's wedding in Hawaii; I'd been a bit hurt that she wasn't bringing me, but I didn't know anyone involved and she swore she'd be back in two days. She'd hired a small private jet, and I'd seen her off that morning at the tiny Santa Clara Airport. She hugged me hard, so hard I actually grunted and squirmed a little. "Oh," she said, "I'm going to miss you." She said it in a way that made my stomach clench. "Mom," I almost said, "don't get on the plane." Instead I handed her the little blooming succulent I'd made for her, potted in compost that we'd made, and a mug with her face emblazoned on the side that a school friend had jokingly given me. Mom had looked at it and laughed. "I love the plant, but the *planter...*" She hugged me again, took the plant, and said, "Don't ever forget how much I love you." Then she walked into the plane.

Auntie Consuela had driven me to school then; it was the first day of May, the sky blue, the weather breezy but warm.

The plane had taken off. An hour to the west it had run into an unlikely storm and gone down. They'd found some charred metal floating in the Pacific but nothing else.

I almost asked, "Then how do they know she's dead?" but I realized how naïve it would sound. Of *course* she was dead. No one survived a plane crash at sea during a storm, not even someone like my mother.

Still...there'd always been the rumors about her—that she'd been Wiccan, or Pagan, or Neo-Druid, that she read tarot cards and created potions and read astrological charts. I'd never seen her actually do any of those things, but then there were a *lot* of things I'd never seen her do. She'd spent most of her days locked away in her home recording studio, producing masterpiece albums at the rate of one every five years. I was occasionally allowed to go in and watch as she bent over her piano, her thick, long, brunette hair falling around her as she tried out notes with fingers and then voice, but most of the time the studio was locked to keep me out. I'd sneak up and press my ear against door; sometimes I heard music, her singing... but other times the sounds were strange, guttural. Those sounds would show up in her recordings and Mom would tell me they were *my* squeals as an infant, sampled and transformed.

Tonight, after our set, Maisie and Jed and I had left the stage at the Troubadour, sweaty and happy (it'd been a good show), and there was a man waiting who followed us back to our small dressing room. "Hello, Keev," he said. He was a man in his late fifties, long graying hair, glasses, slender build, jeans and a plain black T-shirt; he looked familiar, but I couldn't place him. A journalist, maybe? No, he didn't look like one of them. A...?

"It's me—Jamie."

Even with a name, it took a second before the memory fell into place: Jamie Koenig, my mother's recording engineer. He'd often been the only other person in the studio with her; he'd traipsed through our living room on his way in and out, usually smelling of weed, kind enough to tussle my hair or tease me but plainly more interested in making music with the Goddess. I'd never known for sure if Jamie and Mom had been lovers, but they'd certainly been a couple in that studio.

I hadn't seen him since she'd died, and he'd aged twenty years in five. I said his name and we hugged, then pulled back to eye one another. "Did you see the show?" I asked.

He grinned and nodded. "I did—it was goddamned good, girl. Your mother would be so proud of you."

Maisie and Jed stepped around us to help our roadie Pedro pack up our gear, and I went into the dressing room with Jamie. "Are you still in Northern California?" I asked. Jamie had sometimes lived in a guest house on our ten-acre estate in Sonoma County, although he also had his own (smaller) house nearby.

"No," he said, "I'm here in L.A. now. It's...well, you know, it's where the work is."

Of course, I thought, *with Mom dead there was no reason for him to stay up north.*

I abruptly realized I didn't know what to say to him. I hoped he wasn't expecting some long reunion over dinner where we'd exchange endless stories about Mom.

He laughed and said, "Wow, can you believe 'Sliding on Glass' becoming the year's biggest hit?"

I had to admit, the money had been nice but the publicity..."Yeah," I said, "it's been a weird year."

A strange expression crossed his face. "For you, too?"

"I mean, you know...seeing Mom everywhere again."

For a split second I saw something like naked fear in his expression, but then he caught himself and exhaled in relief. "Oh, right—all the ads and so forth."

I wondered what he thought I'd meant. But his next question left me far more perplexed.

"Keev, what would you do if your mom came back today?"

I just looked at him for a bit before answering, "I don't know. That's a strange question."

He forced a laugh, shook his head. "It is, I know. Just...well, I suppose the song coming back just brought so many memories..."

He was in love with her. I knew it just then, with zero doubt. For a split second I even wondered if Jamie could possibly have been my father, but I seemed to have inherited my absent father's guitar-playing skill.

Jamie stepped back, dropped his head. "Well, I just wanted to drop by, say hi..." He gave me an abrupt, clumsy hug and then turned to go. I almost called after him to take my number, stay in touch...but realized there was no point.

Maisie walked by just then lugging an equipment case, but she paused when she saw me. "Are you okay? Who was that guy?"

"That was...I'll tell you later."

That night I awoke from a dream of my mother reaching out to me through foggy darkness. I had that terrible experience of waking with no idea of where I was, but then the sliver of city light coming around the edge of the curtains reminded me: a hotel room in L.A.

Then...

"Keeva..."

My name, whispered. But I was alone. The air conditioning vents were rattling, down the hall I heard laughter...

I tried to tell myself the whisper had been unreal, imagined, a holdover from the dream. That it hadn't really sounded like my mother.

* * *

Three nights later I was home again, at the obscenely huge house surrounded by the vineyards Mom had loved; the property taxes were insane, but I'd been left enough money to cover them. The inheritance also allowed me to keep Consuela on, now well past retirement age but still spry and sharp enough to help me keep track of dates and amounts.

She had filled the house with fresh flowers and hugged me as I staggered in, another tour behind me, ready to begin creating the new songs that would lead to the next album and tour. Once I was settled, I asked her, "Did you ever see Mom... well...doing anything strange?"

Consuela looked at me curiously. "Strange how?"

I felt self-conscious. "I don't know, like...you know, like some of the things they say about her."

"That she was a bruja?" She burst into laughter.

"Was she?"

Now my beloved Auntie Consuela, who in many ways felt more like my real mother, bustled away into the kitchen. "What put these thoughts in your head? Let me make you a cup of my special tea—you'll feel better."

She still hadn't answered the question. But the tea—a mix of herbs that Consuela grew in the garden just outside the back door—melted my concerns away, at least for a while.

The dreams that night, though, were vivid. I didn't remember all of them, but the one that stuck in my head when I woke up had taken place in the recording studio: I followed Mom, always just out of reach, through the dark house until we came into the studio. The lights were out here, too, but there were candles placed around the board, positioned in dishes so the wax wouldn't drip onto the controls. The air was scented with a heady smell I couldn't identify, and there were papers strewn about. I stepped up to examine them, squinting to read them by candlelight, and I saw they were covered in my mother's broad, curling handwriting but in a language I couldn't make out. One page looked like a list of ingredients or instructions; another was a complicated scrawl of some kind of symbol.

And then I was in my own bedroom, light coming in through the window, that intoxicating smell still filling my nostrils.

I knew those pages. I'd seen them among my mother's papers that I'd gathered up after her death, stored away in boxes in a shed out back.

I dressed quickly, ignored Consuela's queries, went out there, started pulling down boxes and going through them. Contracts, notes, photos, clippings...

There they were. Exactly as I'd seen them in the dream, but there were many of them, all written in those words I couldn't parse. I pulled out my phone, took photos of some of them, put the boxes back, returned to the house.

I held out the phone to Consuela. "Did you ever see these? Do you know what they were?"

She squinted at the screen before nodding. "Oh, yes—your mama made those in her studio, but I never knew why."

For the first time in my life I wasn't sure I believed her. Consuela had always prided herself on her honesty, so I had no reason to doubt her, but...

"Did Mom teach you how to make your special tea?"

She stared at me with what looked like mock indignation. "No! That is a recipe that my abuela taught me, not your madre."

"Sorry," I said, confused, wandering away.

I thought of Jamie next and wished I had exchanged numbers with him, but it turned out he wasn't hard to find. He was getting a lot of work in L.A., largely because of his reputation as my mother's engineer. Calls to a couple of producer friends yielded up his contact info.

He was surprised to hear from me, but pleased. "Jamie, can I ask you something about Mom?"

"Of course."

"Do you remember seeing her writing things down in the studio, drawings and notes?"

He hesitated before answering, "Yes, I remember."

"Do you know what any of it means?"

Another long pause before he came on again. "Could I...can I come to see you? At the house, I mean?"

I almost asked him *why*, but this was Jamie, who'd always had his own way of doing things. "Of course. When?"

"I'll drive up there today. I can be there by early evening."

I almost asked, "Why the rush?" Jamie always had jobs lined up; was he just walking out on some, and for...what? But I agreed, ended the call, told Consuela Jamie was coming. She was pleased—she'd always liked him—and started bustling around, getting his old guest house ready.

At some point in the afternoon I found myself sitting in the studio—*her* studio, now *my* studio—and wondering what exactly had taken place here.

I would find out soon, from the only person left alive who knew.

* * *

Jamie made it around seven in the evening, just as the sun was setting. He had a small case with him that he set down as we hugged; then he turned to just breathe in the place where he'd spent so much time.

We went into the house, where he and Consuela embraced. We had dinner, poured shots of tequila, and finally he said, "Let's go into the studio."

The tequila didn't dispel the small chill that passed through me.

Once inside, Jamie took the seat behind the console with a sigh. "Oh, the magic we made here..." He paused to look at me as I leaned against the closed door. "It really *was* magic."

I took another sip, looking for alcohol to bolster my understanding. "She was very special..."

Jamie looked down as he said, "That's not what I mean." After a few seconds he stared into my eyes and said, "Your mother wasn't just a genius musician—she was also an extraordinary *magician*. I'm talking *real* magick."

Somehow I'd known – I'd *always* known – but it still felt strange hearing it finally out in the open.

"Those pages she wrote..."

Nodding, he said, "She said it was the language of nature."

"So she really was a..." A bitter laugh preceded the words: "...a *witch*?"

Jamie smiled, bemused. "Well, yes and no. Here's the thing about magick: it's all around us, all the time. Music itself is a form of magick: how else can you explain that plucking a string or pounding on a skin or blowing into a metal tube can render sounds that make us cry or laugh or dance?

"But your mother tapped into other sources as well. She was born with the gifts: she could channel the world's magick, and she did."

I wanted to *dis*believe, to scoff...but there was something in that studio, something primal and real. I knew I had not inherited my mother's skills—I played guitar, not keyboards or magick—but even so I could feel the atmosphere in the room, how it vibrated, how it prodded at the edge of awareness. What Mother had created here was so powerful that it had survived even after she was gone.

"You can feel her in here," Jamie said, his voice soft.

I nodded.

And then I asked, "Jamie, are you my father?"

He shook his head sadly. "I wish. No, Liz seduced Arly Scott—your father—with magick as much as sex. That's why he's never been interested in you—because that's what she cast. She wanted full control of you."

"Why?" I'd loved my mother, but I'd never felt that she'd taken much of an interest in my life. She was too busy creating songs...and spells.

"Because you are..."

Jamie burst into tears. It was unexpected and intense. I stopped myself from putting my arms around him because he also stood and walked away from me. "I'm sorry, I shouldn't have come." He started for the door, waving his hands as if to dispel spirits.

I ran after him. "Wait—Jamie, what—"

He grabbed his overnight bag and headed for his car. I ran past the baffled Consuela, catching up as he climbed behind the wheel. "It's late now, just stay here, your old guest house is ready—"

"I can't stay here, I know what she..." He caught himself, trailed off, started the engine, said, "I'm so sorry, Keev," and drove off, leaving me stunned, baffled, full of dread.

What did he know? Why had he fled like someone running from something awful?

Should *I* be running, too?

I wasn't surprised when Jamie didn't take my call the next day.

* * *

I tried to put Mom behind me to work on my own music; I had a record company and managers already filling my inbox with polite queries. I'd written down some ideas for songs during the tour and it was time to start working on them.

I was halfway through the second song when I realized I was writing it on the grand piano in the studio.

I didn't play piano. My usual guitar sat untouched in its case.

The song was good—*very* good. It sounded like something my mother would have written, with a chord progression that felt as if it had been pulled from the mists of Celtic history, one of *her* obsessions.

The lyrics weren't from my notebook. The song was called "Regeneration." It was about the cycles of nature, how death gave way to new birth.

I dropped a pencil I didn't remember picking up and fled from the studio—*her* studio.

I needed to be out of that house, free of her influence, so I hurriedly packed a few things and my guitar, threw them into my car, told Consuela I'd be gone for a few days, and left. I had no idea where I was going, just...*away*. From here, from her.

I drove south down the 101, through the verdant hills of Northern California, past oak trees and affluent small towns full of tech millionaires, headed inland to the 5 and kept going. I pulled off at a place called Buttonwillow, got gas and fast food, called my manager Ali, had him book a hotel room and studio space for me, and kept going. I was in L.A. two hours later, nursing a bottle of whiskey and watching whatever came on the hotel room television.

My mother, of course. Liz Oakes, the Goddess; an old interview being rebroadcast.

I set down the drink and moved closer, looking at her with new knowledge but less understanding. Why had she wanted me? What had her life really been like? I knew these were questions that most people asked about their parents at some point, but I had one that they didn't:

What was she?

* * *

The next day I arrived at the recording space Ali had gotten me, a small but storied venue owned by a legendary session guitarist I was pleasantly in awe of. He welcomed me with a warm smile, told me the place was all mine for the next week, offered to set me up with grass or blow or other musicians. I thanked him and was relieved that he left before I pulled out my guitar.

As I started to work, my fingers felt oddly clumsy; I began to sweat in the air-conditioned room. I'd never had an anxiety attack, but I thought it probably felt like this—heart racing, head pounding, shaking.

There was a piano five feet away. I itched to play it, to feel my fingers race across the keys the way they always had—

Always had? No, I'd...I didn't...

I hadn't escaped her. It wasn't the home studio or the house in Sonoma; it was *me*. I was...

I was the vessel.

Yes.

That wasn't my thought, but it was in my head.

* * *

It wasn't hard to track down Jamie; I found him at another studio across town. When I poked my head into the booth, he saw me, frowned, said something to his assistant before following me out.

He nodded at an unused, dark studio. "We can talk in there." He went in first, flipped on the lights, closed the door behind us, turned to face me.

"You have to tell me," I began, my words spilling out in a rush, "you have to be real with me: is my mother dead?"

"Yes, but...no. I don't understand everything she did, but I know one thing: she was afraid of what she'd become. Not the magick part, but the rock star, the Goddess, who was pursued wherever she went. She'd installed extra security measures in her home and even then felt exposed. She wanted to escape that, so she...well, I guess you'd say she crafted a way out."

Jamie looked at my face—saw whatever I was feeling—and added, "I don't mean she faked her death, nothing so trite. She absolutely died. But she died... *magickally.*

"Think about her passing: she died in a machine that was buffeted by charged air, that burst into flame, and that fell into water. She got on that plane having spent years working towards what was coming, designed to involve all four elements: air, fire, water, earth."

"But she crashed at sea," I said. "Where does the earth come into play?"

He took a deep breath before fixing me with his gaze. "*You*, Keev."

"Me?"

"Do you remember what you did that day?"

"I'll never forget any part of that day. I..." I broke off in realization. "I gave her a little cactus plant."

Jamie nodded.

"But how could she have known I'd do that?"

"Because...she made you do it." Jamie's voice trailed off. Then he faded away.

Everything faded away—Jamie, the studio, the very air. In their place was...

My mother. Liz Oakes stood before me, framed by eternal gray nothingness, looking exactly as she had on that day in 2018 when she'd boarded the hired jet. She beamed at me with maternal warmth and pride, her voice sounding normal and human when she said, "Hello, Keeva."

I felt tears spring up, I had to hold myself back from reaching for her, but I was angry, too. "I don't understand," I said, my voice slightly choked, "how are you here? Are you dead, or alive, or...?"

"My body died, just as I planned. I called on the four elements to remain on this plain afterward in spirit form while I waited."

"Waited for what?"

"For *you*," she said, tilting her head, her expression beatific.

"For me? Why? What..." I didn't even know what to ask.

"For this moment in your life. I've guided you every step; I chose your father for the skills his blood would bring, I molded you so carefully, I planned my death to happen as you turned eighteen so you'd be an adult, I've watched as you've progressed in your career until this moment, when you've achieved exactly the right level—you're well-respected but not so famous that you can't do as you please out in the world."

"I don't..." The next word that came out of me was, "NO." *No, I almost said, I'm my own person, you were barely even there when I was a child, you gave me your genes, your security, but YOU DID NOT MAKE ME.*

But deep down, at my most secret core, I knew it was true. It was as if I could already feel her there, moving within me, testing, manipulating.

"Think about your gift," she said softly.

I knew what she meant: that plant, that fucking ridiculous plant. I remembered now: taking a cutting from an aloe behind the house, scooping compost from our bin into the mug, and the whole time some little part of me wondered why this

HER ONLY SINGLE

BY DEVAN BARLOW

My song's moment may be over
but the tape goes ever on
The executives chose me
gave me a song
a dance
a sequined skin
For one fabulous year
I was everywhere
underscoring joy seduction heartbreak
(In the back of your mind
among the shreds of that decade
you remember my hit
as one catchy chorus)
Until it all became too much
for a body as human as mine was then
and I became
only, always,
my cassettes
Pieces of the plastic have chipped
GET YOURSELF TOGETHER
NO ONE CARES WHETHER YOU FEEL UP TO IT
Hinges squeak as the case opens
Pain spikes through my joints
crescendos along my back

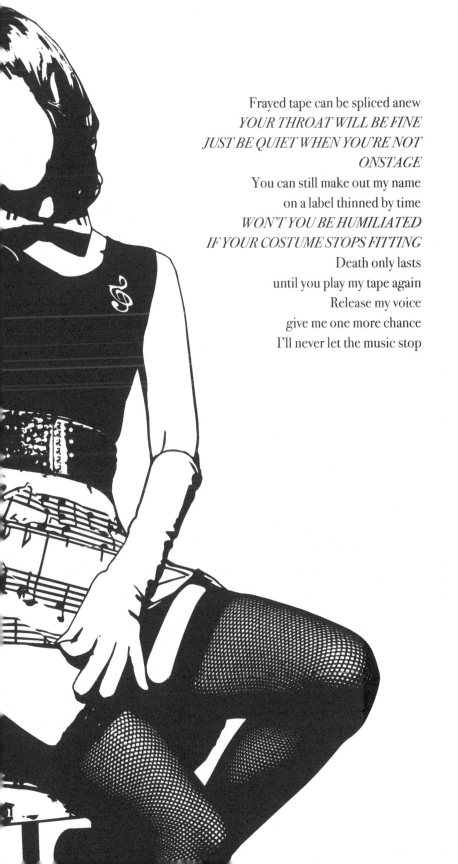

Frayed tape can be spliced anew
YOUR THROAT WILL BE FINE
JUST BE QUIET WHEN YOU'RE NOT
ONSTAGE
You can still make out my name
on a label thinned by time
WON'T YOU BE HUMILIATED
IF YOUR COSTUME STOPS FITTING
Death only lasts
until you play my tape again
Release my voice
give me one more chance
I'll never let the music stop

I WILL NOT SCREAM

BY JOHN PALISANO

Antonia's smelled like rain, pouring so hard it made a curtain across the huge, open windows. A couple sat near one of the windows, unfazed. Maria wished they were closer. Behind the bar, Antonia Camarera worked hard at polishing a glass. Maria looked at her watch. Eight o'clock. Showtime. She fretted E minor on her beloved red Córdoba guitar. She strummed and fingerpicked with her left hand using the rajeo technique she'd learned as a teenager.

Usually, the first chord and minor scale run would get everyone's attention, especially when the guitar was plugged into the house PA with a nice warm compressor and reverb added to the signal.

Did they wince? She looked at the two men by the window to be sure. As she began her first fandango, Maria shut her eyes and let the music envelop her. *It doesn't matter if there are only a few people here, I must always give everything.*

Her fingers flew easily. She didn't think in terms of notes or hand placement. The notes just came; she felt like an antenna channeling music from some faraway place. *This! This is why I do this. Surely, they are feeling it, too. Even if it's only two people, that connection will be enough.*

Going on her feelings, Maria played deeper. She felt her heart racing. The intensity overtook her until the song met its crescendo. She found the natural conclusion and strummed the final chord. Satisfied with her grand opening, Maria opened her eyes. The couple were at the register cashing out. One glared at her and took his hands away from his ears. As they left, Antonia looked at Maria, sighed, and nodded.

Maria's stomach clenched.

The rain sounded louder. The PA buzzed. Her cheeks got hot. She found the volume on the guitar and lowered it.

"No. No," Antonia said from the bar. "It's okay. It's empty because it's almost a hurricane in Key West. The music will tell people we are open and a warm place to hide."

Maria forced a smile. Steeled herself. "Yes. Of course."

She raised the volume just enough. "Good evening. My name is Maria Sonido." She went into a soleá. The slower, melancholy piece felt and sounded appropriate. Lowering her head, she kept focused on the music. The rain sounded like a shaker and provided a gentle rhythm. She glimpsed movement near the back of the restaurant, near the windows. Had someone heard the music from the street and stopped to listen? Someone watched her, she was sure.

Peering up, her gaze met that of not a person, but of a solitary cat. Its eyes were bright yellow and stood out against its dark, silky coat.

Hello there.

Standing on the large windowsill, the cat flicked its tail.

Maria finished the piece and smiled. "At least someone likes my song."

"Oh, don't be silly," Antonia said. "Everyone loves your songs. It's just a slow, stormy night. Don't worry."

"I don't bring in any customers," Maria said. "I drive them away."

"Nonsense. You provide the perfect ambiance."

"I only wish my music reached more people." At that, she looked at the cat. It perked up and she smiled and waved. "What do you think?" she asked.

The cat hopped down from the windowsill and made its way to her.

"See? El Gato approves." Antonia nodded and leaned on the bar.

Reaching down to pet its head, Maria smiled. "Si," she said.

* * *

Keeping her head down against the rain, Maria's right hand felt frozen from carrying her guitar case. Leaving Antonia's, Truman Avenue was nearly empty. She dreamt of being as notable a flamenco musician as Manolo Sanlúcar, Tomatito, Vicente Amigo, or even Paco de Lucia, but only a woman. *There are too many men. There is Charo and Shakira, of course, but the world needs more balance.*

She stepped into a deep puddle. "Shoot," she said, annoyed she hadn't even seen it. She'd worn her nice leather boots, too. Already wet on the outside, they were then soaked inside, too. They'd take a while to dry out and she still had several minutes to go until she reached her apartment. As soon as she looked up, she felt someone watching her again, and she was sure it was more than a stray cat. It was not good to be a lone woman on the streets in the dark, of course. The city was relatively safe, she knew, but there were always exceptions. "Don't be the exception," she whispered and hurried her steps, careful to look around. She didn't spot anyone or anything amiss, but she still felt chilled. Was it from the weather or from fear? *Both*, she decided. *It's a combination. Just get home.*

The rain came harder as she approached Angel Street, racing to get through the storm. Only a block away, from over her shoulder, she noticed a man in a trench coat and wide hat rush around the corner behind her. He was following her. He'd have a knife. A gun. Something to strangle her with. Probably had his eye on stealing her guitar. *No. It's all I have. It's my everything.* She tried to carry the guitar in front of her to protect it.

She walked as fast as she could without running, her heart racing. She clasped her keys inside her left pocket and worked them so one would stick out between her fingers, ready for action. *The Devil is out tonight. I can feel it. Lord protect me.*

Hurrying toward the arch that led up to her apartment's stairs, Maria looked over her shoulder again.

The figure was almost upon her. She tightened her jaw and turned her back to the dress shop's steel door. She was too far from her steps to make it, so she waited and grasped her keys tighter.

"Evening." The woman lifted her hat and smiled. She wore bright red lipstick and her long curly blonde hair cascaded around her face.

"Evening," Maria said, deflated, yet relieved. It wasn't a man, after all. Well, women can be killers, too, of course. But not tonight.

The woman hurried away, oblivious to Maria's fear.

She made it in record time to the arch, rushing under it to minimize standing under the curtain of rain pouring down. With fourteen steps to the top, Maria stopped halfway up. A familiar face stood on her doorstep, looking down with bright yellow eyes, dripping wet.

"You!" Maria said. "How brave of you to follow me home." She got up to the top step. "You are looking for a place to stay, aren't you?" She bent down and petted the cat's head. The cat lifted its chin and shut its eyes. "I don't even know if I can have a pet here." She sighed. "But I don't think one night would hurt, especially with the rain, and especially because you're the only fan of my music."

As soon as she opened the door, the cat bolted inside and went right for one of Maria's dining table chairs. She'd set up three white, circular café tables, doing her best to mimic the setting of one of her most cherished items—a photo of her parents on their honeymoon in Barcelona, framed on the small fireplace. Long gone, it was her way of keeping them alive.

She put the guitar case down against her daybed. Hanging her wet jacket and hat, she went to the kitchenette. "What do I have for you?" Peering at the cat, who was also wet, she smiled. In the fridge, she found some almond milk, poured some onto a cup plate, and put it down. "There you go." The cat jotted over and drank.

Maria opened the window near her bed which led onto her patio. Mist covered her face, so she shut it halfway. She was used to sleeping with her windows open so she could smell the ocean.

Once she finished changing into her sweats and wrapping her hair in a towel, she went back to the kitchen. The cat was almost done so she bent down to take the saucer. As soon as her hand got close, the cat scratched her.

She jumped back. "Ow!" The wound wasn't deep or long, but it stung. Cat scratches were always the worst, she remembered. "That's the thanks I get?" She huffed away. "Fine. Keep it."

The cat, for its part, kept working, lapping every last drop.

Maria washed the scratch in the kitchen sink for a moment, dried it with a napkin, then shut out the overhead lights. "I've got an early day. Goodnight, and no thanks for scratching me." Hurrying over to the bed, the light from the street was enough for her to make her way. She was asleep within minutes of her head hitting the pillow.

* * *

"How was your night?" Shyla busied herself grooming a small white terrier while Maria filled in the acquisition form. There was always something to do at Koconut Kennels.

"A new friend came home with me last night."

"Oh?"

"A stray cat. It showed up at Antonia's and followed me home."

"Are you going to adopt it?"

Maria held up her arm with the scratch. It stretched from her elbow to her wrist, its width the size of a straw. "Maybe if it doesn't do this anymore."

Shyla stopped clipping the white terrier and bent over to look at the scratch. A green discoloration surrounded the wound "A cat did that? It looks seriously infected. Did you clean it?"

"Not like I should have. I was tired." She noticed areas of swelling and dark discoloration.

"Put some ointment on it. Should be fine."

"Should be." Maria wasn't so sure. "I just wish I had more than a single cat coming to these shows. I'm pretty sure Antonia won't be able to keep me on for long."

"At least you have us," Shyla said. "There's no shortage of work here."

Maria looked at the stack of intake forms on the desk and sighed. "As much as I love you and all the animals, I just wish my music was my career."

Shyla turned back to the terrier. "Who wouldn't?"

* * *

During lunch, while Maria ate her salad and leafed through the Key West Citizen, her face flushed. Soon, her head burned with fever. All her joints were sore. She looked up at the sun but didn't forget the storm from the previous night. *Probably caught a bug,* she reasoned, *from walking home in it. That's all.*

The rest of the workday was harder and harder for her to make it through. She tried to make her rounds throughout the kennel but didn't last long before she tracked down Shyla. "I think I'm coming down with something. I'm trying to power through this but it's not working"

Shyla nodded. "You look like hell. Maybe it's that infection. Are you going to be okay getting home?"

"Sure."

"Take care of that arm and get some rest. If you feel the same in the morning, take the day off. Keep me posted."

"Will do."

* * *

By seven o'clock, Maria found herself sweating through her sheets as a high fever surged.

She looked at the picture of her parents and remembered something she'd almost forgotten her mother once said after some other girls at school picked on her for bringing her guitar to school. "The Devil gives you three voices, my child: one to speak. One to sing. And one to scream. Each has a price. Which is why it's good to say nothing and walk away."

"But Mamma...Agnes started it. She said my hands are too big."

"Too big? Or perfect for guitar?"

"Perfect to wring her boney bird neck with so I never have to hear her ratty voice again."

As angry as she'd been, Maria knew her mother was right. It wouldn't be long until she'd be done with middle school, done with Agnes, and the moment would pass. She wrote the poem down and kept it ever since, framing it and bringing it with her wherever she lived as a reminder.

> The Devil gives you three voices:
> One to speak
> One to sing
> And one to scream

I will let nothing make me scream.

She rolled over, trying to find a cool spot on her mattress, but it was futile. The cat watched her, unfazed by her predicament. "I suppose you're looking for dinner, right?"

It meowed.

Maria made herself get up. "Fine. Just let me rest after this."

She struggled through gathering the milk and saucer again and was mindful to stay clear after so as not to suffer another scratch. The first still ached and burned, even after she cleaned it again and applied the proper ointments. Even with the wound care, the bruise had darkened and spread. The bumps had turned a sickly greenish yellow. *Cat scratches are the worst.* Sometimes they stung her for weeks after.

She went back to bed, her head dizzy. Even with the cool night air coming in from the patio, she still felt overheated. Her eyes felt heavy, and she shut them. A few moments later, she felt the cat hop on the bed with her. "Well, hello," she said, her voice ragged and raw.

When she looked down, she saw the cat on its back, legs up, purring. "Oh, so now you're appreciative." She reached down and gave a cautious pet to the cat's belly. It didn't try scratching her. Instead, it remained docile. "Now that I've got a good look at your underside, I can name you. You look like a Lily to me. Yes. That fits. Lily. Welcome home."

* * *

Her head burning up, Maria fell into a deep, uncomfortable sleep. Even in her dreams, she felt persistent aches throughout her body. Her ears rang as if she'd just gotten out of a loud concert. The high pitch irritated her and scared her; present even in her dreams. What if she was losing her hearing? It'd mean the end of playing music. What else would be left?

The high pitch turned into a high A note. She recognized it––played on the 17th fret of the high E string. From there, the note cascaded down a step to the G, and then a melody formed. She heard every note clearly. Simple, but catchy.

She heard the chords. Just a basic A minor progression, but arpeggiated and accented to support the top melody.

It was too good. She thought about getting up and transcribing it.

No. Don't get up. This is just another of your lucid, fever dreams. It's probably not as good as you think it is and you need your rest.

The music persisted.

As did another piece.

If I don't get up now, I'm going to lose these.

She made to move, but something was on her stomach. She felt it breathing. Lily. Her new friend had come to keep her company.

A third piece played in her mind; it was impossible they came so fully formed. What to do?

She blinked several times. *Remember them*, she told herself. *Keep thinking of them over and over again. The Córdoba is at the foot of the bed.*

Okay. She pushed up. "Sorry, Lily." The cat hurried off as soon as its perch was unstable. Maria's head spun worse than earlier. Didn't matter. She had to push through. It would only take a few minutes to capture inspiration, then after she'd be able to go right back to sleep.

Sitting on the end of her bed, Lily watching and listening attentively, Maria grabbed her guitar, pressed record on her phone, and played. She shut her eyes. *Remember.* Her fingers found the notes without trying. It was as though some mystical force was playing through her. She didn't have to think, she just had to sit upright long enough to allow being puppeteered into playing the pieces.

It was a blur. She played for an hour as more music came to her effortlessly. The color and light of the music stopped abruptly as though someone pressed a giant, supernatural stop button. She dutifully put away her guitar and fell back on the bed.

Could it have been? An impossible instrumental hit? How many were there? Especially in an age of computerized music made with artificial voice tuning and predictive songwriting. She wondered if she had something like Herb Alpert's "A Taste of Honey" or Chuck Mangione's "Feels So Good," only from a Tocaora.

Lily hurried up and snuggled under her arm as she lay back down. "Aren't you a little good luck charm?" She laughed and Lily meowed the deepest, longest meow she'd ever heard. Realizing the recorder was still going, she reached over to the nightstand and turned it off. She felt better. Impossible, she knew, and likely just adrenaline, but she was back asleep within moments.

* * *

"At least it's not raining tonight," Maria said as she set up on Antonia's stage for the first time in nearly a week. "Maybe there will be some people tonight."

There were already three tables with guests dining and drinking.

"I hope I don't scare them away with my music again."

"I sure hope not," Antonia said. "The receipts have been brutal the past few weeks."

Maria knew what that was code for. She'd been in such positions many times before, playing for restaurants. When things trended down, cuts were made, and the first thing to go was usually live entertainment. Anything that could be seen as superfluous to running a place.

Just dive into the music. The next forty-five minutes are yours, regardless. Enjoy playing through the PA and hearing the acoustics of the room.

Maria lifted her guitar and put it on her thighs. It was like another part of her body. She wrapped her left hand around the neck. Her fingers found their positions without thinking and she strummed. The minor chord echoed throughout the restaurant. The high notes rang true while the lower strings were strong, reminding her of a piano.

The diners took notice. She had expected them to ignore her, as usual, but one fellow held his fork in the air with food on it and stared. What had changed? *Well, best not to think about it and just play. Probably something on TV over your head. Maybe another storm's coming and they're worried about the lightning.*

She wasn't sure what she was going to play at first, so Maria ran through some scales and basic core changes to warm up. Then she remembered she had an entire batch of new songs she could try. The only trick would be in trying to remember them. She had the recordings on her phone but couldn't stop to listen to them between songs to remind herself of how they went. That would be ridiculous, so she did her best to remember the melody of the first song she'd been gifted during her fever dream.

Maria was surprised the melody came without her trying. The notes rang true. She couldn't believe it was happening. Usually when she had a good night, nobody witnessed it. That night, Antonia's had a good number of people and they seemed primed and open to listening to her music.

On top of being able to play the new song, it was as if she didn't even have to look down at her hands to know where she was on the fretboard. It was though she were on auto pilot. She took the opportunity to look out at the people and take it all in. If people weren't smiling, they were paying attention at least. She didn't see anybody eating their food, but she did see them sipping their margaritas. She knew that would bode well for their bar tabs, which would make all the difference at the end of the night. She might be able to keep her gig after all.

The natural conclusion of the first song played out and she stopped. Before she had a chance to second-guess what was happening, she was met with a warm round of applause. How wonderful! Her dreams were coming true.

She took a deep breath and said, "thank you" into the guitar microphone. Antonia waved and gave a big thumbs up. She returned the gesture.

Now for the next song.

Again, she was able to recall the chords, structure, and melody. Expecting the first songs to have been a fluke, Maria didn't look up until halfway through, even though she didn't need to—it was as if the pieces were ones she'd played her entire life.

Confident she was doing well, far ire in the back, sitting peacefully on the same ledge where she'd first seen her, Lily watched intensely, her eyes glistening like fire in the night, her tail twitching. "This one's for you," Maria said. "My good luck charm." She always made it to the shows. After all, Lily came and went as she pleased. Maria left the window cracked just enough so Lily could go out onto apartment's balcony.

The patrons around Lily were still paying attention, although Maria was glad to see many had started to dive into their food. She also saw three people at the bar ordering second rounds. *What an amazing night.* And it continued for the rest of her first set. The place got so busy she barely had time to put her guitar down to grab water before it was time for the second set.

"Beautiful night," Antonia said. "The crowds love you and they keep growing."

"I don't believe it," Maria said.

"Enjoy it."

"Every second."

* * *

After the set concluded, a young lady approached Maria as she was putting her guitar in its case.

"I couldn't get the second song you played out of my head. I have to hear it again."

"That's so wonderful of you to say, but I don't have any recordings to sell at this time."

"Fair enough, she said. "I'll just have to come back and see you again next week."

"I think that sounds wonderful."

Maria went home happy. The tips were substantial. Antonio was thrilled. It was one of the best nights that Maria could remember.

Lily followed her home.

* * *

As soon as Maria had pulled the covers up to her neck, she felt a sticky feeling on her left fingertips. Blood. She hadn't even noticed while playing or coming home– the adrenaline had been so high. Before she could get out of bed, Lily hurried up and lapped the blood off one of her fingers. Maria recoiled. "Hey, don't do that. What's wrong with you?"

She shooed Lily off the bed, and went to her kitchen sink and ran her fingertips under the water for a few moments. She didn't want to cover them with Band-Aids. Doing so might make her calluses soften. *Wow. I haven't torn through my calluses and ages. It didn't even feel like I was playing hard.*

When she was curled up back and snug under her covers, she felt Lily jump on the foot of the bed and stare at her. "What? Are you just gonna stand there all night, or are you gonna come to sleep too?"

Lily curled up around her middle, walking in a circle three times before plopping down. Maria pet her head and Lily leaned into it, purring. The gentle sound soothed Maria and before she knew it, she was out cold, reliving the show in her dream.

* * *

After another successful show the following evening, and drawing even more patrons, Maria sat the bar, happy she'd resigned from Koconut Kennels, taking in compliments as she picked at her platter of flautas. She thought she had a moment to breath when it was broken by a very well put together woman. "Hi, Maria," she said. "I'm Rebecca Cleary. I work for Club Music."

Maria knew what that meant, and who she was. "Pleasure to meet you."

"Likewise," Rebecca said. "It's hard not to notice your crowd here. I love your music. This is the third time I've come."

Trying to calm herself and not give away her excitement, Maria mustered a quick *thank you* and put down her fork. She saw the tears and scars on her fingertips, courtesy of Lily. So, too, did Rebecca. She curled her fingers into a fist to hide them away. "Callouses," she said. "Been playing a lot." Maria hid them like she hid the scratch on her arm under long sleeves. It looked worse than ever. She told herself she'd have it looked at but didn't want to take the time.

Rebecca laughed. "I imagine." She looked at the food. "I don't want to interrupt your meal, but I did want to talk to you about coming to Club Music. I'm sure you'd do well."

"Wow," Maria said. "Really?"

"Really."

Was this how it happened? It was this easy? Had her break finally just walked in?

It had.

"No joke." Rebecca took out her phone. "Can I send you an offer? We can discuss more details in the morning."

"Yes." Maria was sure her voice was shaking. She gave Rebecca her info.

"Do you have any recordings?"

"Antonia has several she recorded right off the PA," she said. "I can get you a copy, no problem."

"That would be great. Please."

Antonia, who'd heard the entire conversation, nodded and smiled, thrilled. Rebecca left and Maria finished her food like there was no tomorrow.

* * *

Sleep was short-lived. Maria played the conversation with Rebecca over and over in her mind. *You deserve this. You've been waiting for this. It's your time.* She listened to sounds out on the street. Cars rolled by. People talked. Life! Even her street seemed to be renewed.

She woke from feeling tingling on her fingertips and found Lily chewing on them, her tongue slurping fresh blood.

"Hey!" Maria shot upright, pushing Lily from her bed. "Stop that. I told you not to do that." She felt flushed. Repulsed. "Blood is not breakfast."

Lily hopped back on the bed and again went for her fingers. "No!" Swatting as hard as she could, Maria knocked Lily to the floor. Lily looked at her, shocked, her ears folded back. When Maria got up, Lily hissed.

"How dare you?" Maria hurried to the front door. "Out with you. I've had enough. You can come back when you don't attack me. I gave you a home. What have you ever done for me? I don't feel safe with you. You have to go." Lily didn't move. Maria was enraged. She made to kick the cat, but Lily scooted out of the way, returning the gesture with a swat of her paw and nails. She missed Maria, but the intention was clear.

Maria grabbed her broom and swept it toward Lily. "This is not all right. I will not have you biting me and scratching me. I don't need you. Get out!"

Before the broom could touch Lily, she scooted out the front door. She cowered down and looked back, her belly close to the ground. For a moment, Maria felt bad, regretting her choice. Then she saw a trickle of blood on the broom handle—blood Lily had drawn while Maria had slept—and felt righteous. She slammed the door. She made sure the doors and windows leading to her balcony were shut, too. "I will not have such a beast," she said. "I won't." When she caught her breath, she shook her head. "And she made me scream, the little devil."

* * *

Soon, Maria's wounds went away, and so, too, did the crowds. The shows went from four nights, to three, then quickly back down to one. Rebecca ghosted Maria. There was no deal to be had. With no crowds came no gigs. Antonia just couldn't hold on to her any longer. And Shyla had already found a replacement for her at the kennel.

Maria went to her balcony. Once more, her street was dark and quiet. She looked at her fingertips, closed shut, misshapen, bulbous. *How can these ever work to make such music again?* Her heart was heavy. *It was Lily that gave me my luck. I should have never sent her away.*

She had an idea. Taking her guitar from its case, she decided she'd be bold.

Bringing it out onto the balcony, she sat at her café table and strummed. Ah. There it was. That beautiful ringing sound. The cord echoed off the opposite buildings and reverberated down the street. It was so loud, which is why she'd never dared try such a stunt before.

Going into a faster, pulsing progression, Maria felt lost and carried by the music again. She shut her eyes. *There it is. Yes.* She wasn't sure what the next day would bring, but she would figure it out. She felt people watching. Listening. A crowd on the street, enraptured like they were at Antonia's, she was sure.

A thumping like thunder came. A storm, she was certain. God was coming to show approval. It got louder, the crowd larger. She didn't want to look up and ruin the moment. *Just be in the moment. Play with everything. It's all you have. It's all you've ever done. It will fix this.*

The thunder became so loud it overtook the guitar. She concluded and opened her eyes. A bright blue hot-rodded Honda Civic had parked opposite her building and blared electronic music. It hadn't been thunder or God; it'd been partiers anxious to let everyone know they were there.

Something smashed against her balcony. A bottle. She didn't move, she was so shocked. "Hey lady? Why don't you go back inside with that crap?" someone yelled.

Maria's heart sank countless fathoms. How could someone be so cruel? Before they could throw anything else, she retreated, their laughs like hyaena's while she did.

As she made her way through the door, she caught her wrist on the end of a tuning peg, and the sharp, needle-like end of the string cut deeply. Her wrist gushed. Inside, she quickly wrapped it with a wash towel, having no bandages big enough on site.

"Where are you, Lily?" she asked. "I need you."

Knowing she had to clean it, she took her bottle of mescal from the top of the fridge. She looked away as she unwrapped the towel from her wrist and poured a big splash onto the wound. Burning pain made her scream. She wrapped the towel around her wrist again and squeezed as though it were a baseball bat. She had to apply pressure.

She eyed the mescal. *Why not?* she said and poured herself a shot.

One shot became two, which led to three, then four, until the mescal was all gone. Her head spinning, she retreated to her bed. *Good job. she scolded herself. Way to face your problems.* She looked at her guitar. "Tomorrow, I'm going to sell you. I'm sorry. It's too painful now." The thumping in her head matched the rhythm of the party car outside. She wished they'd go away.

Footsteps startled her. Lily. She'd come back. Staring at her, Lily stood at the foot of her bed. Maria went to pet her and noticed the bloodstained towel. She didn't have enough strength to reach Lily, but at least everything had gone quiet. "How'd you get in here? Everything's locked." She closed her eyes for a moment, so fatigued. "It must be your magic cat powers." Lily curled into a ball at her side and purred. "Do you forgive me?" Maria asked. "I hope you do. You'll always be my little good luck charm."

Maria remembered the crowds and the music and thought. maybe she 'd hang on to her guitar, after all. She recalled the feel of the frets and the sharp sting of the strings. Heard the notes flow as though they leaked from her fingertips.

* * *

"Hello? Maria?" Antonia knocked on the front door. She felt bad about having to let Maria go the prior weekend, but the business couldn't sustain her. She brought her a plate of food. "Are you in there?" She made to knock again, but as she did, the door opened a crack and Lily ran out. "Hey!" She watched the cat hurry down the stairs and go out into the street.

Inching the door open, Antonia had to cover her nose and mouth. The stench of rot was overwhelming. She spotted a big spot on Maria's bed. When she got closer, she saw that it must have been blood. Near the bed, she saw Maria's guitar.

She put the food plate down and went to the bathroom, the only other room in the studio. Maria wasn't there.

Antonia called out her name, but inside she sensed Maria was gone. But where?

* * *

Several days passed but Maria never turned up at any hospitals. Her body was never found. She'd left everything behind: her purse and wallet. Her phone. Her guitar. The detectives turned up nothing.

It was as though she just vanished.

The detectives took her statement and shot some photos even though there was no body, nor signs of foul play. The blood could have been from any number of non-fatal occurrences, they claimed. "She could have cut herself," one detective had posited. "Even a small nick can bleed a great deal. It's also contained to the bed."

Nodding, Antonia had agreed. Maybe Maria had just taken a last-minute siesta somewhere.

Soon, the landlord reclaimed the apartment. Antonia paid for it to be cleaned and for Maria's belongings to be put into storage.

* * *

"One day, you will come back. I know you will."

She wondered, though, what had become of Lily.

Antonia looked out at her patrons and at the small altar she'd made in an ofrenda shadowbox behind the bar. She'd had Maria's guitar mounted up nearby. In the box, she put some pictures of Maria she'd found at her apartment, along with the flowers, since dried, that were on her table. The centerpiece was a small poem she'd written.

> The Devil gives you three voices
> One to speak
> One to sing
> And one to scream

She wasn't sure what it meant. Maybe it was some lyrics? But there was something about it she loved, so into the ofrenda it went.

With one more thing to do to mark the first anniversary of her friend's disappearance, Antonia bent down and opened her tablet. She found one of the recordings of Maria playing and started it. Beautiful music played again throughout the restaurant. She shut her eyes and imagined Maria there, sitting on the small stage, strumming and playing her heart out. *I miss her so much. Where did she go?*

Antonia was lost in the music until she felt someone watching her. When she opened her eyes, she saw a familiar face staring at her from the bar.

"Lily?" she said. "Where have you been hiding? You must have heard the music playing. Do you miss your friend, too?"

Lily raised her head, and Antonia took it as a cue to pet her. No sooner had she reached to do so than the cat swatted, her nails scratching Antonia's forearm.

"Why you little..."

Lily rushed away, making it all the way to the back of the restaurant, where she stopped for a moment on the same window ledge from where she'd first arrived. "Do you know what you did?" Antonia shouted. Lily's tail twitched as she stared at Antonia from her spot on the windowsill.

Antonia shook her head. "You little demon."

She wrapped the scratch with a bar towel, reached down to the PAs volume, and turned it up a notch. *I'm not going to let this ruin this celebration.* Maria's music played on.

And then she sang along with Maria's music, her voice soft but sure.

> *"The Devil gives you three voices*
> *one to speak, one to sing, and one to scream with.*
> *But I will not cry out until I see my friend again.*
> *I will not."*

Maria lifted her scratched arm and the towel fell away. The scratch looked much worse than she'd expected. It went deep, already infected.

Behind the cat, Antonia saw rain. Another storm arrived.

Lily's tail twitched in time with Maria's music. She meowed three times, each getting stronger, the last as loud as a scream.

LOVELY PIANO OF RICH MAHOGANY

BY A.J. BARTHOLOMEW

A lovely piano of rich mahogany and ivory-keyed
Unknowingly bought with a sinister need
Play the piano, play
It'll force you to stay
And play and play and play until your fingers bleed.

A CONCERT IN MERZGAU

BY R.L. CLORE

Though most of my memories of Merzgau were fragmentary and vague, I clearly remember the smell of the train station on the day I left with my mother—coal smoke, oil, and the scent of musty linen from the woman boarding ahead of us. A similar smell greeted me as I stepped off the train at the same station over twenty years later. Only three others exited the car with me, and an immediate sense of abandonment settled in as I crossed under the shelter of the platform. The doors to the station were scaled in peeling red paint, the round windows cracked; in some places, slivers of glass were missing altogether. The interior fared no better: the black and white checkered tile was filthy, streaked in gray mud; the bench cushions in the lobby were the same shade of red as the doors, the upholstery as cracked as the windows; a chandelier bereft of its crystal swayed slightly overhead from the rumbling of the trains—the skeletal memory of something splendid. I made my way to the front doors to await the car I'd arranged for.

I'd read that a few factories still operated in Merzgau; a fact I found hard to believe upon leaving the station. An ashen wasteland lay before me, the skyline a dizzying zigzag of jagged, tumbling ruins. Chimneys stood in empty plots, entire walls leaned against their stronger brethren. I hurried out from beneath the blackened awning frame for fear it would come down on my head; turning round I saw the entire front of the station was scorched. Any hopes I'd entertained of gaining my bearings were dashed. It looked as if there had been no effort to rebuild. The street in front of the station was barely serviceable, messy blotches of tar and gravel the only attempts at repair. There were no memories for me to recover from these ruins.

A black car idled a few yards from the entrance. I walked to the driver's side window and knocked on the glass, my knuckles clearing little circles in the fine, gray coat that covered the vehicle.

"Mr. Vogl?" the driver asked, rolling down the window. He was a plump man, older, with dark circles under his eyes.

"Yes."

"Help you with your bag?"

"No, thank you. I'll hold onto it." The driver pulled a lever; the rear door opened and I took a seat, placing my bag beside me. The interior of the car appeared clean.

"Where you headed?"

I removed the letter from my coat pocket, smoothing the wrinkled paper on my lap, noticing my knuckles were smeared in gray.

"Twenty-two Beckmann's Row," I answered, reading from the envelope. The return address of Frederick Vogl, my father.

The driver took us away from the center of town. Though the buildings improved a bit as we went, there was still a noticeable lack of vegetation. I saw only small clumps of grass and low shrubs; both blade and leaf were painted in the same gray that all of Merzgau seemed awash in. It felt as though even nature had ceased her work the day after the fire—no cleansing rain allowed to wash away the ash.

"I've heard of the industry in Merzgau," I said. "The factories?"

"There's an old engine factory. Well, makes parts, at least. What you want to know?"

He had me stumped. I had no interest in engine parts, only wishing to confirm that there was some work in this place, as well as people to do it.

"You in the business?" he asked in response to my silence.

"No. I'm a musician," I answered.

"Oh? What do you play?"

"Piano."

"Ah, don't want to go mucking about in factories then. Need to keep all your digits!"

He chuckled a laugh full of phlegm that ended in a coughing fit. I was relieved when the car slowed in front of a low, gray building.

"This is it," the driver announced as he brought the car to a stop. I paid and thanked him, taking my bag and stepping out into the barren evening light of Merzgau. It appeared to be a one-story apartment building, a door and single window marking each residence. Letters differentiated the doors and I realized with a shot of panic that no such letter was listed on the envelope, just the street address. I loathed the idea of knocking on each door until I found my father, but it seemed I had no choice and there were only eight units, besides.

I began with A. My knock caused the door to swing inwards, revealing a room lost to darkness. There was a dry rustle of rat or draft somewhere in the shadows, but it was clear no one lived here. The light from the doorway revealed a broken table and a stained, sagging sofa against the back wall. Apartments B through E were just as empty. I began to worry. It seemed clear that no one lived here; the car had already left, and I could hardly expect to find a working telephone among the debris of these abandoned apartments to call for another.

The door to F swung gently open, a flickering glare of candlelight reflected on its surface.

"Zachary?" A brittle voice called from within. "Is that my boy, Zachary?"

I didn't answer immediately, but instead walked slowly toward the open door.

"Hello?" The voice called again.

"Yes, I'm here," I answered, stopping short of the threshold. I could see nothing beyond the door save the play of light on the wall inside.

"Come in. Don't be frightened."

A request that did nothing to calm me. It was regrettable enough that anyone lived in this dismal little building full of empty apartments—but that it should be my own father, alone—both pained me and caused me to wonder what sort of a man could tolerate such circumstances.

"Why should I be frightened?" I answered, trying to sound jovial. The answer was in his face as I crossed the threshold. He cowered behind the door, stooped over, looking up at me with one watery eye deeply recessed in a face ruined by scarred tissue. A wild tuft of gray hair stood out from the side of his head over his left ear. I tried to remain stoic as he closed the door behind me.

"My," he said, shuffling over to a little table to light a few more candles. "How tall and handsome you've become."

The increased light revealed the extent of his deformity. One eye was completely closed up beneath the webbed ridges of flesh, his mouth but a wet gash, oddly off kilter over a chin that melted into his neck. His nose was a nub on either side of which were two misshapen nostrils, like holes hastily poked by a crude instrument. It was clear walking was a challenge as he shuffled toward a brown easy chair. He gestured for me to sit on a wooden bench more suited to a park than a living room. I reflexively brushed the bench with my hand before I sat. My palm came away gray.

"I have a lot of explaining to do, of course, but I'll have to be quick. The show starts in just two hours and it will take at least thirty minutes to get there," he said.

"The show?" I asked.

"That's right."

This explained the final two lines of the letter that had brought me back to Merzgau: *Come see your father. I have something to show you.*

"I didn't know how to reach you before," he said. I moved my feet nervously, feeling grit between my soles and the wood floorboards. "I didn't know where you and your mother had gone to until someone showed me the announcements in the paper. There you were, listed among the students that had been admitted to Bildsen Music Academy. I was so proud."

"Well, it certainly took me long enough," I said, uncomfortable accepting his praise. "I'm nearly thirty."

"Oh," he waved his hand, disturbing the candle flame. "No matter about that. You have talent."

"Thank you." I stole a quick glance about the room. There were no furnishings besides the table, chair, and bench. The wallpaper was falling away along the top, its original color impossible to distinguish under the grime. A short, darkened hallway led to what I assumed were the bedroom and bathroom.

"I was caught in the fire," he continued. "Didn't know what was what for a long time, healing up in the hospital. By the time I walked out, everything was gone. The city, you, your mother. How is she?"

"Fine. She works as a typist, a government job. Very healthy for her age. I doubt she'll be retiring anytime soon."

"No, not your mother," a twitch at the corner of his mouth. Selfishly, I felt

R . L .   C L O R E

cheated. There was nothing in this face that could resemble even the faintest memory of my father. The hands curled up in the sleeves of his dirty shirt could scarcely hold a cup, much less hoist up a six-year-old boy. I wondered how he'd managed the letter. "She was always doing, couldn't slow her down. Even when she was pregnant with you, just kept at it."

"How have you been?" A preposterous question, but I could think of nothing else and wanted to drop the topic of my mother. I was guilty, caught between my father's wishes and my own to be truthful with her. He'd made it clear in his letter she was to know nothing of his survival nor my trip here. *I died in that fire as far as we're both concerned.*

"I'm managing. Harald takes me to eat every day, a show every now and then," he became quiet, scratching his bald head.

"I see."

"That's why you're here. A show, like I said."

"Not to see you?" I asked. I was too uncertain to feel angry or hurt; but the question had come out curt. I regretted it immediately.

"No. I had nothing to offer you, as a father. You can see that. I can't work. I sleep twelve hours a day. You'd both get sick, just at the sight of me. I thought you might not even believe it was me, had I been able to find you. But then, when I saw that you were a musician, I thought, 'Now, *now* I have something to offer him.' You can't hear anything like it anywhere else, Zachary. Not in the Opera House in the capital, not in the grand theater of Eisenhal. Nothing like it."

I was at a loss. I could muster no response. I stared stupidly at the dirty floor. My curiosity as a musician was piqued, despite it all.

It was another hour before Harald came to pick us up in his car. Words began to come naturally and I filled the time with stories about my and Mother's life in Bildsen. Talking was something of a struggle for him, the words he'd already spoken taking much out of him; so he just listened hungrily to my accounts of life outside of Merzgau, grunting with approval, even managing a chuckle or two. The impact of his grotesque appearance lessened with each moment that passed.

"I was working at the hospital, transporting patients," Harald explained as he drove. He was a burly, bearded man that I estimated to be in his fifties. "I carted Mr. Vogl around during his recovery, to the cafeteria, from his room to surgery."

"And you still take care of him."

"It's nothing. Just down to the diner, a film now and then."

"No, you deserve my thanks."

Through the clouded glass of the windshield, clumps of buildings emerged, a few street lights shone. I could see little of the landscape in this area of Merzgau as dark had fallen. Harald's concentration was set on avoiding the numerous potholes, no small task in the dark, and he offered no response to my gratitude.

A large sign loomed just ahead, lights along its edge, proclaiming the building beneath it to be the Merzgau Concert Hall in spray painted stencil letters, an ambitious name for the dilapidated old house. Nothing about it, save the sign and the number of cars parked in its yard, indicated that it was anything but a private residence. Men stood smoking on the porch, silhouettes crossed the windows, and warm light spilled out of the open door. It was, at least, the cheeriest sight I had seen thus far in the burnt out city.

Harald pulled into the yard, tires crunching in the gravel that had been spread over the spacious lawn.

"I'll be back in a couple of hours," he said. "Your father will need help out."

"You aren't coming with us?" I asked, surprised.

"It's not something I enjoy," he said quietly, turning away.

"Thank you for the ride."

"No bother."

I helped my father out of the back seat. He leaned heavily on my arm as he hoisted himself up and removed a cane from the car.

"I know it doesn't look like much," he said apologetically. "We've all moved to the edge of the city, a ring around a smoldering hole."

He said this with an odd tone of approval, as if it were precisely the way things ought to be. Approaching the porch slowly to accommodate my father's uncertain gait, I noticed all the men gathered at the entrance and tarrying in the yard suffered from scarring, in varying degrees, similar to my father's. Not one among them had escaped the fire unscathed. Fortunately, my father's condition had acclimated me, and I was able to move into the house without gawking. Still, it was overwhelming to be surrounded by them, each new face or bare limb a unique variation of ruined flesh.

The house had been gutted. The ground floor had been turned into one great room with only the supporting timbers remaining. A bar stood on the left side of the room, the floor littered in cigarette butts and peanut shells. The refuse mixed with the persistent grit that I had accepted as a fact of life in Merzgau. Even the men milling about, standing around little round tables, seemed ashen, their shirts and jackets streaked in gray, the soles of their shoes caked in mud. I checked my own and saw with dismay that I, too, had trucked it in. I felt a strong impulse to leave, that the mud had somehow marked me as resident.

My father had no interest in the bar or any of the men in the great room. He greeted no one, instead heading straight for the staircase that ran up the rear wall.

"The stage is upstairs," he informed me. "I want to get us good seats."

The second floor had been similarly repurposed into one L-shaped room. The stage had been built into the corner; red fabric hung on the wall behind it. Rows of mismatched chairs filled the rest of the space. Elegant ladder backs that would be perfectly at home in a fine dining room sat beside scarred barrel backs, rocking chairs and wheelchairs. We made our way to the front, settling for the second row as the first was already filled.

"There now," my father groaned as I helped him sit. "Can you see all right?"

"Yes, just fine." We said nothing further while we waited, the room filling slowly. The rest of the audience was equally silent, following some unspoken rule. The creak of chairs, labored breathing and muffled, wet coughs made me squirm in my chair, crossing and uncrossing my legs.

Finally, the room went dark. The lights didn't dim as in a proper theater, but simply went out. Large flood lights installed sloppily at the foot of the stage came on, trained on the backdrop, flooding it with harsh, white light. The drapery stirred, low voices spoke behind it. The dimensions of the room made this seem impossible, that anyone could fit in the little corner behind the stage, never mind the hospital bed that was trundled out, its wheels squeaking loudly in the silence. A head poked out from under the gray blanket that covered the bed: a shiny, pink scalp resting on a stack of pillows. The face of the bed's inhabitant tested the resolve I had built. The only feature remaining identifiable as human was a glistening wet hole, the edges of which were so scarred, the orifice resembled a sphincter rather than a mouth. Dark hollows sunk into the pale tissue below his brow were revealed by stark shadows cast by the stage lights. Two tubes snaked from his nostrils, attached to a cylindrical bellows so large that it required its own cart. It expanded and collapsed with mechanical regularity. More tubing ran from under the blanket, hooks below the breathing apparatus laden with swollen, transparent bags filled with cloudy fluids. My eyes followed the tubes to the bed, studied the contours of the man's body beneath the blanket. A single, limbless lump lay under the thin fabric.

For a moment, the man was alone on stage, the hiss of the machine filling the room. I looked over to my father, but his single eye was fixed ahead. Every man in the room sat rapt, waiting. Two stools were brought out by stagehands, along with a jointed metal stand; it brought to mind the type used in dentist offices, only a microphone was affixed to the end rather than a light—positioned alongside the bed, the microphone pointed towards the bedridden man's mouth.

A drummer emerged from behind the curtain, a shirtless behemoth of a man. A metal drum the size of a thirty-gallon trash can was harnessed in leather, the strap around the man's neck sinking into his fat. His left arm was the good one, though even it required a metal prosthetic, affixed to which was the thickest rute I'd ever seen, perhaps twenty rods bound together. His right arm lay against his large belly, withered and useless. He carefully took his stool, positioned stage left. He wore a simple mask of burlap, holes cut for his eyes and mouth.

The room filled with a hollow clang as rute met drum. There was a liquid undertone to it, a sloshing that must have emanated from whatever the barrel held. He began a martial tattoo that rode atop the lapping liquid, imbuing his rhythm with a languid flow. It was a hypnotic marriage of the metallic and organic, incongruously soothing and jarring.

From stage right emerged a spindly little man with bulging, rheumy eyes, a violin held tight against a chin that jutted out proudly, despite the scarred tissue that seemed determined to pull it in toward his concave chest. Long, gray strands of thin, brittle hair swayed with his first stroke, a plaintive, uneven note that seemed to rise up from my own stomach. It shrieked over the foundation laid by the drummer. I thought of scripture, something moving across the face of the deeps.

Finally, the man in the bed vocalized. It was an enormous exhalation, dry and crackling, yet airy. It stirred those drumming waters and gave lift to the tattered notes of the violin. There was nothing there of the human voice as I knew it. No words were formed, no melody unfolded, only this terrible breath of a living corpse, amplified by a method I couldn't ascertain.

There was composition, distinct changes in rhythm and flow, but no progression. The music, as it was, built up to nothing. It was as empty as days spent meandering through debris-littered streets, despondent as ash-filled rooms too barren to hold memories. Lurking between the drum, breath, and violin—a void, a negation of interfering sound, an aggressive silence. I reached out for my father's deformed hand.

I was lost for a time, my musical training wrestling with the sounds that engulfed me, every principle I'd learned ignored by the trio. Just as I'd accepted what I was hearing, allowing immersion to soothe away confusion, the violin became erratic, the drum uneven, the sigh a rasp—a sickly, jagged crescendo. It was a hollow chaos—each element turning away from one another into their own individual demise. The drummer struck his last dripping beat; the violin howled off over the horizon and the breath became a wheezing death rattle. The silence that followed was immense.

I thought the performance was over, both hoping for it to be so and wishing for it to continue—but the stage lights remained on, the musicians kept their positions. A stagehand emerged; first adjusting the breathing apparatus, then moving the microphone even closer to the vocalist's mouth. The bellows slowed its rhythm. No longer a dry gust of gritty wind, the vocalist's performance was a low, steady groan. Though a quick motion, I caught the violinist trading his bow for another. The drummer stood, hugging his instrument with one arm and swaying at the waist in a slow circle, his ruined arm dangling to and fro, each slosh from his drum matching the length of the vocalist's exhalation. The violinist took up his bow, inclined his head, and ground out the tone of a broken machine, a failing gear, metal against metal. All three came together in a kind of monotonous, overwhelming harmonic tone, a monk's chant for the end of things.

The stage lights went out, leaving us in total darkness. A hum rose from the men around me. It seemed every throat around me aided the trio. My father's hand, still in mine, managed a weak squeeze. Whether the gesture was meant to comfort me or encourage participation, I didn't know. I couldn't go that far. I already had the mud of Merzgau on my shoes and its music in my ears. That was enough.

Each tone, the length of which seemed lead by the vocalist, became longer, weaker, and lower. It was aural death vibrating in my chest. I felt alone among these men. I was spectator, intruder, and stranger.

As the last tone petered out and the house light snapped on, I found I couldn't look up, afraid I might meet someone's gaze. As the men around us rose to their feet, my father waited patiently beside me as I gathered myself.

"There now," he finally said. "Wasn't that something?"

I said nothing as I stood, but managed to muster the courage to look around me. Some of the men were still struggling to their feet, others were solemnly descending the staircase—but not all of the chairs were empty. Three men remained: one was slumped over, chin on chest, eyes closed; another gaped at the ceiling, eyes and mouth wide; the last was curled up in a wheelchair, knees to his chest, head nestled against the backrest.

"For some," my father said, "it sends them off. You see, you understand."

We carefully navigated the staircase, my father leaning on his cane and gripping my arm, I in a daze, the music whirling about in a newly formed cavity at my center, sloshing, pounding, screeching, and grinding. I managed to operate the phone at the bar, arranging for a car to take me away from 22 Beckmann's Row.

The ride back to the apartment was silent. Harald had the decency to refrain from asking how I'd liked the performance. When we arrived, the car I'd arranged for was already waiting for me. There was no late train; I'd have to take my chances with Merzgau's only hotel.

"Stay if you like, save yourself some money," my father offered. It was a matter of courtesy. We both knew there was no reason to lengthen my stay. We shook hands and I took a final look at him. In the headlights of the hired car I could see just how deep the gray grit of Merzgau had become embedded in him. It was in every crease of his scarred face, every fiber of his worn clothes; I thought I saw a film over his eyes as they seemed too dull in the electric light.

So I left him for a second time to that dead, ashen city, my departure stirring little in the way of emotion; I was too empty and too full of the music of Merzgau.

SING TO THE GOD OF SLUGS

BY MAXWELL I. GOLD

hated those awful tones and cursed melodies; bemoaned by the Cyber Gods, and sung by the inane, delusional, and sycophantic worshippers, who danced in the muck and majesty, drenched in bile beneath the shameless and monstrous God of Slugs. Chorused through star-webs of shadow and static, pulled along each painfully, dull-pizzicato step, they followed, trailing the neon pink sludge to the craven altar where songs were chanted in low hums.

Lazily perched atop the corpse of an ancient volcano, Or'Thrag, the God of Slugs, lingered in a palace of obsidian, rock, and heat. Contained in the fiery belly of a nameless mountain, the vinegar-like bitter smell of its fat, hulking body filled the crater, happily swallowing the prayer-songs and dirges which flowed upwards into the beady-eyed, slug god.

Below, I watched, afraid and hypnotized by the spectacle of a thousand men who waded through the tropical woods towards the summit.

Building towards a terrible crescendo in mad, desperate admiration, the ground itself cracked where—between the mud and water—billions of sparkling veligers, volcanic snails, and cephaloid horrors crawled from the depths; eager to hear the music and sing the songs in praise for the monster at the top of the dead mountain.

No longer could the mountain contain the gluttonous contentment of that vile god, who, stuffed with darksome adulation, spilled forth from the summit with unspeakable, symphonic ululations.

Blood raced down my ears, escaping from my broken skull as if there was some other refuge in the world away from the hideous, slug-god. It was too late for me, for the world even, when the song was sung, the last moments of my miserable life were painted in blood, mucus, and those awful, cursed melodies.

SONG OF THE GUQIN

BY FRANCES LU-PAI IPPOLITO

船夜援琴	*Evening Qin on a Boat*
鳥棲魚不動，夜月照江深。	Birds alight, fish don't move; the moon shines on a deep river.
身外都無事，舟中只有琴。	Outside the physical nothing matters; on our boat there is only *qin*.
七絃為益友，兩耳是知音。	Seven strings appease my friend; ears knowing music
心靜聲即淡，其間無古今。	Hearts tranquil; there is no past or present.
- 白居易 *(772-846)*	– Bai Juyi (Tang Dynasty 772-846)

一悲伤
(One, Anguish)

The house smelled of old music. Stale and sour, a scent that reminded Ji-Lan of acid-eaten sheet music secreted and forgotten in a library basement. She nudged the door open wider and the smell thickened like rice porridge as dust flecks whirled their escape into the fresh spring air.

It was like no one had been in the cottage for years. And perhaps no one had, Ji-Lan considered as she watched drops of rain catch the dust and sink them into the muddy red clay beneath her Dollar Store flip-flops.

She felt a tug on her sleeve and looked down at her son, Caleb.

"Mama? Where are we?" he asked, crinkling his nose at the smell.

Ji-Lan smiled and crouched to his height. He was nearly eight, small for his age, with serious, mirthless gray eyes and dark curls. She waved her arm at the half-opened door, a movement that sent her thick braid of black hair whipping across her shoulders.

"Are you ready to see our new home?"

Caleb tipped his head to peer past Ji-Lan's pale face and her tired brown eyes, to the doorway and a hall extending into the dim cottage.

He looked so much like Joon, especially the eyes, she thought as the rain dampened and weighed straight the curls on his forehead the way showers did to her husband's bangs.

Caleb shrugged. "I wanna go home."

"Honey, we're not going ba—"

"No! No!" The little boy broke in, shaking his head. "What if Baba can't find us? What if he doesn't know how to get here?"

"Caleb—"

"Baba came back! Why don't you believe me?"

Ji-Lan reached for Caleb to calm him but he moved away.

Her heart clenched.

"Caleb, please," she whispered as the rain grew heavier, chilling the air, making the boy shiver.

She didn't want to talk about Joon's suicide or his note.

Well, not really a note, Ji-Lan corrected herself. Notes, lines, staves, and annotations on a sheet of paper that Ji-Lan stuffed into her wallet without reading.

Ji-Lan pulled one of Caleb's hands into hers and rubbed his fingers. They were ice cold and so thin she could feel the dents of bones beneath his paper skin.

"Xiao Guai-Guai, I'll show you the waterfall after we unpack. I promise you'll like it here." Ji-Lan led him into the cottage.

* * *

The inside of the cottage was covered in superstition. Wispy banners stretched in scarlet panels on the walls, each emblazoned with gold-inked script that Ji-Lan recognized as the words for protection and peace. Smaller protective talismans were stamped across the surfaces of doors, cabinets, and drawers, littering the cottage in yellow and red joss paper.

Ji-Lan sniffed. This explained the smell of old paper. The house was strangely shrouded in seals and wards. But, perhaps, it wasn't strange for the visitor quarters of a Taoist temple to be covered in protections. When she'd visited more than twenty years ago, her class had stayed in downtown Portland, driving up the hill to the temple during the day. She'd seen the cottage behind the temple, but the priests hadn't taken the children in.

"Mama?" Caleb called from another room. Ji-Lan had left him on a couch with a blanket to warm up while she checked the kitchen.

Neither Caleb nor the blanket were on the couch when Ji-Lan returned to the living room.

She wiped her nose. The smell of decaying paper was strongest here. The windows sealed shut, curtainless, and plastered with paper fu. Sheets of joss paper taped or glued to the glass pane, one on top of another, like striations of limestone accumulated over decades.

"Caleb?" she called, wandering down the hall to a bedroom that was more a closet. A twin mattress laid directly on the wooden floor, bare except for a quilt the color of ash. It was the blanket she'd wrapped Caleb in. In the living room, the quilt had appeared a light blue. In the bedroom, it was gray, as if the room had siphoned the colors out.

Where'd he go? she wondered, examining the stitches between threadbare patches on the quilt. Too faded now for Ji-Lan to make out the pattern and images.

Ji-Lan dropped the blanket onto the mattress and headed into a shared bathroom that connected the two bedrooms. Dirty white tiles lined the bathroom floor in neat rows except where squares had broken off like missing teeth.

"Ugh," Ji-Lan mumbled when she noticed a puddle of brown water under the exposed sink pipes.

She had expected the cottage to be in better condition. Nestled on the grounds of the temple, it was advertised as a retreat for visitors in search of respite and peace. It had also been cheap. With the security deposit from their Los Angeles apartment, Ji-Lan had cobbled together two months' rent.

Enough time for me to find work and a better place. Though she knew the internet connection and phone service were spotty in the forest and it'd be difficult to advertise and teach virtual violin lessons. Even harder to find work with a symphony.

But none of that mattered.

Caleb was disappearing before her eyes. His waist half of what it was, his skin a wraith-like pallor.

Soon after Joon's suicide, he withdrew into himself, stopped playing with his friends at school, preferring to spend recess scribbling sharps and flats on his worksheets and notebook. When he got home, he immediately changed into pajamas and slipped into bed, humming a song she didn't know.

When Ji-Lan asked him what he was doing, his answer was always the same, "Waiting for Baba. He comes when I sleep."

The day her son refused to eat, Ji-Lan broke the apartment lease and packed up her ailing Mazda for the two-day drive north to Oregon. Of all places to go, Portland wasn't the most obvious. No family or other ties. But she had fond memories of lush autumn forests carpeted in moss and golden chanterelles, and a Taoist temple built on a secluded hill behind a silver waterfall. She'd especially loved that thunderous cascade, the deafening plunge of water that drowned all other noises.

"Caleb?" Ji-Lan called again as she entered the second bedroom. This room was slightly larger than the first, but also minimalist with a single mattress and no furniture or windows.

Where could he have gone? The cottage was no more than 900 square feet.

"Mommy!" Caleb's voice was muffled as if from a distance.

"Where are you?"

"Help me Mommy!"

Ji-Lan hurried to where Caleb's voice seemed to be coming out of the wall. There, she spotted a doorknob that had been painted with the same white as the bedroom. She twisted the knob, cracking the paint around the hinges of a door that blended into the walls.

"Caleb?"

"In here."

Ji-Lan opened the door and stepped in. The closet was deeper than it appeared and the wall did not extend the full length of the closet. She trailed her hands to the end of the wall and felt a space behind the edge. She took out her cellphone, switched on the flashlight, and peeked around the wall. There was another wall and Caleb sandwiched in the space between them. His thin arms wrapped around a wooden box, wider than his chest and taller than his head.

"Caleb, what on earth are you doing?"

"I can't move it," Caleb panted and leaned into the box with his chest, but only managed to rock it side-to-side.

Ji-Lan scowled. "You'll break it. Come out!"

"I want to see what's inside." Caleb hugged the box, lacing his fingers together and pressing his cheek against the wood. "Please? Please, Mommy?"

Ji-Lan hesitated. Caleb hadn't wanted anything other than his father in a long time. What harm would it be to bring out the box? It looked like a trunk. Probably empty or full of superstitious junk. Just like the rest of the house. Would anyone care? After all, someone had stuffed the trunk in the back of a closet and forgotten about it.

"Alright, Caleb," Ji-Lan said. "Come out. I can't reach it with you in there."

When Caleb scooted by her, she gripped the top of the trunk with one hand and pulled. The trunk rocked a sharp corner into her ribs. She tried again, digging in her fingernails. This close, she saw that the trunk looked more like a coffin. Sized for a child.

No, that was silly. It was a trunk. An old trunk. The talismans were getting to her.

The trunk was constructed from a hardwood, possibly redwood or mahogany. On the back, Ji-Lan found brass hinges, the middle one missing, leaving an imprint of its prior existence. On the frontside, three bent metal latches secured the trunk shut. Ji-Lan touched a latch, fingering the goose-pimpled rust.

Caleb tapped Ji-Lan's arm. "Mommy, I want to do it."

"It's heavy. We'll do it together," Ji-Lan said, crossing her legs to sit.

Caleb climbed into her lap. He felt and looked like a bird. Keen eyes, sharp nose. Body weightless and hollow-boned, ready to take off into the sky. Ji-Lan resisted the urge to trace his collarbone that jutted out under his T-shirt. Instead, she showed him how to wiggle the three latches free.

"Oh wow!" Caleb exclaimed as the trunk sighed open.

Inside laid a seven-stringed zither the color of midnight.

"Beautiful," Ji-Lan said as she lifted the black instrument out of the trunk. "Caleb, close the top."

"What is it?" Caleb asked as Ji-Lan set the instrument on the trunk.

"A guqin."

The guqin stretched nearly four feet from head to foot with scalloping long edges that tapered one end to the other. Seven strings were drawn across. By the outermost string, an inlay of mother-of-pearls dotted a constellation of finger positions marking white translucent stars in the shellac of night.

As a violinist, Ji-Lan knew that the guqin worked on similar principles—a soundbox formed of wooden planks glued together, strings vibrating, and sound holes.

"Can I play it?" Caleb asked, his fingertips reaching. He plucked a single string. A dulcet tone revibrated. Caleb grinned.

"We should put it back." Ji-Lan was uneasy. The instrument was obviously expensive and well-cared for. Stored; not forgotten. Ji-Lan hoped the jostling hadn't damaged it.

Caleb squirmed in her lap to meet her gaze. "I want to play more."

"I said no."

He frowned. "You always say 'I can't do this. Can't have that.' You did that to Baba too! Maybe that's why he was sad all the time. Maybe that's why he died!"

"Caleb!"

"It's true!" He crossed his arms and glared. His pinched expression full of disappointment and hurt. So much like Joon's on the night she told him he had failed them and that she was taking Caleb back to Minnesota.

Had Caleb heard them arguing? Did he blame her?

She stroked her son's cheek and touched her forehead to his.

"I know it's been hard. But—"

A loud knock came from the front door.

She sighed.

"Stay here," Ji-Lan said, scooting Caleb off her lap. "I'll see who that is."

二桥

(Two, Bridge)

Two men were at the cottage door. One young, mid-twenties with a boyish face round like the moon and a body burly and strong as a water buffalo's, barely fitting into his blue tunic. The other was naturally taller, but bent by age to stoop below the younger man. Both bowed low to Ji-Lan when she opened the door.

"Yes? Can I help you?" she asked.

"Hello Mrs. Yi. I am Zhang. The senior daoshi here at Gong Qing Temple and this is my assistant Tom," the older man said, still bowed.

His tone was soft, and measured, carrying a polite restraint that matched the way he was dressed. Tang shirt. Long cuffed sleeves. Black linen. Frog buttons queued from mandarin collar to waist. Pristine white pants, the fabric swaying like wisteria in the breeze. But when Zhang straightened from the bow, he teetered.

Tom immediately caught the priest's elbow. The younger man easily supported the frailer older one. In fact, he looked like he could lift Zhang with one muscular forearm and carry him up a mountain if needed.

"Thank you, child." Zhang patted Tom's arm. When he did, Ji-Lan noticed black leather gloves covering both of his hands.

Zhang chuckled. "Mrs. Yi, as you can see, the disciples fuss over me. I came to ask if you will join us at the temple? Guests are provided breakfast and dinner each day during their stay."

"Oh! I wasn't aware. And I haven't been able to buy groceries. We just arrived."

"Ah, then, you must come tonight. Mind you, our dinners are simple. Pickiness is not encouraged. We..."

Zhang stopped at the sound of a plucked string. The low bass note holding firm in the stillness of the forest for several beats like a bear's yawn after a winter's nap.

As the first note faded, another was plucked, followed by a flurry of more, some twanging into whines.

Glissando, Ji-Lan thought. Sliding a finger across a plucked string.

Caleb.

He had disobeyed her.

Daoshi Zhang turned to Tom, his face pale. "That sound...the guqin?"

Tom nodded, his expression tensing into a scowl.

Ji-Lan felt the need to explain. "We found a guqin and my son...well, you see... we meant no harm. If anything is broken...," she said, nervous. She hesitated to offer paying for the damage, worried at the cost of repair or replacement for an instrument like that.

Zhang waved away her concerns. "Please, may I meet your child?"

"Uh, oh, yes. Please come in."

Upon entering the cottage, the daoshi's gaze lingered on the windows blocked by paper fu to the talismans that dangled from the ceiling. He and his disciple shared a look.

"Mrs. Yi, it's been a while since I've visited this house. Too long. I neglected to remember the conditions before the Trustees rented it out," Zhang said, apologetic. "I've been ill, still recovering."

"It is...rustic," she said.

"Rustic," Zhang repeated the word slowly as they continued down the hall, past the dingy bathroom, to the bedroom.

The guqin continued to play when they reached the bedroom doorway. Taking a lively turn. The notes sprinted fast and syncopated from the young boy's fingers rushing across the strings.

Caleb sat at the guqin—brow furrowed, eyes closed, shoulders square. Both hands working the strings, ignoring his spectators.

"Finally," Zhang remarked in a whisper. "It's returned. Fifteen years." He pointed at the dark instrument against Caleb's chest.

"Yes," Tom answered, his eyes narrowed and his mouth tightened. The veins on his neck pulsed

"Excuse me? What returned?" Ji-Lan asked.

"Pardon me, my dear, I was rambling," Zhang said. "That guqin has a history of being difficult to play. Your son is very talented."

"Thank you. Caleb has always been musically inclined. A hazard of having two musical parents."

"Ah, do you play?"

"I teach violin."

"Your husband?"

"He plays many things." Ji-Lan said, before adding, "He *played* many instruments. He died last year."

"My sympathies, Mrs. Yi." Zhang gave her a gentle, fatherly look that stirred to life what Ji-Lan refused to feel. Something wild beat in her chest and keened in her ears. Ji-Lan pursed her lips together to cage the panic, focusing her gaze on Caleb, at his concentration and improvisation, at his fingertips pressing, stroking the strings.

"The white dots are hui, finger positions on the strings for harmonics," Zhang explained. "Your son is testing them. He plays by ear?"

Ji-Lan nodded. It was easier to talk music. She could manage that. "Caleb is teaching himself the places for each note. He is listening for octaves."

"A musical prodigy? He can't be more than five?"

"Eight. He's small for his age. He has not been well since my husband...that's why we came. For a change."

"A change? I see. He plays well, though I'm sorry to say that he must stop."

"Of course!" Ji-Lan made her way to Caleb. "Caleb, stop," she said softly in his ear.

He played on. Eyes shut.

"Caleb," she said. This time, squeezing his shoulder. His eyes opened, groggy. He gave Ji-Lan a confused look. Meanwhile, his fingers kept going. The left hand pressing and gliding on the strings while the right hand plucked.

"Mommy?"

Ji-Lan placed her palms on the back of his hands, stifling the music.

"We didn't mean to use it without permission," she told Zhang and Tom.

Zhang wore a curious, excited expression as he looked at Caleb, but chuckled. "You misunderstand." He thumped his belly. "Dinner is starting and temple meals are eaten punctually and in complete silence. Let's head that way."

* * *

"You found the guqin in this house?" Zhang asked, sitting on a folding chair in the living room.

They had returned after dinner with more disciples to "spruce up" the cottage. Tom directed a team of teenagers who wore faded blue tunics as uniforms. One pair was busy scrubbed joss paper off the windows. Another took measurements for curtains. And others fixed wiring for additional ceiling lights. As they worked, Tom rifled through a tool box, searching for a wrench to staunch the bathroom leak.

"Yes, in the closet," Ji-Lan answered. "Do you know who it belongs to?" Ji-Lan observed the efficiency of the disciples working in silence. Caleb sat on the floor nearby, watching the progress. One hand resting idly on the trunk where the guqin had been returned.

"I know who it *belonged* to," Zhang answered.

"Can you return it?" If her violin were missing, she'd desperately want it back.

"Ji-Lan, may I call you Ji-Lan?"

"Sure."

"Ji-Lan, grief is like this water," the priest swirled his glass in his gloved hand. "Many stages and forms. For some it is a monsoon that floods at the start and every season after. Reappearing on schedule." He took a mouthful and swallowed. "For others, it flows in a cycle—a never-ending river, self-sustaining and tame in its chosen path until it becomes a part of who we are. To the point we might forget its presence." Another sip.

"And for a few, it is alive and unpredictable. A pressure mounting behind a dam or a rip current snatching you to sea. Ready to drown you at the moment of release." He gave Ji-Lan a meaningful look.

"I am sorry if I am blunt." He turned his attention to the disciples.

She did not mind the man's forwardness. It was only that she was already drowning. Gulping for air. Her lungs filled with tears she refused to cry. The anger kept her afloat. She'd be alright if she held onto the rage.

"It's okay," she said after a time.

"The guqin belonged to my brother. It went missing when he died fifteen years ago."

"I'm sorry."

"We were very close. He was murdered, stolen from us." Zhang's face hardened, the gloved hand strained against the glass. "The guqin is a symbol of that thievery."

"Can I have it?" Caleb had been listening.

"Shh, Caleb! That's not—"

Zhang raised a hand to stop Ji-Lan. He pulled himself up shakily. Tom rushed over to help the man hobble to Caleb.

Zhang peered into the boy's eyes. "What would you give me in return? What is your offer?"

"Offer?" the boy asked.

Ji-Lan was uncomfortable. They had no money to buy the guqin and a gift was inappropriate.

"Open the case." Caleb did as Zhang asked, his eyes glowing as soon as he saw the instrument. His fingers immediately seeking the strings like they were reeled in.

Zhang watched the boy carefully. "This guqin is very special. You can't expect me to part with it for nothing."

Caleb wrung his hands together. "Anything! I would give anything! There's nothing I want more."

"Daoshi..." Ji-Lan sensed Caleb's desperation and was anxious. A mother's heart wished to give her child everything.

Zhang looked at Ji-Lan and winked. Then he turned his attention back to the boy and stroked his chin as if mulling. "Will you care for the instrument? Never leave it behind? Treat it as if it were a part of you?"

Caleb nodded, eagerly.

"Will you promise to practice every day at the temple? Learn from Tom?"

Surprise passed over Tom's face, but he remained quiet.

"Yes! I promise!"

"Well then, I suppose we have a deal." Zhang held out his hand and the boy shook it. "It's yours."

Caleb smiled wide and brought his face close to the row of hui.

"You're mine," he whispered to the guqin.

"Daoshi, that's very kind of you, but let me pay, maybe over the next few months. I haven't found work."

"My brother was all the family I had. And my hands..." Zhang took off a glove to show the scarred, torn skin and gnarled digits. "...will never play again. You're doing me a kindness." His hand tried to fist, but the joints had fused in places, limiting the motion.

"I'm sorry, I didn't know."

"An accident at the temple, the same day my brother died. If you truly feel like you must pay me, let it be a favor I ask in the future."

"Please, please, mommy?" Caleb pleaded.

Ji-Lan sighed, but nodded.

三 漸強
(Three, Crescendo)

Three weeks in, Ji-Lan did not know how the daily practices were going because Caleb never played for her. However, he had improved in health. He'd gained weight, even grown an inch, and a rosy color was returning to his cheeks.

Most of all, he had stopped asking for his father.

Instead, he talked about the guqin.

"Mommy, did you know my qin is made from Paulownia wood? And the hui from ivory and bone."

"Hmm?" Ji-Lan answered, exhausted after an afternoon and evening of violin classes. Daoshi Zhang and Tom had connected her to a music school across the river in Washington state. The pay was generous. But the rush hour commute was two hours unless she decided to return after dinner.

Luckily, the temple provided Caleb with meals, and for the evenings she ran late, Daoshi Zhang and Tom offered to let Caleb stay overnight with them. At first Ji-Lan hesitated to rely on strangers, but the daoshi insisted.

In fact, the temple insisted on providing practically everything. After the disciples left the first night, Ji-Lan realized she did not pack shampoo or soap. And then, as if summoned by unspoken needs, a basket of toiletries appeared at her door the next morning. The same happened with clothing, coats, food, or household supplies. When she asked about the costs, Daoshi Zhang said, "Taoist hospitality."

Despite the generosity, she missed Caleb and the privacy of a little family. Disciples came at random times into the cottage. But at least Caleb was eating, growing stronger. And she needed to work more than anything else if they were to find a permanent living situation.

"Mommy? Are you listening?" Caleb asked.

"Hmm? What honey?"

"Daoshi Zhang says there were master players who played well enough to please gods and demons. That is what I want. I want to be,..what was the word Daoshi used? Oh, 'legendary.'"

"Uh huh, that would be wonderful honey. Are you going to play for me?" Ji-Lan wandered from the living room to the bathroom, searching for a clean blouse to wear for work the next day. Caleb trailed behind her.

"Not yet. Daoshi Zhang says I need more practice."

She headed into Caleb's room and saw the guqin on his bed. Tom had built wooden frames for their mattresses. Caleb's was a tall frame and the guqin perched several feet above the floor.

"Caleb, don't leave your guqin on the bed. It could fall off and break."

She sighed, but stopped her search to examine the instrument. It was beautiful and sleek. More impressive after it had been cleaned and polished. Ji-Lan touched a string. Smooth as silk, taut. Ji-Lan looked closer. The strings were black, like her own hair. If she were honest, it looked a bit like hair.

"Don't touch it!" Caleb stood in the doorway, shaking in fury.

"Caleb, I was just looking at it."

"You're not allowed," he growled. "Only me."

"What kind of nonsense is that? Who told you that?"

"It's not for you. A qin has only one master. You'll ruin it."

"Caleb Yi! Don't use that tone with me!"

"Mine," he hissed and stomped into the room, inserting himself between Ji-

Lan and the qin. He slapped her hand off the strings.

Ji-Lan stared at her stinging hand in shock. Silently, she counted backwards from twenty.

Do not act in anger. Keep control.

She took another breath. "Caleb, put the qin away. Bedtime. No stories tonight."

She shut the door behind her.

* * *

Ji-Lan sat in a small office waiting for her next student who was running late. Her gaze shifted to the music stand and she felt her spine stiffen straight into the practiced posture of a musician. Her back ached more than it used to, but it was her hand that she cradled as if it had been sliced apart.

What was she going to do? Punish him? Take away the guqin? Keep him from taking lessons?

Ji-Lan shook her head.

He was finally better. Eating. Sleeping. Talking. And hadn't he lost enough already? But...something was not right. She felt it. Caleb was changing.

She missed Joon. So much. She missed raising their child together. She missed his reassurances that they would be fine. She missed his optimism. She missed his idealistic certainty.

She taught other people's children how to play, but she never had the patience to teach her own child. Joon had been the patient one. He showed Caleb how to hold his first bow. How to pull it across the strings. And then find the notes with his fingertips.

The note.

Ji-Lan sniffed and wiped her tears on her blouse sleeves.

Joon.

Why?

Ji-Lan reached into her pocket and took out the crumpled sheet, her hand shaking.

She opened the sheet and placed it on the music stand.

He'd named it "Harmony."

Ji-Lan picked up her violin. Rested her chin. Straightened her back, raised the bow. And played.

* * *

"Why do I have to miss lessons today?" Caleb whined from his booster in the car.

"Because we're spending time together."

"Can I bring the qin?"

"Absolutely not. String instruments hate salt and sand." Ji-Lan started the car down the winding dirt road to town.

"I wonder why they're here," Ji-Lan slowed the car as it approached three disciples standing in the road. She rolled down her window. "Hi there, we're heading to the coast for a couple of days."

The boys glanced at Ji-Lan but remained in the road, partly blocking the way.

"Boys, can you get out of the road?"

The three teenagers didn't move out of the road, but one leaned to whisper in another's ear.

"I won't go," Caleb tugged the door handle, but it was child-locked. "I want to stay with my qin. It needs me."

Ji-Lan looked at her son in the rear-view mirror. "You have been practicing every day for weeks. And, I still haven't heard you play. Besides, I took the days off. We can get ice cream, set up our beach tent, and build sandcastles." She maneuvered the Mazda around the group of boys who stared at her silently. It was odd the way their three heads turned as if one, following the car. She shivered. The temple had been great, no doubt. But she was ready to put Caleb back in school with normal kids.

She reached the bottom of the hill and turned onto the main highway for the coast.

"Caleb, I thought that today, we could talk about Baba. I know you wanted to tell me about his songs and I was always busy. I'm here now."

"I don't care about Baba! I only need my qin." Caleb yanked on the handle, rattling it loudly, surprising Ji-Lan with his strength. Unable to open the door, he unlatched his belt and pushed the button to roll down the window.

Ji-Lan immediately locked the windows from her driver's panel. "Caleb! Get back in your seat!"

"A gentleman never leaves his qin...never leaves...never...never. I promised. Never leave," Caleb babbled to himself, banging his fist on the window, and then slid out of the mirror's sight.

Ji-Lan craned her neck to see the backseat, nearly swerving off the road. Caleb was in the foot space. Twisted. Eyes rolled back, the whites showing, foam bubbling out of his mouth. Black veins smoked and slithered like maggots under his skin.

"Oh my god! Caleb!" She switched lanes. Cut off a pick-up truck. Skidded into the shoulder. Parked, she climbed into the backseat and gathered Caleb into her arms. His body was sturdier with the weight gain, but cold and clammy. Ji-Lan wept as she dialed 9-1-1.

* * *

"Trauma seizures are common. Caleb has been through a lot of stress with your husband's passing," the pediatrician spoke softly in the ER as Caleb napped on the hospital bed behind the closed curtain.

Ji-Lan wiped her eyes. "We've seen specialists in Los Angeles. Nothing helped. I thought...I thought moving here would give us a new start."

"You said he's been eating? Is happier?"

"He is happiest when he has his instrument."

"Then I would say he's making progress."

"But..."

"But?"

"He won't play for me. I don't know what he does at the temple. He says he's practicing while I'm working." She swallowed a sob. "I don't know what to do."

"The temple?" the doctor looked puzzled.

"On top of the hill, by the waterfall."

"I didn't know anyone went up there anymore. There was an accident many years ago, before I moved here."

"Accident?"

The doctor shook her head. "Don't know the specifics. In any case, I'm glad it brings Caleb comfort." The doctor glanced at the clock. "Mrs. Yi, it's late You've both been through a lot. Take your son home and get some rest." The doctor circled her name on the discharge papers. "Call me in the morning if anything changes."

* * *

When Ji-Lan pulled into the driveway, the headlights lit the faces of two men waiting at the cottage door.

Daoshi Zhang and Tom.

What do they want? she thought, irritated. These unannounced visits were exhausting. ohe constant interruptions. The strange way they knew her schedule, habits, and needs.

No more.

In the morning, she'd find a place closer to work. Start over. Really start over this time.

Ji-Lan edged the car slowly down the band of dirt that made up the driveway. The car jounced over the exposed root of an ancient cedar tree. Ji-Lan peeked at the rearview mirror. Caleb's head lolled to the side, but the jostling didn't wake him. She'd have to carry him in. But first, she'd send the men away.

"Caleb and I are too tired for a visit this evening. We're going straight to bed," Ji-Lan said as she got out.

Zhang ignored Ji-Lan, talking directly to Tom. "Get the child."

Ji-Lan froze. What did Zhang mean "get the child"? Was Tom helping her carry Caleb into the house?

"Thank you Daoshi, but I can manage. He's already asleep. But we'll come by the temple in the morning."

Neither man acknowledged what she'd said. Instead, Tom strode past Ji-Lan and took ahold of the backdoor handle.

Ji-Lan slid in front of Tom, blocking the door with her body. "I said I can take him in." She crossed her arms. "I was going to wait until the morning, but I guess I'll tell you now. We'll be moving next month. I need to be closer to work."

Tom let go of the handle and looked at Zhang. Zhang gave him a slight nod. It was a small, barely perceptible movement but it made Ji-Lan's skin tingle with a cold sweat. These men. How much did she know about them? Or this place?

The calm quiet of the temple's location suddenly felt isolated and suffocating.

The cascade of the waterfall in the distance had been soothing at night, but it would be hard to hear cries for help over the roaring water. In fact, she couldn't even use her phone with the poor cell reception.

Her breath hitched. Dread twisted in the pit of her stomach.

Tom's eyes met hers and when his didn't leave her face, she knew he was taking Caleb from her.

"Stay away!" She pushed against the man, doing little to move him. Tom grabbed her arm and shoved her out of the way.

He opened the car door and lifted the sleeping boy.

Ji-Lan scrambled up. She caught Tom's arm, prying to release Caleb from his grip.

"Put him down!"

"It's too late," Zhang said. "Caleb needs the qin. The bond is too strong. They cannot be separated for long. There's nothing you can do."

"Let him go! You're crazy! You're all crazy!" Ji-Lan grabbed for Caleb's dangling foot, but Tom shifted the child's body and kicked the back of Ji-Lan's legs. He was strong and precise. Practiced. Her knees buckled and she landed face down on the driveway.

It hurt to breathe. But she forced herself to inhale, gaining a mouthful of dirt and hair. She gagged and pushed up to standing, using the side of the car for support.

She lunged after Tom again.

Tom watched her come and slipped aside with Caleb still clutched in his arms. She fell forward, propelled by her own shaky momentum, and tripped over the tree root. This time, Tom followed to where she'd landed. He raised his foot to stomp and she covered her face and chest with her arms.

She heard the bone in her forearm crack before the pain stole her breath. She gasped, wide-eyed, as the searing agony blossomed and her vision blurred.

"Leave her," Zhang instructed. "Take him to the temple. Once he plays, the qin will do the rest. We must be ready."

Through the pain, Ji-Lan listened rather than saw the men walk away, the crunching of gravel beneath their feet, the footsteps dwindling to the silence of the starless evening. Soon all she heard was her heartbeat and her raspy, labored breath. She braced her arm and crawled slowly to a sitting position, crying out from the ache and swelling.

The pain was unbearable, but more than that was a numbing tingling sensation that swarmed like bees in her skin. She pulled the phone from her pocket. Raised it to the sky.

No reception.

Stumbling, she stood and walked. One breath. One step.

Caleb.

She passed by the waterfall. Cascading water roared and rumbled. Cold sprayed her face. She was close. The stone steps of the temple entrance were a few feet from the waterfall. She climbed the steps, counting each one to counter the shock, and held the railing with her good arm for support.

Luckily, the temple doors were never shut. But once inside, Ji-Lan didn't know where to go. The temple was ancient with serpentine hallways above and below ground. That much she remembered from her childhood tour. They could have taken him anywhere inside.

Except.

Music.

Plucked strings.

The guqin.

A song that raced and glided faster than any song she'd heard before. The rapidity and volume of notes played by someone with incredibly quick hands. Too fast for her to catch the melody before it ballooned into another, a melding cacophony. A train of snakes gorging on each other's tails.

She followed the music to a set of speakers in the temple office. Two curved monitors showed rows of surveillance video squares. Some of temple meeting spaces. Most of the cottage. The outside. The inside. Kitchen. Living room. Bedrooms. Bathroom. Shower. Ji-Lan shuddered.

They had been watching the whole time.

But the horror of that revelation was nothing. All that could wait.

Caleb.

On the screen, he was in the dining room, sitting atop a table, the qin in his lap. His hands floating above the strings. His eyes open, unblinking.

Ji-Lan staggered in the direction of the dining room. Stumbling down a sloped corridor that descended to the lower floor. Below the electric lamps, monastic paintings and poetry lined the walls. The light shined on the drawn faces of grinning monks, who stared at Ji-Lan with eyes that trailed after her like shadows. She pressed on, ignoring the burning and freezing sensations in her swelling arm.

When she reached the dining room, she saw Caleb crossed-legged on top of the table. The qin balanced on his lap. His fingers darting furiously, blurring in their speed. His face in a trance. His eyes blood red. A group of twenty or so teenage disciples stood in front of him, their faces tilted upwards to the ceiling. Their bodies swaying like river reeds.

"Caleb!" Ji-Lan shouted and started to run for him. But someone grabbed her by the neck and waist. Someone incredibly strong. Tom.

She flailed, restricted by the unrelenting grasp and the broken bone. Tom held on, dragging her to the back of the dining room where Zhang sat and watched Caleb.

"Why are you doing this? Let us go!" Ji-Lan sobbed. "He's just a little boy."

"Ji-Lan, he is more than a little boy. Much more," Zhang said.

Caleb's hands no longer plucking the strings. The music continued. The strings playing on their own. The song's tempo becoming too fast to follow.

"What have you done!?"

Zhang laughed. "Me? No, my dear child. I did nothing. The qin chose Caleb. It was done before I even met you. I am only ending what should have ended fifteen years ago. It will never stop. Look for yourself," he said.

With both hands, Caleb returned to strumming and the strings flew off the pegs, lengthened and stretched through the room. The far ends of the black strings aimed for each of the disciples' heads. Some strings flew fast with the twang of a bow. Those penetrated quick into the foreheads and out the back of heads. Grisly pink and grey hung on the lines like tassels. Others hit foreheads, but took time to fully break through. Those strings twisted like drills, burrowing into the young men, whose lithe bodies shuddered with each turn as if they wanted to escape but could not will their limbs to move.

Caleb lifted into the air with the qin, levitating a few feet above the table.

He was like a child flying a kite. Doing exactly what Ji-Lan had wanted to do with him at the coast. Except his kites were made of children, tethered and wielded by the qin in the sky, the instrument connected to the earth by cords running through the brains of teenage boys.

The music switched into something softer, muted. Caleb's expression changed to satisfaction and pleasure. His face glowed. His cheeks flushed. A smile. Round bulges traveling down his throat as if he were swallowing.

"It feeds the emptiness in your son. His grief, like yours, is bottomless. Like my brother's was. Like mine," Zhang said, bitterly. "The difference is that you and I are not hungry. We are full of rage."

"I don't understand." Ji-Lan fell to her knees, suddenly weak. "What's happening to him?"

"Something that has happened time and time again whenever it appears. The instrument sucks the life out of others. It will consume everything. Everyone. But not this time. I won't fail again." Zhang took out a six-inch stone dagger from the folds of his robe. Engraved on the patinaed handle were vines encircling the ankles of dancing women. "I severed the strings and destroyed the qin once." He shook his head. "At the cost of my hands. I could not save my brother once the bond was broken. The qin stole his remaining life force to save itself and disappeared."

Zhang unsheathed the dagger, the stone sheath falling onto the floor. "I know better now. The master must die first, but at the moment of the strongest connection, when the musician has mastered the instrument as your son now has."

"No!" Ji-Lan jumped up. "I won't let you."

Tom restrained her.

Zhang gave her a pitying look. "You can't save him. I wish it were me instead. Unfortunately, Ji-Lan, this is the favor I must ask of you. To let me end the cycle."

"Daoshi, I will go," Tom said.

"No, this is my burden. Keep her quiet."

Tom nodded and covered Ji-Lan's mouth.

Zhang crept against the wall, clutching the dagger to his chest. He took small steps toward the center of the room. Closing in on the table where Caleb feasted on the energy of the other children. He approached from the rear, getting within inches of Caleb's back. As he drew the dagger to strike, Ji-Lan stomped hard on Tom's foot. He released her mouth and she screamed, "Caleb! Watch out!"

The boy's eyes opened and he looked at his mother with a glimmer of recognition. And then turned his head around like an owl's, the skin at his neck twisting into accordion folds. He smirked at Zhang and opened his mouth.

Loose, unanchored strings launched like ravens out of his throat, spearing the old man through flesh and bones.

"Daoshi!" Tom ran to catch Zhang as he fell, but a string coiled around his leg and held him in place as others crept up his legs, his waist, his chest, and head, cocooning him in a spider's purse.

The song grew louder. The qin strings needled into Caleb's fingertips. The scent of blood mixing with the percussive primal strumming of notes. Running toward Caleb, Ji-Lan covered her ears and yelled, "Caleb! Stop! It's Mommy!"

But the music played on. Cacophonous strumming, no meter, no pattern. All noise.

"Caleb!"

She reached the table where he sat, strings fused to his fingertips, vibrating in song, snaking through the room to find the bodies of boys who were still alive. To siphon their remaining life. The rest of the guqin hovered high above Caleb, safe from the splatters of blood.

Ji-Lan got within a step of Caleb, before the strings stopped her.

They wrapped a black vine around her. She fell to her knees at his feet.

"Caleb," she coughed. "Caleb." She yanked at the strings strangling her throat. But they were silky and sharp—hard to hold, biting into her fingers.

"Please Caleb," she gasped. "Don't you remember? Mommy? Baba?" Her vision was blurring, red spots appearing.

She was going to die, she knew it. But if she was, she wanted Caleb to know.

"I love you. He loved you too," she whispered and began to hum the bars of Joon's last song, "Harmony." She closed her eyes as the strings tightened, but kept humming. Her voice growing quieter and quieter as she fell sideways.

The noise died down.

A new melody emerged from the guqin.

It was Joon's song, playing back.

Matching the notes Ji-Lan hummed.

At first, the strings notes were hesitant, unsure, but growing louder, strident. Full and synchronized .

The strings released Ji-Lan.

"Caleb?" Ji-Lan said, crawling to her son. Meeting his eyes.

Caleb looked at his mother and dropped his hands. The string tension eased, letting the teenage boys fall to the ground. The room became suddenly quiet, except for the gurgles of Zhang and the dying disciples.

She saw that Caleb's fingers quivered, wanting to flex the attached strings. And she also saw the blade of the dagger on the table next to him.

"Mommy, I can't. I can't control it." He showed her his hands—palms raw and bleeding. The nails worn to the skin. The qin's strings splintered deep into fingertips.

"It's okay, baby. I'll help you. Concentrate on me. Look at me."

She climbed on the table, sat next to Caleb, careful to tuck the knife under her thigh.

"I used to know his songs," he said, tears streaming down his face. "I don't remember them anymore. Mommy? Why can't I remember Baba?"

"Shh, you're tired."

"I want to go home."

"Okay, Baby. I promise I'll take you home. But I need you to do something for me." Ji-Lan's left hand gripped the knife tight.

"Okay, Mommy."

"Close your eyes."

He nodded and shut his eyes.

She raised the knife and sliced.

Straight across Caleb's fingertips where the strings meet flesh, cutting into his skin and bone.

He collapsed into her arms; blood poured from his hands onto hers.

She picked him up, bracing his back in her working arm and biting her lip when the pain in her broken one reached new heights as she rolled his legs into the crook of her elbow. He was limp and cold, but breathing.

The dagger dropped onto the floor as she stood, but she hardly heard it over the guqin's screech. The melody gone. Strings flailed in the air like headless serpents. And the instrument plummeted from where it hovered, crashing onto the ground. Splitting open.

She ran, never looking back, with her son in her arms through the temple hallways back out into the darkest night.

四尾声
(Four, Coda)

The wood planks of the broken guqin were stacked and bound together by the silk threads. After the failed exorcism, the remaining Taoist disciple, Thomas Wang, of Gong Qing Temple, had, according to the report, taken the instrument pieces to the west wing of DaoGuan Temple, which specialized in cleansing and releasing resentful energy.

Upon receipt, the resident senior priest entrusted a junior priest to expedite the processing of the guqin given the potency of the instrument. They determined very quickly that the guqin was stained with the grief of the original master. Grief was always the worst, the senior priest told his juniors. People grieved with stamina and mourned from their bones—a deep, penetrating pain and suffering that grew roots outside of themselves and into whatever they touched, like a tenacious weed.

A junior priest was instructed to dispel the problematic guqin as soon as possible, but unfortunately, he was new to the temple.

How can this place be such a maze? he wondered, thinking that it was unjust for Master Liu to have assigned him to this freezing, wet temple in Seattle and send Chow to the one in California. He'd spent over an hour walking through the many underground corridors and stone stairways to no avail.

After another long hallway and short staircase past a dry food storage room, the young priest decided that he had found the cleansing room.

His stomach growled in agreement and though there was dust on all the tables and chairs, and a layer over the rest of furniture, the priest tossed the bundle of broken planks and silk strings onto a chair. He cleaned himself off, patted down his yellow robe, and rubbed his hands together, anticipating what might be for dinner that night.

He turned and headed out of the room.

In the lonely quiet, the guqin strings unwound from the planks. A single pluck acquiring a chorus, interrupted only by the sounds of shifting, reassembling wood.

SCORDATURA

BY JESS LANDRY

O dette starts the morning with Bach's "Cello Suite No.1 in G major." There's something about the way the notes pour from her cello as the bow glides across the strings that makes her feel at home. The strings reverberate against the bow, fine strands of a Siberian stallion's hair, the cold metal vibrating on the cello's fingerboard, loose then tight, tight then loose. The way the acoustics in her empty room make her feel like she's happily suffocating, every stroke of the bow pressing tighter against her chest. The bass notes, the high notes, all filling the air around her, squeezing, pressing, against the tall windows in her room. The music holds firm against the stark, white walls, off her cream-coloured bedsheets, perfectly made and ready to welcome her this evening. They bounce off the ceiling, off the herringbone-patterned hardwood floor, against the small door that leads to her bathroom. The notes reverberate through her: in her dark hair and into her pale skin. They seep into her brown eyes, the fabric of her grey dress, through her fingertips and into her bones. She knows this Suite, and many others, like the sun knows to rise.

The bow curves around the C string, a smooth bass note, closing out the Suite. The sun shines in through her bedroom window. Their apartment sits on a corner block of Rue Saint-Martin, another apartment sitting adjacent with her own.

People walk the cobblestone streets four stories down, some passing the shops hand-in-hand, others hurrying along by themselves. Odette sets her cello down and props open the window, the room immediately filling with the aroma of fresh bread from the nearby bakery. An orange tabby sits across the way in the adjacent apartment, sunning itself, eyes squinted and content. One floor up, a man in a red shirt sits on his small cast-iron balcony, tiny cup and newspaper in hand.

Odette looks down and imagines what the cobblestone must feel like under bare toes. Would it be cold? It must be—though the sun's bright, it's no match for the tight Paris streets.

A tap echoes through the apartment followed by two more in quick succession. Odette takes in one last smell of baking yeast and picks up her bow, ready to spend the rest of her day practicing her debut concerto, the one she'll be playing in four days' time at the Palais Grenier—Kodály's "Sonata in B minor," all three movements.

The impossible piece.

* * *

Odette starts the morning with Bach's "Cello Suite No. 1 in G major." Outside, people traverse down the cobblestone street. The cat across the way is in his normal spot, waiting for the sun to peak.

The cold cello strings fit snuggly into the self-made grooves of her fingers like a second home. Down-bow, up-bow, she lets her elbow guide the stroke, the music spilling from her like blood pouring from an open wound. She wonders how that would feel, the blood gushing from her body, out of her shell and pooling at her feet. Would it seep through the herringbone floor? Would it collect in the unused space between her room and the room below, her mother's study? Would it pool and pool until it seeped through the intricate fleur de lis-patterned ceiling, breaking through the plaster and onto her mother, covering her in a sea of red?

She's playing faster now, an eighth above tempo. Her brain tells her to slow but her hands refuse to listen. The cat across the way lays on his open perch, the man in the red shirt sipping his drink and reading the paper one floor above him. Odette longs to be that cat, to be free and lazy, to watch the world without a purpose.

Three quick taps sound from the room below—a stick to the floorboards—a first warning to keep tempo.

The cat's owners don't keep him confined. They open a window for him every morning. He wears a collar with a small bell, and sometimes, when Odette's window is open, she hears it ringing. The cat likely eats the freshest of foods; his dish is probably made of crystal. And at night, he sleeps with his contented look in the centre of his master's bed, nestled comfortably between sheets and legs.

Faster now, almost double tempo.

Three more taps, now with more force, more echo—her second warning.

To be that cat, Odette would walk off that ledge and onto the street below. If she jumped from the window, her fingers wouldn't ache, her hips wouldn't burn; she wouldn't have to practice anymore. Her room wouldn't echo with the taps from below, her mother banging on the floor. If she jumped, she'd be free. She'd feel the coolness of the cobblestone, the rush of air flying past her as the ground quickly approached. Would others rush to her aid, or would they leave her on the street, her body mangled, her bones broken, her blood spilling through the cracks forming a tiny red stream? At least her last breath would be one of fresh bread.

The cat's looking at her now, a contented gaze no longer, but wide, alert eyes as though it's spotted its prey. They lock on one another, nothing but 20 meters and the sweet French air between them. He's sitting up, watching her, watching her play, watching her hands and fingers flail wildly across the cello, his tail swishing wildly.

The cat takes a step towards her, toward the edge of the windowsill, as though an invisible bridge connects them, as though he wants to step off.

With a final stroke, Odette finishes the song, short of breath, cold with sweat. She rests her bow as one loud *thud* shakes the floor underneath her. Her third and final warning, one that always comes too late.

"Odette!" A muffled cry rings out from below.

She turns to the cat. The animal gives his head a shake and takes a step back, into the safety of his home, into the warmth of the sun.

* * *

It's mid-day but the fireplace in her mother's room is lit, the room filled with the smell of burning wood. Her mother sits in front of the flames, her wheelchair parked within a few feet. The back of her head is always the first thing Odette sees. The woman's hair is pulled back in a tight bun, the wear of years staining its colour: a once vibrant dark brown, similar to Odette's, now a muddy, bland tangle. She tries her best to hide the off colour, the wrinkles, the crow's feet, by pulling her hair back as tight as it can go. Her face—*is that how I'm going to look when I'm older?*—is one of corners and angles. Sunken cheeks and hollow eye sockets rest on a paper-thin neck. Underneath the usual black smock is a body diseased.

She's wrapped her shoulders in her favourite fur blanket—one that was given to her while on the Canadian leg of her last tour before the muscular dystrophy overtook her—pulling it closer to her neck as Odette approaches, her thin, wiry fingers attempting to clutch at the fabric.

Next to her, her silver cane, the one she had custom-made before the disease rendered her wheelchair-bound, when she was hopeful that she'd still have the use of her legs. Its wooden stem grows from thicker to thinner with a silver-plated head shaped like that of a crow's, its beak acting as a place to rest her thumb. Both the stick end and the crow's head have found Odette's skin at some point in time; both ends likely to find it again shortly.

"Sit," her mother says without looking up from the fire, her eyes fixated on the flames. Odette sits on the floor, warming her through her clothes. She hears the shuffle of anxious feet from the next room—the hired help scrambling away to avoid her mother's wrath, leaving Odette to take the brunt.

Mother and daughter sit in silence for a moment, like they always do. The flame's reflection in the crow's head catches Odette's eye, and she quickly loses herself in its world, a space of reflections, of opposites.

In the reflected world, are the roles reversed? Would Odette be the former ingénue, a musical prodigy, bound to a wheelchair after the unavoidable disease took hold of her? Would her mother be the child, the up-and-comer with her debut at the Palais Garnier in a few days' time; the daughter of *the* Marguerite Wagner, world-renowned cellist and socialite? Would she stare emptily into the flames, her mind wandering much as it did now, waiting to inflict pain both spoken and forced upon her flesh and blood? Would she sit in this very spot night in, night out listening to her daughter play in the room above her, catching her off moments with the thwack of her cane to the floor, her muscles and joints throbbing?

"I expect you know why I called you."

Odette nods, her gaze shifting from the reflection to the floor.

"Then I also expect you know what to do."

What if once, just this one time, Odette didn't do it? What if she ran, ran to the window, and let herself fall onto the cobblestone street below?

"Odette."

Her mother's voice is stiff, hoarse, much like the woman's final weeks playing the instrument she loved. Before her body betrayed her, betrayed her with an infliction of which there is no cure, just a life of memories of what once was. But Marguerite was a fighter. Even as her fingers curled and her knees bowed, even as her muscle mass slowly wasted away, she pushed. She pushed until her body screamed back, confining her to this chair, this prison on wheels.

This would not be Odette's life.

Not now.

Not ever.

"Odette!"

The woman slams her cane onto the floor, the vibrations shaking through to Odette's bones, rocking her back into the present. She feels her mother's frigid gaze upon her.

Odette stands and moves towards the fireplace, the sound of the crackling logs relieving the room of an otherwise dead silence. She places her hands on the mantle, one devoid of any family photos, any mementos of a childhood. It's lined only with trophies, medals, keys to cities—material things that mean nothing except to that of the beholder. A mantle filled of ghosts, remnants of another life.

Odette brings one hand to the back of her neck and pulls at the button holding up her dress. The fire burns at her face, drying her tears before they can drip from her eyes. The dress falls from her slender frame. She shivers as the air touches her exposed skin.

"You should know better by now," her mother says, picking up her cane with atrophied hands.

* * *

Odette runs to her room, the fabric of her dress clinging to her back. She's never touched fire but the feeling drumming through her body has to be close to it.

Careful not to let her back scrape anything, she sits straight and grabs her bow and cello—this instrument, this piece of wood, the reason for all her suffering. Below, her mother bangs the crow-headed cane against the floor; Odette sees a glimpse of her flesh still dangling from its sharp beak.

With her bow up, Odette begins the third movement of Kodály's "Sonata in B minor," the venom inside her fueling every stroke. She would be better off jumping out the window, that would ruin her mother's grand plans, plans that were originally meant for Marguerite in her prime, now up to Odette to follow through. *The heir to the cellist's throne*, she'd once read in a London newspaper. The article painted her mother in pastels and sunshine, and talked about how her diagnosis was a complete surprise, how it changed for life for the worse.

"But then I turned to my child, my sweet Odette," the article had quoted. *"And I knew that my legacy would live on through this little girl."*

She looks out the window and sees the cat across the way, sunning itself in the late afternoon blaze.

Odette's suffocating; the heat, her rage, the music pushing against the flimsy windowpane.

Her eyes fixate on the cat.

She wills it to look at her, to feel her what she feels.

As Odette plucks at the strings, the cat opens its eyes.

He turns his head towards her.

The tempo increases, the bow movements more frantic than earlier, an organized chaos. Everything Odette has, everything she is, pours from her wounds, from her hands, from her instrument.

The animal sits up, much as it had earlier, its eyes on Odette.

Go on.

She wills it through the music. The cat takes a step toward the edge of the windowsill.

Do it. For the both of us.

She reaches the finale. She's on another plane now, another world where notes and music meld together, where rage and heat are two in the same. Mother's below, waiting for this moment, waiting for her to take one false step, polishing her crow for another round.

Go on.

His little orange paw takes a step.

Go.

Odette's fingers glide over the strings, pressing and relenting in the exact moments where they need to.

As her bow crosses the final note, as she gasps for air, the cat pitches himself off the ledge.

Odette rushes to the window, nearly knocking over her cello. She throws open the pane and sticks her head out.

Four storeys down, the body of the orange tabby cat lies, its little chest heaving, its hind legs twisted in a way that shouldn't be, its eyes looking up to the sky, to Odette.

He takes his last breath on the cobblestone street as people step over him, not a soul stopping to help.

* * *

Odette picks at her plate: coq au vin with scalloped potatoes and herb-garnished peas, a lukewarm glass of water. Wilhelmina, their chef, clinks away in the kitchen, washing and scrubbing dishes. Marguerite eats steadily, ferociously, as though the woman hasn't eaten in days. The fork sits awkwardly in her curled fingers. Her shoulders sit tight, her arms as pointed as her face, her contorted body hidden under a black shawl. With a full mouth, she still manages to speak, spitting criticisms at Odette: her tempo, the pressure of her bow on the strings.

"If I can hear it from one floor below, imagine how it will sound at the Palais."

Under the dim dining room lights, Odette can only see the cat, its mangled body, the possessed look in its eyes as it stepped off the ledge.

Did I make him do that?

She pushes a pea absent-mindedly across her plate, her mother's voice tuning in and out.

"I expect you not to make a fool of me. Do you know how many influential people will be there? Do you know how long it took me to achieve what you've done in so little time? You should be grateful."

Impossible. In her eighteen years of life, never once has Odette willed anyone to do anything. If she had any will, she would've kept it all for herself and certainly not forced a cat to jump to its death.

If she had any will, it would've been her twisted on the cobblestone.

"Odette."

But what if she had? What if there was something inside her that made the animal end its life? Did it feel her heartache through the windowpane? Did it look into her eyes and understand what she wanted it to do, because she wanted to do it herself?

"Odette!"

Her mother smacks her crow's head against the wooden table, rattling the dishes, shaking the water in her glass.

"Have you heard a word I said?"

Their eyes meet, and in them, Odette sees a faint reflection of herself.

"Yes," says Odette.

"Well then, enlighten me." Her mother stares her down, peeling back Odette's flesh and exposing her for the liar she is. Marguerite taps the crow's head against the table, Odette looks down at her half-eaten dinner. She says nothing.

"Upstairs. Now. Kodály's 'Sonata in B minor.'"

Odette thinks to protest. Today could be the day she stands up for herself, when no spills from her lips and she stands tall, taller than her mother ever was, when she walks out the door and never looks back.

She gets up and pauses for a moment, parting her lips, the word at the back of her throat. Mother stares at her, her eyes as black as coal in the room's shadows. Marguerite doesn't take her eyes from Odette, not even as the girl makes her way to the staircase.

"Odette," her mother says, letting her name linger.

Odette stops on the second step, her mother's eyes seem to soften, or they appear to from where she's standing. Marguerite sets the cane down, resting it against the table. Wilhelmina's footsteps creak in the kitchen, the cling and clang from the dishes barely audible.

A wicked smirk spreads across Marguerite's pointed face as she says, "Play it until your fingers bleed."

* * *

Bach's "Cello Suite No.1 in G minor," that's how Odette starts her day. She looks out her closed window across the way to where the cat used to lay. Now that window's closed, the blinds drawn. She had checked last night before going to bed to see if the cat's body was still on the cobblestone but it was gone. No doubt the owners had found him.

First position, bow up.

Slack the wrists, and go.

Music spills from Odette's body. She closes her eyes, imagining the room filling with music in a physical form, like a warm down blanket covering every inch, every nook. Wrapping itself around her, over her tiny, pale frame; engulfing her dark hair, turning it white, as white as her room, as white as snow.

Could I do it again?

Her eyes open, the bow nearly skipping over the strings. She corrects her posture while still playing, her mind now wandering to the place she didn't want it to go.

Fighting her thoughts, she turns her head to the window. The man in the red shirt one floor up from the cat's apartment is sitting on his small balcony, the paper in his hands. He looks to be her mother's age, though his face seems warm.

Try.

She pushes the ridiculous thought from her mind, telling herself that she had nothing to do with the cat's actions, that she, Odette Wagner, daughter of Marguerite Wagner, famed cellist, on the brink of succeeding her mother in talent, soon to have her debut concert at the Palais Garnier in Paris, did not force any creature from its window perch. No, she did not have the ability to sentence creatures to their death.

But what if I do?

She finishes the Suite, letting her bow rest. Then, she takes a breath and brings her bow back to first position.

Second finger on B and first finger on A, second finger to F sharp, first to E. The impossible Sonata reverberates through the room. Her gaze sets on the man, sipping from his tiny cup.

The music pours, her fingers burning. The man doesn't budge.

She's stretching her fingers as far as they can spread, her whole body pushing against the instrument using as much of it to play as her hands. It resounds through

SCORDATURA

her chest and into her veins.

The man doesn't look up from his paper.

Suddenly her back spasms, causing her bow to jump. The pain burns and flares through her skin, her muscles, she even feels it in her teeth. She stops, pulling at the fabric of her light dress that presses against her open wounds from yesterday.

Below, the crow's head bangs once against the floor.

Odette fixes her posture and resumes from the last bar. The crow's head bangs twice more like a muffled metronome. It echoes inside her as she gets near the end, the most intense part of the Sonata.

Tap tap tap.

It's all she can hear, drowning out the sound of her own instrument.

It's all she can feel, the crow's beak tearing at her flesh.

With everything in her, she plays the final note, her bow leaving the strings smoothly. She takes a deep breath and looks out the window.

Her eyes meet those of the man in the red shirt as he steps off his balcony.

Odette runs to her bedroom window, opening it to the sound of screams and the smell of fresh bread. He's twisted like the cat, except this time, people have noticed. People step back as blood spills from his body out onto the cobblestone, slipping between the gaps and trickling down with the slope of the street. His body twisted one way, his face the other looking up at Odette with a hollow stare.

But what if I could?

* * *

The Palais Garnier is full, every crushed velvet seat, every curtain-draped loge, all 1,979 seats filled with faces Odette's never seen before. A massive chandelier dangles high above the crowd, sparkling in the theatre's glow. Her cello sits centre stage in its holder, the bow hanging beside it. The stage lights run over its polished maple surface, illuminating it as though it were on fire. Marguerite Wagner's famed cello, passed down to her daughter. The heirloom of all heirlooms. If only it meant that much to Odette.

She peeks from behind the stage curtains, her hands steady and calm as the faces take no notice of her. They're not here for Odette, not really. They're here for Marguerite Wagner, they're here to appease her, a hurricane of a woman.

252

The auditorium doors open and in comes Marguerite, commanding the attention of all as she's pushed to her seat. Her black dress squeezes her frail frame, her eyes looking forward, not acknowledging the admirers who applaud as she takes her place at the front of the Palais.

The clapping subsides and the lights dim.

With a deep breath in, Odette walks onto the stage.

She takes her seat and cradles her cello into her arms, heavy against her body.

She brings the bow to first position, and begins.

Kodály's "Sonata in B minor," the first movement. The acoustics of the theatre travel the music far and wide, into the ears of every soul in the building. She focuses on the strings as she brings the bow fore and aft, crescendo to decrescendo. The music flows from the Stradivarius just as it did at home, in her room with the window overlooking the street, the cat, the man in the red shirt. The window from where she looked down at the cobblestone, wanting to press her bare feet against them, avoiding the spots where dried blood stuck in between. Would the stone feel like the crow's head? Would the first touch be cold, then would they turn into fire?

She looks up from the strings, her eyes washing over a sea of unknowns. These faces, round and thin, man and woman, these eyes staring up at her, no feelings behind them.

Her eyes find her mother's, the woman with the distorted body in the front row, her eyes burning holes into her, the crow's head in her palm. Under the dim lights, her face looks more angular than ever, a Picasso made flesh. A tight mouth with tight eyes with skin beginning to sag at the jowls. Is that what Odette had to look forward to in her elder years? To look as though she hated every moment, no matter how big or small? Is that what she was to become?

She finishes the first movement and the audience applauds plainly, except for Marguerite.

Odette exhales and begins the second movement. The faces in the crowd stifle yawns and fidget in their seats the more she plays; her mother turns her head to the crowd and notices the same as her daughter. The grip on the crow's head tightens.

At the end of the second movement, Odette cracks her fingers and raises her bow. She begins the third, the final piece of the impossible Sonata.

The faces in the crowd perk up as though she's just screamed from the top of her lungs.

Their bodies stop fidgeting and become taut to attention.

This is what they've been waiting for.

This is what reminds them most of Marguerite.

This is the last Sonata she played.

Odette's fingers pluck and press, her hand rises and lowers, her body pushes against the wooden body of the cello, using it as much as her other extremities. Music pours from her fingertips, her eyes, her mouth. It fills the space in the auditorium, seeping into the skin of the faces watching her.

Odette's fingers feel as though they're moving faster than they've ever moved before; her bow movements making their own breeze.

What happens after this? she wonders. Am I destined to live a life identical to Marguerite? To have others fawning over me, travelling the world to play in famous theatres night after night, to drink myself to sleep and eventually wind up pregnant. To have a child out of spite? To have an incurable disease take over my body? To force everything I wanted for myself upon my child?

Marguerite smirks, her grip relaxing on the crow's head, her thumb flicking at its sharp beak keeping in time with the Sonata.

Odette looks to the crowd; she has their attention now. She has the very breaths in their chests. Their bulging necks that spill from their too-tight lapels, their stomachs that push and scream against the tight fabric of their one size too small dresses. Their eyes hollow, their blank minds. She has them mesmerized. She has them under her influence.

This is not the life I want.

She turns to her mother, the bow stroke faster than Marguerite could ever do. For the first time in her life, Odette sees a look on the woman's face that she's never seen before.

It's not love—it'll never be love.

It's not pride.

It's not contempt or hatred or jealousy.

It's fear.

The raw wounds on Odette's back swell, her chest heaves and heats up, like she could melt the stage from her presence alone. She pulls the cello closer until her and instrument are two in the same—two beings turned to one, one heart, one mind.

She plucks the strings as her mother starts to cough, bringing her hand to her mouth.

Odette plucks again, her gaze not leaving her mother's. The woman coughs and coughs, her other hand on her chest, dropping the crow's head to the cold ground. Other faces in the audience turn to Marguerite, a distraction from the performance.

Odette brings the bow over the strings hard, nearly snapping them. Marguerite pitches forward in her chair, falling next to the crow. The faces stand up around her, rushing to the woman's aid, but Odette keeps on, the music is her and she is the music. She watches as burly men with patches of facial hair reach Marguerite, but before they can help her, they clutch their chests or their heads or their stomachs or their necks. They fall beside her, near her, in the aisles.

The women in the audience stand and scream as bodies from the upper balconies throw themselves off the ledges and onto the patrons below. Men step over women rushing for the theatre doors, people shove one another in a chance to save themselves.

But it's no use.

Odette plucks the strings and the theatre goers fall like dominoes.

As she nears the final bars of the Sonata, she looks at her mother, a woman tangled on the floor, her curled fingers searching for something. She lifts her head with her frail neck and their eyes meet. Blood spills from Marguerite's nose, ears, and eyes, like tears of pride Odette never knew.

Odette brings her bow over the final note, a deep bass tone, holding it for as long as she can.

The blood pours from Marguerite's mouth like a river, the darkness in her eyes fading away into nothingness.

Odette props her cello and stands to the crowd, a sea of silent bodies, their faces looking anywhere but hers.

* * *

Odette starts the morning with Bach's "Cello Suite No. 1 in G major." The way the notes pour from her cello as she brings the bow across, as the strings reverberate against the Siberian horsehairs, the cold metal vibrating under her fingers, loose then tight, tight then loose. The way the acoustics in her empty room make her feel like she's suffocating, every stroke of the bow pressing tighter against her chest. The bass notes, the high notes, all filling the air around her, squeezing, pressing, against the open window in her room.

A quick few swipes and she finishes the Suite, the pressure in her chest releasing. She sits back in her chair. Outside her window, the sounds from the street below rise along with the smell of fresh bread.

Smiling, she sets her cello aside and grabs some loose change from the mantle in her room.

Odette steps outside, barefoot, onto the cobblestone street, the cool stone refreshing on such a warm summer's day.

THE MEN WHO PLAY

BY JANGAR TOKPA

There is a man who looms,
and when he plays it moves you.
Pulls you by your spine.
Pulls you by the ends of your hair.

Spirits enter through the slits in your teeth
and your body synthesizes
creating indents in your bones.
Bending your soul.
Sending you over.

There is a man who peels my fingers back.
Teaches me to snap necks
and roll heads,
place them on stones.
My heart beats at unsteady rhythms
and veins vaporize in the midst of music.

He plays a pulverizing kind of punk.
The type that causes vessels to pulsate.
Where hands slam organs,
when men play chords
and screams tear through your core.
You enter reprise and resurgence
and there are men who play.

WHALESONG

BY SHANNON BRADY

I didn't start out wanting to go to space. When I was a kid, I thought I was going to delve down into the ocean.

My much older cousins lived on the coast—wow, sunlight, imagine that—and they would take me out sailing on their boats. So many memories, most of which probably involved little me bumbling around the deck thinking I was helping, but mostly just getting in the way. But there's only one that lingers in perfect clarity even now.

Wake up, Levi. Do you want to see a whale?

Space mostly smells metallic—even more now, it seems, with the mess around my ship still fresh. And the deck of a standard Caelestis exploration ship is, of course, cold steel instead of sun-kissed wood. But, as I stare out the wall-to-wall viewport, and the great yellow eye too big for it stares back at me, I hold the hole of my trusty flute to my lips just like my cousin did.

They like sounds that are like theirs, see?

Between notes, the only sounds I can hear are my own racing heart and the creaking and sparking of a tiny ship barely clinging to life around me, Ishmael's coffin bobbing treacherously on the ocean waves. Judging from the shredded metal I can see floating behind the dark mass before me, that's still better than the rest of the fleet is doing. All communications are silent, not even static left behind. Who knew that the only thing worse than hearing the dying screams of your crewmates was hearing them stop?

My breath falters, and the meteor-sized pupil in that yellow eye starts to contract, nearly stopping it completely. Hastily, I pick the song back up, its notes long and low and deep as the heart of the sea.

See, Levi, look! That's his tail...and that's his fin! See it?!

He likes it! Keep playing!

A call for friendship, a plea for life—at the moment, they're the same thing. The music of my little flute, flowing through the speakers I desperately hope will keep working, never had lyrics before, but the way I play it, it sure does now: *oh, please, oh, please, oh, please, please, please...*

Out of the corner of my eye, I see a pitch-black tail three times the length of my ship swaying leisurely back and forth. How quickly it could end me, little meaningless me, if it wanted to. Nobody agrees on whether the whales of the abyss have teeth—nobody has ever lived to confirm one way or the other—but does it matter? No. A piece of the vast universe come to life, pulling free, drifting through the cosmos and destroying all it encounters through enormity alone doesn't need to *bite.*

Funny, actually: I never feared drowning before.

Plunged so far into the cold and dark it's impossible to imagine resurfacing, I play by muscle memory alone, too terrified to stop and think. But the notes come perfectly, as if on their own, eager and clear. And then, through the flimsy barrier of steel and quartz glass, from the stars and from space and from my very blood and bones, I hear it.

Listen!

What is it?!

He's singing! He's singing back!

I feel more than hear the bellows that seem to go on forever, matching my tune note for note, and it is the wildest joy and ecstasy any human on or off the Earth has ever known, I'm absolutely sure. Up and down the scale, we sing together, as the mass of darkness steadily but unmistakably begins to pass me and my ship by.

Goodbye, whale! Goodbye! Tell all the other whales we're friends now!

I almost laugh with delight. The blast of unregulated air into my flute sends a sudden, ear-splitting screech out of the holes instead of sweet music.

Everything stops.

Instantly, the pupil contracts to a pinprick. The tail slowly, horribly swings back, with a rumble like a war drum. My stomach drops to the bottom of the sea.

THE DEVIL WENT DOWN TO THE SUBWAY

BY A.J. ROCCA

'm not really a religious person, so I never thought I'd meet the devil. If I was going to meet him, though, last place I suspected was going to be on the platform for the A under Columbus Circle. I'd spent half the night grinding myself down on our conductor's favorite Bartók (I had to get it mastered; I was auditioning for concertmaster the next week) and was running to catch the last train home. I took the stairs in threes and hit bottom just in time to see the doors shutting. The violin case banged my knees as I raced along the yellow line, but it was no use. The train shot down the tube and was gone.

I walked to a stop and panted for breath, case still swinging from my shoulder. It would be a while yet before the next train came in. I wheezed curses at the empty platform.

That's when I started to hear him play.

Amateur violin music is a common part of the city soundscape. I can't count how many times I've seen a busker on a street corner or in the subway stumbling through *The Four Seasons* or hammering out the Allegro from *Eine Kleine Nachtmusik*. Back before high school, I used to always perk up my ears whenever I heard them, no matter how bad they were. Now I was a senior at Julliard, and the only thing I heard was our program for the semester and all my misgivings against our conductor's choice of phrasings. The rest of it was all was just so much noise fading into the background of taxi horns, jumbled accents, and a million walking feet.

Normally I wouldn't have even turned my head, but it was such a strange little tune this busker played. Full of lots of funny trills and arpeggiations, some stuff I'd never even heard done on a violin before. I turned to look over and saw him leaning up against one of the pillars, patchy coat and big ragged black beard spilling over his instrument, swaying with his eyes closed.

Also, the guy had horns. Again, not normally something you'd pay much attention to in New York, but you had to see these horns. I mean they looked bad—all dull and scratched up and chipped—but the thing was that they looked real, not some cheap Halloween prop. The things went right down into his shaggy black head with the skin all puckered up around them just like a billy goat's. One of the horns had a tin cup hanging off it with the word "tips" written on it in black marker.

I decided to go up to him. There was just something about his playing, something you couldn't get out of your ears. It was like classical music, but with lots of slurs and blue notes thrown in; Paganini after a night of hard drinking. I looked around to see if anyone else was there, but the platform was abandoned except for the two of us. It was an entire world of novel musical expression being spilled out with no one there to hear it but me and the rats.

I put down my violin case and undid the clasps. I wanted to try that music for myself, to get it under my fingertips. I'd never tried playing anything like that before, but I figured if some crazy, cosplaying busker could do it, well. I opened the case and took out my Heberlein and tuned a slightly sour G. I tightened up my bow, rosined, and touched the hair to the strings.

The violinist's eyes shot open and his music stopped. "Hey man, you can fuck off with that. This is a solo act."

"Oh," I said. "Oh, sorry." I bent down to slip the violin back into its case, cheeks burning hot. He glared at me the whole time I was at it—one blue eye, one blind—and refused to start again until I'd clicked both clasps shut. Only then did the strange music pour through the empty platform again.

"So uh, you're supposed to be, like, the devil, right? That's your schtick?" I asked after a little while.

"Just call me Bill."

"You mean like Beelzebub?"

"I mean like Bill."

I watched him play for a couple minutes more. I took out my phone to film him, but one deadly flash of the blue and blind eyes and I dropped it back into my pocket.

"So are you here to offer me a deal or something?" I asked.

"What deal?"

"Like you'll make me the next Perlman if I trade you my soul?"

"Soul? What would I want with somethin' like that?"

"Geez, I don't know. Isn't that supposed to be your thing? Collecting lost souls?"

"I collect soda cans sometimes. Gets you five cents a pop. Souls don't get you shit."

Bill's playing thrummed through the mold-heavy air and filled up the subway. He wrapped around peeling pillars, echoed between rust-stained pipes, and slid beneath popped tiles. It was a shock compared to the clean acoustic of the concert hall; Bill's music had the flavor of the place.

"Well, can I ask what you're doing down here then?" I said.

"I don't know. Practicing. Trying to make a buck."

Bill slid down a long legato phrase that sounded like he was thinking about it. He pointed his bow at my case.

"You a musician, right?"

"Yeah."

"I mean a real musician, not just a weekend player. Something you'd give everything for?"

"I'm competing for first chair in the Juilliard orchestra."

"Yeah, yeah," Bill murmured. He stared at me hard with the good blue eye, but it was like the grey one was seeing something else. Something far away.

"Imagine your conductor comes in one day, guy's a brilliant composer, you can't wait to see what you're playing next. He comes in with a big stack of sheets, huge stack, a score that's piled up, up, up through the ceiling, into the sky. You're all excited, and then he flips the page and it's just blank. Page after page after page of it, bar after bar filled up with nothin' but rests. It's four thirty-three plus eternity, and you're just sittin' there with everyone else while this head case beats out rest after rest after rest. He lets all your talent go to waste because no music can be as perfect as his perfect silence. What would you do?"

"I'd probably quit."

"Me too."

Bill played a little slower now, and his music continued its journey through the subway's ocean of negative space. It wandered clean over the platform and down into the track bed, bowed chords broken in time and strange little melodies drifting down, down, down over the crossties. His music went into the tunnel, and I wondered how far it penetrated the darkness.

"Hey man," Bill said. "If you're gonna stand there and bug me all night, least you can do is throw in a buck."

"What?"

Bill tilted his head to give the little tips cup hanging from his horn a jangle.

"Oh. All right."

I got out my wallet and dropped a five in the tin cup along with the change that was already in there. Bill gave me a little busker's bow to the tintinnabulation of quarters and dimes. I was surprised when I felt the air whoosh out about a minute later and another train pulled up alongside the platform. The doors slid open and waited.

"Well, what are you staring at?" Bill asked.

"There's not supposed to be another train here yet."

"Train company owes me a favor, and I feel kinda sorry for you. Just get out of here."

Before then, I had just been going along with Bill's whole devil thing. Half believing, half not-believing, you know. That train gave me the creeps, though. It looked like some kind of older model, and it seemed sooty somehow even though my fingers came back clean when I touched the corrugated metal. I went to the open door and peeked my head inside. There were no people there, only shadows.

"This isn't some kind of trick, is it?"

"What?"

"I mean this isn't the train to hell or anything like that, right?"

"Man, there ain't no hell. There's just the devil, and the devil's homeless."

"Oh. Okay, well, thank you."

I got on the train and took the nearest seat that didn't already have a shadow sitting in it and put my case across my knees. There were two dings, the doors closed, and I heard Bill start up again as we pulled away. The train took me back home and back into my life, back into stuffy practice rooms and internal auditions, but it also took me further than that. The train took me to gypsy jazz corners and cool blues bars, down to smoky basements and up to cellists' apartments on the twenty-first floor. I never did reach first chair at Julliard, but the train took me past that to other concert halls in other cities. Along the way were YouTube videos, TikToks, and movie studios; we even hit the Grammys on a hip-hop collaboration before we reached the end of the line. The shadows in the train shifted as new light pierced its windows. The train changed to a boat to take me out to Odessa, São Paulo, and Tokyo. The boat changed to a radio wave to take me out to Sirius, Cygnus X-1, and Alpha Centauri. And everywhere we went my music went with me, changing and growing, never stopping.

But before we came to my music, the train took me to the end of Bill's. The sound of his playing followed for a while as we picked up speed, then grew fainter and fainter down the tunnel until I couldn't hear it anymore. I tried my best to write a little of it down, but I don't think I saved even a single note.

POSSESSION NO. 239 IN E MAJOR, OP. 1

BY HAILEY PIPER

There's a ringing in her ears as Brooke collides with smaller, firmer bodies, and then all sound snaps into clarity around her—first a laughing chorus at a nearby table, and then the busy restaurant's dull roar, and then the unified grunt ahead as two figures stumble back. She can't remember what distracted her, what she was getting up for, maybe to get away. A lost and crewless ship can smash into any port.

But this is no port, and she is no ship. Apologies spill out in a torrent, for being a klutz, an elephant, a great beast with two left feet, and she prays through tensed nerves that she won't get yelled at for a change.

The strangers turn to her fully, each slender face flashing lighthouse-bright eyes. They lean up in unison, two skinny girls with drunken smiles.

"It's alright," one says, her voice humming with a tuning fork's touch, reaching through limb and bone. The other titters beside her.

Brooke stands stiffly, unsure whether or not to retreat. "Forgive me."

"Forgiveness," one of the girls says. "Does she think we're sweet?"

Brooke's having a hard time telling them apart, as if she's the drunk one and seeing double. They don't look exactly alike, but they're both narrow, short, dark-haired creatures with wavering stances and kind smiles.

One of them reaches out a slender hand and closes it around Brooke's fingertips. "No," the stranger says. "*You're* sweet." Her friend or duplicate takes the other hand.

A pleasant cold fills Brooke's fingers, and her jaw slides down in a slight gape, lost for words or understanding. If she could sing her feelings, she would. Here she is, this big clumsy creature, assumed by everyone to be a fortress, a bruiser, a thunderstorm of a violinist, and she's never known what to do with that.

And yet these strangers have closed their hands around her fingertips as if she were a porcelain figurine. Too much pressure and she would crack. They met only seconds ago, and yet the strangers understand she is delicate. She could break down crying right here if she weren't so stunned by the gentle confidence in the strangers' faces or the sureness in each one's tender grip.

And then a rougher grasp takes Brooke's thick bicep. It tugs back, prying her fingers from the strangers' hands, urging her against a hard chest—Lena.

Her face of confident bones and looks leans past Brooke's shoulder. "I apologize for her."

And without letting her get the strangers' names, without hearing their odd replies, Lena leads Brooke away.

* * *

Brooke thinks she says, "I can walk myself," but it comes so softly that she isn't sure. Lena's grasp squeezes the words up from her red-fingernailed grip, an ache in Brooke's arm, but the pressure won't push the words high enough. Despite her softness, she's meeker than a dog's squeaky toy.

Lena sits her down at their round table, full of Lena's friends, and whispers in Brooke's ear. "I would really appreciate if you didn't make things difficult for me for one night."

"It was an accident," Brooke says.

"Don't argue at the table," Lena says, easing back. "You know I need to look out for you, but don't you know you can't make a scene here? This is a restaurant. A nice one."

Half of what Lena's saying is in her words, but the other half is what's unspoken around them. Yes, this is a nice restaurant. Not the kind of place Brooke would have ever ended up on her own.

Her gaze slides over the warm lighting, busy waitstaff, wealthy patrons in fine dresses and suits, especially the ones forming a circle at Lena's table. She commands their attention at times, waves it at others, this petite pale creature with her swept-back blond hair and her black suit and her status. Their respect for her is unwavering.

And what exactly sits beside her? Not another friend, certainly no peer to these people. Brooke isn't even really a girlfriend, let alone a trophy wife. What then, a charity case? Sponsor a confused giant in a flashy yellow gown when she arrives at your neighborhood? Look how kind Lena is to care for such a life, having stumbled straight out of fairy tales and into the orchestra.

"Brooke, do you hear me?" Lena asks, and her voice is the playful lilt of presentation. See how patient she is. Her attention turns to her friends with a bemused shrug. "Meds."

The friends nod. One woman with algae-green hair and a white dress waves at Brooke. "I get it, hon," she says. "I'm the same at night."

Pity hurts almost as much as Lena's annoyance. Are these people judging or apathetic? Their only impression of Brooke's value is her violin skill, and in her time with Lena, those strings and that bow and the knot that once lived in her shoulder all feel like the experience of an alien presence.

She stumbles up from her seat, needs to get away again. The awareness of the table is crushing her. Best she hide somewhere, or else the next sound they hear will be her crying.

"I need to use the ladies' room," she mutters.

Lena has a fire in her eyes but a coolness in her voice. "I'll go with you, so you won't get lost."

Brooke opens her mouth, but nothing comes out. This nice restaurant is not her territory, and she doesn't know what kinds of bodily excuses are acceptable here.

"Lena Hawke?" a gruff voice asks. "Is that you? It's me, Christopher, remember?"

Lena turns from Brooke as a gangly man approaches the table, likely a forgotten colleague. The nearby friends have no idea how quickly Lena can discard people, how she's done it to those who came before Brooke and would thoughtlessly do it to those who would come after.

But Brooke will remember him, even if Lena can't. His presence forces her to let Brooke go. Can't make a scene in a restaurant.

She hurries around tables, letting the surrounding chatter engulf her. She's thought of leaving Lena before, finding another orchestra, abandoning before abandonment, forgetting before being forgotten.

But she never seems to get any farther than the ladies' room.

* * *

You would think a giantess could swallow a little poison like Lena Hawke. They were only together because Lena found something of merit in Brooke—inspiration, arousal, some unnamed un-word. She chose Brooke to join the orchestra's violinists, to stay at Lena's side and attend her and touch her, but not when everyone's looking.

To enter this world was to be awestruck. To be at Lena's side was to be at the right hand of genius.

But novelty has a shelf life. Even genius can become ordinary, and whatever the hell Lena used to see in Brooke, nowadays there is exhaustion squirming underneath.

The real poison isn't the threat of being forgotten. It's that Brooke sometimes wonders if she loves Lena, and she knows Lena doesn't wonder the same. That's the double-edged sword of affection. That's what all the love and breakup songs are about, that special poison that lands you crying in a restroom stall. A giantess should be able to handle a little poison, but this big girl has bigger feelings, and heart-poison taints all facets of love.

If only she could act as tiny as she feels. Real love wouldn't make her feel so small. But what is she supposed to do?

She can't even think, can only cry harder.

Two voices hum outside the restroom stall, and Brooke catches her quiet sobs in the hitching wetness of braking tires on a wet road.

"Odd song," one voice coos.

"A crooning," says the other in a sinking note.

Brooke wipes her face with toilet paper and emerges from the stall. She needs to get her face together, get her *feelings* together, and march back out there. For another night, she can be tiny in the way Lena likes.

The humming figures slide to Brooke's sides, and in the broad mirror, she recognizes the drunk girls she stumbled into earlier.

"Look at those hands," one stranger says.

That surprised, almost pleasant cold from earlier takes hold of Brooke as if the strangers have again gripped her fingertips, leaving her overwhelmed, maybe even flattered. She's never thought much of her hands before, but these two appear fascinated.

"Calloused fingertips." The other hums a little louder. "You do music."

"New hit single," they say together.

"Am I single?" Brooke asks. She can't really tell. She's a tall dirty secret that Lena carts around in broad daylight.

The strangers waver on their feet. One digs into her purse—Brooke didn't notice purses before—and smiles into its darkness.

"Global sensation," one says, giggling.

"World domination," says the other, and her hand emerges from her purse clutching a glass syringe, its sharp needle dripping with liquid glitter.

Brooke spins at the sink, forgetting to shut off the water. Her damp hands tense in rising, ready to shove the syringe-wielding girl away.

But the mirror has confused her as to who's on the left and who's on the right, and the only correct person in the world is Lena. She's known all along that Brooke can't take care of herself. She would deserve to be smug if she could see the syringe plunging into Brooke's neck right now.

"Melody's servants," the unarmed girl says.

"Like you, we have this music." The syringe-wielder steps back, the glass glittery with residue. "And we keep it, and we give it, and we—"

* * *

This is your most violent effort, but if anyone can understand violence, it is a player of violins. The wordplay tickles the sensitive underside of her soul. You've always known how to charm them, and it's only desperation that forced you to coalesce in that syringe, in the servants' hands.

But now there is Brooke. She has the space for you, and she knows your

Melody as a piece of her heart, like the callouses on her left hand's fingertips. She's known to touch you, but now she can know your touch.

The space within the violin player, played by the sound of a violin.

Those calloused fingers thrum beneath your musical command down her belly. Between her legs. It is a standing wet dream in a place too nice by mortal standards for your harmonious eternity, but the physical is a suggestion and the hard surfaces are only barriers to repel and amplify every note.

There is no sight here. There is only pregnant emptiness and the musical promise it offers. In moments, Brooke has no need for hands. You can touch everything, the Melody of conscious ecstasy that grabs every true music lover. They don't even know they've let a living creature inside them, only the need to tap their feet or drum their fingers, to hum along to a song with a tune beyond their capability, or to weave their heads in the air as if a conductor like Lena were directing their neck muscles.

Brooke imagines love. You *are* love.

Instrument plays the player and slides sound from her throat. A tongue of violin strokes one risen note atop another until a high A note on the E string crests in tears of gasping relief down her cheeks and a trembling cry from her core to the world.

It is the first time in many years she has felt held by a presence greater than herself.

* * *

The ladies' room door bangs open, and Lena marches across the tiles. "Always getting lost in yourself, aren't you?"

She sounds almost playful, and Brooke finds herself standing at the mirror, searching its reflection for a face she can't find. Not the drunk girls, the servants—they're gone already.

Brooke nonetheless knows she isn't alone, and not because of Lena. Because of you. She hasn't realized quite what you are yet, but she knows you're there. A small glittery dot on her reflection proves at the very least that one of your servants jabbed her neck with the needle and set her playing like a vinyl album.

Lena grabs for Brooke's wrist, taking her away, but Lena doesn't realize she's grabbing two souls. You're barely making your presence known yet. Only the echo of a hum in the depths of Brooke's throat and an aftershock down her legs, desperate to tap their feet.

But you're with her now. Not in that syringe or the ether, but *With. Her.* It isn't going to last long, but what a night it's about to become.

* * *

"Quit bouncing your leg," Lena says at the table. "You're shaking the wine glasses."

She thinks she's speaking to Brooke, and that's somewhat true. Brooke is used to sitting perfectly poised, understanding that her every muscle must work in a web of synchronization both to effectively play the violin and to play it in tandem with the rest of the orchestra. It is the only activity during which she quits feeling like a giant living in a Lilliputian world.

But you're here, and Lena's kind of talking to you, even if she doesn't know it. You're the one playing the violinist, and you're the one bouncing her leg. Although Lena can't possibly know you're here at the table too, she has kept Brooke as her plaything for this long, and only she gets to decide when she's done playing.

And she does not share. A domineering hand lands on Brooke's kneecap and forces her leg against the restaurant's thin carpet. Brooke winces as nails dig into her flesh.

"Don't," Brooke whisper-sings.

"Do better," Lena says, and her eyes glance to her friends. To them, she looks like she's confiding in Brooke, and maybe that's true, but you hear everything too. "I can't be your mentor and your conductor and your babysitter." And her side piece, but that goes unspoken in the space between words. "At this rate, I might as well bring a man along. They can handle themselves sometimes, and at least then I could get fucked tonight instead of dragging you in a drunken stagger."

"You can get fucked now," you sing. Too quiet for anyone but Lena to hear, and you sound like Brooke when you're playing her tongue, but the effect is a slap across Lena's face.

"Are you serious?" she asks. "This is what you want tonight to be?"

Brooke continues not to answer, and you pause briefly from playing her.

Lena's fingernails dig deeper into Brooke's flesh. "Do you have the faintest thought what I'm responsible for? I practically keep the world spinning. Can you imagine what that is, caretaking an entire orchestra *and* you, Brooke? You have no idea the stress you put me through."

Your non-calloused non-fingers strum Brooke's spine. "Then go," she sings.

"What?" Lena snaps.

"Let go," Brooke says, and her great hand is an eclipse over Lena's.

Lena slides back fully into her seat and aims an encouraging grin across the table at her well-dressed, better-mannered friends. She's supposed to put on the show for them—perfect control, master of music and souls.

But they aren't paying attention. For one instance, Brooke knows something Lena has yet to figure out, that each person in this restaurant has their own world inside, and it is full of doubts and hopes and hungers that have nothing to do with Lena Hawke.

Brooke spots a couple of them now—the drunk girls, your servants. They're standing between other tables, getting in the way of waitstaff, watching with wide eyes while giggling behind their hands. Brooke isn't sure anymore that they're drunk. She isn't even sure that they're human. You can't correct her by playing music down her nerves, but you can calm her as she again launches from the table as if it keeps belting her across the room.

Brooke reaches your servants. "What did you do to me?" she asks them, not angry but worried.

You keep trying to soothe her, but it's a kind of control, isn't it? Lena has tried the same—to cage the giant, to vacuum-pack these big feelings into a manageable size. You can do better than some *conductor*. She tells music where to go; you *are* music, and you can flow with any instrument of flesh, any scale of talent and inclination.

A good musician knows to trust her instrument, and music knows to trust its instruments too.

One of your servants leans her smile into Brooke. "Only half of music is the sound you hear," she says.

"The other half is the space between sounds," the other says and then titters.

"Sound alone is formless."

"Space alone is silence." The second servant grins. "And that's what Melody needs, her bare half."

"She is the sound," says the first. "You are the space."

They're too honest for Brooke's own good. She almost can't feel anything, this bold declaration that within her stretches a hollow mountain, only good for filling up with some other presence. You want to comfort her, but the sound of you will only confirm what your servants have said.

In the absence of musical relief, that control returns to Brooke's side—Lena, rushing between Brooke and the servants, telling them to get lost.

They raise their eyebrows and burst into laughter, but they go. Part of them is like music too, floating around and shadowing their present circumstances. Flesh can't fight music. Lena can't win in the end.

Not even with Brooke. She presses close, hugs her arms around Brooke's frame, tells her she is sorry and will look out for her. It would be sweet in a private place without the restaurant's rumbling commotion.

Without the table of friends watching from afar. Brooke has danced to this tune before, the damsel in distress rescued by powerful Lena, and she's seen the aftermath, too. Does Lena really care? Or is she only doing this for control, not of music but of perception. What a strong woman. What a good caretaker she is for clumsy, confused Brooke.

You feel these doubts pulsing between the two women like a song on repeat. Eventually, it can drive you mad. And you're not the only one.

"It isn't just what they put in me, is it?" Brooke asks. "It's us, too. You are the sound and I am the space."

Lena's face falls. "I don't know what you're trying to say, but don't do this here."

"I know."

Brooke returns Lena's embrace, briefly, fleetingly, and then slips back, and then she's pulling you up from inside her, inviting you to play.

And you oblige.

"*Yooou* can't make a *scene* in a *restauraaant*," Brooke sings, booming and ferocious. "But we're *different*, and I *caaan*."

She keeps retreating, knocking her hips into seats, catching the fitful glances of disturbed diners. Lena reaches after, but she can't pursue in a place like this. They truly are different.

Had your servants injected you into Lena, she would have caught you between her fingertips and squeezed you dripping until she'd absorbed every piece of you. Her possessive nature is almost a kindred spirit. It isn't like you haven't slipped through two hundred and thirty-eight people before, though each more kindly than Lena. The two of you wouldn't have worked.

But Brooke is different. Her space is important. Necessary.

And Brooke is important, too. She is a big girl with bigger feelings, and now that emotional enormity shares space with you, and neither of you can act tiny. You never knew how, and she's forgetting by the note.

She can be music. Both of you as one thing. The sound and the space between.

You wind yourself in a circle inside her like fingers around a radio dial turning the volume up and up to blast music through her veins. There are destinies for this song beyond her pleasure, past the high A note. She's ready to help herself. To help you.

That stringlike sound flows from her skin, strangling nearby conversations. There's a tongue on hers, and fingertips down her vertebrae, and a bow gliding along her soul, or at least these are the ways she perceives you within. The more you let her pretend to understand, the better your unity.

Music trusting instrument, instrument trusting player. You let yourself become the space and allow the sound of her, the *her* of her, to spill up.

Brooke opens her mouth, and everything comes out. Music cannot prowl a space like a carnivorous animal, and it shouldn't be caged in Lena's mental zoo. It is cloudlike, filling the air, becoming thin or thick as is its pleasure.

You are the giant now, and that is why you needed Brooke to be your violin.

Her skull thrums with new instrumentations, and they pound past her lips in a vivacious river of strummed-upon cellos, teased cymbals, and a ferocious saxophone.

Lena should be stepping back now. She should have the wherewithal to know you're beyond her control, but she still can't sense you. To her, you're simply a phenomenon that Brooke has manifested to spoil the evening, and maybe that's what she deserves to think. She's so used to deciding when a song ends—radio fadeout, closing moments in a concert, humming until she has something to say—that likely she and most other mortals in this world have never truly heard what it sounds like when one of your kind reaches completion.

She should find out.

Brooke sways in an awkward dance as the sound of you echoes through her space. She isn't suddenly graceful for your presence, but even in the most stubborn of onlookers, there's an inkling that she doesn't dance alone. You're her partner to lean on, like Lena never could be. Not an invisible physical presence, but the intangible miracle of music. A partner no one can see, but everyone can feel.

Lena finally shrinks back. Her limbs curl against her core like the legs of a dead spider, but no matter how small she makes her body, it can never compare to the cramped space inside her soul.

For once, a piece of her life is truly outside her hands. Brooke dances, and Lena gawks, and you aim to finish yourself the way a needle never could, be it part of a record player or a syringe.

Beyond the awestruck diners, the delighted and embarrassed and the damned, your servants giggle themselves silly. They're the only ones who know what's about to happen.

"World domination," one says.

The other can barely get her words out through her joy. "Global sensation."

You swell to a brassy roar, every semblance of instrumentation reaching its crescendo. A new climax builds inside Brooke, and beneath the music comes her moaning and screaming and transcendental frenzy. This is your new hit single, and it has the striking power of an avalanche.

And Brooke? She's better than any syringe at injecting you into the world.

Her nerves flare across her body, a plunger closing off all the space inside her and forcing you out in a new sharp breath of violence. She becomes no space. All sound. Everything around her is the space instead, waiting for you.

Across the restaurant, into the onlookers, you burst forth beautiful and unrelenting. This is what all the love and breakup songs are really about, the systemic invitation for destruction, but no one here has ever heard that kind of music reach its true end before.

And they've never felt a true end to themselves, either.

You're an earthquake made of a violin's kiss, shaking the fragile strings that band the universe together until they begin to snap and split away from each other. Every physical object has a frequency at which it shatters.

Wine glasses.

Eyeballs and eardrums.

Even human bones.

But what an experience to hear a song end. To know that it is spreading through the air, and for those far enough away to survive the gentle lick of its aural tongue, there can be inspiration. There can be offspring, and new songs to come. You are a majestic source of musical pain.

And Brooke, at the center of it all, is too overjoyed to understand or care about the gory tremor rocking through the area. There is only her moment with you as your joined ecstasy bursts through every nearby pillar of flesh and blood.

At least the last sound they'll hear is the rhythmic fadeout of your laughter.

SLOW HEAD KARAOKE

BY ROBERT BEVERIDGE

"I know she wasn't trained to operate//on me."

- Jody Chan, "music video where Taylor Swift is a cardiac surgeon & I am a dying bird"

The radio is up, up, up, the pantheon
of static a 100% attendance rate
in the middle of a field somewhere.
I can't even remember the name
on the last welcome-to sign we saw
and that must have been four
hundred miles ago. It's very green,
however, the stalks higher
than our eyes can go, the clouds
above an impossible shade.
What is this crop around us? I have
no idea. (Not that this is odd.)
The gas is getting low, I hope there's
an exit soon, and it seems
you've been asleep for longer than usual.
I'll sing another sixteen bars
with the crows in the air who match
your T-shirt, try to get the GPS
to find a signal, get us to our destination,
wherever that may be.

CONTENT NOTES

Tears Like Rain, by Tim Waggoner - None.

The Brazen Bull, by Sofia Ajram - Gore, self-harm (implied).

Oil of Angels, by Gemma Files - Teenage death, gore, language.

This Loaded Gun of a Song Stuck in My Head, by Paul Michael Anderson - Child death, blood, mental illness (implied), self-harm (implied).

Pack Up Your Sins and Go to the Devil, by Elis Montgomery - Jazz.

Everybody Loves My Baby, by Mercedes M. Yardley - Domestic abuse, physical abuse, murder, blood, gun violence.

The Lung of Orpheus, by Jonathan Duckworth - Language.

I am He, by Premee Mohamed - Murder, occult.

Pied Piper, by Carol Edwards - Disturbing imagery.

Mixtape, by V. Castro - Domestic violence, murder, gore, sexual assault (implied), language.

To the River, by Corey Farrenkopf - Teenage death, gore.

The Prodigy, by Philip Fracassi - Child death, satanic elements.

Red, Black, & Blue, by Linda D. Addison - Disturbing imagery.

Instruments of Harm, by Julia LaFond - War.

Electric Muse, by Virginia Kathryn - Language,

Ambient, by L.B. Waltz - Language, child death.

Vinyl Remains, by Chad Stroup - Gore (mentioned and depicted), drug use (mentioned), self-mutilation, language.

Goddess, by Lisa Morton - Language, witchcraft.

Her Only Single, by Devan Barlow - Death.

I Will Not Scream, by John Palisano - Blood.

Lovely Piano of Rich Mahogany, by A.J. Bartholomew - None.

A Concert in Merzgau, by R.L. Clore - Disturbing imagery.

Sing to the God of Slugs, by Maxwell I. Gold - Disturbing imagery.

Song of the Guqin, by Frances Lu-Pai Ippolito - Child harm, gore, murder, suicide (referenced).

The Men Who Play, by Jangar Tokpa - None.

Scordatura, by Jess Landry - Animal harm, emotional abuse.

Whalesong, by Shannon Brady - None.

Devil Went Down to the Subway, by A.J. Rocca - Language, satanic elements.

Possession No. 239 in E Major, Op. 1, by Hailey Piper - Language, sexual imagery (implied).

Slow Head Karaoke, by Robert Beveridge - Drug use (implied).

ABOUT THE AUTHORS

SIDE A

Tim Waggoner has published over fifty novels and seven collections of short stories. He writes original dark fantasy and horror, as well as media tie-ins, and his articles on writing have appeared in numerous publications. He's a four-time winner of the Bram Stoker Award, has won the HWA's Mentor of the Year Award, and been a finalist for the Shirley Jackson Award, the Scribe Award, and the Splatterpunk Award. He's also a full-time tenured professor who teaches creative writing and composition at Sinclair College in Dayton, Ohio.

Sofia Ajram is a multidisciplinary artist based in Montreal. Prior publications include The Arborglyph in the anthology *Lost Contact*. Their latest project, *Bury Your Gays: An Anthology of Tragic Queer Horror* (serving as Editor) releases April 2024. When they're not writing, they can be found goldsmithing at Sofia Zakia or moderating the Horror forum on Reddit. Find them at @sofiaajram on Twitter.

Born in England and raised in Toronto, Canada, **Gemma Files** has been an award-winning horror author for almost thirty years. She has won the Shirley Jackson Award for Best Novel (*Experimental Film*, CZP) and the Bram Stoker Award for Best Achievement in a Fiction Collection (*In That Endlessness, Our End*, Grimscribe). She has a new collection out now (*Dark Is Better*, Trepidatio) and one upcoming (*Blood From the Air*, Grimscribe).

Paul Michael Anderson is the author of *Standalone* and the collections *Bones are Made to Be Broken* and *Everything Will Be All Right in the End: Apocalypse Songs*. He lives with his family in Northern Virginia.

Elis Montgomery is a speculative fiction writer from Vancouver, Canada. She is a member of SFWA and Codex. When she's not writing, she's usually hanging upside down in an aerial arts class or a murky cave. Find her at @elismontgomery on Twitter.

Mercedes M. Yardley is a dark fantasist who wears red lipstick and poisonous flowers in her hair. She is the author of *Darling, Beautiful Sorrows*, the Stabby Award-winning *Apocalyptic Montessa and Nuclear Lulu: A Tale of Atomic Love*, *Pretty Little Dead Girls*, and *Nameless*. She won the Bram Stoker Award for her story "Little Dead Red" and "Fracture," and was a Bram Stoker Award nominee for her short story "Loving You Darkly" and the *Arterial Bloom* anthology. Mercedes lives and works in Las Vegas. You can find her at mercedesmyardley.com.

Jonathan Louis Duckworth is a completely normal, entirely human person with the right number of heads and everything. He received his MFA from Florida International University and his PhD from University of North Texas. His speculative fiction work appears in *Pseudopod, Beneath Ceaseless Skies, Southwest Review, Flash Fiction Online*, and elsewhere. He is an active HWA member.

Premee Mohamed is a Nebula, World Fantasy, and Aurora award-winning Indo-Caribbean scientist and speculative fiction author based in Edmonton, Alberta. She is an Assistant Editor at the short fiction audio venue *Escape Pod* and the author of the *Beneath the Rising* series of novels as well as several novellas. Her short fiction has appeared in many venues and she can be found at @premeesaurus on Twitter and on her website at PremeeMohamed.com.

Carol Edwards is a northern California native transplanted to southern Arizona. She grew up reading fantasy and classic novels, climbing trees, and acquiring frequent grass stains. She currently enjoys a coffee addiction and raising her succulent army. Her poetry has been published in numerous periodicals, digital magazines, blogs, and anthologies, most recently in *Beyond the Sand and Sea* from Southern Arizona Press and *#SPIRIT* from White Stag Publishing. More of her poetry is forthcoming in *Under Her Eye* from Black Spot Books. Her debut poetry collection, *The World Eats Love*, released on April 25, 2023 from The Ravens Quoth Press. Follow her at @practicallypoetical on Instagram and on Twitter and FB at @practicallypoet.

V.Castro is a two-time Bram Stoker Award nominated Mexican American writer from San Antonio, Texas now residing in the UK. As a full-time mother, she dedicates her time to her family and writing Latinx narratives in horror, erotic horror, and science fiction. Her most recent releases include *Alien: Vasquez* from Titan Books, *Mestiza Blood* and *The Queen of the Cicadas* from Flame Tree Press, *Goddess of Filth* from Creature Publishing, and *The Haunting of Alejandra* from Del Rey. Connect with Violet via Instagram and Twitter @vlatinalondon, on TikTok @vcastrobooks, or at VCastroStories.com. She can also be found on Goodreads and Amazon.

Corey Farrenkopf lives on Cape Cod with his wife, Gabrielle, and works as a librarian. His work has been published in *Three-Lobed Burning Eye*, *SmokeLong Quarterly*, *Reckoning*, *Bourbon Penn*, *Tiny Nightmares*, *Flash Fiction Online*, *The Dread Machine*, and elsewhere. Follow him at @CoreyFarrenkopf on Twitter, on TikTok at @CoreyFarrenkopf or on the web at CoreyFarrenkopf.com.

Philip Fracassi is the Stoker-nominated author of the novels *A Child Alone with Strangers*, *Gothic*, and *Boys in the Valley*, as well as the award-winning story collections *Behold the Void* and *Beneath a Pale Sky*. His stories have been published in numerous magazines and anthologies, including *Best Horror of the Year*, *Nightmare Magazine*, *Black Static*, *Southwest Review*, and *Interzone*. Philip lives in Los Angeles and is represented by Copps Literary Services. For more information visit him on social media, or at his website at PFracassi.com.

Linda D. Addison is an award-winning author of five collections, including *The Place of Broken Things* written with Alessandro Manzetti, & *How To Recognize A Demon Has Become Your Friend*. She is the recipient of the HWA Lifetime

Achievement Award, HWA Mentor of the Year and SFPA Grand Master of Fantastic Poetry. She is a member of CITH, HWA, SFWA, SFPA and IAMTW. Vist her at LindaAddisonWriter.com.

Julia LaFond got her master's in geoscience from Penn State University. She's recently had flash fic published in *The Martian Magazine, White Cat Publications*, and *Thirteen Podcast*. In her spare time, Julia enjoys reading and gaming. Find her at JKLaFondWriter.wordpress.com.

Virginia Kathryn is a songwriter and storyteller based in northern Colorado. As a musician, she has participated in workshops hosted by the Silkroad Ensemble, Richard Thompson, and other traditional/folk musicians. Her debut album is available on all streaming services, and she is currently working on the next. She participated in the Futurescapes workshop for writers of speculative fiction in 2018 and 2021. Her stories transform trauma into nightmares, as a reminder that memories are like dreams—we can always choose to wake up, but sometimes, they haunt us even in waking.

SIDE B

LB Waltz has been publishing creative works for over 20 years under various pseudonyms. They enjoy taking walks, biblically accurate depictions of angels, and reading about botanical folklore.

Chad Stroup is also the author of such novels as *Secrets of the Weird* (Grey Matter Press) and *Sexy Leper* (Bizarro Pulp Press), as well as the short story collection *Teeth Where They Shouldn't Be* (Oddness). When not writing, he is also the vocalist for the band Icepield and a fierce drag queen by the name of Jenn X. No, he doesn't sleep much. Stroup received his MFA in Fiction from San Diego State University. Follow him on Instagram @chadxstroup.

Devan Barlow is the author of *An Uncommon Curse*, a novel of fairy tales and musical theatre. Her short fiction and poetry have appeared in several anthologies and magazines including *Solarpunk Magazine* and *Diabolical Plots*. She can be found at her website DevanBarlow.com.

Lisa Morton is a screenwriter, author of non-fiction books, and prose writer whose work was described by the *American Library Association's Readers' Advisory Guide to Horror* as "consistently dark, unsettling, and frightening." She is a six-time winner of the Bram Stoker Award®, the author of four novels and over 150 short stories, and a world-class Halloween and paranormal expert. Forthcoming in 2023 from Applause Books is *The Art of the Zombie Movie*. Lisa lives in Los Angeles and online at LisaMorton.com.

John Palisano's nonfiction, short fiction, poetry, and novels have appeared in countless literary anthologies and magazines such as *Cemetery Dance, Fangoria, Weird Tales, Space & Time, MCFarland Press*, and many more. He's been quoted in publications such as *Vanity Fair, the Los Angeles Times*, and *The Writer*. He's won the Bram Stoker Award© for excellence in short fiction and was recently President of the Horror Writers Association.

A.J. Bartholomew is a write poet from Northern Virginia. She has published several short horror stories in anthologies and magazines including *Hell's Mall, Hell's Highway, Ink Stains vol. 14*, and *Cosmic Horror Monthly*. One day, she hopes to publish a book of horror limericks. When she is not writing, she is typically playing with her cat.

R.L. Clore lives and writes in rural North Carolina.

Maxwell I. Gold is a Jewish-American multiple award-nominated author who writes prose poetry and short stories in cosmic horror and weird fiction with half a decade of writing experience. Five-time Rhysling Award nominee, and two-time Pushcart Award nominee, find him at TheWellsoftheWeird.com.

Frances Lu-Pai Ippolito (she/her) is a Chinese American writer, judge, and mom in Portland, Oregon. Her writing has appeared or is forthcoming in several venues including *Nightmare Magazine, Flame Tree Press's Asian Ghost Stories and Immigrant Sci-fi Stories, Strangehouse's Chromophobia, Startling Stories, Mother: Tales of Love and Terror, Death's Garden Revisited*, and *Unquiet Spirits: Essays by Asian Women in Horror*. Frances also co-chairs the Young Willamette Writers program that provides free writing classes for high school and middle school students. You can find her on IG @francespaippolito and Twitter @frances_pai.
Jangar Tokpa is a writer from Plymouth, Minnesota. She is currently pursuing a Bachelor's in Environmental Science.

Shannon Brady is a fiction author who specializes in fantasy and horror. Her previous work can be found in such publications as *Queer Sci Fi, Jerry Jazz Musician, Dark Peninsula Press*, and *Third Flatiron Anthologies*. When not writing, she can be found baking, reading, or petting dogs.

Robert Beveridge (he/him) makes noise (xterminal.bandcamp.com) and writes poetry on unceded Mingo land (Akron, OH). Recent/upcoming appearances in Five Fleas, Dreich, and Sein und werden, among others.

A.J. Rocca is a writer and English teacher from Chicago. He specialized in the study of speculative fiction while pursuing his M.A., and now he writes both SFF criticism as well as his own fiction. A.J. plays the violin, and for a while his main source of income was fiddling for change on the street. While his busking days are over, he continues to love music.

Hailey Piper is the Bram Stoker Award-winning author of *Queen of Teeth, No Gods for Drowning, The Worm and His Kings* series, and other books of dark fiction. She's an active member of the Horror Writers Association, with over a hundred short stories in *Pseudopod, Vastarien, Cosmic Horror Monthly*, and elsewhere. She lives with her wife in Maryland, where their occult rituals are secret. Find Hailey at HaileyPiper.com.

ABOUT THE ARTISTS

Sinan Kutlu Kuytuoğlu is an artistic director and illustrator from Istanbul, Turkey. With a penchant for horror and several national commercial design projects under his belt, he marries a phenomenal artistic vision with an understanding of how to use images to invoke dread.

Frank Walls is an American artist best known for his dark, surrealistic fine art, fantasy illustration, and similarly ominous heavy metal musicianship. Walls' interests in heavy metal music, dark art, and horror films paved the way to his emergence as the lead vocalist for bands like Embalmer and HateWorks in the mid to late 90's. His passion for fine art underlined his guttural vocals, and he produced CD and t-shirt art for bands like Incantation and Crypt Kicker, while front lining others. Walls is celebrated for his contributions to game companies like Fantasy Flight Games, Wizards of the Coast, and Alderac Entertainment. He now hails from Hawaii where he teaches Art and Design, works as a freelance illustrator, and pursues his passion for painting and music.

ABOUT THE EDITORS

Jessica Landry is a screenwriter, director, and Bram Stoker Award-winning author. Her original horror feature, *My Only Sunshine*, was accepted into Whistler Film Festival's Screenwriters Lab in 2020 and is in development. In 2022, she was accepted into the CFC/Netflix Project Development Accelerator, NSI's Series Incubator Program, and TIFF's inaugural Series Accelerator. Jessica has written several MOWs, including *List of a Lifetime*, which was nominated for a Critics' Choice Award. She also released her collection, *The Night Belongs to Us*, in March 2023; co-edited the Bram Stoker Award-, British Fantasy Award-, and Shirley Jackson Award-nominated anthology *There Is No Death, There Are No Dead*; and has an original story in *Aliens vs. Predator: Ultimate Prey*, released March 2022. Find her online at JessicaLandry.ca.

Willow Dawn Becker is an award-nominated editor, a writer, an actress, and a marketer. She is also the CEO and Editor-In-Chief of Weird Little Worlds Press. Her most recent anthologies include the award-winning *Mother: Tales of Love and Terror* which was co-edited with Christi Nogle and *Humans are the Problem: A Monster's Anthology*, co-edited with Michael Cluff. You can find her short fiction at *Black Fox Literary Magazine, Space & Time Magazine*, and *Irreantum*, among others. You can purchase her book *Leto's Children: Book 1 of the Leto Trilogy* at WeirdLittleWorlds.com and follow her at @WillowDBecker on Twitter, on Instagram at @TheOnlyWillowBecker, or at WillowDawnBecker.com.

Through the lens of speculative fiction, **Jason Andress** explores the darker corners of imagination. Parallel to this, he offers insights into the technological landscape through his non-fiction. He lives in Washington state with his wife, various progeny, and a three-legged dog. You can find him on the information superhighway at JasonAndress.com.

Pete Lead (he/him) is a half-Chinese, half-Anglo Australian living in New Zealand. He is a speculative fiction author, narrator, slush reader, and workshop facilitator. By day, he is a coach and advisor for startup companies around the world, and likes to teach and perform improv comedy on the side. He has a story forthcoming at *The Dread Machine*, and hopefully many more to come. Find links to Pete's work and workshops at PeteLead.com

Christopher Degni is a 2019 graduate of the Odyssey Writing Workshop and a recovering prescriptivist. He writes about the magic and the horror that lurk just under the surface of everyday life. He lives south of Boston with his wife (and his demons, though we don't talk about those). He was part of the editorial team for the Stoker-nominated *Mother: Tales of Love and Terror*, and you can find his writing in *Stupefying Stories, NewMyths.com, Sherlock Holmes and the Occult Detectives, 99 Tiny Terrors*, and the upcoming *99 Fleeting Fantasies*.

Krysta Winsheimer is a freelance editor living in central Virginia. She is a senior editor at *Run Amok Books* and spends as much time as possible being a first reader for several publishers of speculative, crime, and translated fiction. When she's not enjoying time with her husband, kids, or pitbull, she likes to sit in her garden while reading stories that pair well with an existential crisis. Find her online at MuseRetrospect.com.

THANK YOU!

Without the support and help of you, our incredible backers, fans, and friends, Weird Little Worlds would cease to be. We'd like to give a special thanks to these phenomenal **Rock Star backers**:

Chris & Jessica Baxter
Melanie Briggs
Kyle Becker
Cheri & Steve Becker
Ichabod Ebenezer
Roni Stinger
Beth Barefoot
Nick Bouchard
Tiffany Smith
Bryce Stidham Segars
Roth Schilling
Kenny Endlich
Eileen Gettle
Rachel Redman
David Worn
David A. Ward
Rachel A.

Alison Palmer
Emily Walter
Claire Rowe
Ernie Ridley
Tom Finnegan
Jeffrey A. Greene
Christopher Smith
Chad Bowden
Dustin Skaggs
Scott Casey
Paul Buchholz
Edward P. Abbott
Genghis Mike
Chris McLaren
Heather St. Clair
Chris Padar
Taryan Kayihan

Carl & Allie Duzett
Dan Bugbee
Holly Wolfe
L.L. Garland
Steven Duane Allison Junior
Richard Wood
Kenneth Skaldebø
Emiliyan Gikovski
Sarah Duck-Mayr
PunkARTchick (RAD)
Jason McDonald
Rachel Anfinson
Jonathan Gensler
Christine Blackwicks
Lisa M. Gargano
David Swisher

And to our **Producers**:

Kyle Vincent Lemmon
Jacob Adamson

Victoria Lisowski
Andrew Harding

Justin Lewis
Gaylene & John Adamson

WEIRD LITTLE WORLDS

Weird Little Worlds Press is an independent publishing house designed to bring light, understanding, and communication into the publishing industry and the world. Through telling stories, we believe we can impact the world for good.

Through speculative fiction in the areas of science fiction, fantasy, horror, and adventure, we believe that we can bring the world greater perspective; allow readers to experience both fun and well-crafted stories that lead them towards personal joy and fulfillment; open up conversations about how we treat ourselves, each other, and the world around us; and inspire positive actions at the individual, family, and community levels to make the world a more harmonious, inclusive, and loving place.

As such, we avoid any content that relishes in evil, including excessive profanity; "splatterpunk" or unnecessary gore; prurient violence, especially sexual violence or abuse or violence against children; graphic sex of any kind; and extreme political viewpoints couched as fiction.

We seek after, as Paul said, "Whatsoever things are true, honest, just, pure, lovely, and of good report." But, we also believe that good fiction must include true evil in opposition to good, and so we appreciate the frightening as well as the fearless; the glorious as equally as the gruesome.

And above all, we are a press of transparency, decency, and love. We are here to spread goodness. We work together as a team—both internally and with our followers and fans. Join with us at **WeirdLittleWorlds.com.**

SECRET TRACK

It should be noted that all parties who have witnessed the phenomenon agree upon one thing: it is not the cassette tape itself that is the source of the evil, but the act of playing it.

As for myself, I read the notes, as did you, regarding each of the songs, initially prepared to simply put the tattered cassette into the deck that I'd borrowed from an elderly neighbor and prove to myself it was just another viral prank.

And yet...as I sorted through the documentation—written in scrawling script at first, then on typewriter, then on dot-matrix pages with feedholes half torn at the sides—I realized that no *one* person had accumulated the complete library of "liner-notes," as we used to call them when I was growing up in the 90s. No *one* person had heard the entire cassette all the way through. Or if they had, only one soul had been able to capture a single song's essence before some untimely end.

At least, that is my hypothesis, since there is no one alive to tell me different.

You know the story—the tape was found in a small cave outside of Pahrump, Nevada, by an internet caver, Jeremy Schall. His few thousand online followers became instantly engaged when he stumbled upon the cassette with just three words written upon it: *Do Not Play.*

Along with the tape, police investigators say that the sheaf of documents must have been stored, even though close inspection of the initial video does not indicate that there was anything in the cave except the tape, which, as dark as it was, must have been nearly impossible to see against the forgotten coal cache.

The investigation almost overlooked the evidence in relation to his disappearance over a month later. His estranged wife, Elyse, was the one who made the connection, frantic at his disappearance and finding nothing unusual except for the papers and cassette left on his bedside table after he had failed to pick up their daughter from school. Her statement reflected that Jeremy, much like the unfortunate soul highlighted in "Vinyl Remains," had become reclusive in the weeks leading up to his disappearance. The transcript of the 911 call included an unusual focus on music, music that she could not identify and that the on-scene officers could not hear. And this is when I was called to investigate.

I'm a forensic psychologist, and when I'm not working on creating profiles of white collar criminals and divining motivations of local gang leaders based on social posts, I sometimes get a rare call for something "other" that the beat cops don't know what to do with.

And so, after hearing the story, I hesitated before playing the cassette. Call it superstition or maybe a "gut feeling," I decided to focus my efforts on the notes surrounding each song rather than listening to it myself.

I tell you this because I fear that we are all wrong. Playing the tape is not the only danger.

For me, it began with the strange tale of the "Brazen Bull." The notes indicated a song from within the depths of some horrific murder machine—powered by God or man—the author never states. Upon reading the scrawling, seemingly ancient notes, I felt the hairs on my skin stand up straight. The image was so visceral, it was as though I could hear the song myself.

But, this is the magic of the written word. We are able to cross times and locations to share in a mental moment with the author, regardless if they are dead or alive. Much like music, I suppose.

I brushed the experience off easily, however. I am a writer, myself, and a painter when life becomes too stressful. I have been known to have an active imagination, at least that is what my wife, Connie, tells me, especially when it comes to the things of the macabre.

But with each entry into the strange pile of documents, I felt more ill at ease. More untethered from my reality. The shadows crept after me when I read the cramped, feminine script discussing the mob events of "Everybody Wants My Baby." I read the zine, covered in personal notes, and was immersed in a dank and crowded punk club, dancing towards the end of the world with the Electric Muse. Even though I had not heard the music myself, just reading the notes made me somehow connected to those who had written them. And I began to hear.

But what no one can tell you, I suppose, is what it *sounds like*. Like in the strange tale of Brooke who is consumed and possessed by music itself, or the man who gives his last breath to know silence…no one can explain the sound of something that transforms reality. It must be experienced.

And so I have taken great pains not to hear the tape. Not even once. I thought that would protect me from the fate of the others, but I am no longer sure.

I have started to hear them in my dreams, the voices of the *Playlist of the Damned*. At least, I think that is who they are. They whisper their words in my mind. And I know that I have become obsessed with what they are saying. The words I've read rephrase themselves, take on tone, and snatches of notes play in my head—an earworm that can't be unremembered or unlearned.

What's strange is that the music I hear makes me want to create. It is not benign music. It is music with a motive. It wants me to *do*.

My wife has noticed the change. I sit down at the piano that was given to me when my mother died—a lovely upright Steinway—and I pick out notes, like Keeva, even though my last lesson was over 30 years ago. I have gone out of my way to the music store (more than once) to "test" the electric guitars, fingers cramped in chords that are vaguely familiar, though I don't know why. I saw out ugly lines of cat screetches on borrowed fiddles, like poor Josh with his demonic gift. And though the music never quite adheres to my throat or comes out as I hear it in my mind, I close my eyes at night and breathe that dusty, dark song of Merzgau.

Connie tells me to take time off. Let the beat cops work on the case of Jeremy Schall. I tell her I will, I have. And, yes. I have indeed given the documents and cassette tape back to them. It is safe and sound in an evidence box somewhere in Southern Nevada.

But I couldn't let it go without at least attempting to keep a bit for myself. That's why it came to me, I believe. *They* knew I could do what no one yet had done.

The dual tape deck is a thing of beauty. It took a week of looking and a quick eBay win to deliver it to my doorstep. Anyone who was young in the last part of the 20th century knows how easy it is to just press the Record and Play button at the same time and make a copy of a copy of a copy...

I have made my copies in the darkness, when no one was watching. I have been careful not to hear it myself, ears pugged, in the shower, on the other side of the house. I can her them humming, though, despite my best efforts. And my song in the shower has become a strange, choking sound of longing. If only I could hear them with my own ears...

But soon, we will all hear, won't we?

The little packages have all been sent—to the radio stations, in mail boxes, laid on doorsteps, dropped at McDonalds. Shiny, plastic cases with a pristine cassette tape in each of them, courtesy of the National Audio Company. Neat, printed labels for each song. Handled with gloves and great care.

I know that most who see them will never hear them. They might not even know what they are. But the cassette tape is coming back, they say. And the right ones...the *right ones* will know. Like the sound of the Devil's sweet music in the subway, the *Playlist* will call them home.

And for the rest of the world? There is always this book. A love letter to entropy. A guide on what it's like to slowly lose yourself in the madness of a poisoned obsession. Music for the end of the world.

I hope you have enjoyed reading it. This is my gift to you. This is their gift to all of us. A crack in your reality that will slowly unwind you and drive you downward.

And as for me? I have done what I was sent here to do: grow, and be illuminated, and fill the world with the music of the damned.

Soon, I will finally rest myself and join the others. The "Play" button calls to me like a lover. I have still never heard the melodies of the songs with my own ears. But they come to me as snatches of forgotten melodies, haunting me between the place of sleep and wakefulness. And I think, somehow, I am writing a new song to add to it.

I cradle the tape deck in my arms, naked, and waiting for whoever will come to claim me.

I would be lying to say I am not afraid. My bowels are weak and watery. My mouth is dry. And the sounds of far off screams are trickling into my head like a descant. A backbeat of ancient drums and a choir of earthen voices surround me, suffocating me in ecstatic harmony.

When I open my mouth, the sound of the universe will fall inside of me and I know that wherever it is, the *Playlist* will include my voice. And, if you've read this far, it will one day include yours, too.